D1516137

SKYSCRAPERS OF OZ

STORY

YOSHINO SOMEI

ART

ROW TAKAKURA

NEW YORK, NEW YORK

Translation, Adaptation & Design - Kitty Media
Retouch and Lettering - Junemoon Studios

Skyscrapers of Oz ©2001 by Yoshino SOMEI & Row
TAKAKURA. All rights reserved. Original Japanese edition
published by TOKUMA SHOTEN PUBLISHING CO., LTD
Tokyo. English version in U.S.A. and CANADA published by
Kitty Media under license granted by TOKUMA SHOTEN
PUBLISHING CO., LTD.

Kitty Press Office of Publication
519 8th Avenue, 14th floor
New York, NY 10018.

ISBN: 1-58655-999-0

Printed in Canada.

Fourth Printing

WWW.KITTYMEDIA.COM

YOSHINO SOMEI

Birthday: October 28 • Scorpio • Blood Type: O

Born in Tokyo, lives in Chiba

Seeing my own characters brought to life outside of the novel is magical! But the real Oz is OOXX…You might be able to see a building very similar to theirs on a certain street here…?

ROW TAKAKURA

Birthday: January 17 • Capricorn • Blood Type: O

Born in Fukuoka (still lives there)

I'm so happy to have my first series and novel-based manga published in a single volume…it's a dream come true. Somei Sensei, thank you so much! Because of my inexperience, your wonderful novel has become quite risqué…please forgive me! By the way, Yoichi is my type!

SKYSCRAPERS OF OZ

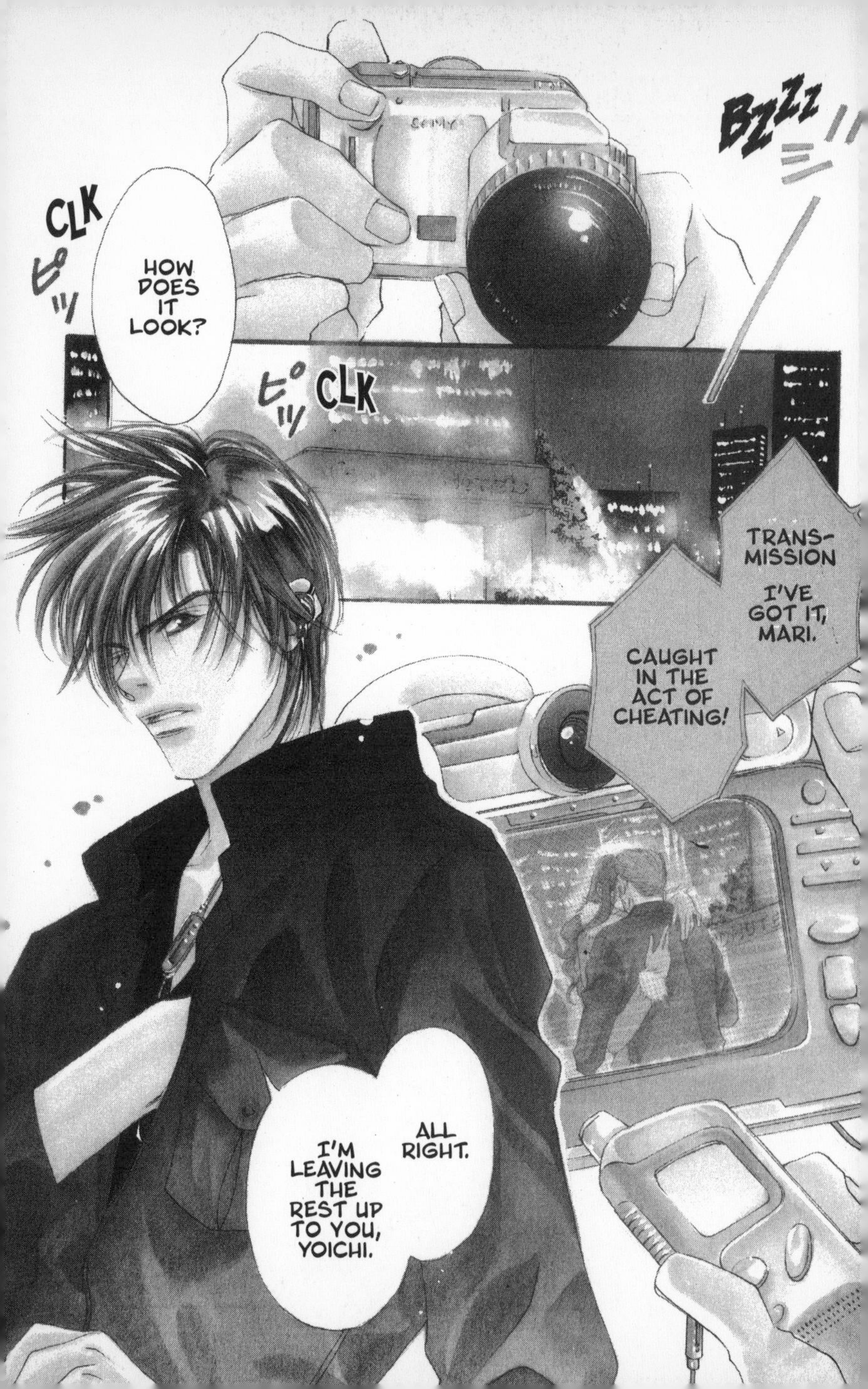

BZZZ
HOW DOES IT LOOK?
CLK ピッ
ピッ CLK
TRANS-MISSION
I'VE GOT IT, MARI.
CAUGHT IN THE ACT OF CHEATING!
ALL RIGHT.
I'M LEAVING THE REST UP TO YOU, YOICHI.

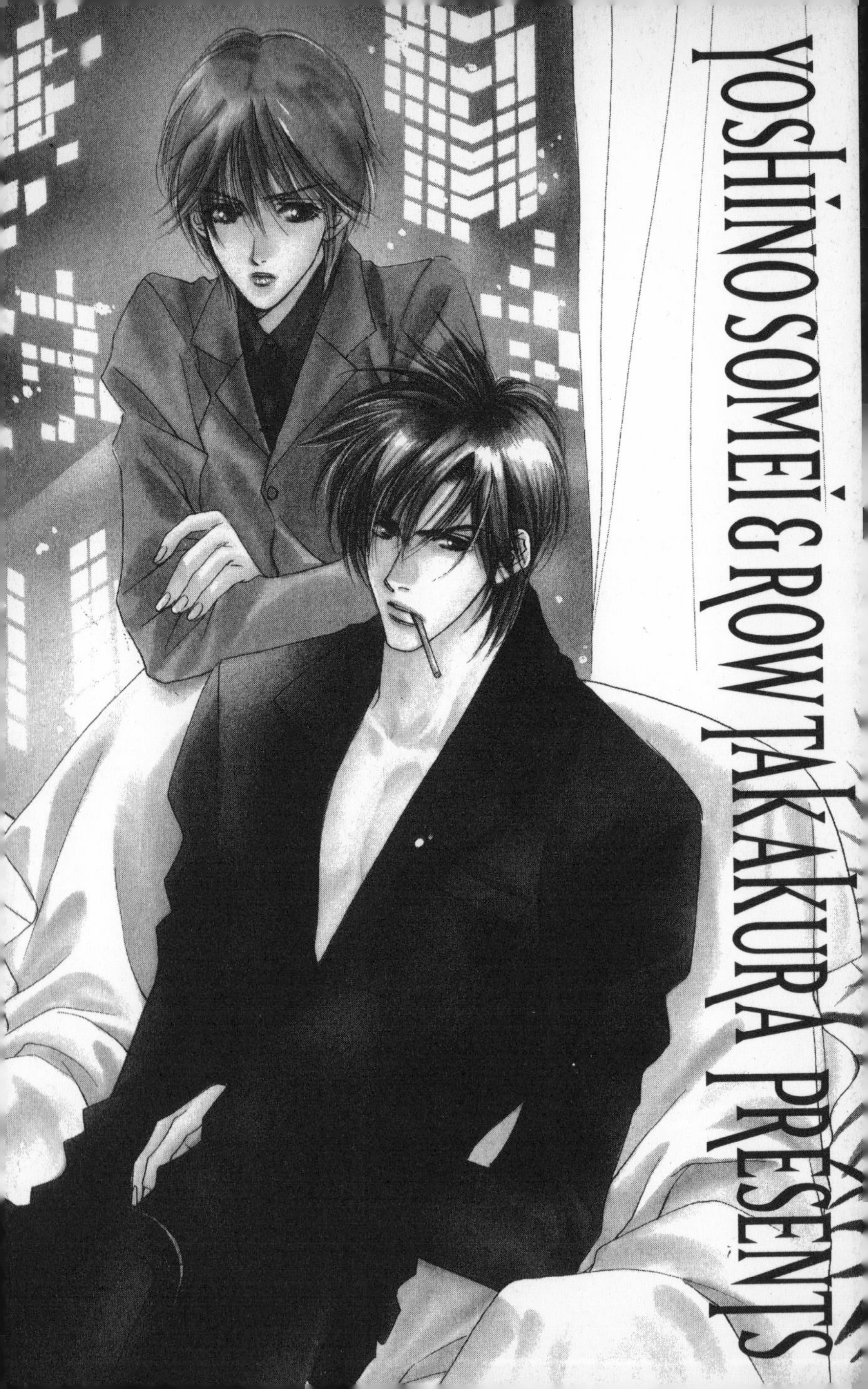
YOSHINO SOMEI & ROW TAKAKURA PRESENTS

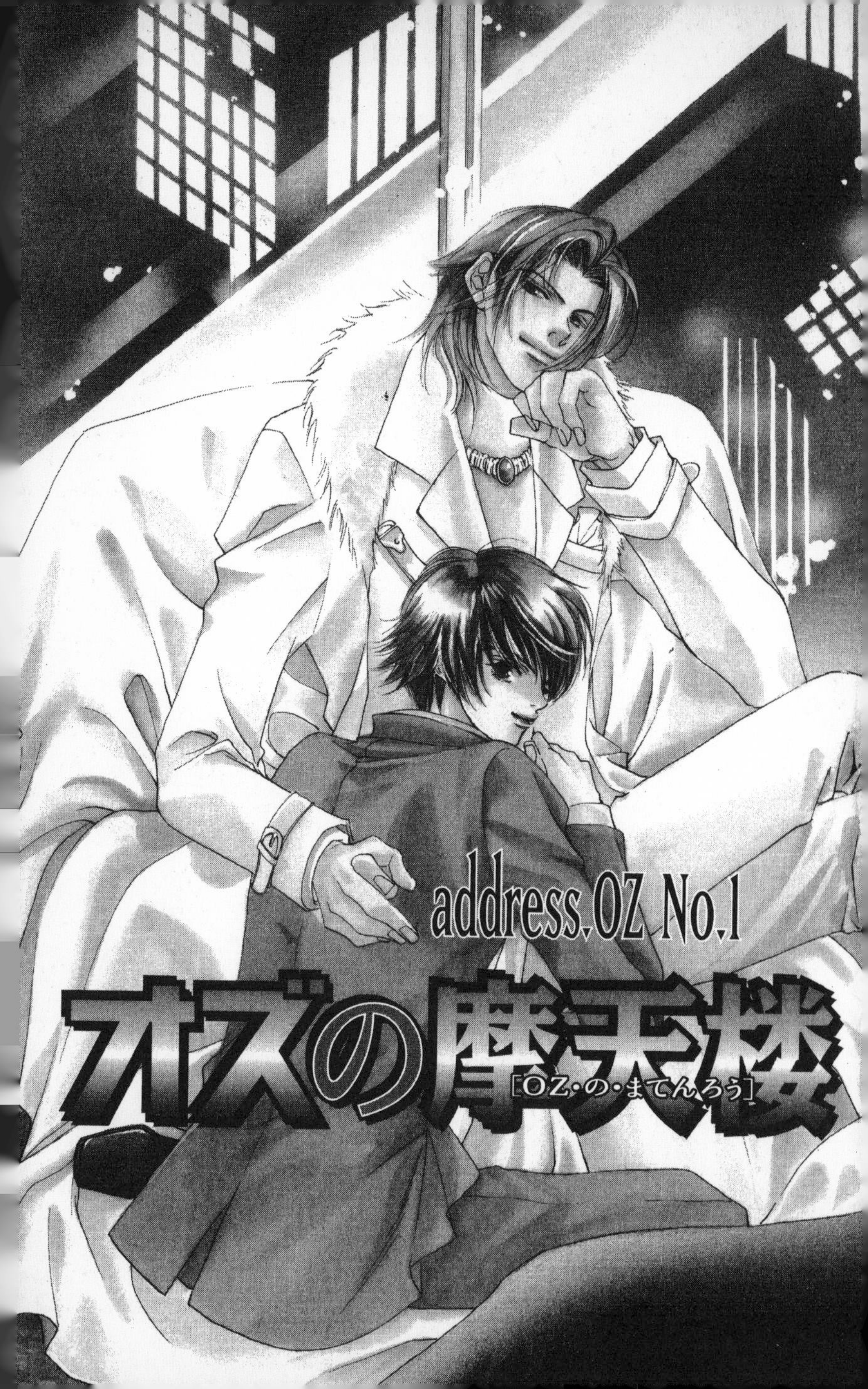
address.OZ No.1
オズの摩天楼
「OZ・の・まてんろう」

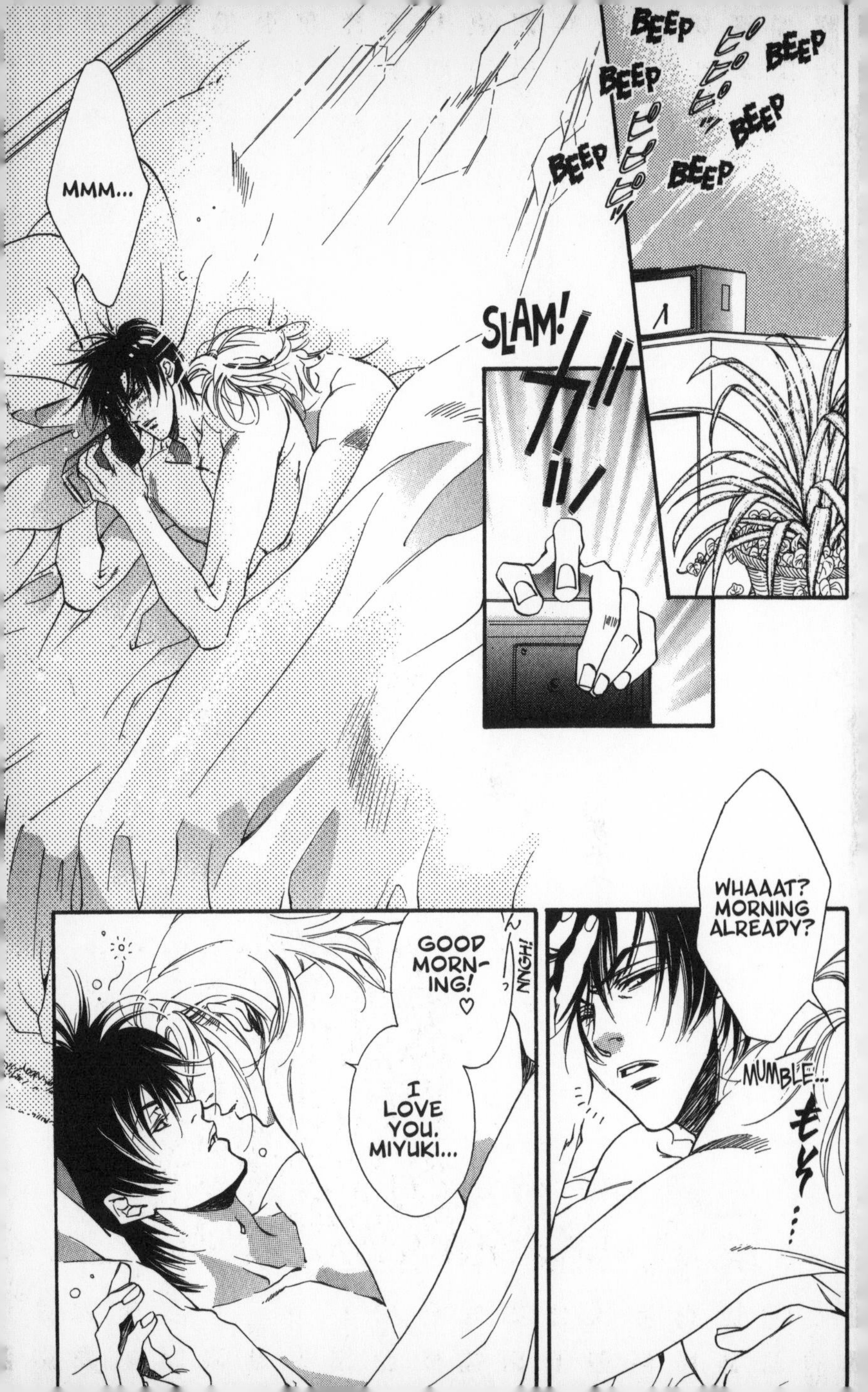
BEEP
BEEP
BEEP
BEEP
BEEP
BEEP
ピピピピッ
ピピピッ
SLAM!
ガッ
MMM...
WHAAAT? MORNING ALREADY?
MUMBLE...
もぞ...
GOOD MORNING! ♡
NNGH!
んー…っ
I LOVE YOU. MIYUKI...

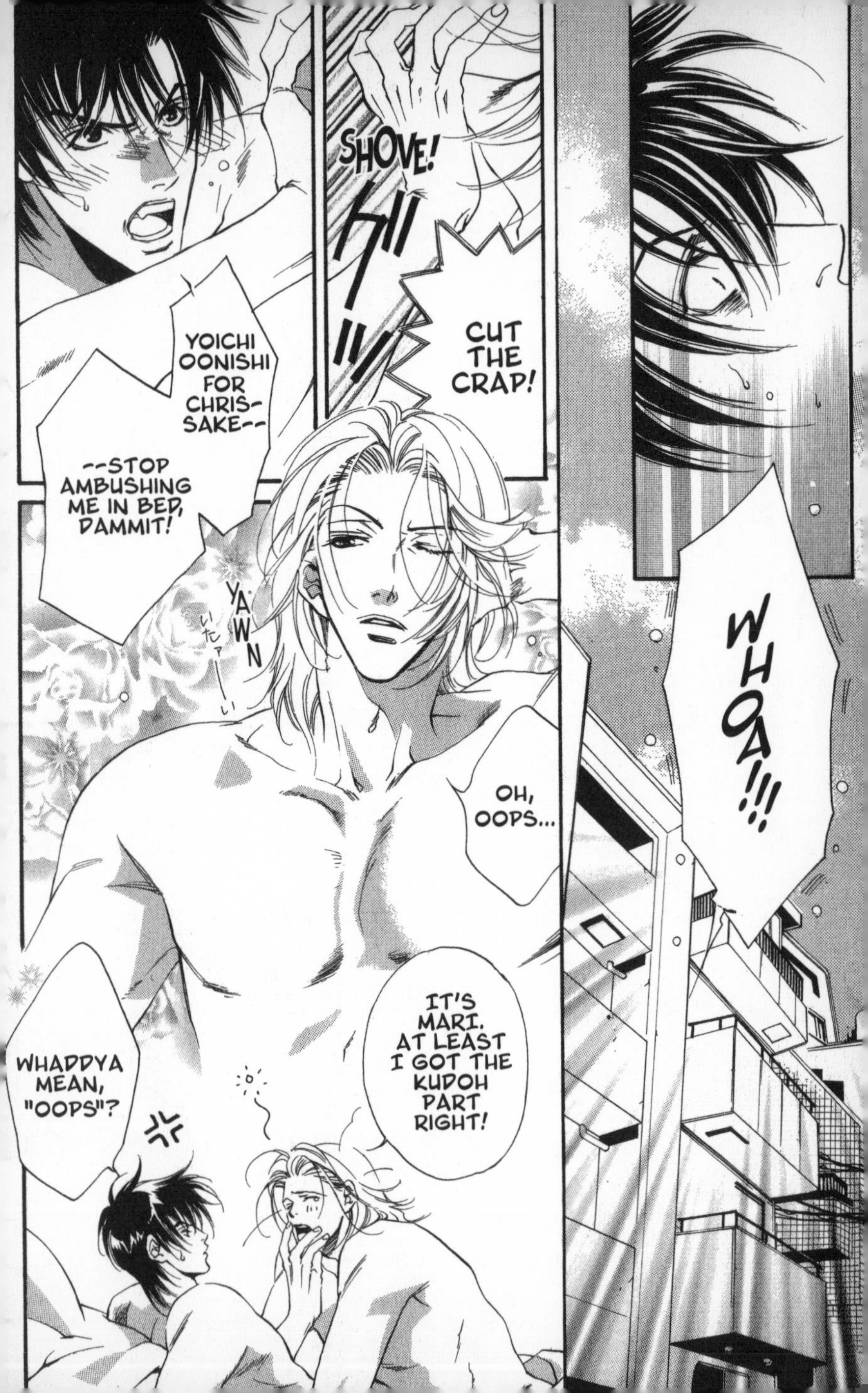
WHOA!!!
SHOVE!
CUT THE CRAP!
YOICHI OONISHI FOR CHRIS-SAKE--
--STOP AMBUSHING ME IN BED, DAMMIT!
YAWN
いたァーーい
OH, OOPS...
IT'S MARI. AT LEAST I GOT THE KUDOH PART RIGHT!
WHADDYA MEAN, "OOPS"?

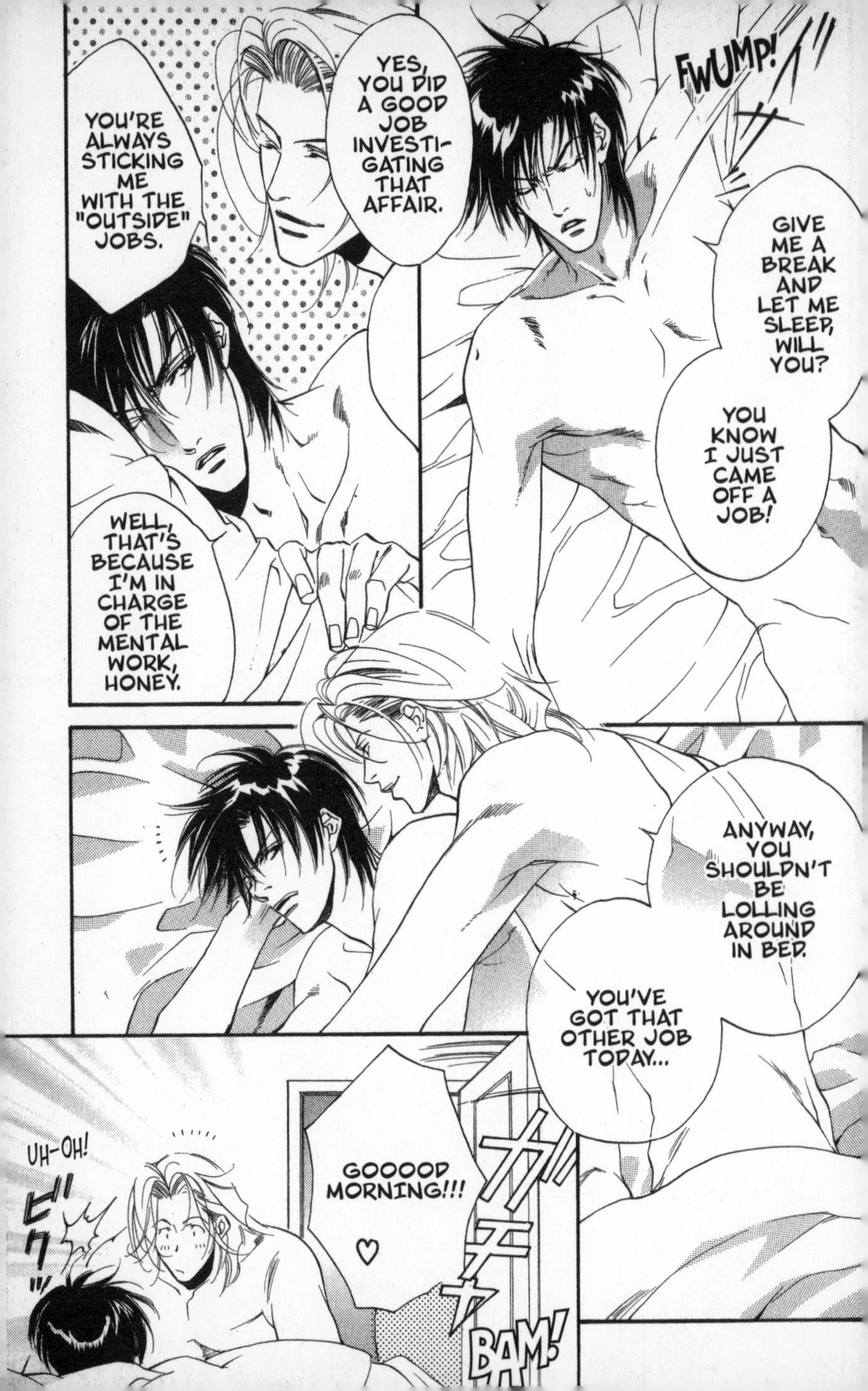
FWUMP!
GIVE ME A BREAK AND LET ME SLEEP, WILL YOU?
YOU KNOW I JUST CAME OFF A JOB!
YES, YOU DID A GOOD JOB INVESTIGATING THAT AFFAIR.
YOU'RE ALWAYS STICKING ME WITH THE "OUTSIDE" JOBS.
WELL, THAT'S BECAUSE I'M IN CHARGE OF THE MENTAL WORK, HONEY.
ANYWAY, YOU SHOULDN'T BE LOLLING AROUND IN BED.
YOU'VE GOT THAT OTHER JOB TODAY...
ガチャ
BAM!
GOOOOD MORNING!!! ♥
UH-OH!
ビクッ

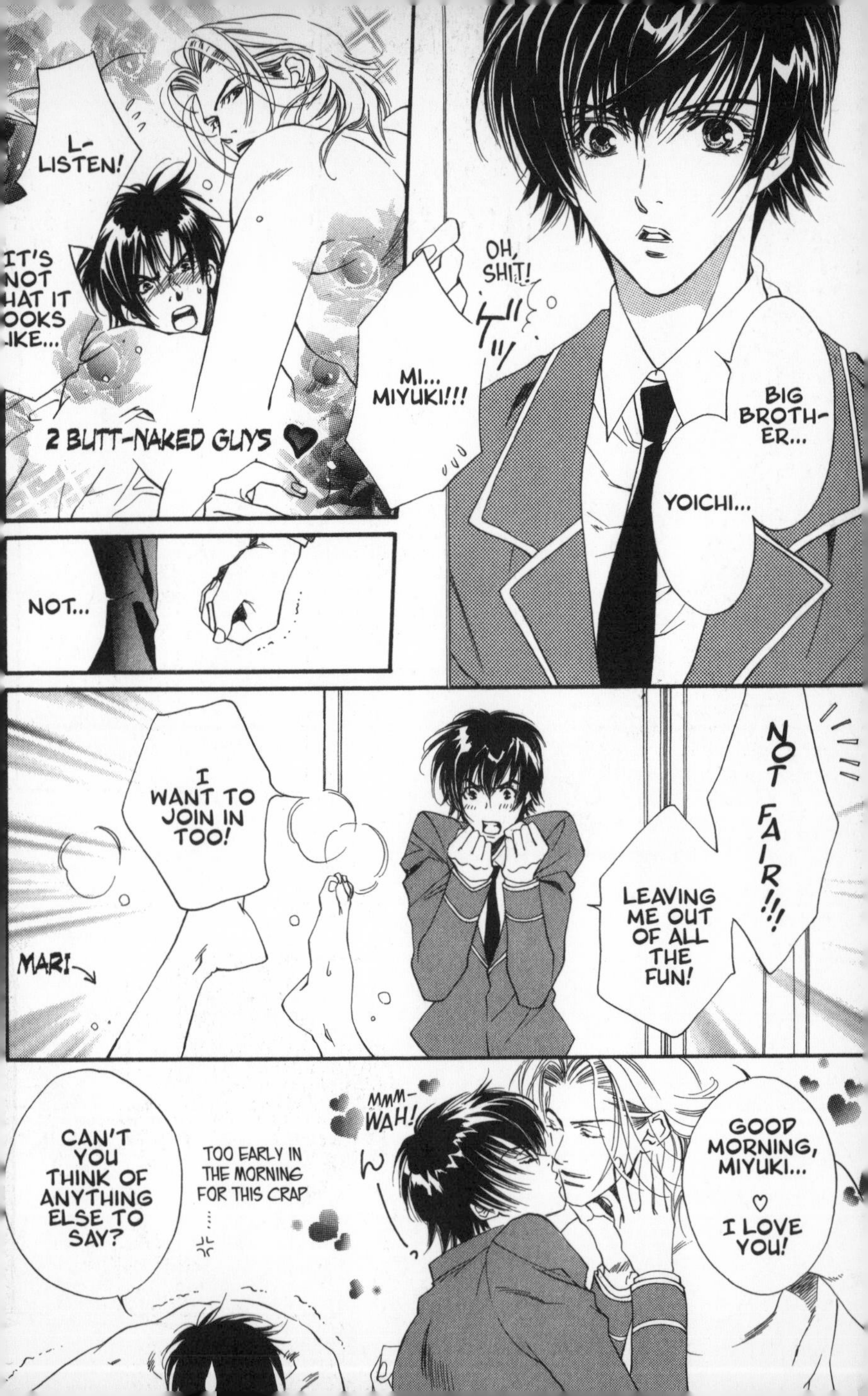
BIG BROTHER-ER...
YOICHI...
OH, SHIT!
MI... MIYUKI!!!
L-LISTEN!
IT'S NOT HAT IT OOKS IKE...
2 BUTT-NAKED GUYS ♥
NOT...
NOT FAIR!!!
LEAVING ME OUT OF ALL THE FUN!
I WANT TO JOIN IN TOO!
MARI
GOOD MORNING, MIYUKI... ♡ I LOVE YOU!
MMM-WAH!
TOO EARLY IN THE MORNING FOR THIS CRAP
...
CAN'T YOU THINK OF ANYTHING ELSE TO SAY?

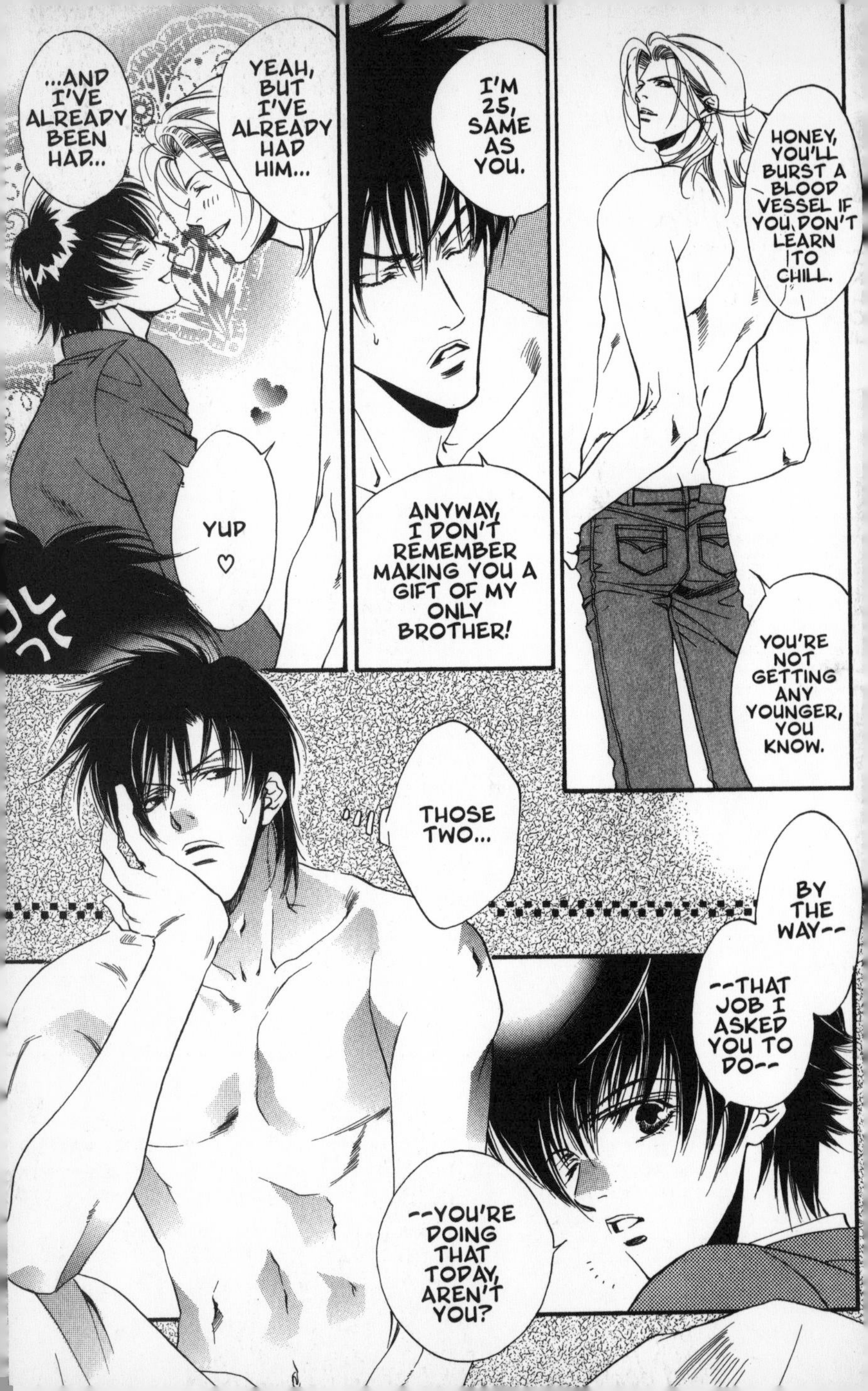
HONEY, YOU'LL BURST A BLOOD VESSEL IF YOU DON'T LEARN TO CHILL.
YOU'RE NOT GETTING ANY YOUNGER, YOU KNOW.
I'M 25, SAME AS YOU.
ANYWAY, I DON'T REMEMBER MAKING YOU A GIFT OF MY ONLY BROTHER!
YEAH, BUT I'VE ALREADY HAD HIM...
...AND I'VE ALREADY BEEN HAD...
YUP ♡
THOSE TWO...
BY THE WAY--
--THAT JOB I ASKED YOU TO DO--
--YOU'RE DOING THAT TODAY, AREN'T YOU?

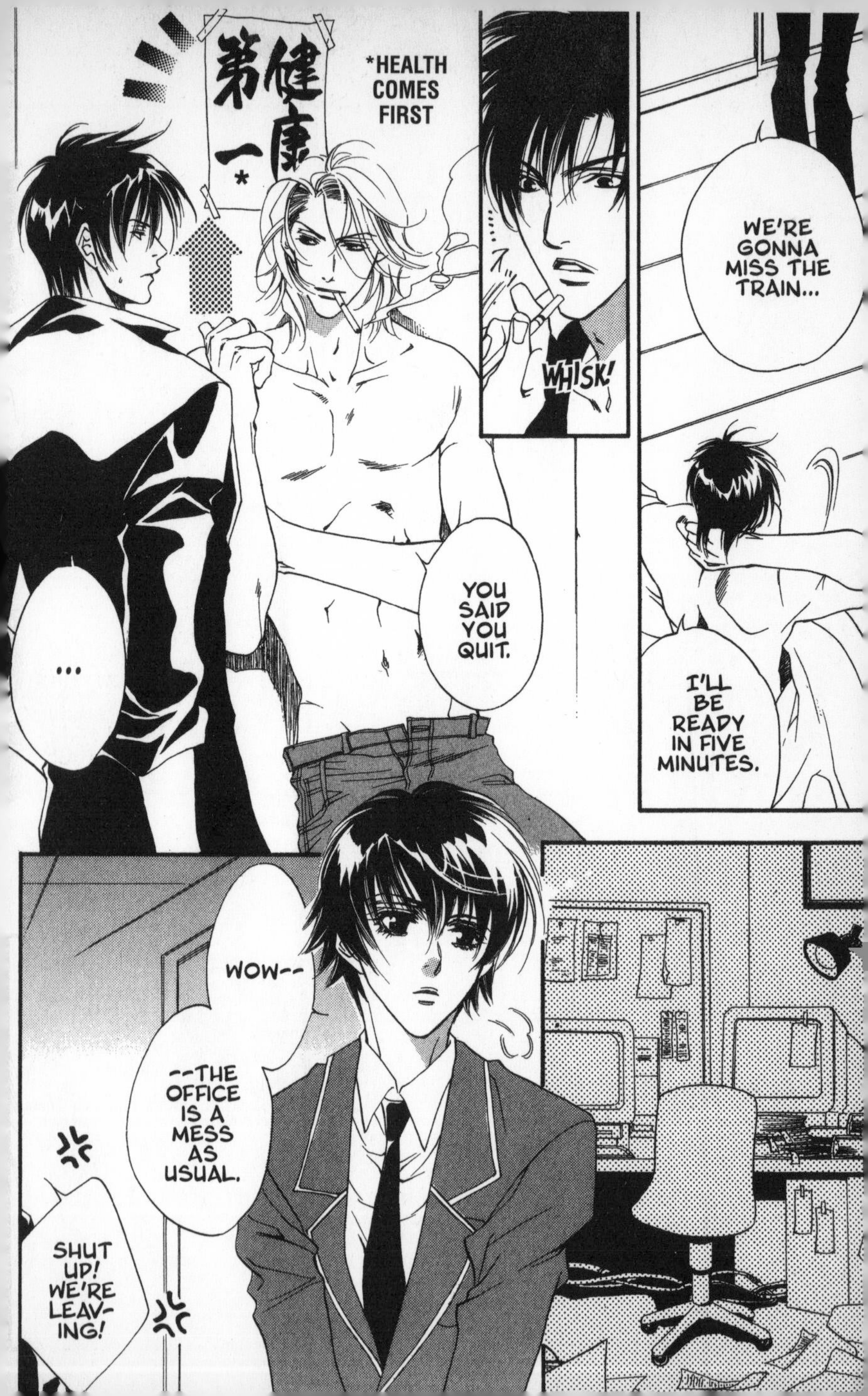
WE'RE GONNA MISS THE TRAIN...
I'LL BE READY IN FIVE MINUTES.
WHISK!
健康第一*
*HEALTH COMES FIRST
YOU SAID YOU QUIT.
...
WOW--
--THE OFFICE IS A MESS AS USUAL.
SHUT UP! WE'RE LEAVING!

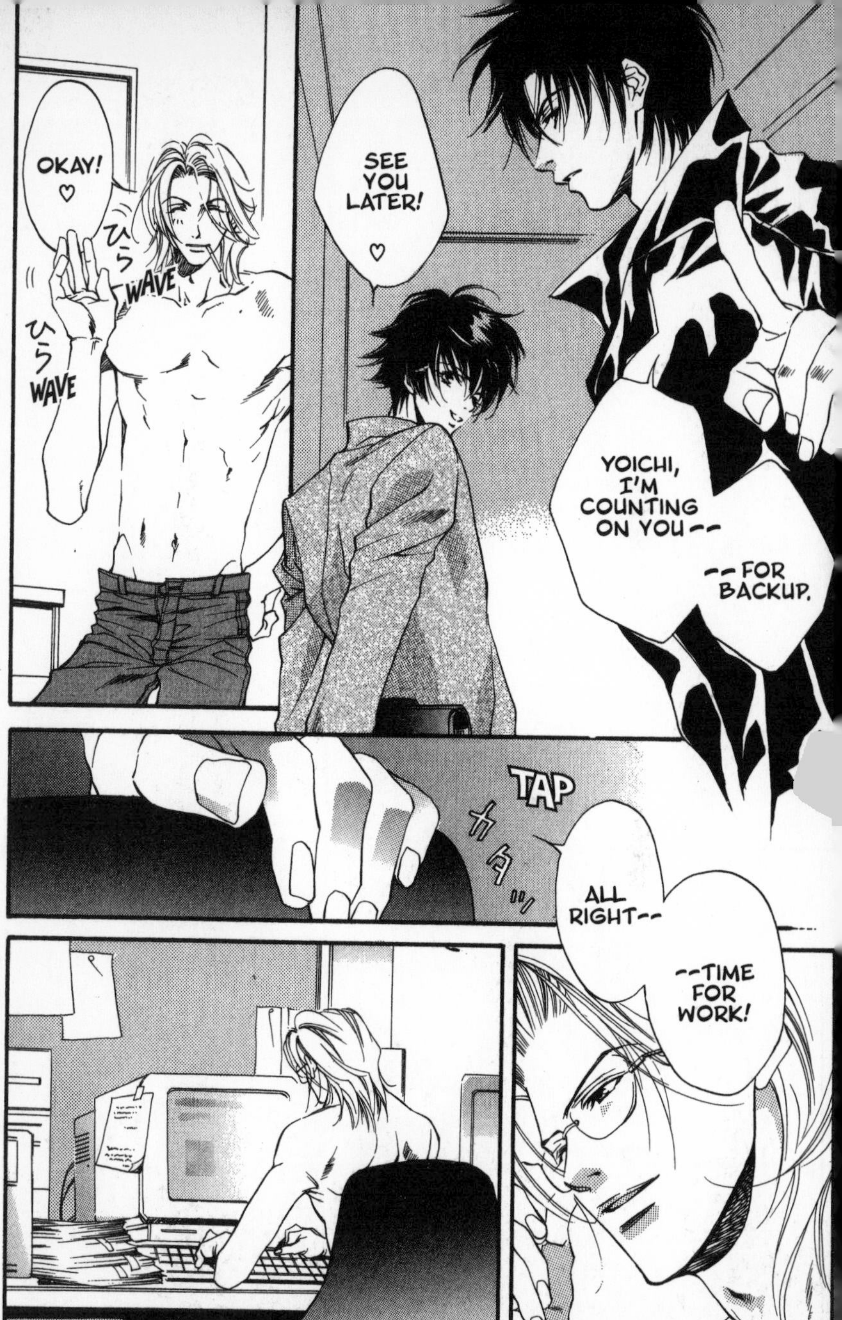
YOICHI, I'M COUNTING ON YOU--
--FOR BACKUP.
SEE YOU LATER! ♡
OKAY! ♡
ひら WAVE
ひら WAVE
TAP カタッ
ALL RIGHT--
--TIME FOR WORK!

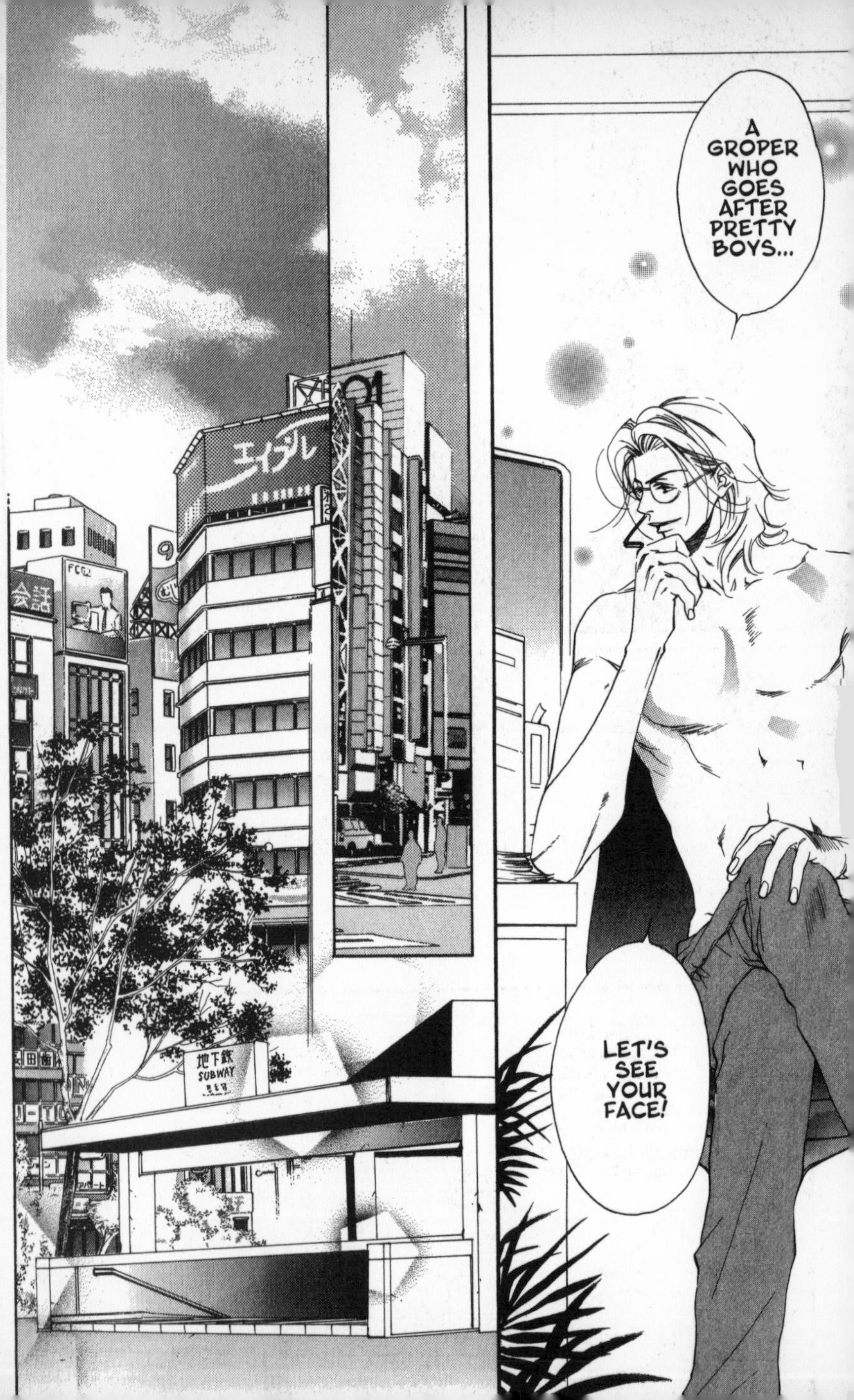
A GROPER WHO GOES AFTER PRETTY BOYS...
LET'S SEE YOUR FACE!
地下鉄
SUBWAY

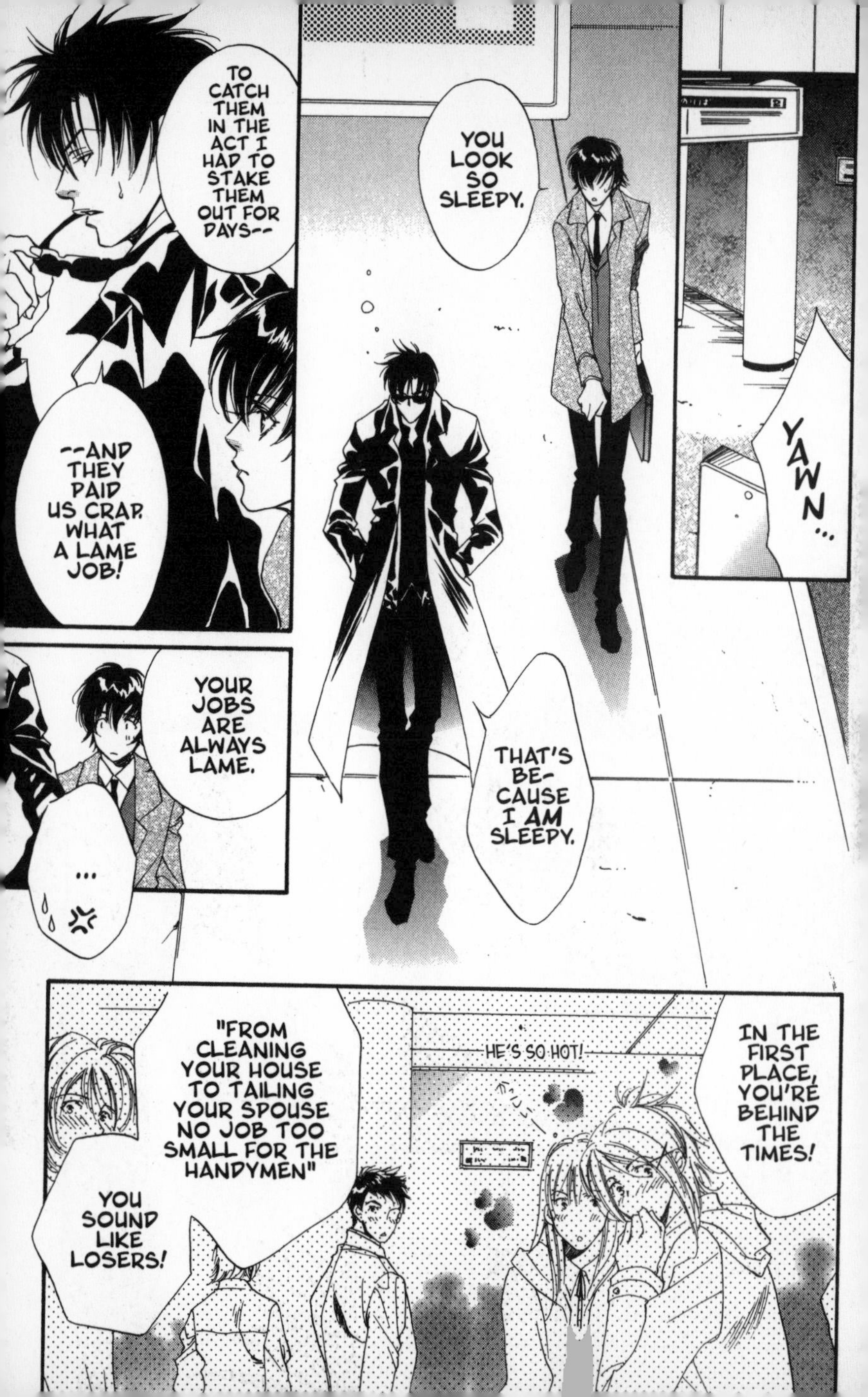
YAWN...
YOU LOOK SO SLEEPY.
THAT'S BE-CAUSE I AM SLEEPY.
TO CATCH THEM IN THE ACT I HAD TO STAKE THEM OUT FOR DAYS--
--AND THEY PAID US CRAP. WHAT A LAME JOB!
YOUR JOBS ARE ALWAYS LAME.
...
IN THE FIRST PLACE, YOU'RE BEHIND THE TIMES!
HE'S SO HOT!
"FROM CLEANING YOUR HOUSE TO TAILING YOUR SPOUSE NO JOB TOO SMALL FOR THE HANDYMEN"
YOU SOUND LIKE LOSERS!

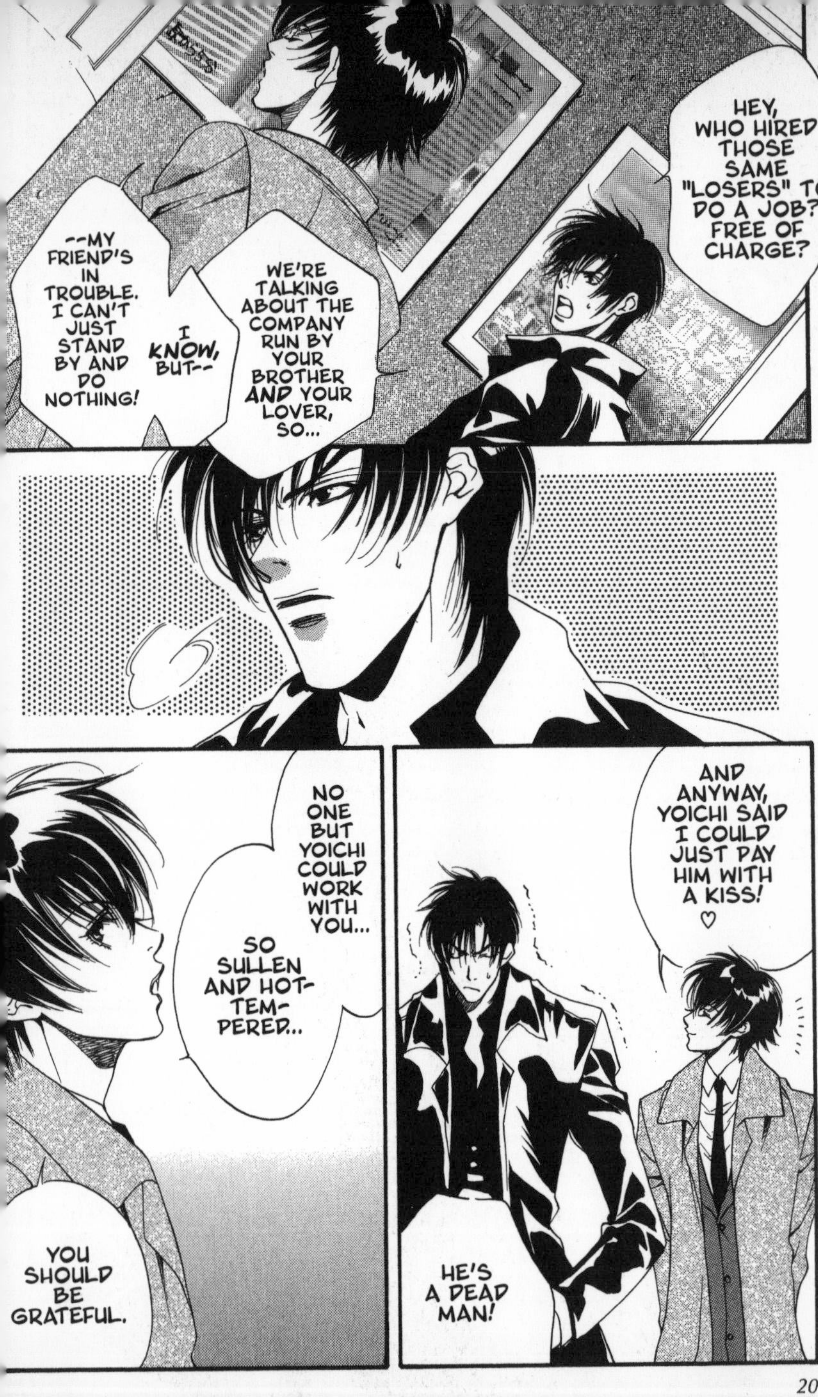
HEY, WHO HIRED THOSE SAME "LOSERS" TO DO A JOB? FREE OF CHARGE?
WE'RE TALKING ABOUT THE COMPANY RUN BY YOUR BROTHER **AND** YOUR LOVER, SO...
I **KNOW**, BUT--
--MY FRIEND'S IN TROUBLE. I CAN'T JUST STAND BY AND DO NOTHING!
AND ANYWAY, YOICHI SAID I COULD JUST PAY HIM WITH A KISS! ♡
HE'S A DEAD MAN!
NO ONE BUT YOICHI COULD WORK WITH YOU...
SO SULLEN AND HOT-TEMPERED...
YOU SHOULD BE GRATEFUL.

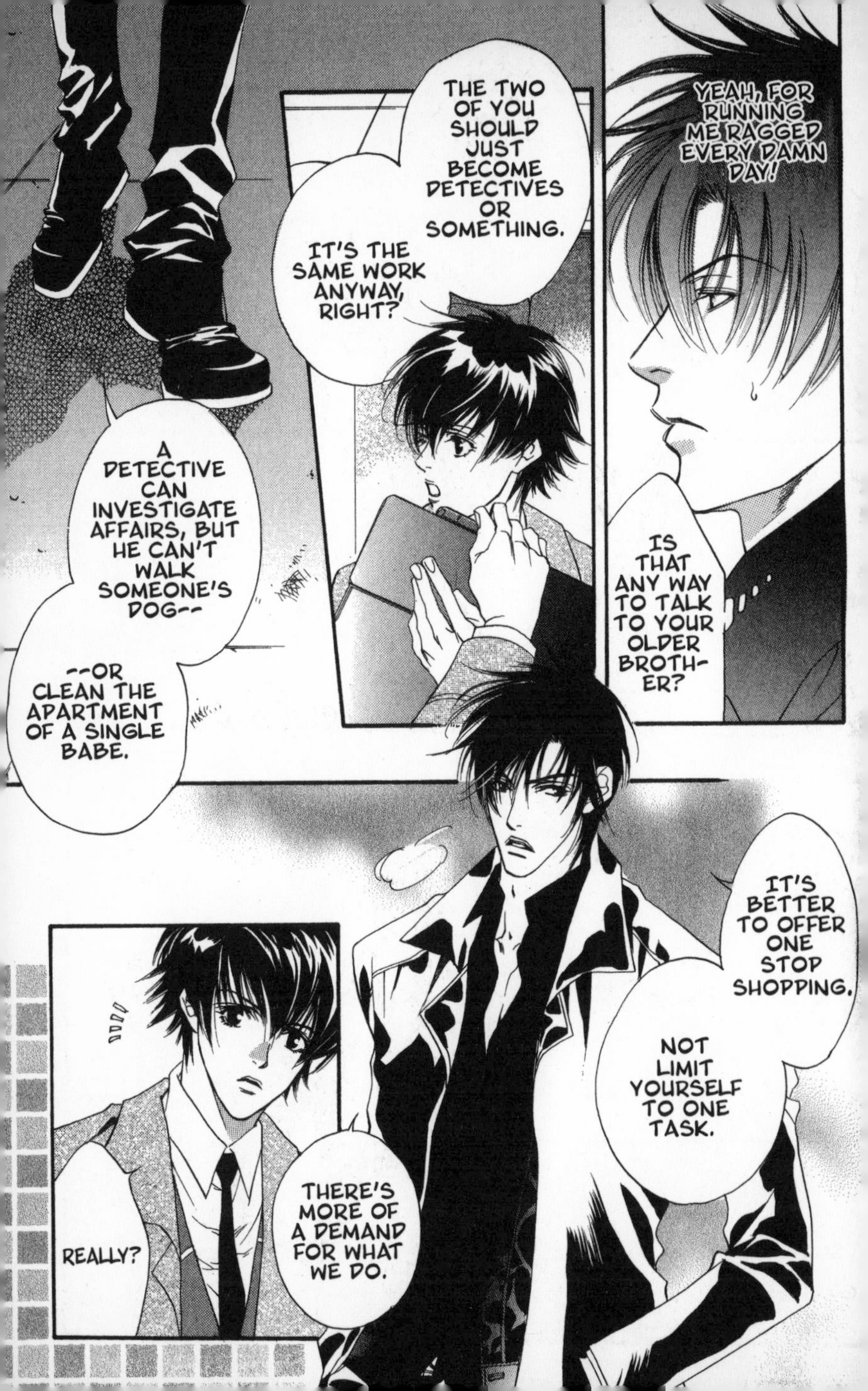
YEAH, FOR RUNNING ME RAGGED EVERY DAMN DAY!
IS THAT ANY WAY TO TALK TO YOUR OLDER BROTH-ER?
THE TWO OF YOU SHOULD JUST BECOME DETECTIVES OR SOMETHING.
IT'S THE SAME WORK ANYWAY, RIGHT?
A DETECTIVE CAN INVESTIGATE AFFAIRS, BUT HE CAN'T WALK SOMEONE'S DOG--
--OR CLEAN THE APARTMENT OF A SINGLE BABE.
IT'S BETTER TO OFFER ONE STOP SHOPPING.
NOT LIMIT YOURSELF TO ONE TASK.
THERE'S MORE OF A DEMAND FOR WHAT WE DO.
REALLY?

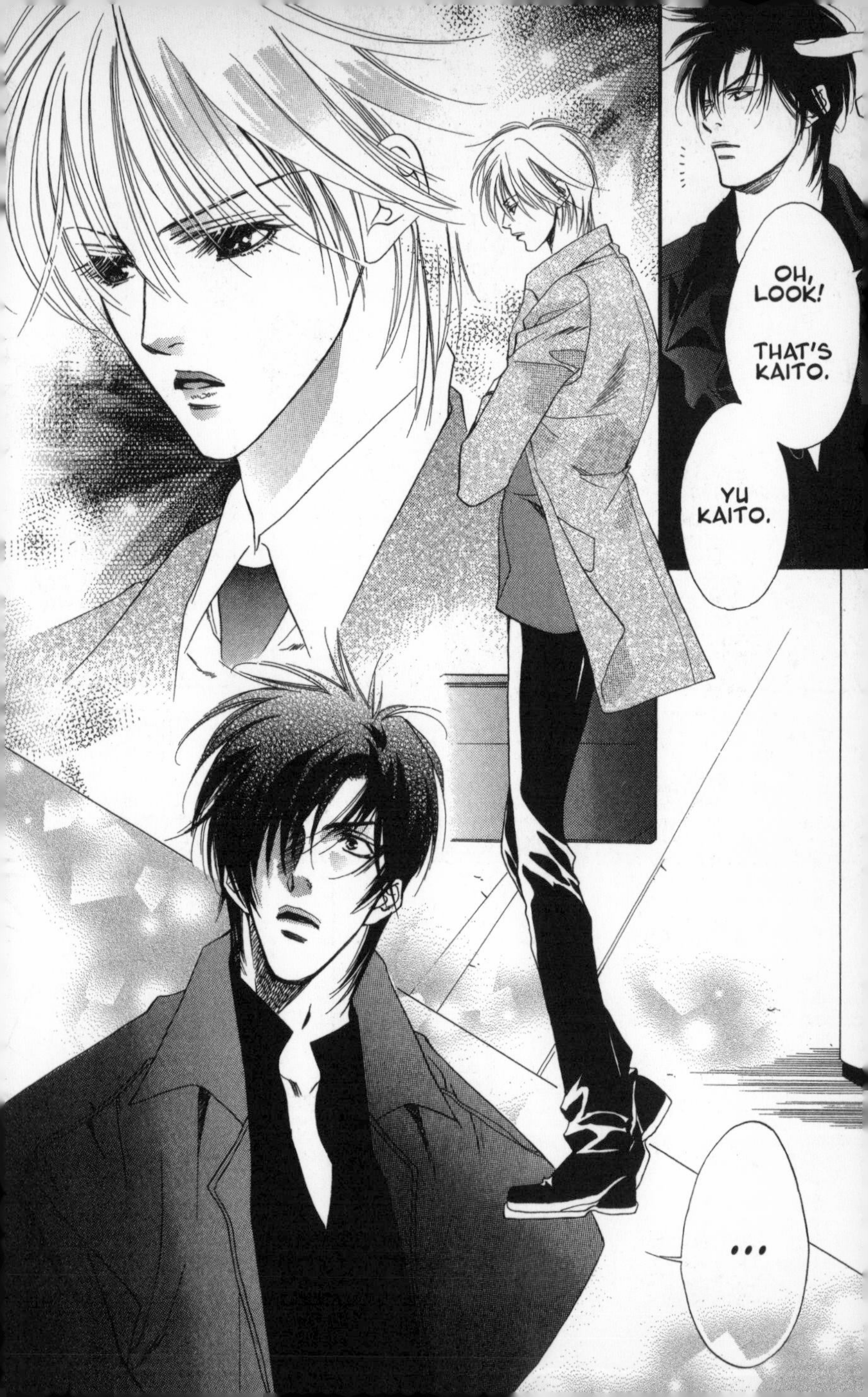
OH, LOOK!
THAT'S KAITO.
YU KAITO.
...

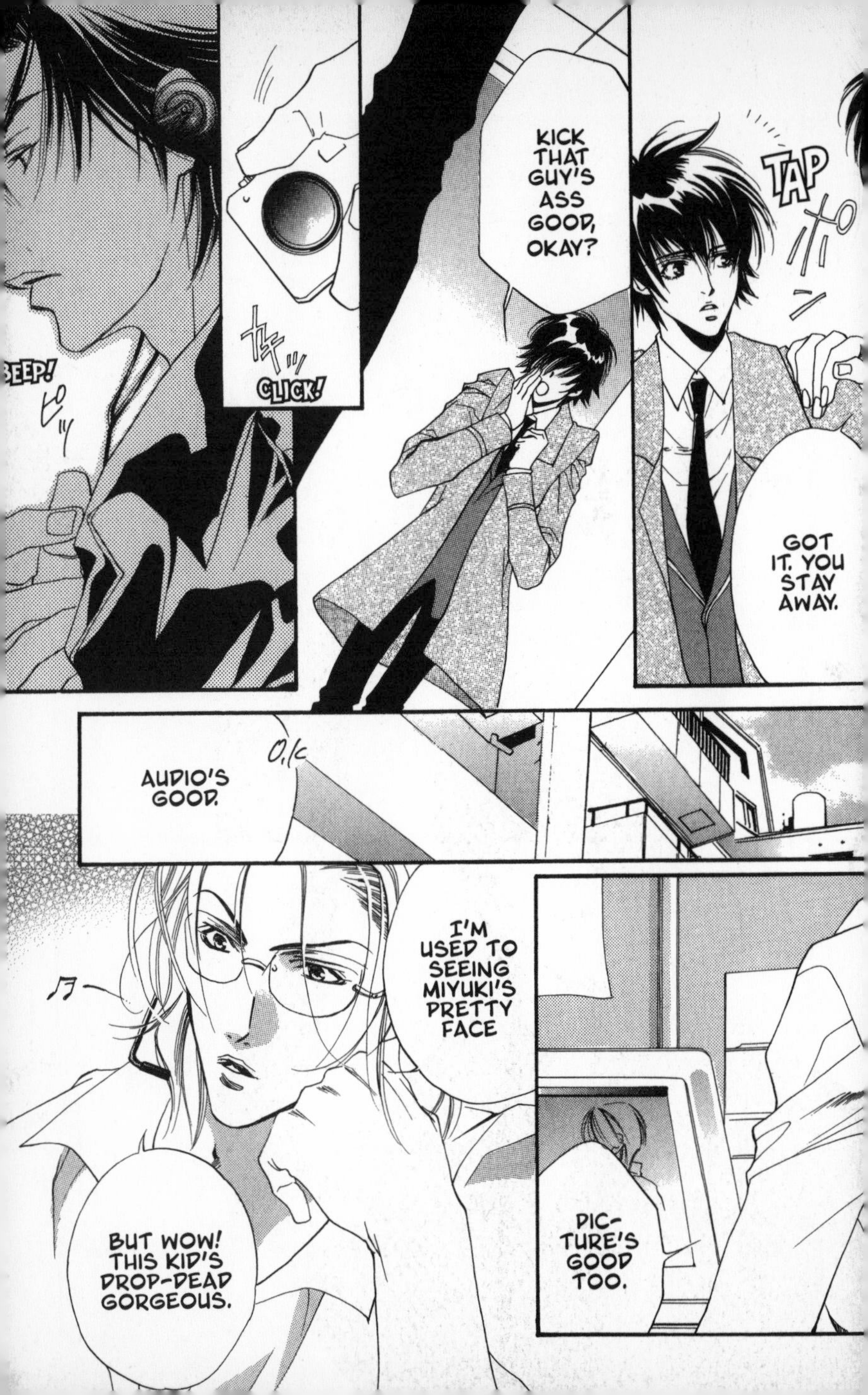
TAP
GOT IT. YOU STAY AWAY.
KICK THAT GUY'S ASS GOOD, OKAY?
CLICK!
BEEP!
AUDIO'S GOOD.
PIC-TURE'S GOOD TOO.
I'M USED TO SEEING MIYUKI'S PRETTY FACE
BUT WOW! THIS KID'S DROP-DEAD GORGEOUS.

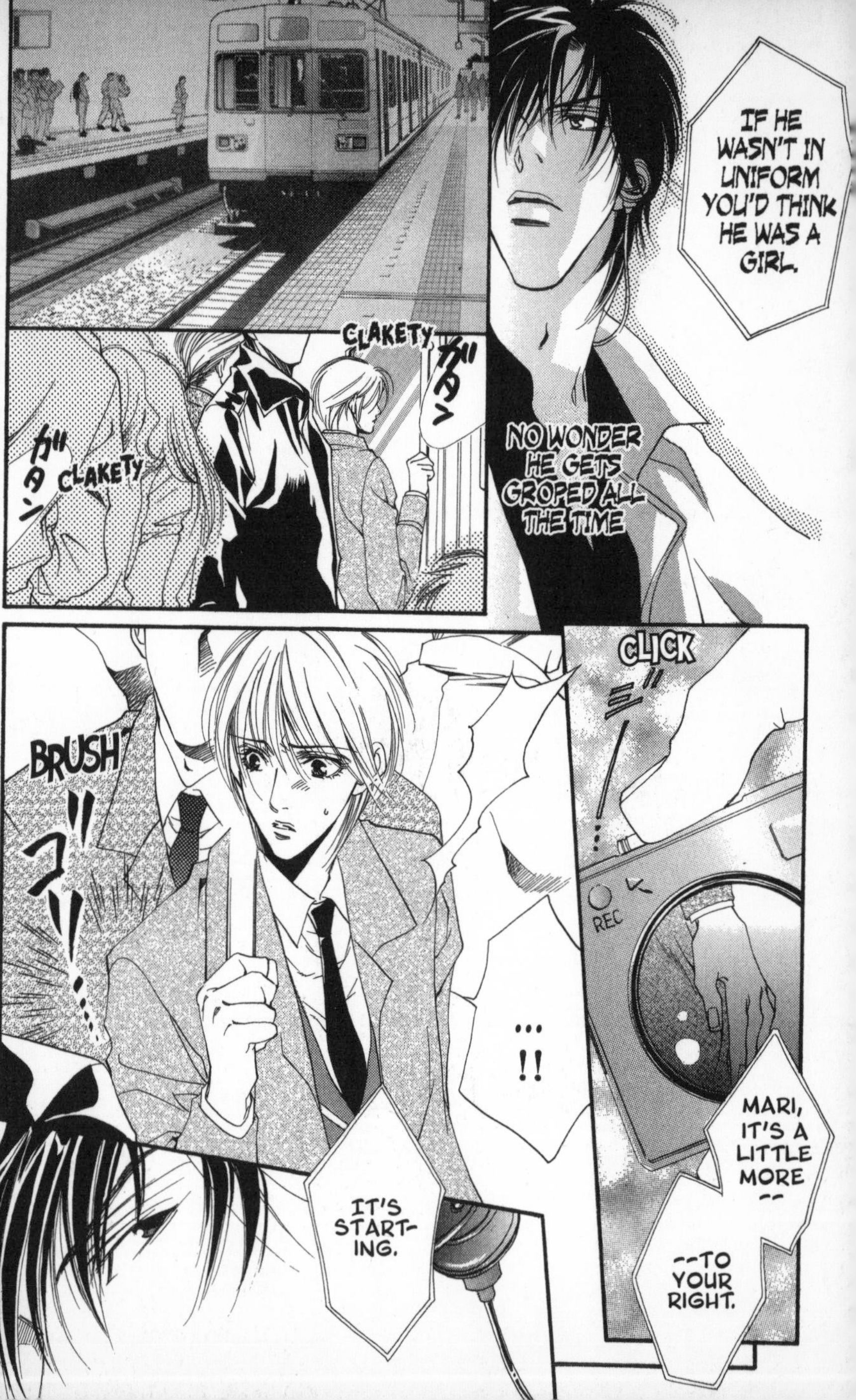

IF HE WASN'T IN UNIFORM YOU'D THINK HE WAS A GIRL.
NO WONDER HE GETS GROPED ALL THE TIME
CLAKETY
ガタン
CLAKETY
ガタン
CLICK
MARI, IT'S A LITTLE MORE --
--TO YOUR RIGHT.
BRUSH
...!!
IT'S STARTING.

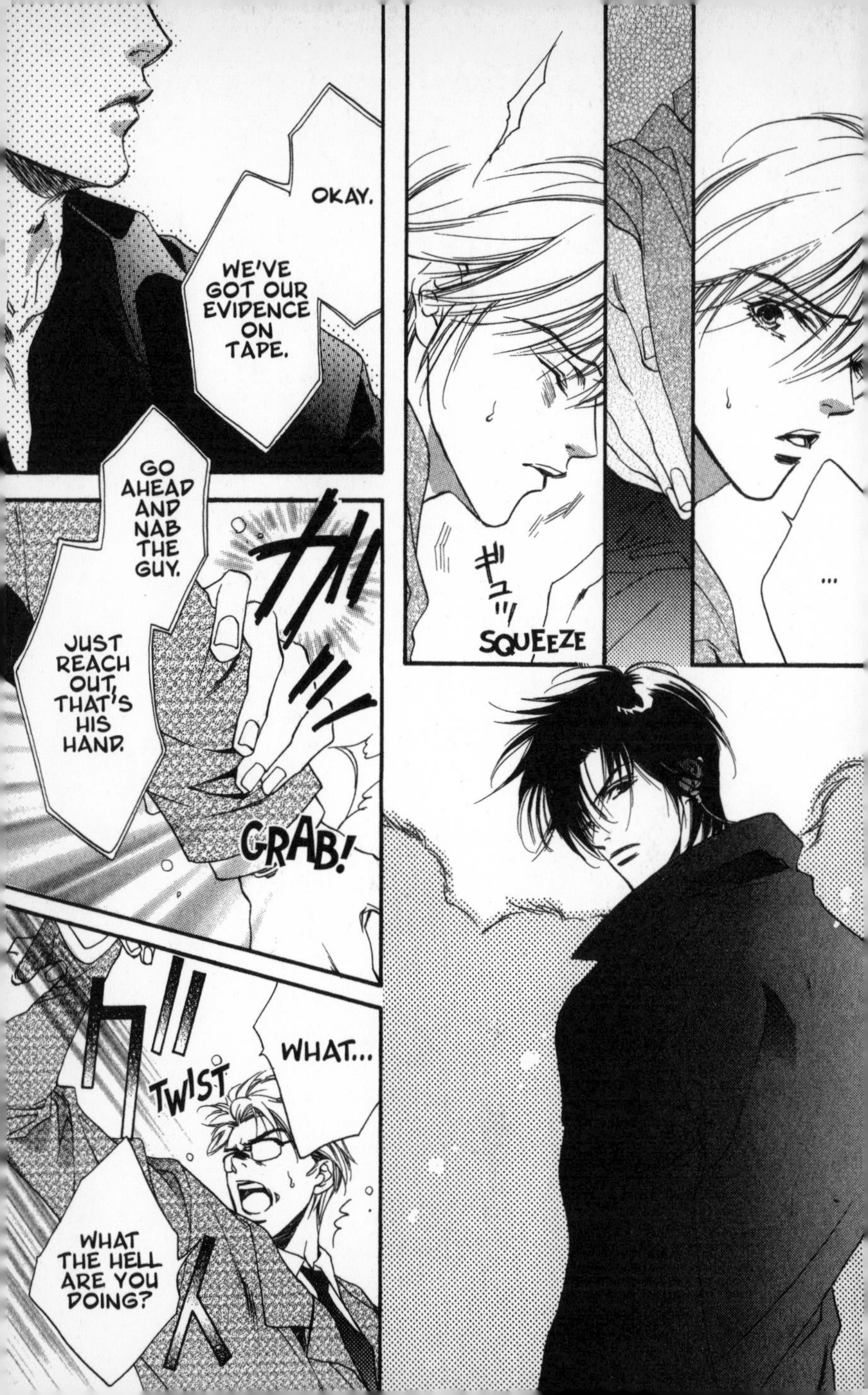
...
ギュッ
SQUEEZE
OKAY.
WE'VE GOT OUR EVIDENCE ON TAPE.
GO AHEAD AND NAB THE GUY.
JUST REACH OUT, THAT'S HIS HAND.
GRAB!
WHAT...
TWIST
WHAT THE HELL ARE YOU DOING?

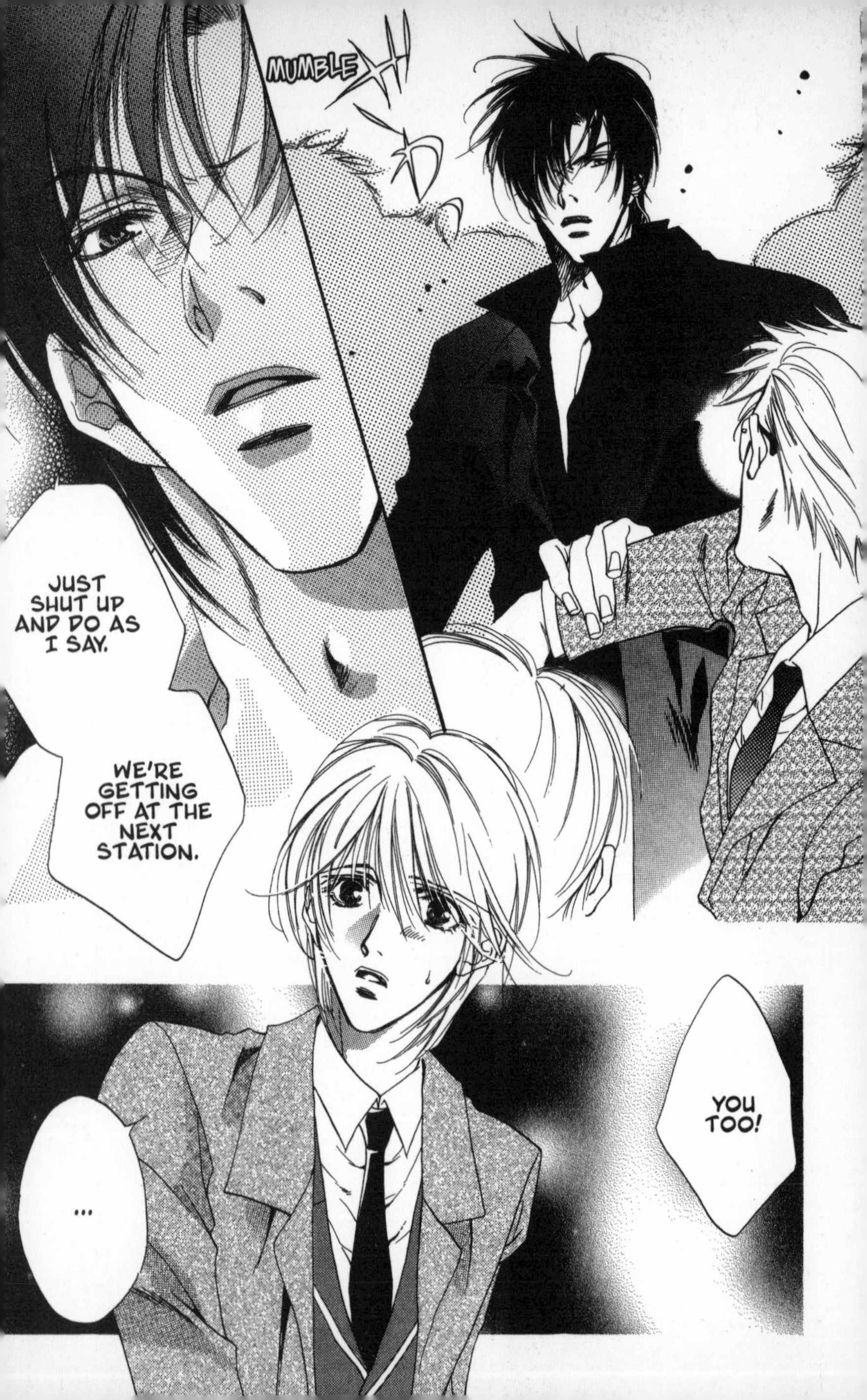
MUMBLE
JUST SHUT UP AND DO AS I SAY.
WE'RE GETTING OFF AT THE NEXT STATION.
YOU TOO!
...

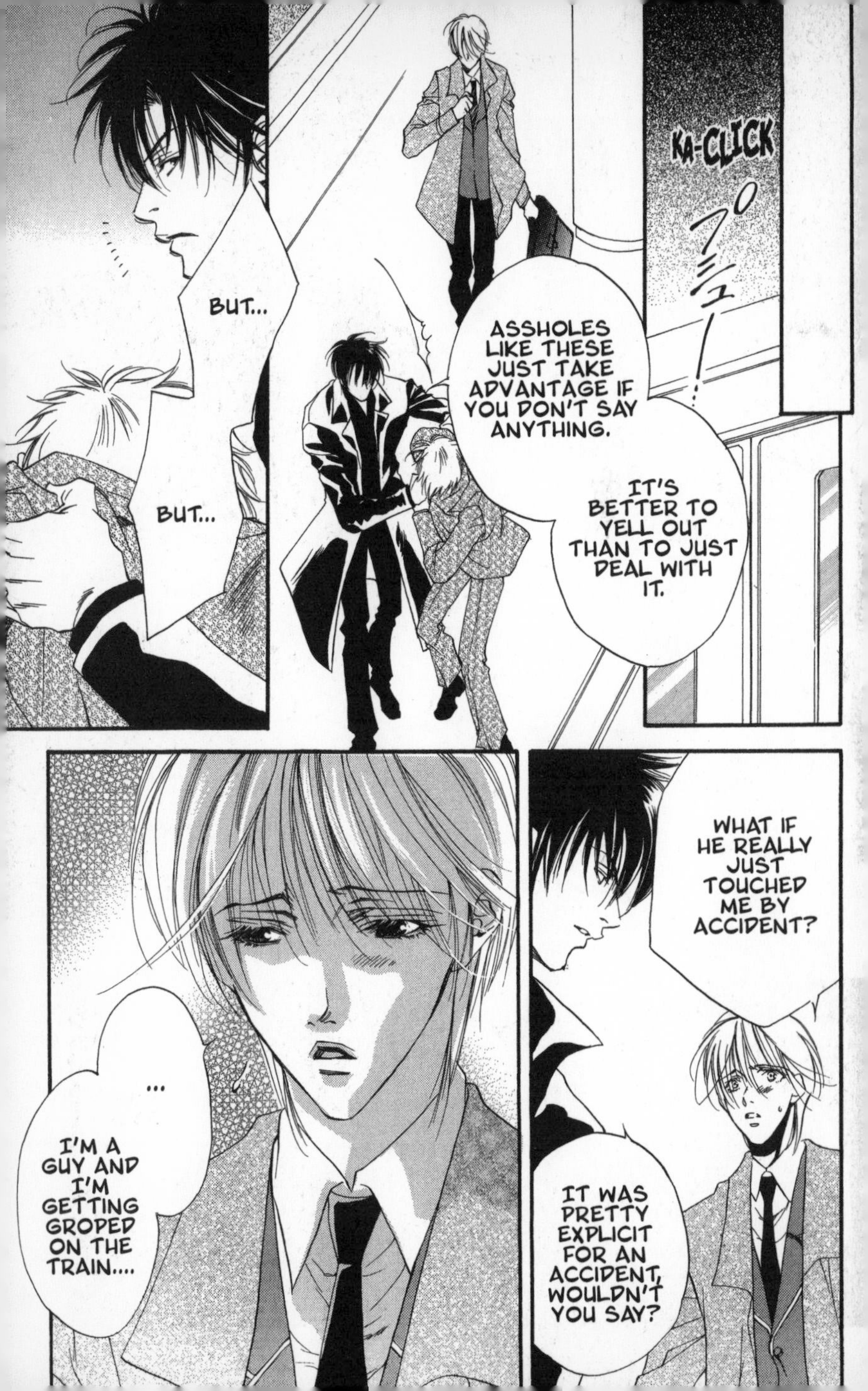
KA-CLICK
プシュー
ASSHOLES LIKE THESE JUST TAKE ADVANTAGE IF YOU DON'T SAY ANYTHING.
IT'S BETTER TO YELL OUT THAN TO JUST DEAL WITH IT.
BUT...
BUT...
WHAT IF HE REALLY JUST TOUCHED ME BY ACCIDENT?
IT WAS PRETTY EXPLICIT FOR AN ACCIDENT, WOULDN'T YOU SAY?
...
I'M A GUY AND I'M GETTING GROPED ON THE TRAIN....

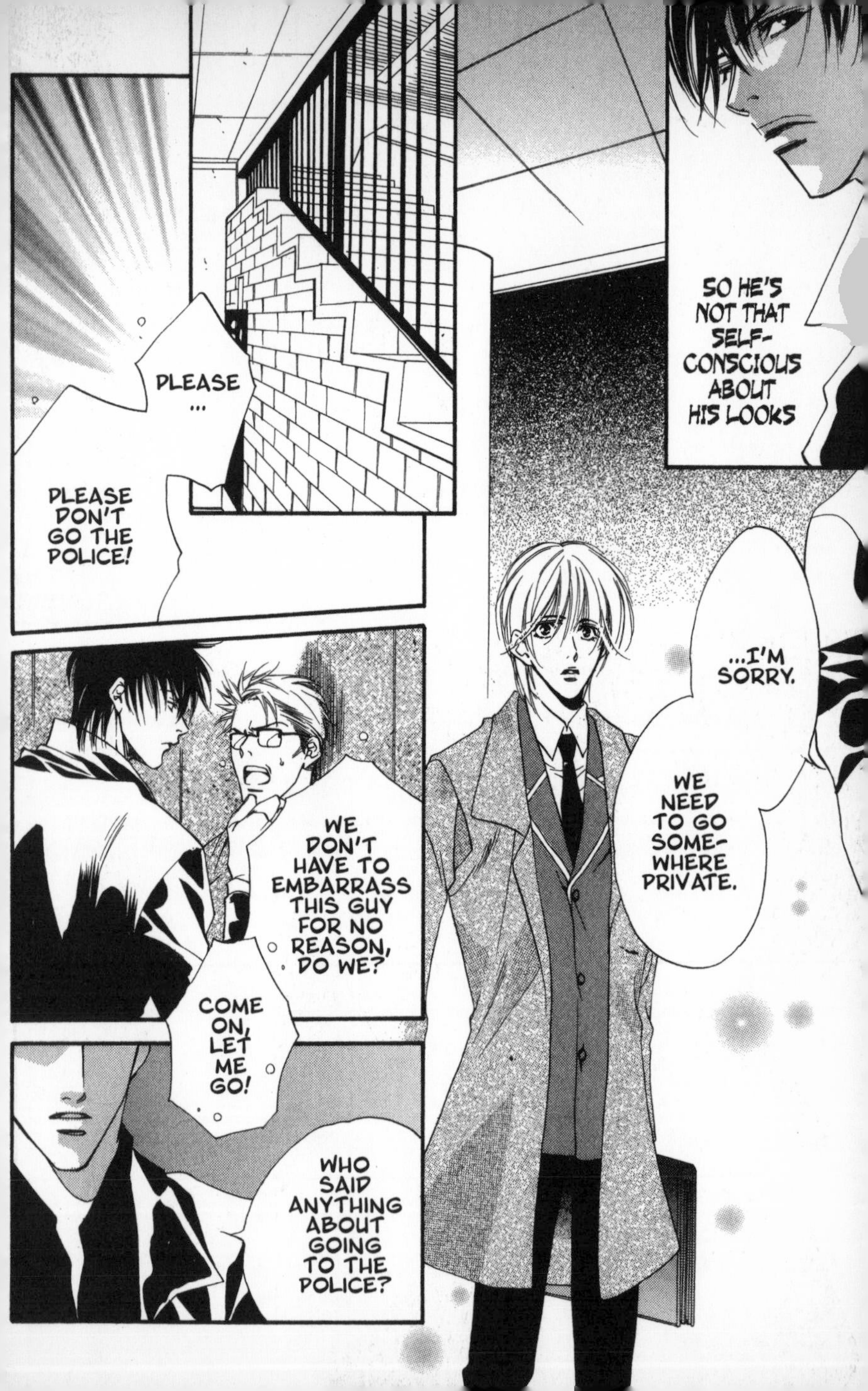
SO HE'S NOT THAT SELF-CONSCIOUS ABOUT HIS LOOKS
PLEASE ...
PLEASE DON'T GO THE POLICE!
...I'M SORRY.
WE NEED TO GO SOME-WHERE PRIVATE.
WE DON'T HAVE TO EMBARRASS THIS GUY FOR NO REASON, DO WE?
COME ON, LET ME GO!
WHO SAID ANYTHING ABOUT GOING TO THE POLICE?

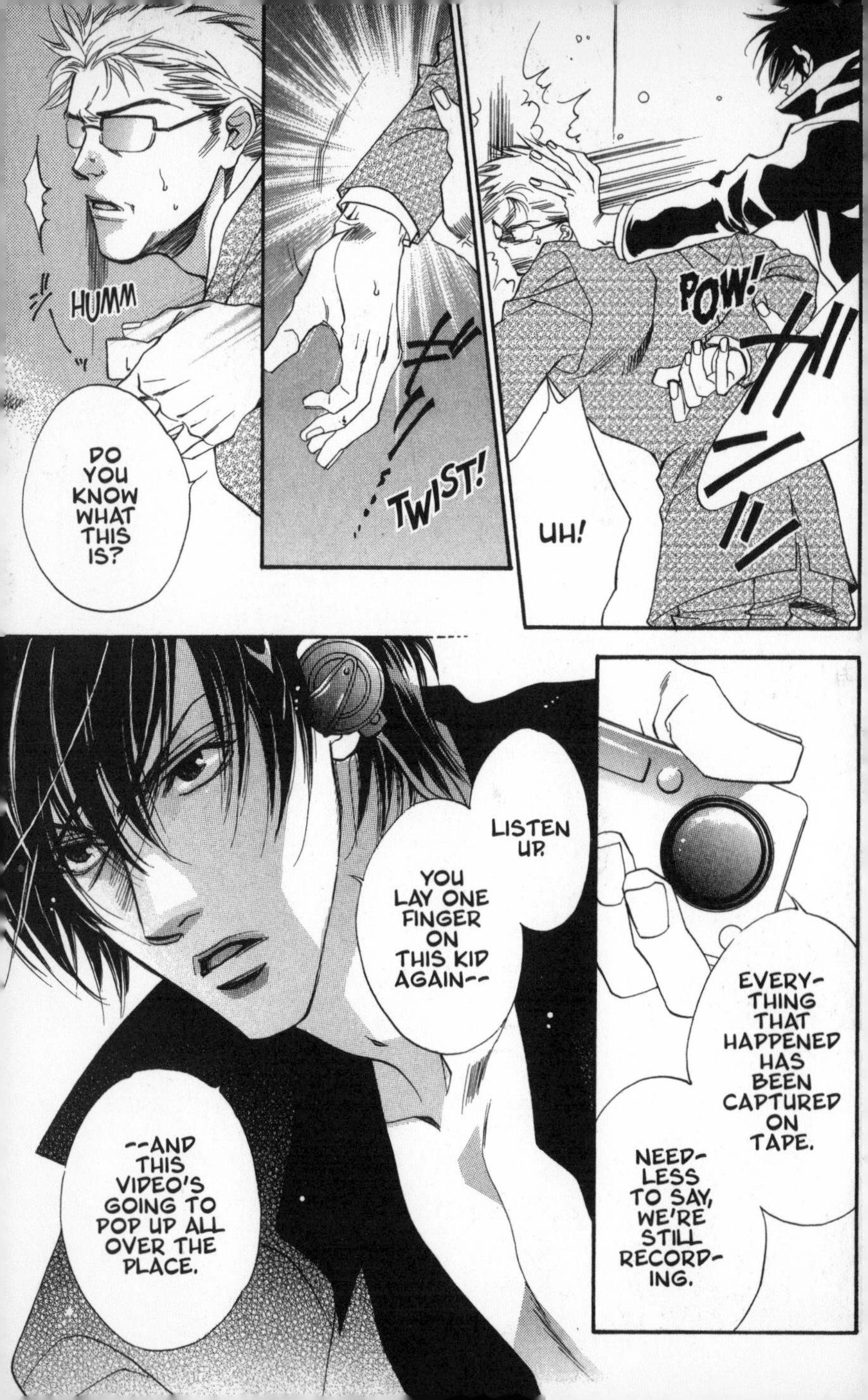
POW!
UH!
TWIST!
HUMM
DO YOU KNOW WHAT THIS IS?
EVERY-THING THAT HAPPENED HAS BEEN CAPTURED ON TAPE.
NEED-LESS TO SAY, WE'RE STILL RECORD-ING.
LISTEN UP.
YOU LAY ONE FINGER ON THIS KID AGAIN--
--AND THIS VIDEO'S GOING TO POP UP ALL OVER THE PLACE.

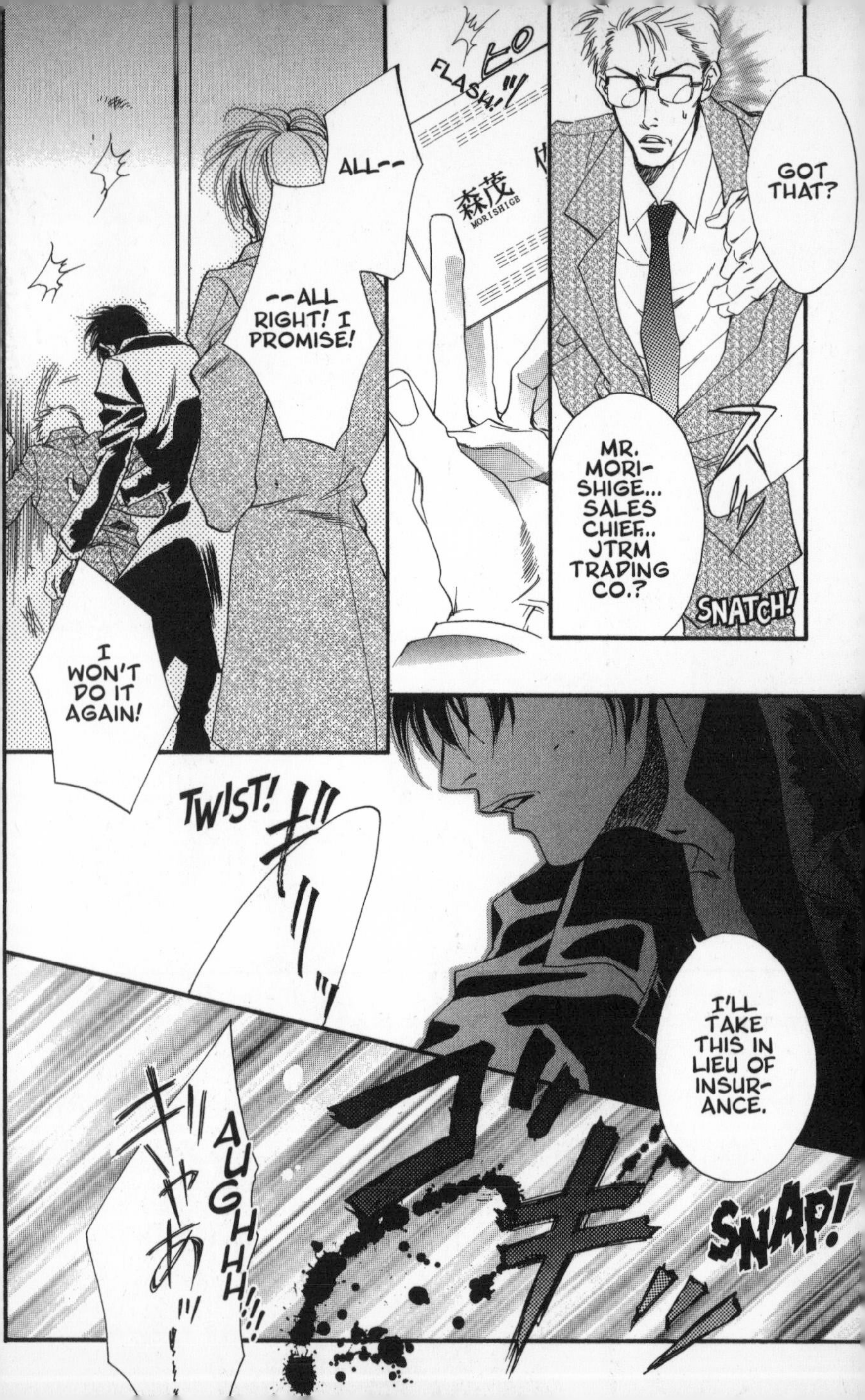
GOT THAT?
MR. MORI-SHIGE... SALES CHIEF... JTRM TRADING CO.?
SNATCH!
FLASH!
ピ
森茂
MORISHIGE
ALL--
--ALL RIGHT! I PROMISE!
I WON'T DO IT AGAIN!
I'LL TAKE THIS IN LIEU OF INSUR-ANCE.
TWIST!
ギリ
SNAP!
ゴキ
AUGHHH!!!
ぎゃあ

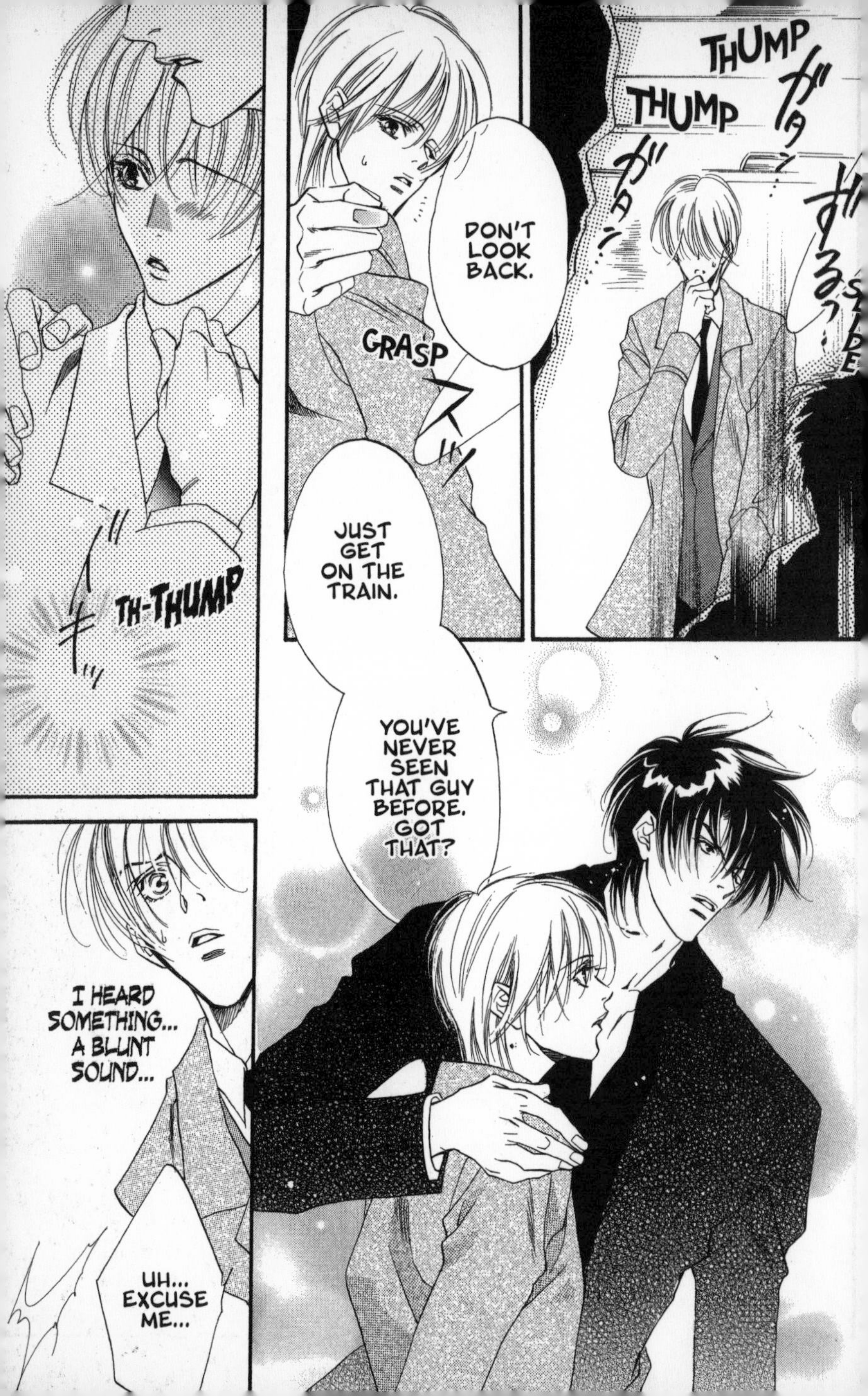
THUMP
THUMP
SLIDE
DON'T LOOK BACK.
GRASP
JUST GET ON THE TRAIN.
TH-THUMP
YOU'VE NEVER SEEN THAT GUY BEFORE. GOT THAT?
I HEARD SOMETHING... A BLUNT SOUND...
UH... EXCUSE ME...

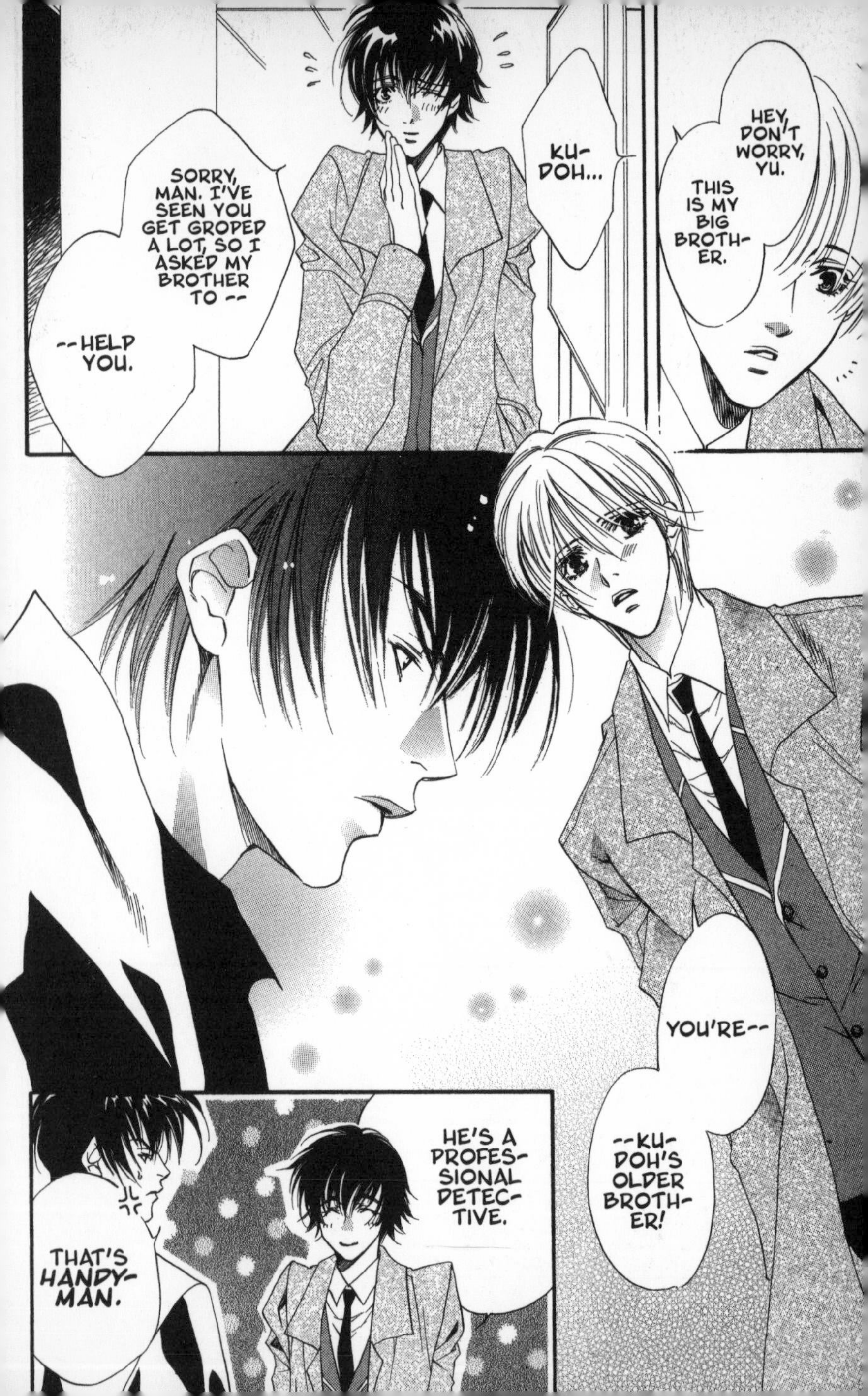
HEY, DON'T WORRY, YU.
THIS IS MY BIG BROTHER.
KU-DOH...
SORRY, MAN. I'VE SEEN YOU GET GROPED A LOT, SO I ASKED MY BROTHER TO --
--HELP YOU.
YOU'RE--
--KU-DOH'S OLDER BROTHER!
HE'S A PROFESSIONAL DETECTIVE.
THAT'S HANDYMAN.

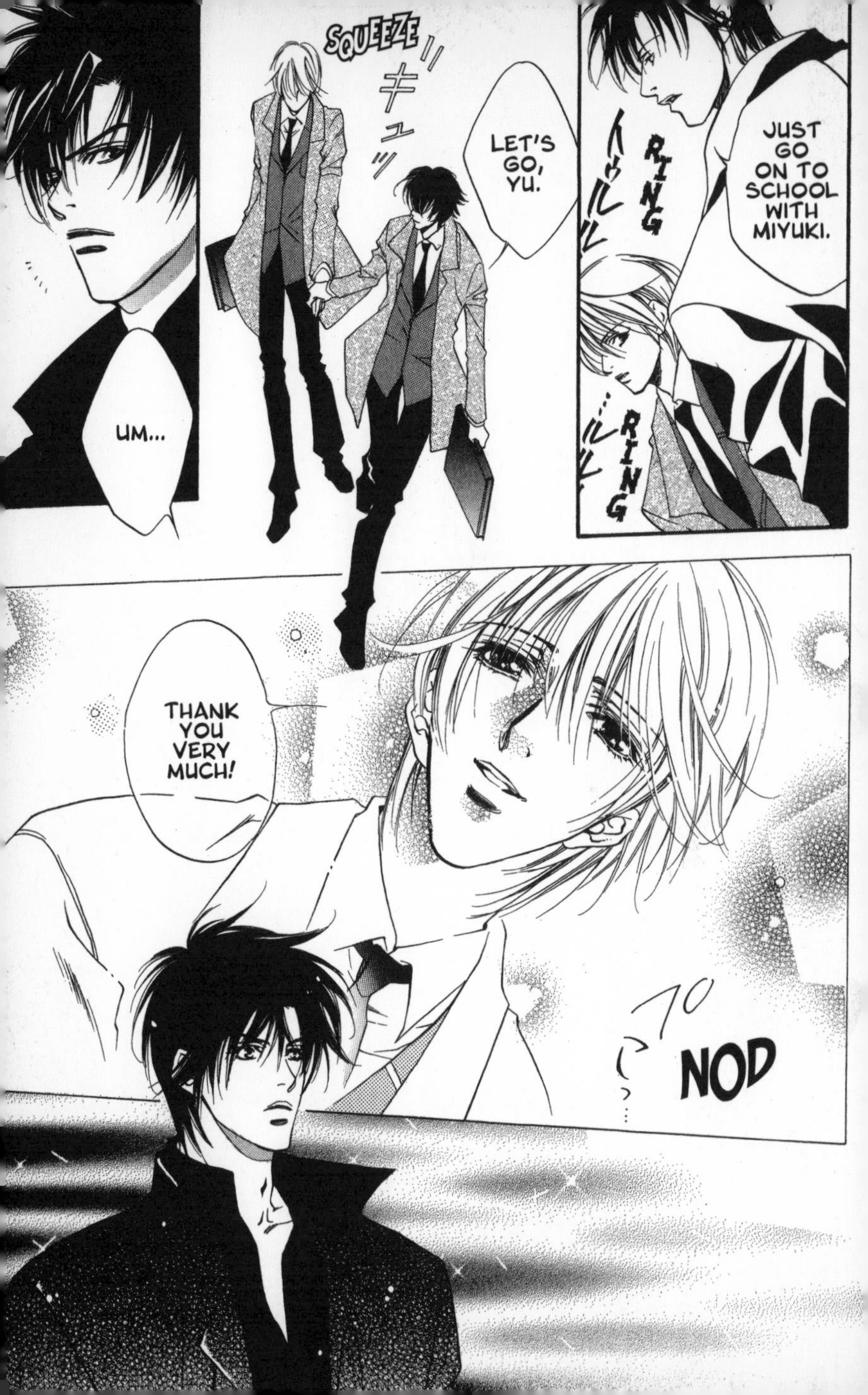
JUST GO ON TO SCHOOL WITH MIYUKI.
RING
RING RING
SQUEEZE
LET'S GO, YU.
UM...
THANK YOU VERY MUCH!
NOD

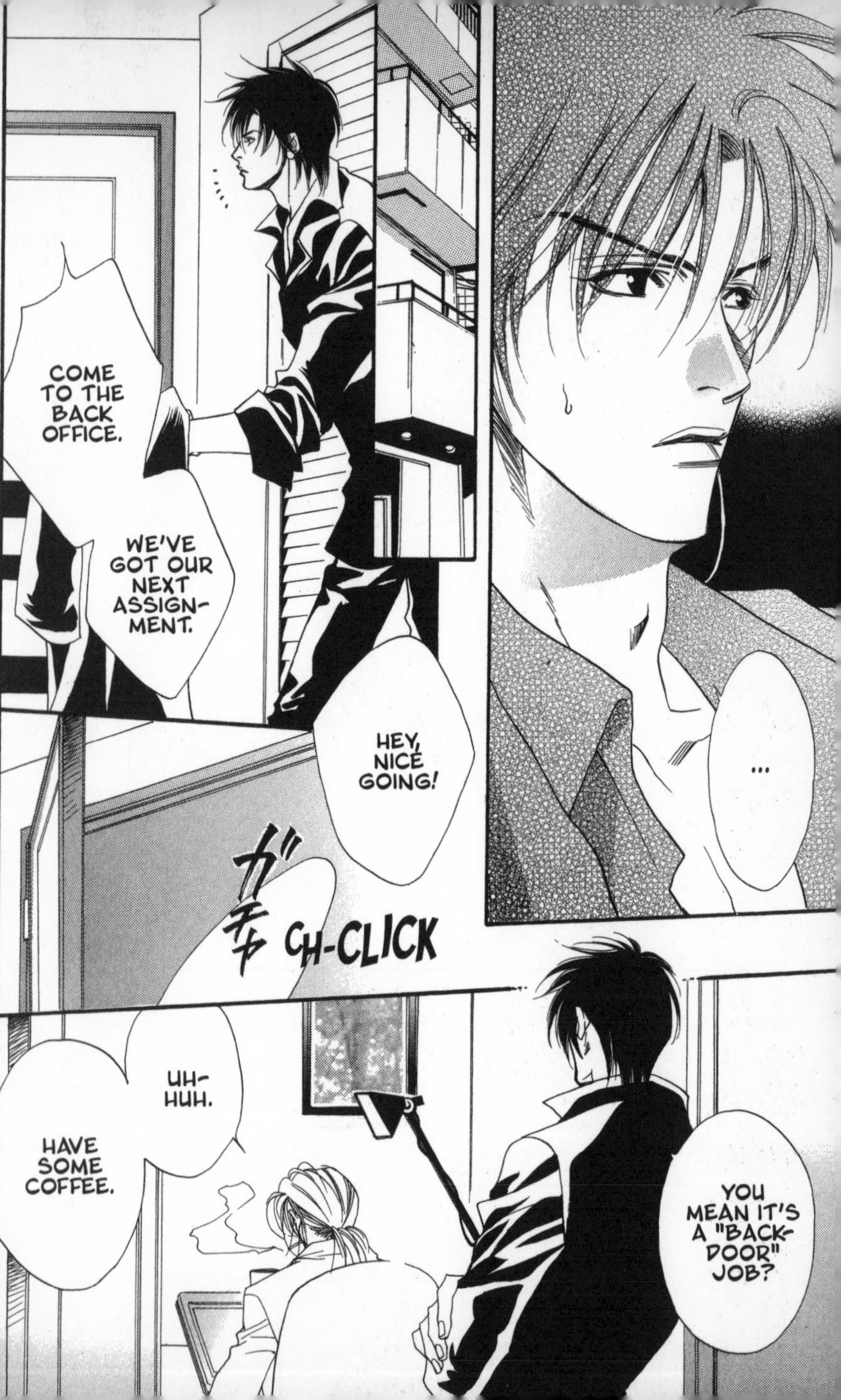
...
....
COME TO THE BACK OFFICE.
WE'VE GOT OUR NEXT ASSIGNMENT.
HEY, NICE GOING!
ガチャ
CH-CLICK
YOU MEAN IT'S A "BACK-DOOR" JOB?
UH-HUH.
HAVE SOME COFFEE.

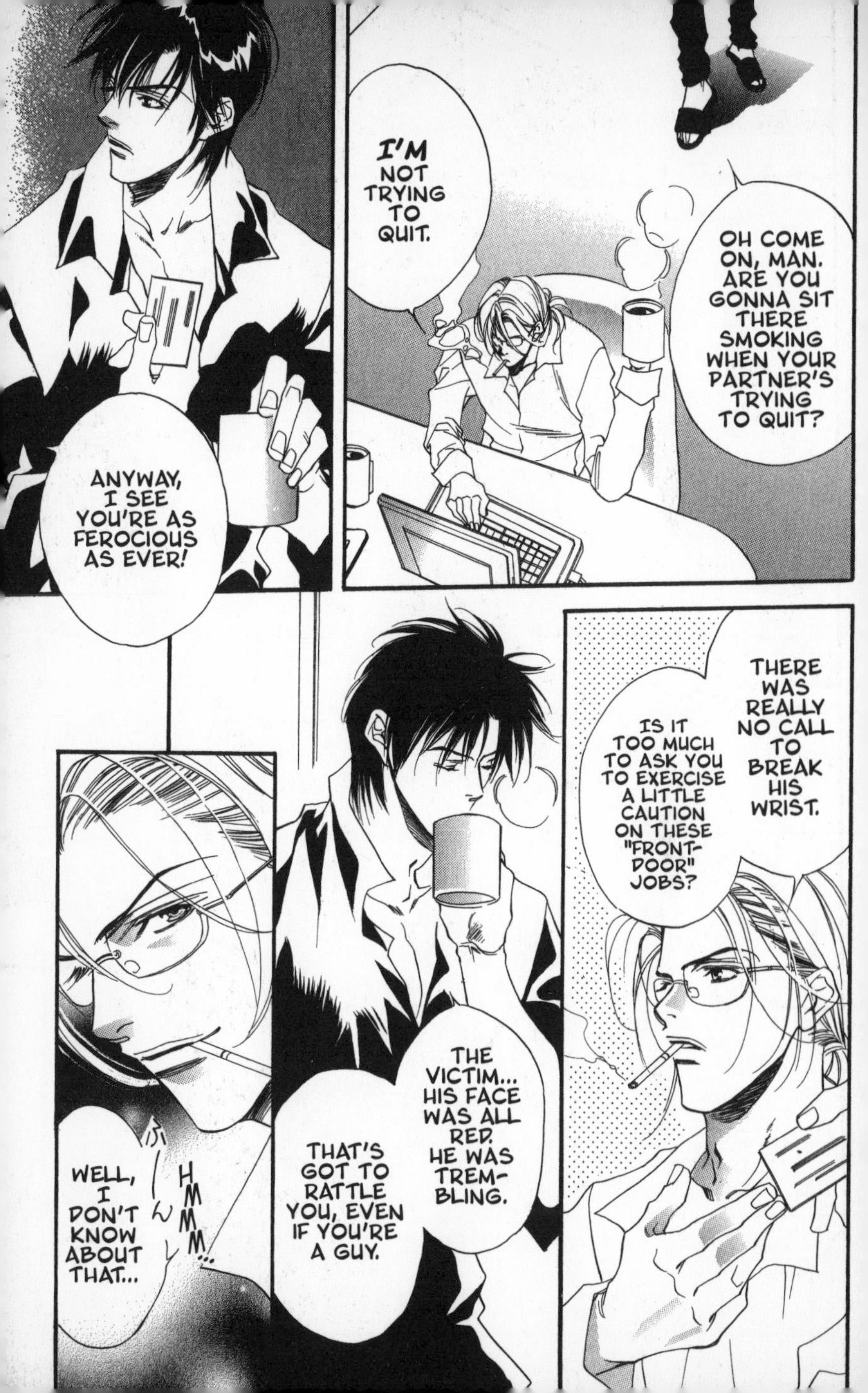
OH COME ON, MAN. ARE YOU GONNA SIT THERE SMOKING WHEN YOUR PARTNER'S TRYING TO QUIT?
I'M NOT TRYING TO QUIT.
ANYWAY, I SEE YOU'RE AS FEROCIOUS AS EVER!
THERE WAS REALLY NO CALL TO BREAK HIS WRIST.
IS IT TOO MUCH TO ASK YOU TO EXERCISE A LITTLE CAUTION ON THESE "FRONT-DOOR" JOBS?
THE VICTIM... HIS FACE WAS ALL RED. HE WAS TREM-BLING.
THAT'S GOT TO RATTLE YOU, EVEN IF YOU'RE A GUY.
HMMM...
WELL, I DON'T KNOW ABOUT THAT...

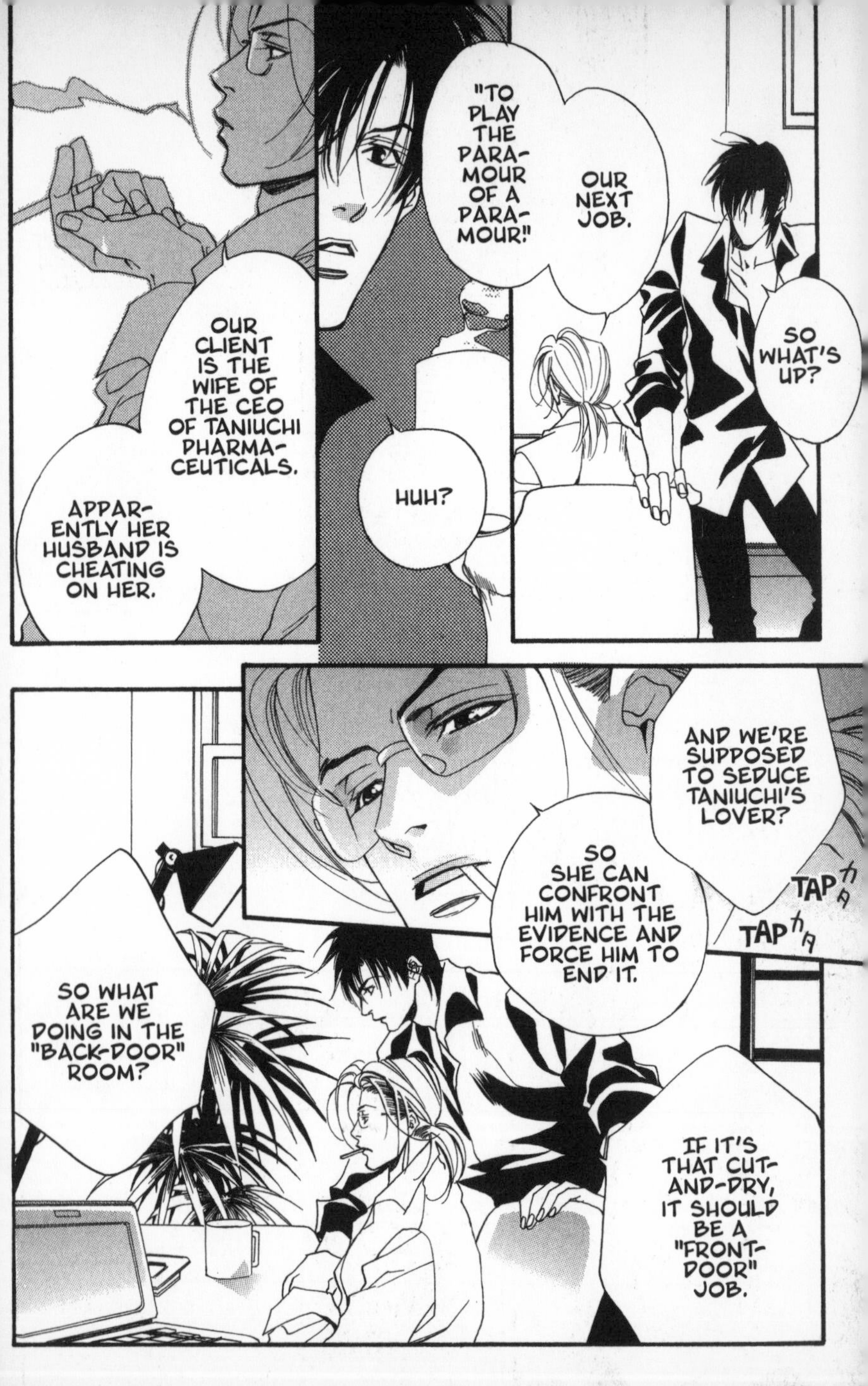
SO WHAT'S UP?
OUR NEXT JOB.
"TO PLAY THE PARAMOUR OF A PARAMOUR!"
HUH?
OUR CLIENT IS THE WIFE OF THE CEO OF TANIUCHI PHARMACEUTICALS.
APPARENTLY HER HUSBAND IS CHEATING ON HER.
AND WE'RE SUPPOSED TO SEDUCE TANIUCHI'S LOVER?
TAP
TAP
SO SHE CAN CONFRONT HIM WITH THE EVIDENCE AND FORCE HIM TO END IT.
IF IT'S THAT CUT-AND-DRY, IT SHOULD BE A "FRONT-DOOR" JOB.
SO WHAT ARE WE DOING IN THE "BACK-DOOR" ROOM?

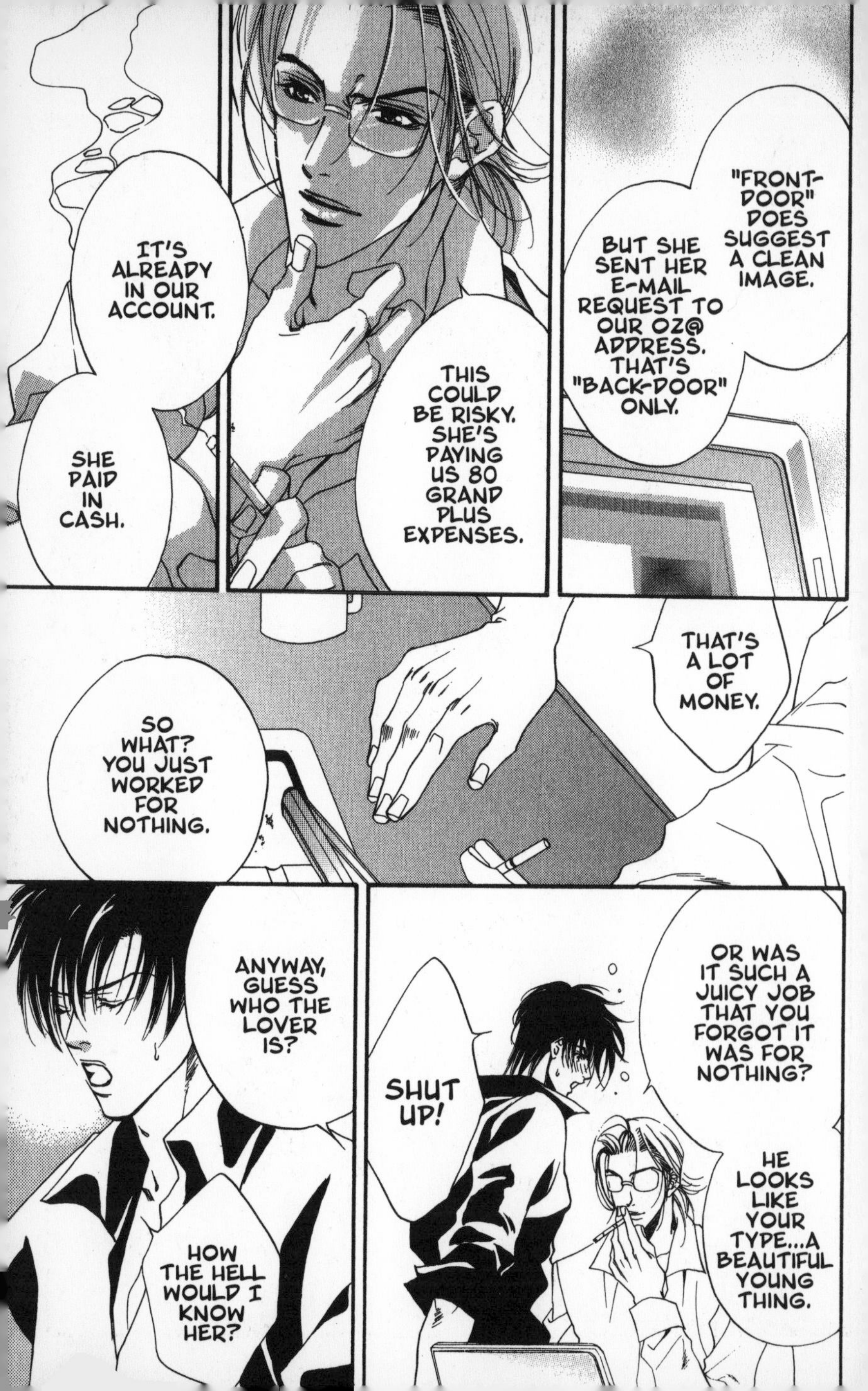
"FRONT-DOOR" DOES SUGGEST A CLEAN IMAGE.
BUT SHE SENT HER E-MAIL REQUEST TO OUR OZ@ ADDRESS. THAT'S "BACK-DOOR" ONLY.
THIS COULD BE RISKY. SHE'S PAYING US 80 GRAND PLUS EXPENSES.
IT'S ALREADY IN OUR ACCOUNT.
SHE PAID IN CASH.
THAT'S A LOT OF MONEY.
SO WHAT? YOU JUST WORKED FOR NOTHING.
OR WAS IT SUCH A JUICY JOB THAT YOU FORGOT IT WAS FOR NOTHING?
SHUT UP!
HE LOOKS LIKE YOUR TYPE...A BEAUTIFUL YOUNG THING.
ANYWAY, GUESS WHO THE LOVER IS?
HOW THE HELL WOULD I KNOW HER?

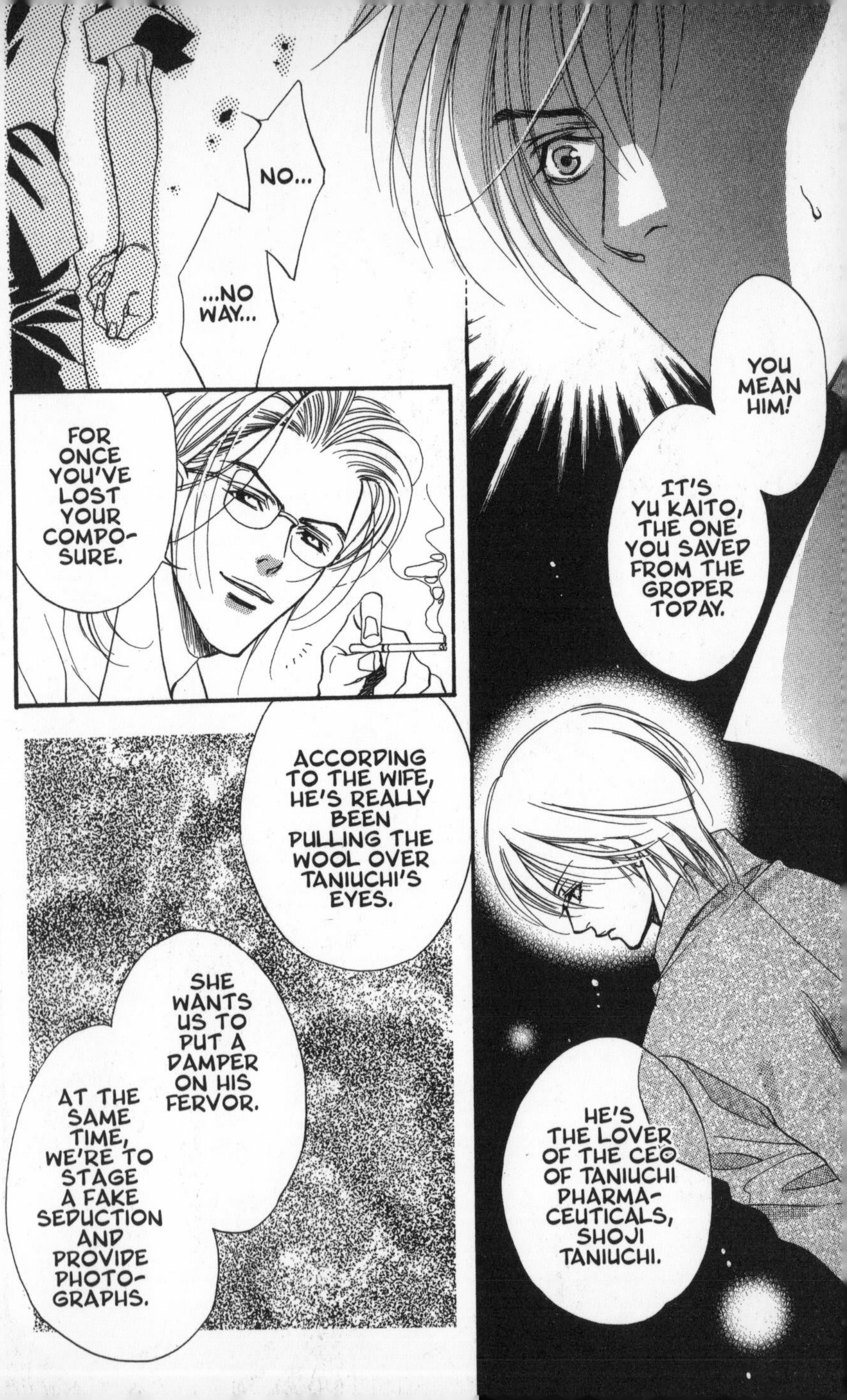
YOU MEAN HIM!
IT'S YU KAITO, THE ONE YOU SAVED FROM THE GROPER TODAY.
HE'S THE LOVER OF THE CEO OF TANIUCHI PHARMACEUTICALS, SHOJI TANIUCHI.
NO...
...NO WAY...
FOR ONCE YOU'VE LOST YOUR COMPOSURE.
ACCORDING TO THE WIFE, HE'S REALLY BEEN PULLING THE WOOL OVER TANIUCHI'S EYES.
SHE WANTS US TO PUT A DAMPER ON HIS FERVOR.
AT THE SAME TIME, WE'RE TO STAGE A FAKE SEDUCTION AND PROVIDE PHOTOGRAPHS.

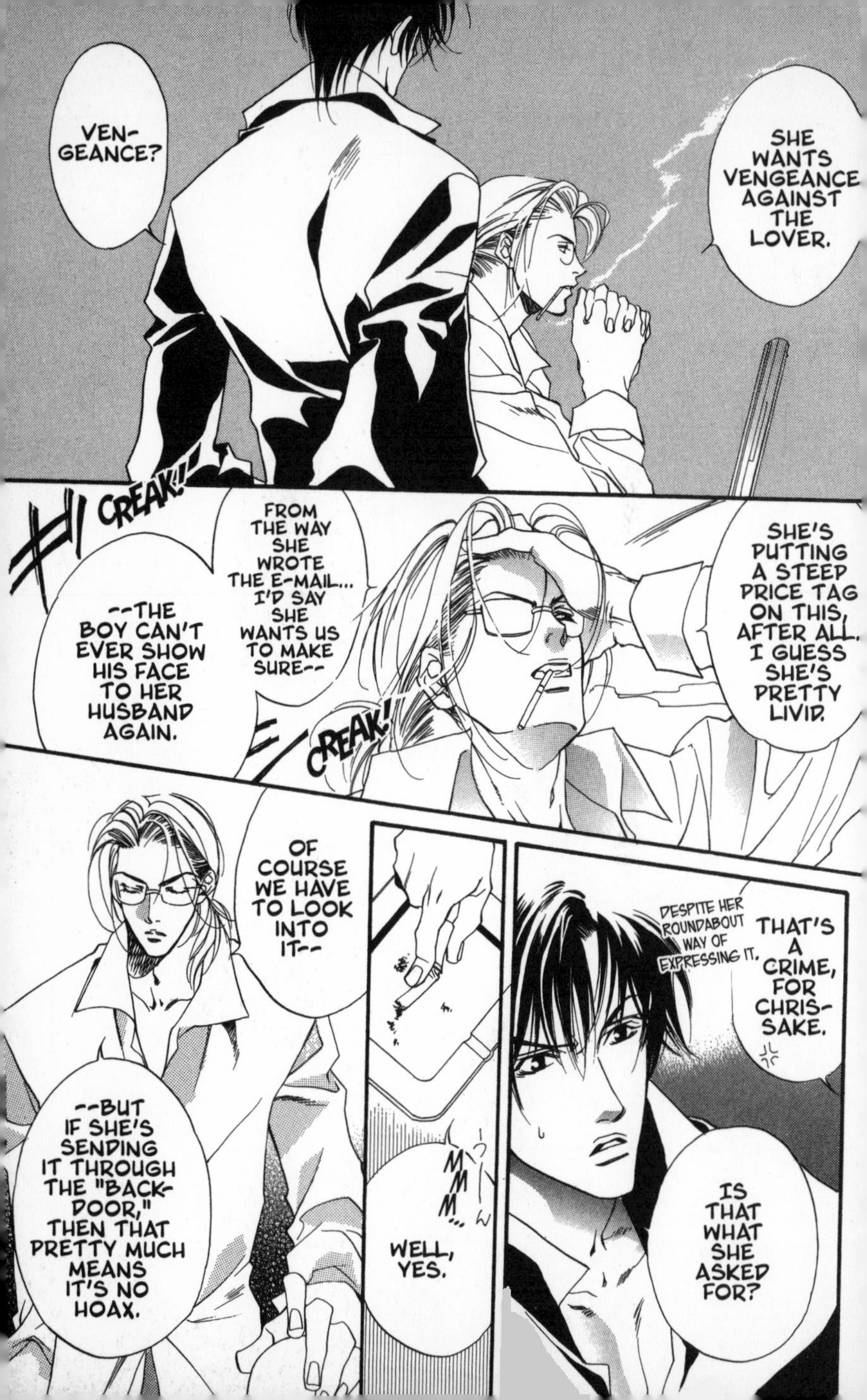
SHE WANTS VENGEANCE AGAINST THE LOVER.
VEN-GEANCE?
SHE'S PUTTING A STEEP PRICE TAG ON THIS, AFTER ALL. I GUESS SHE'S PRETTY LIVID.
CREAK!
FROM THE WAY SHE WROTE THE E-MAIL... I'D SAY SHE WANTS US TO MAKE SURE--
--THE BOY CAN'T EVER SHOW HIS FACE TO HER HUSBAND AGAIN.
CREAK!
THAT'S A CRIME, FOR CHRIS-SAKE.
DESPITE HER ROUNDABOUT WAY OF EXPRESSING IT.
IS THAT WHAT SHE ASKED FOR?
MMMM...
WELL, YES.
OF COURSE WE HAVE TO LOOK INTO IT--
--BUT IF SHE'S SENDING IT THROUGH THE "BACK-DOOR," THEN THAT PRETTY MUCH MEANS IT'S NO HOAX.

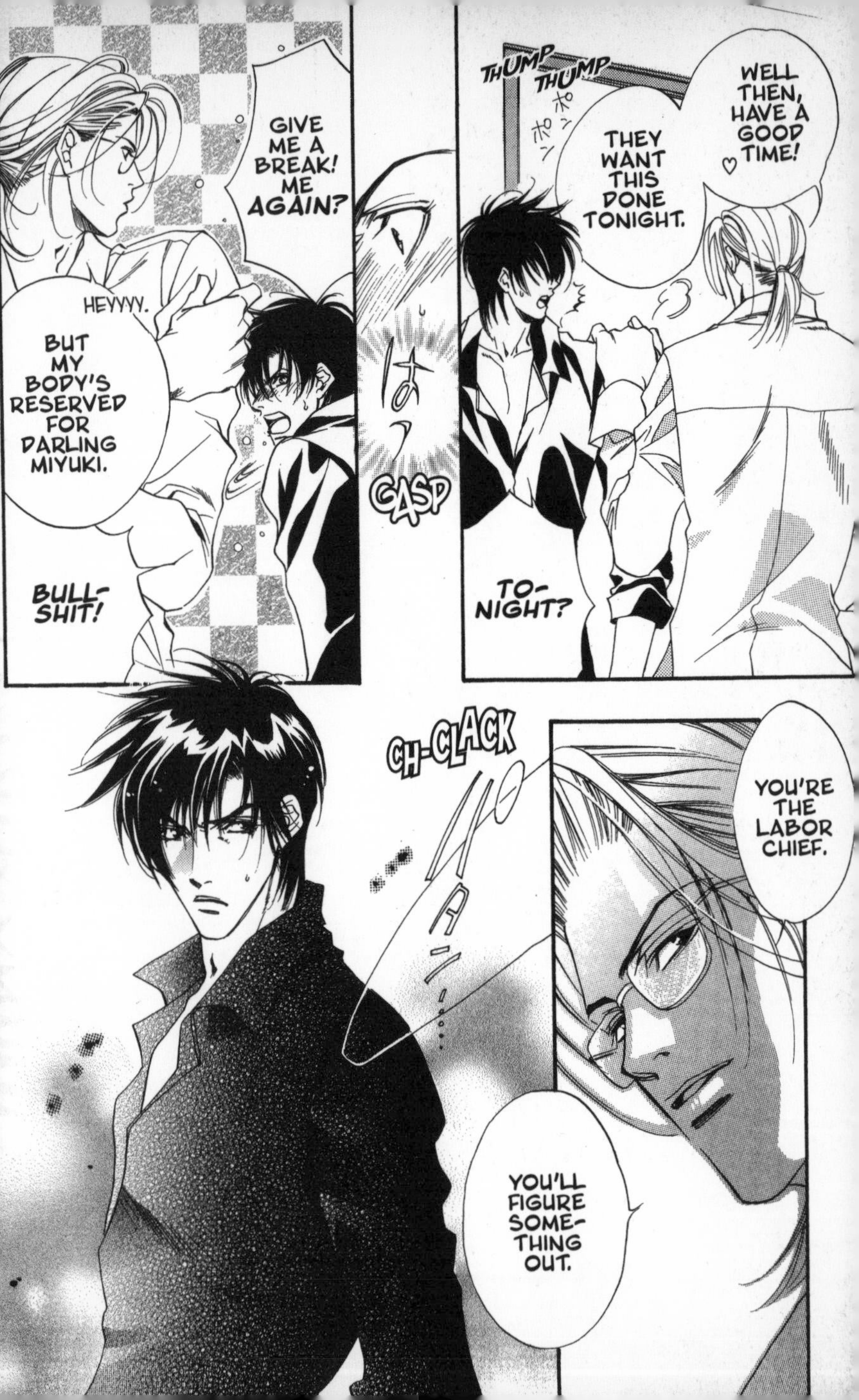
WELL THEN, HAVE A GOOD TIME! ♥
THUMP THUMP
ポン ポン
THEY WANT THIS DONE TONIGHT.
TO-NIGHT?
はっ
GASP
GIVE ME A BREAK! ME AGAIN?
HEYYYY.
BUT MY BODY'S RESERVED FOR DARLING MIYUKI.
BULL-SHIT!
YOU'RE THE LABOR CHIEF.
YOU'LL FIGURE SOMETHING OUT.
CH-CLACK

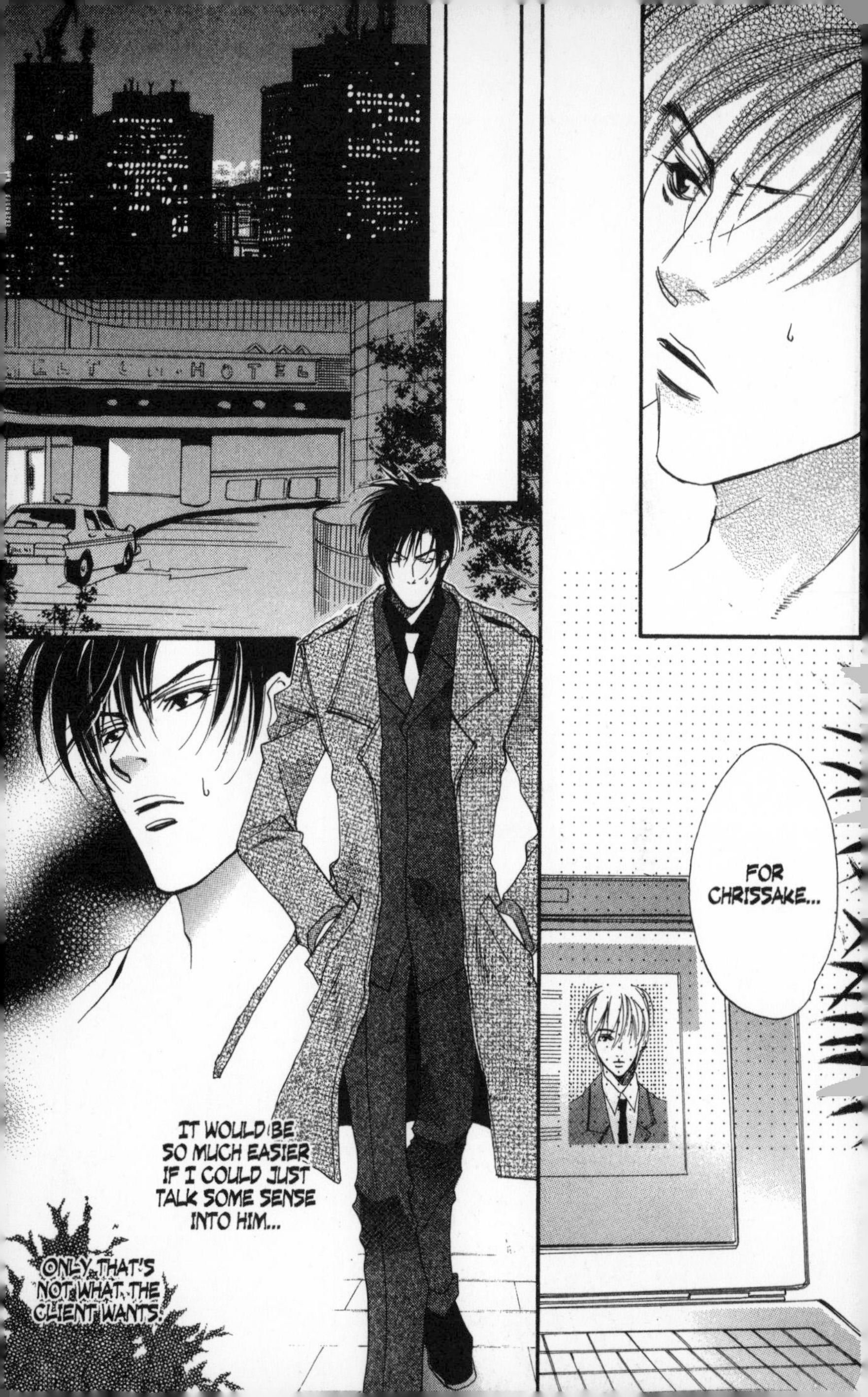
FOR CHRISSAKE...
IT WOULD BE SO MUCH EASIER IF I COULD JUST TALK SOME SENSE INTO HIM...
ONLY THAT'S NOT WHAT THE CLIENT WANTS.

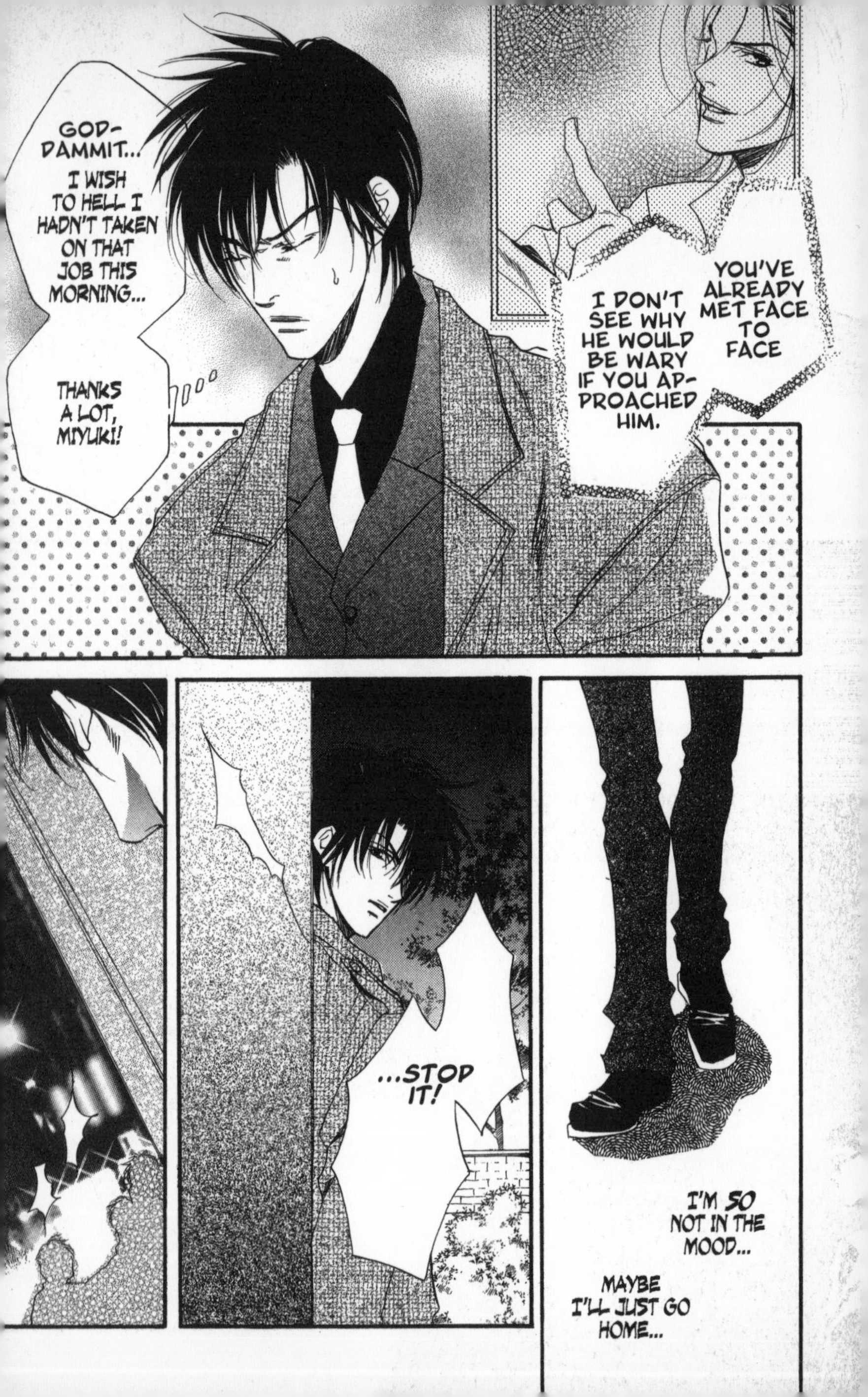

YOU'VE ALREADY MET FACE TO FACE
I DON'T SEE WHY HE WOULD BE WARY IF YOU AP-PROACHED HIM.
GOD-DAMMIT... I WISH TO HELL I HADN'T TAKEN ON THAT JOB THIS MORNING...
THANKS A LOT, MIYUKI!
I'M SO NOT IN THE MOOD...
MAYBE I'LL JUST GO HOME...
...STOP IT!

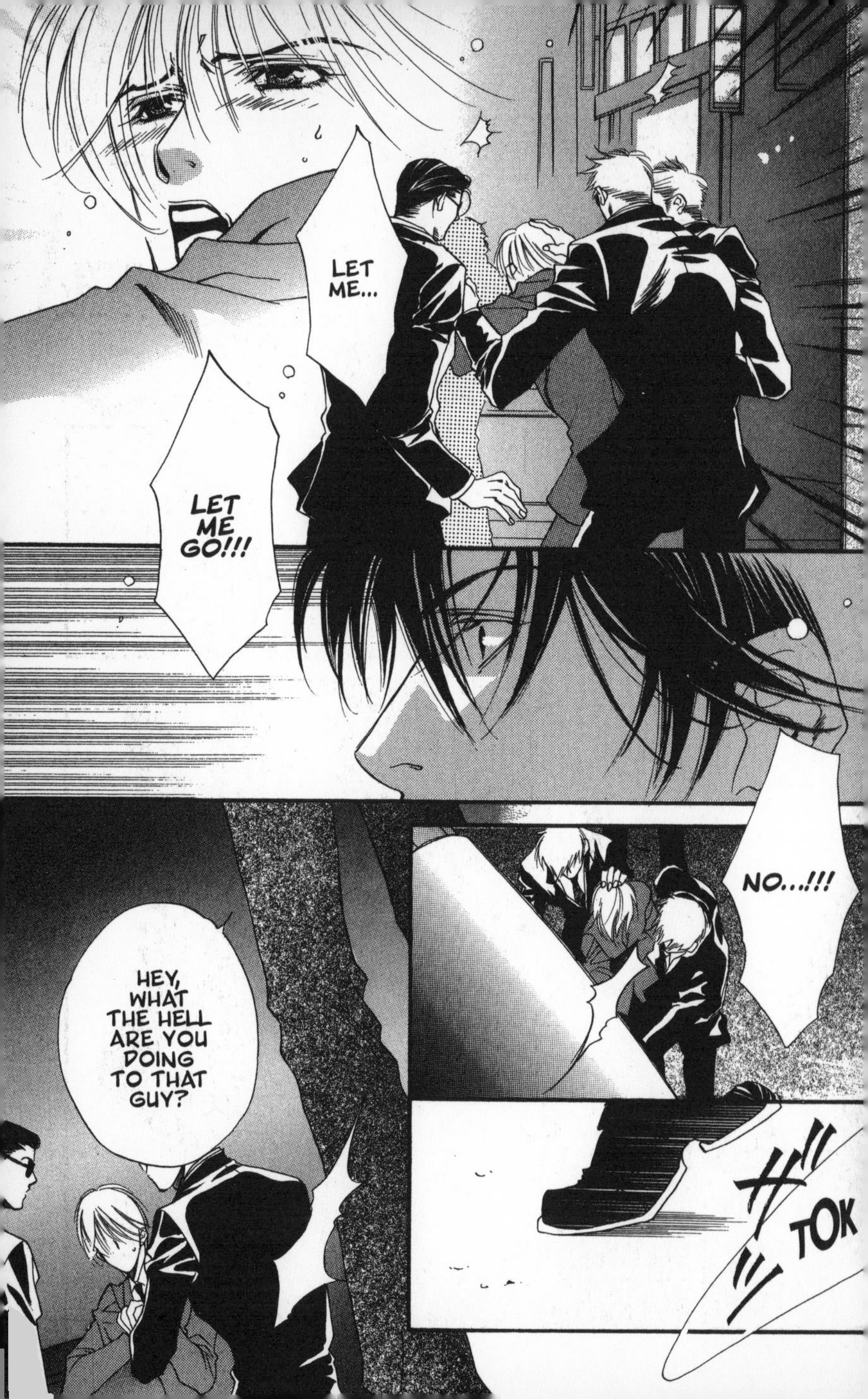
LET ME...
LET ME GO!!!
NO...!!!
ザッ
TOK
HEY, WHAT THE HELL ARE YOU DOING TO THAT GUY?

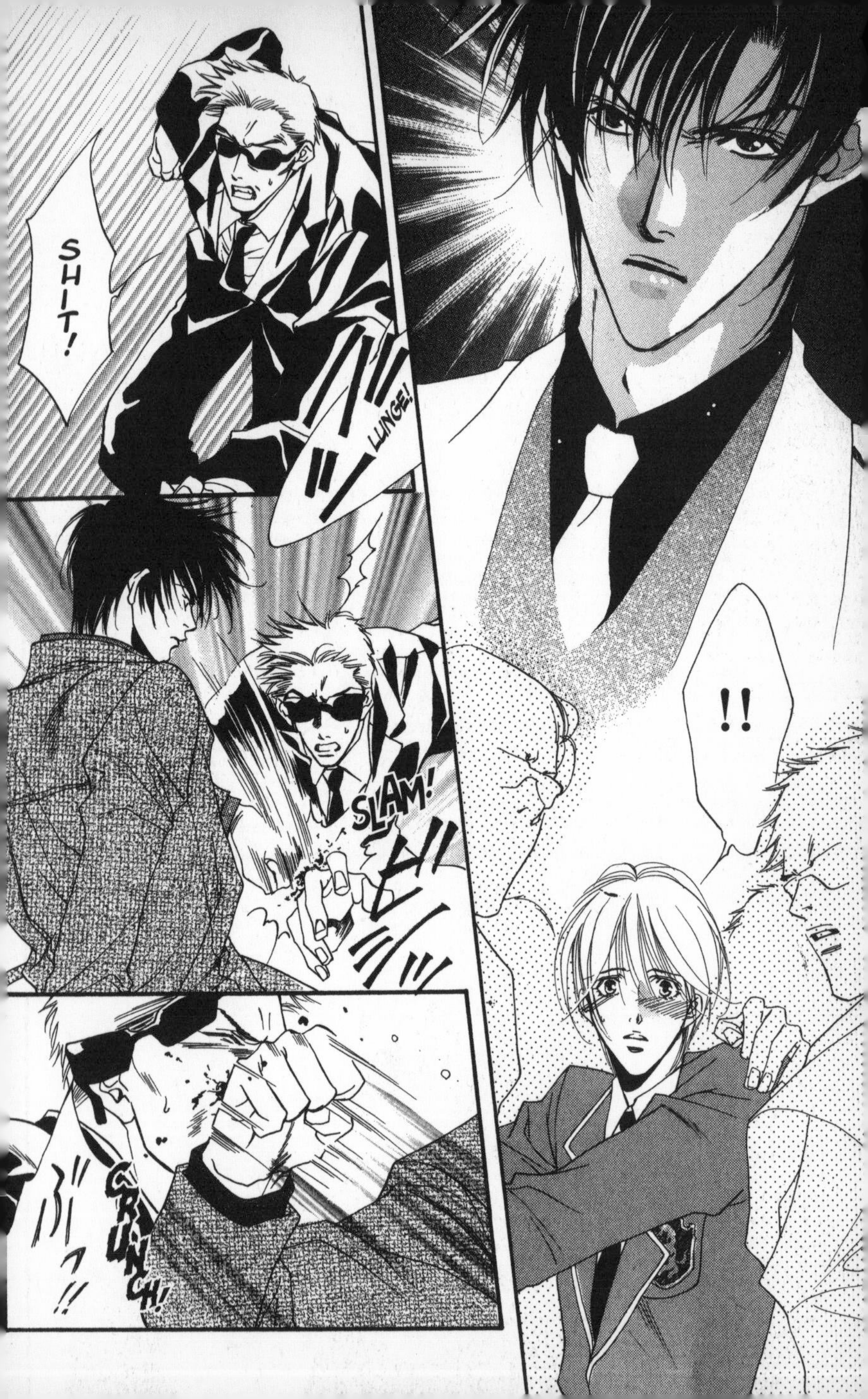
!!
SHIT!
LUNGE!
SLAM!
CRUNCH!

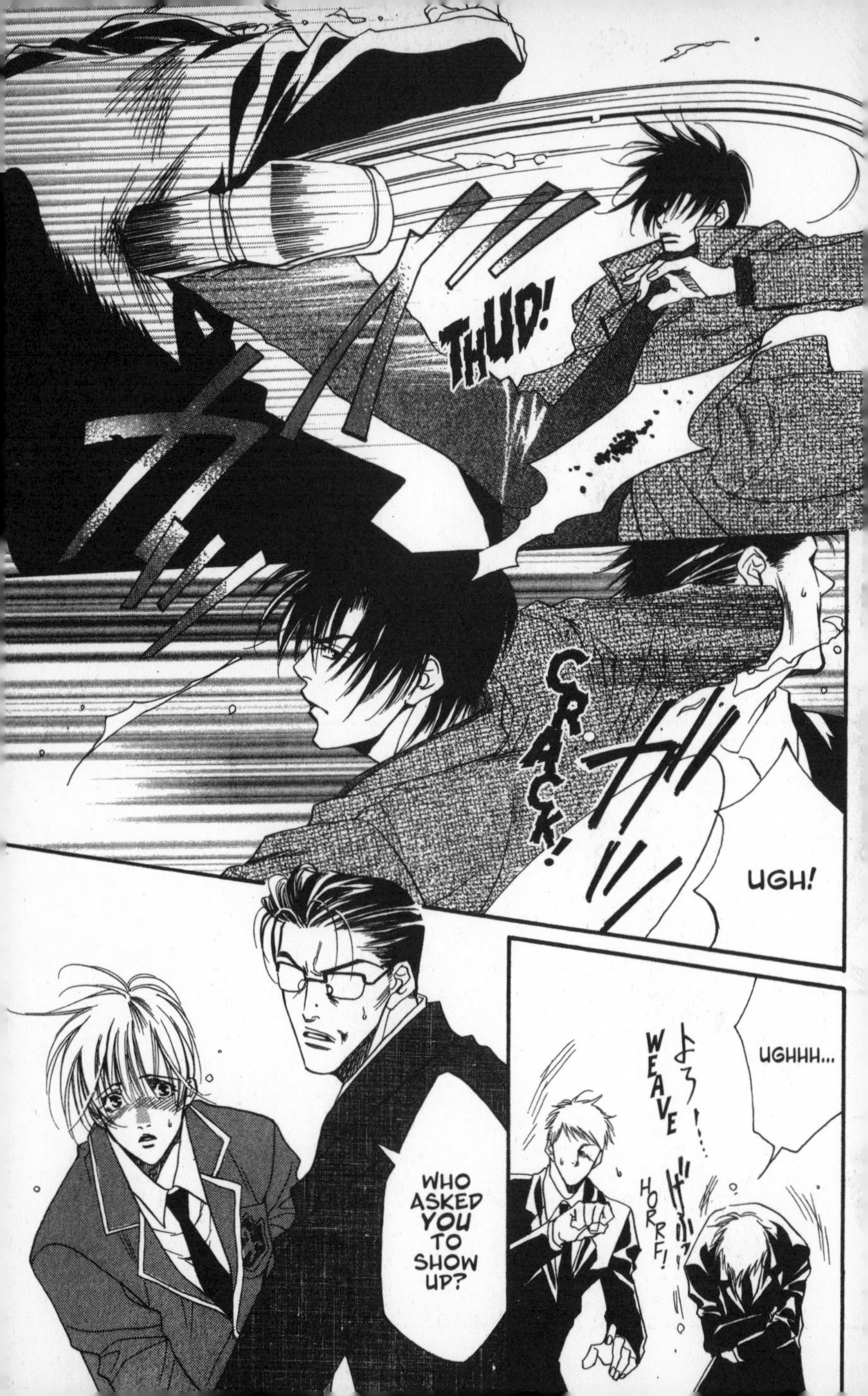
THUD!
CRACK!
UGH!
UGHHH...
よろ
WEAVE
HORF!
WHO ASKED YOU TO SHOW UP?

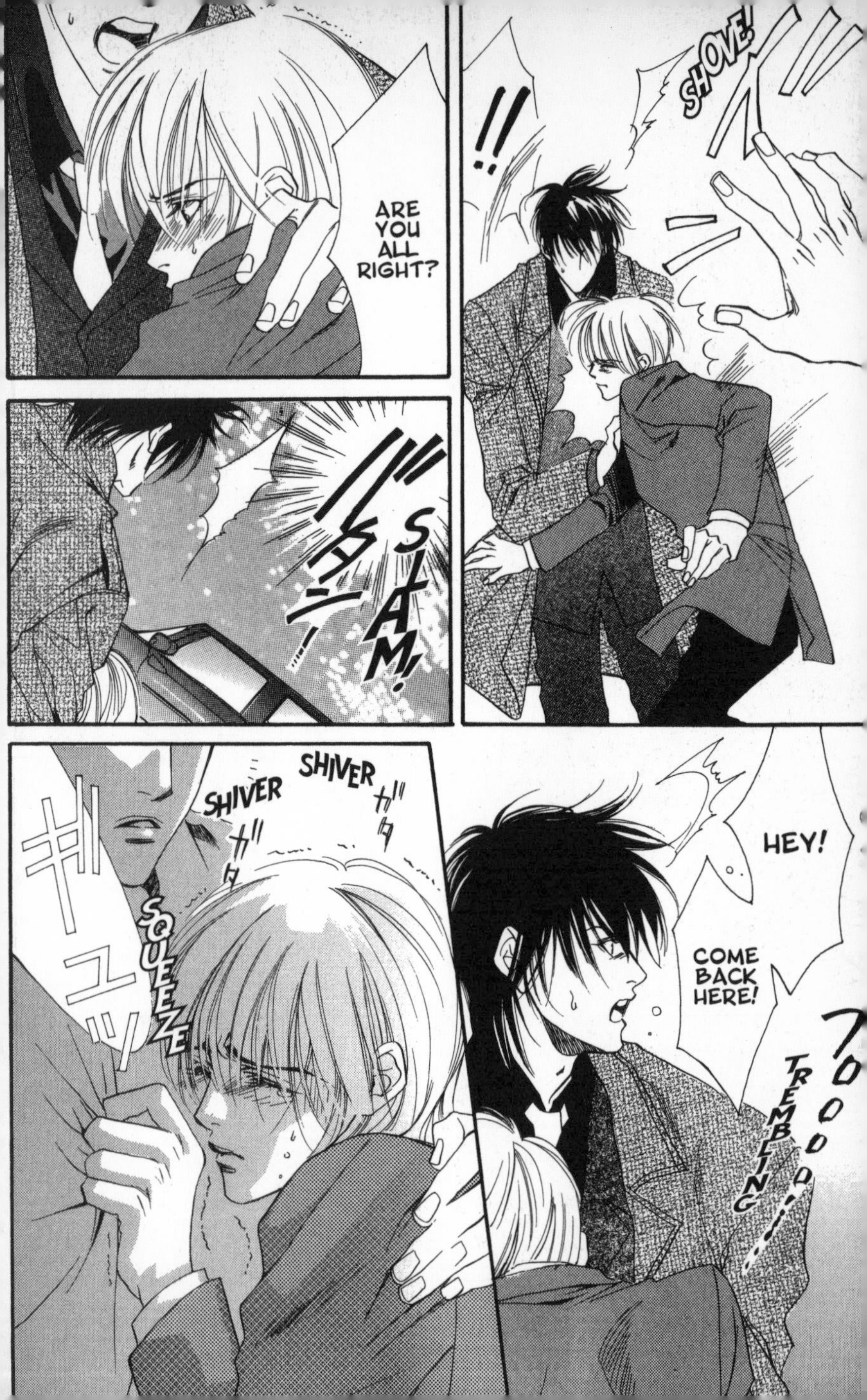
SHOVE!
!!
ARE YOU ALL RIGHT?
SLAM!
HEY!
COME BACK HERE!
TREMBLING...
SHIVER
SHIVER
SQUEEZE

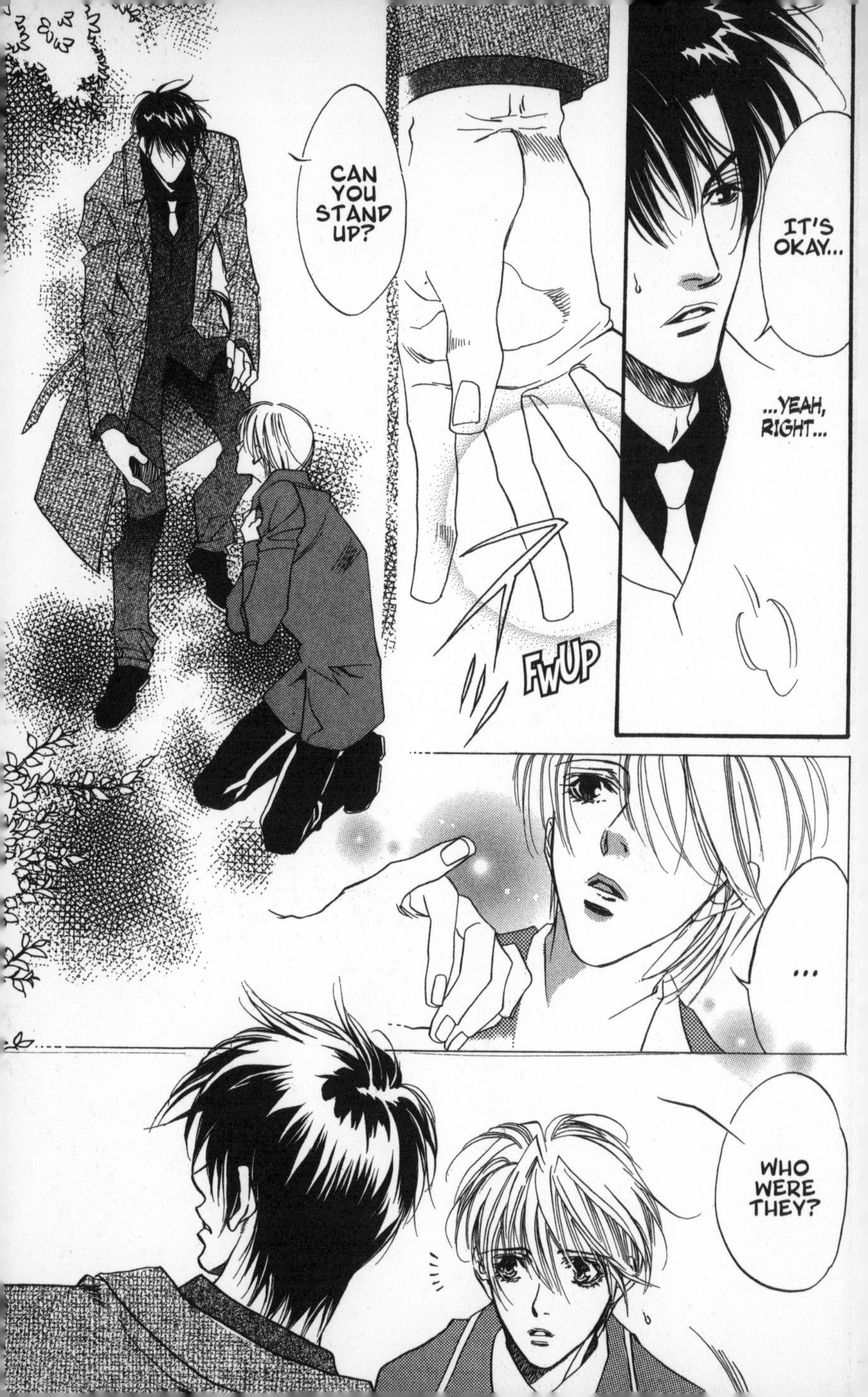
IT'S OKAY...
...YEAH, RIGHT...
FWUP
...
CAN YOU STAND UP?
WHO WERE THEY?

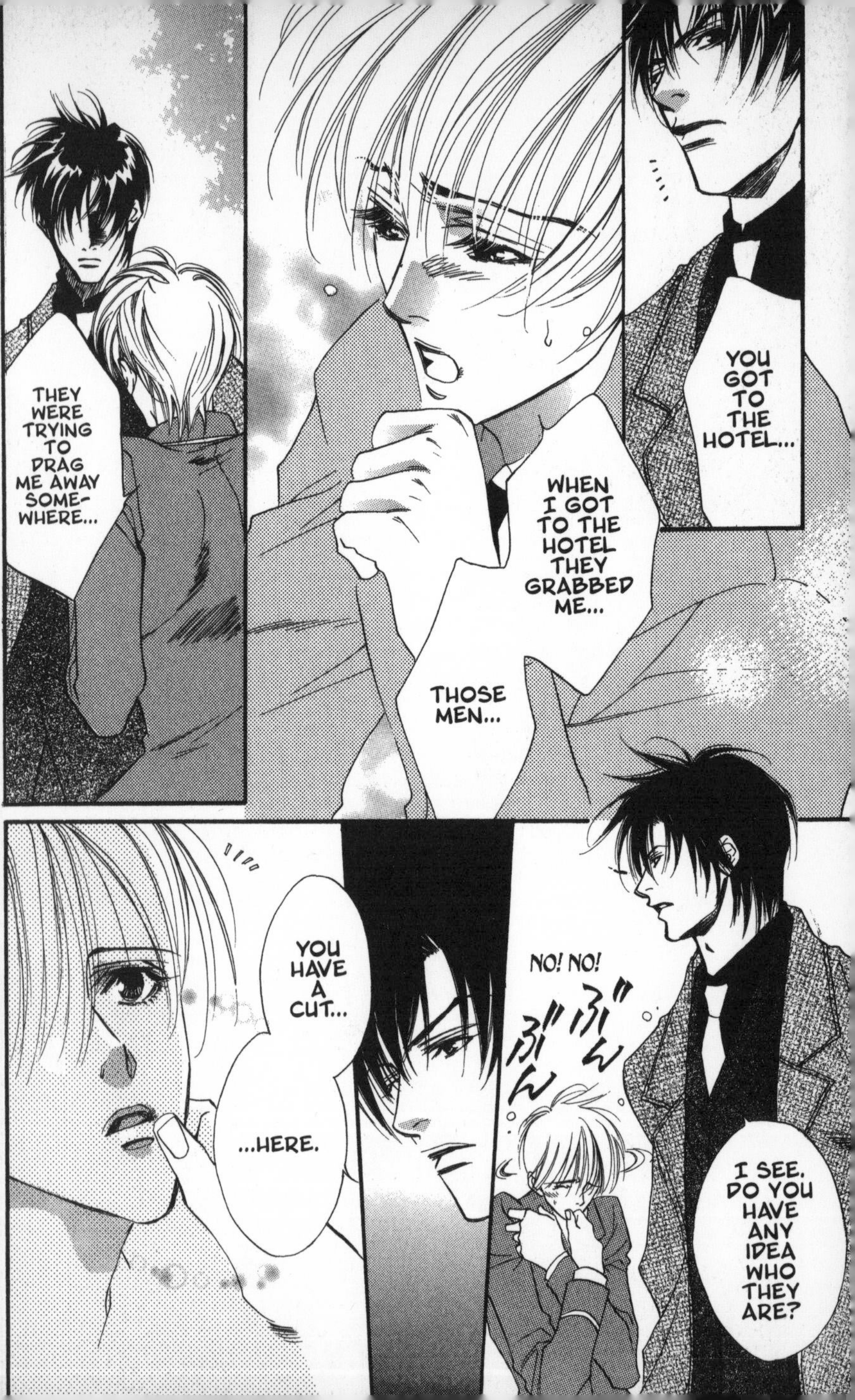
YOU GOT TO THE HOTEL...
WHEN I GOT TO THE HOTEL THEY GRABBED ME...
THOSE MEN...
THEY WERE TRYING TO DRAG ME AWAY SOME-WHERE...
I SEE. DO YOU HAVE ANY IDEA WHO THEY ARE?
NO! NO!
ぶんぶん
YOU HAVE A CUT...
...HERE.

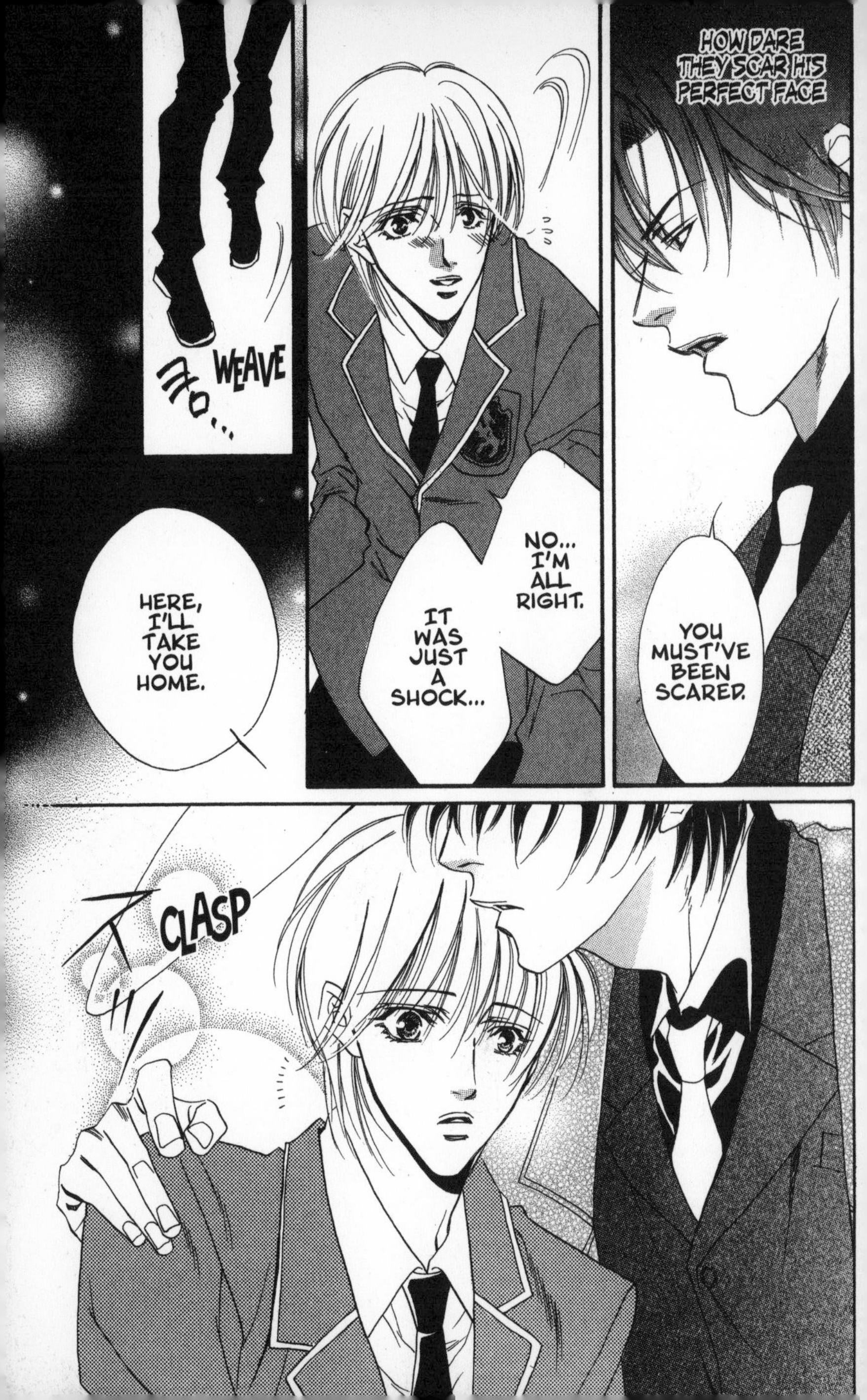
HOW DARE THEY SCAR HIS PERFECT FACE
YOU MUST'VE BEEN SCARED.
NO... I'M ALL RIGHT.
IT WAS JUST A SHOCK...
WEAVE
ヨロ...
HERE, I'LL TAKE YOU HOME.
CLASP

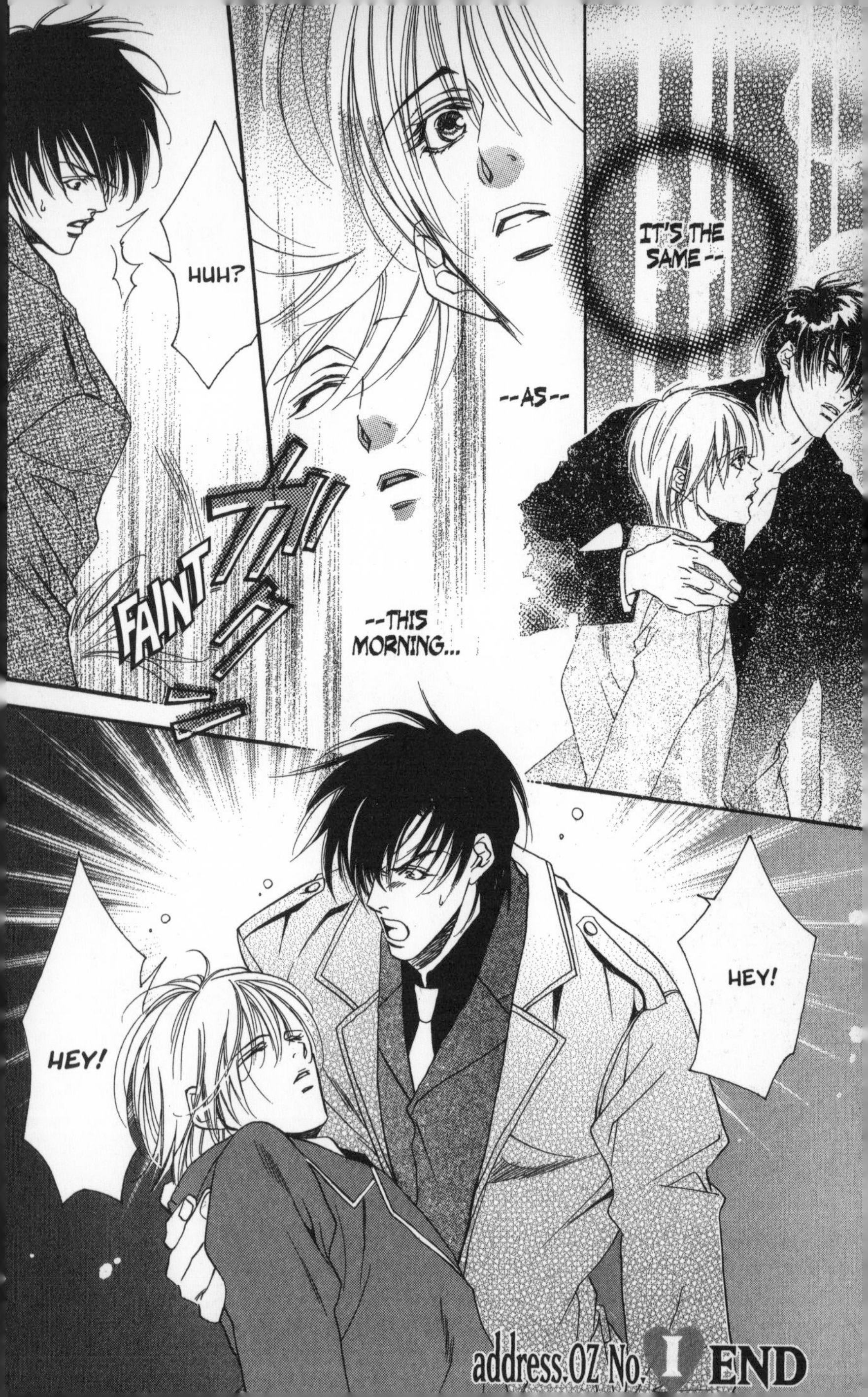
IT'S THE SAME --
--AS--
--THIS MORNING...
HUH?
FAINT
HEY!
HEY!
address.OZ No. I END

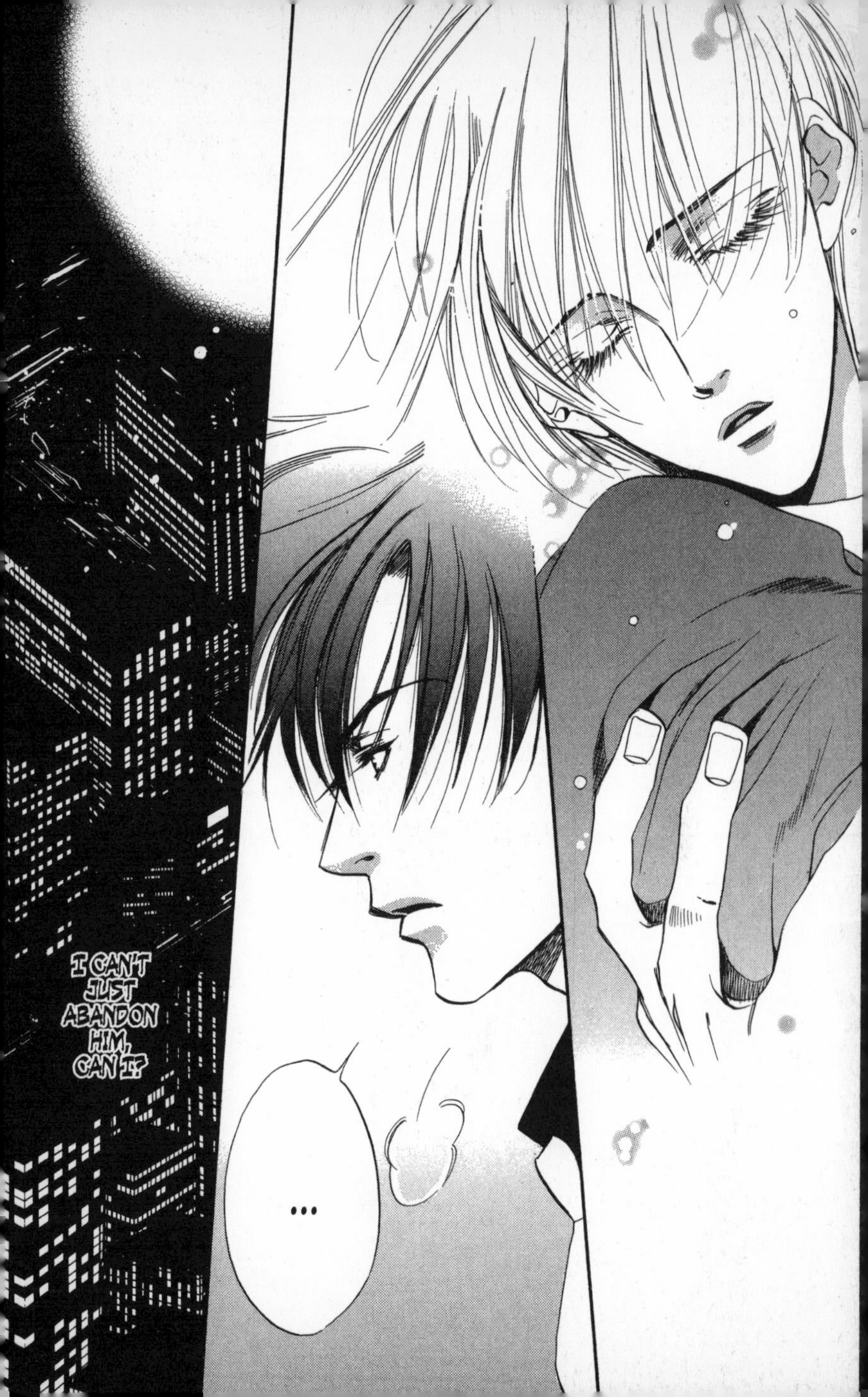
I CAN'T JUST ABANDON HIM, CAN I?
...

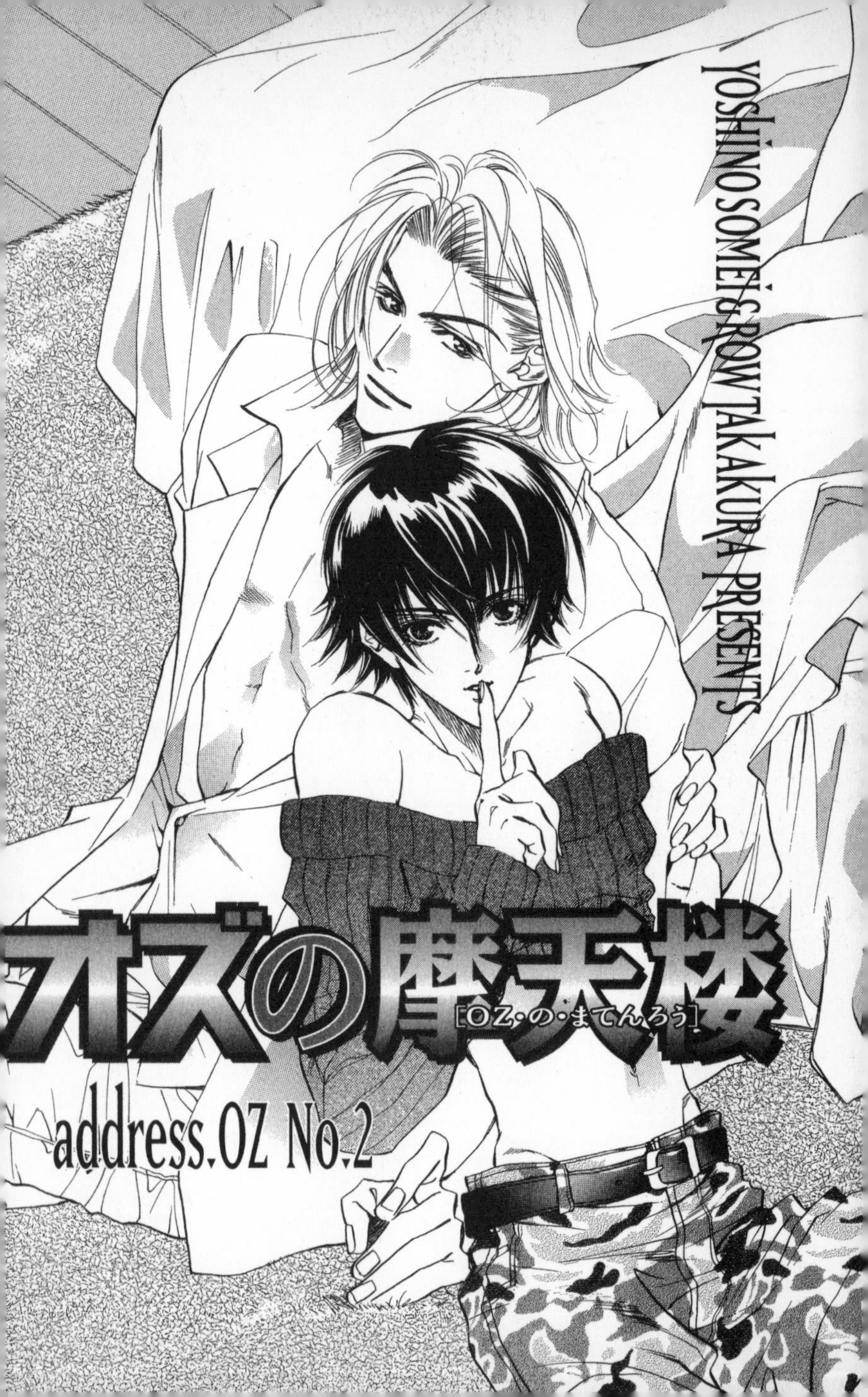
YOSHINO SOMEI'S ROW TAKAKURA PRESENTS
オズの摩天楼
[OZ・の・まてんろう]
address.OZ No.2

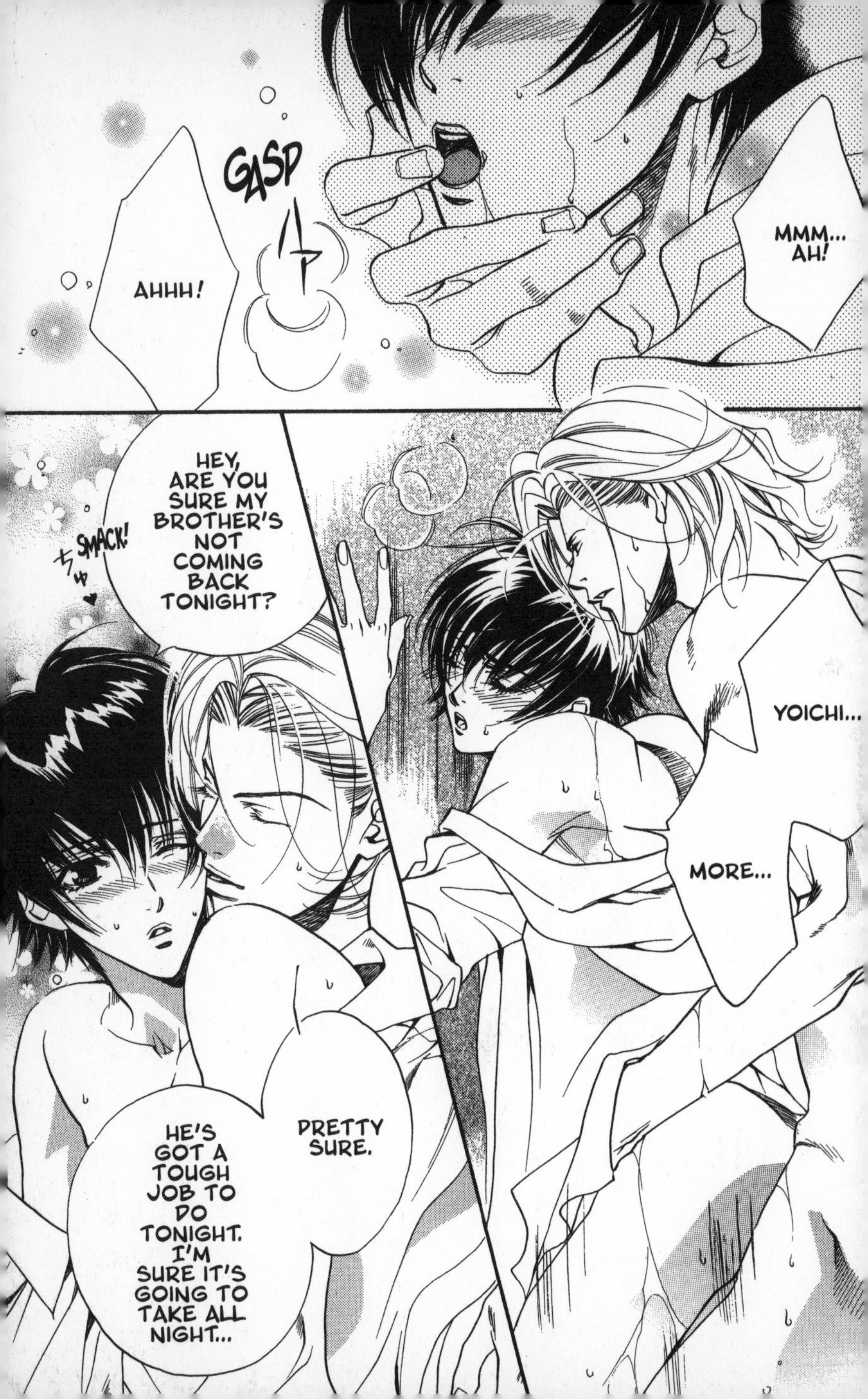
MMM... AH!
GASP
AHHH!
YOICHI...
MORE...
HEY, ARE YOU SURE MY BROTHER'S NOT COMING BACK TONIGHT?
SMACK!
ちゅ
PRETTY SURE.
HE'S GOT A TOUGH JOB TO DO TONIGHT. I'M SURE IT'S GOING TO TAKE ALL NIGHT...

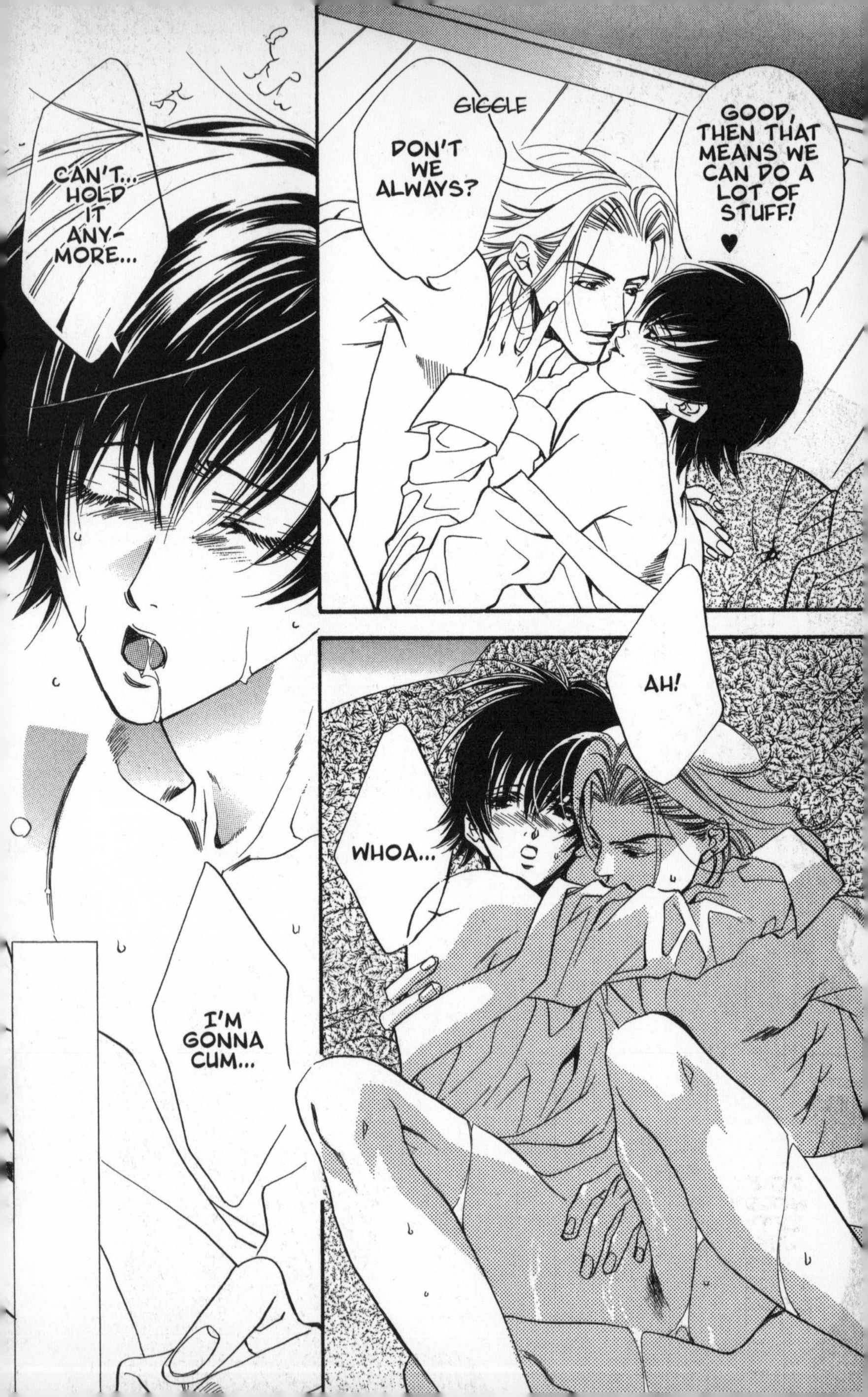
GOOD, THEN THAT MEANS WE CAN DO A LOT OF STUFF! ♥
GIGGLE
DON'T WE ALWAYS?
AH!
WHOA...
CAN'T... HOLD IT ANY-MORE...
I'M GONNA CUM...

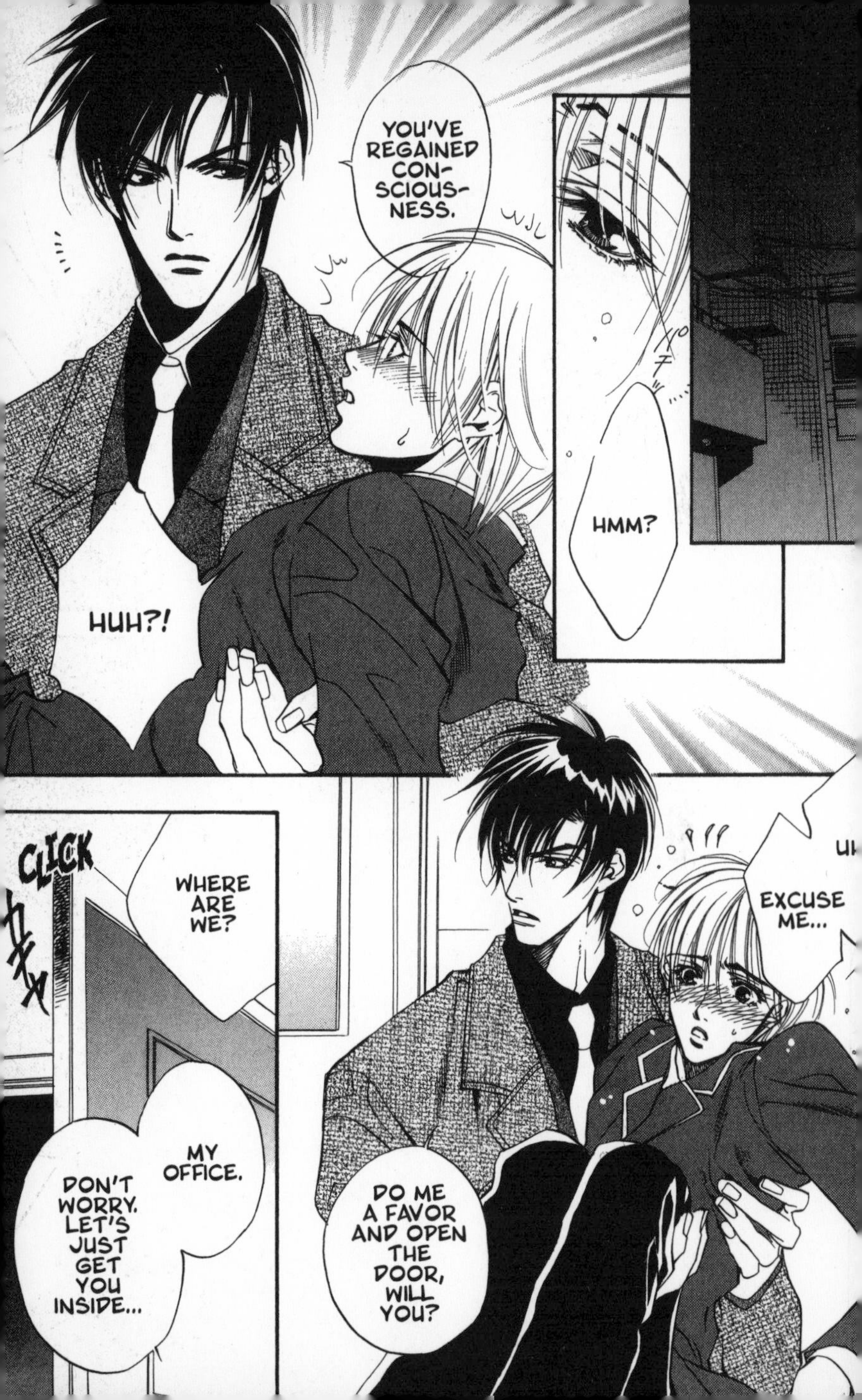
HMM?
YOU'VE REGAINED CON-SCIOUS-NESS.
HUH?!
EXCUSE ME...
DO ME A FAVOR AND OPEN THE DOOR, WILL YOU?
CLICK
WHERE ARE WE?
MY OFFICE.
DON'T WORRY. LET'S JUST GET YOU INSIDE...

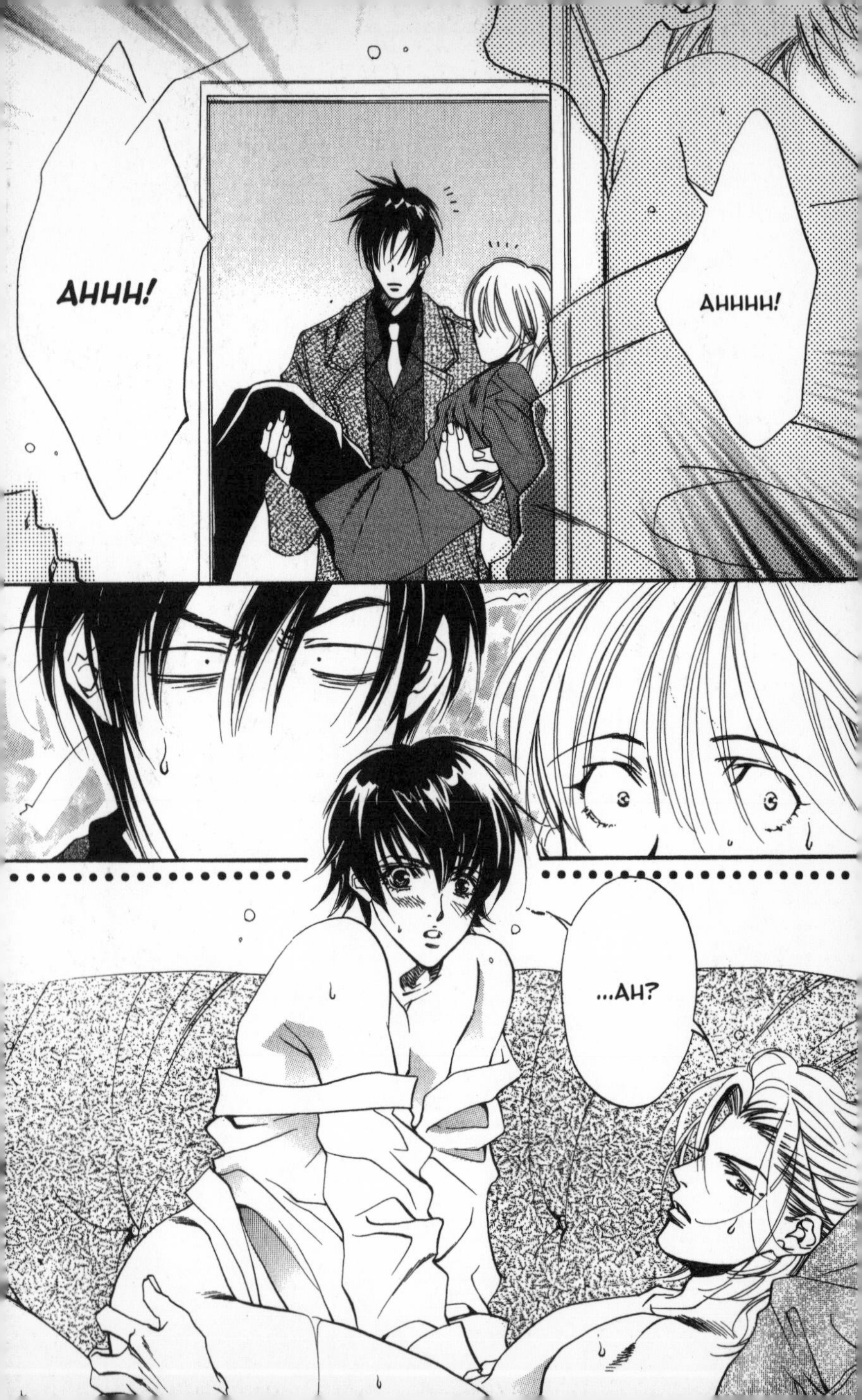
AHHHH!
AHHH!
...AH?

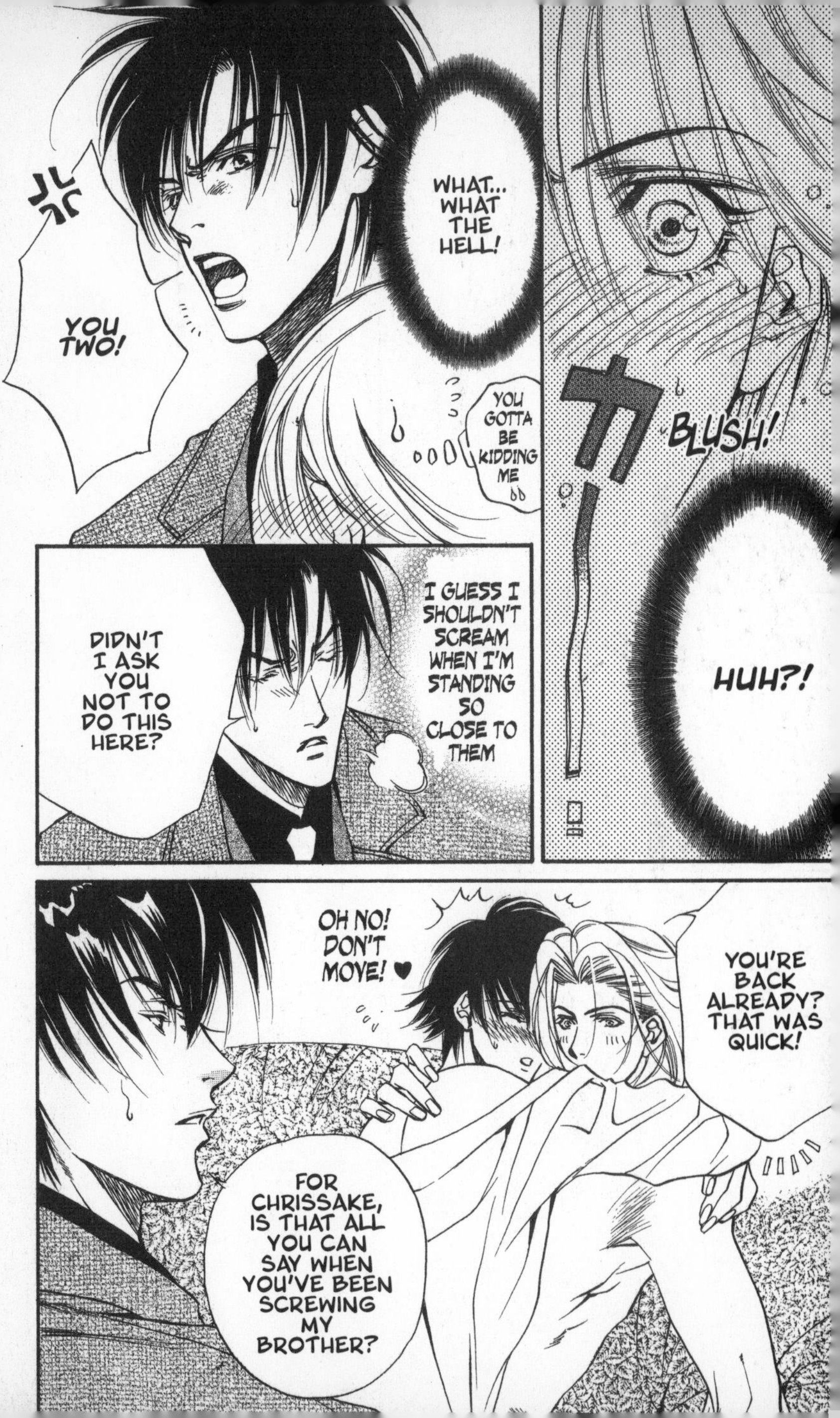
BLUSH!
HUH?!
WHAT... WHAT THE HELL!
YOU GOTTA BE KIDDING ME
YOU TWO!
I GUESS I SHOULDN'T SCREAM WHEN I'M STANDING SO CLOSE TO THEM
DIDN'T I ASK YOU NOT TO DO THIS HERE?
YOU'RE BACK ALREADY? THAT WAS QUICK!
OH NO! DON'T MOVE! ♥
FOR CHRISSAKE, IS THAT ALL YOU CAN SAY WHEN YOU'VE BEEN SCREWING MY BROTHER?

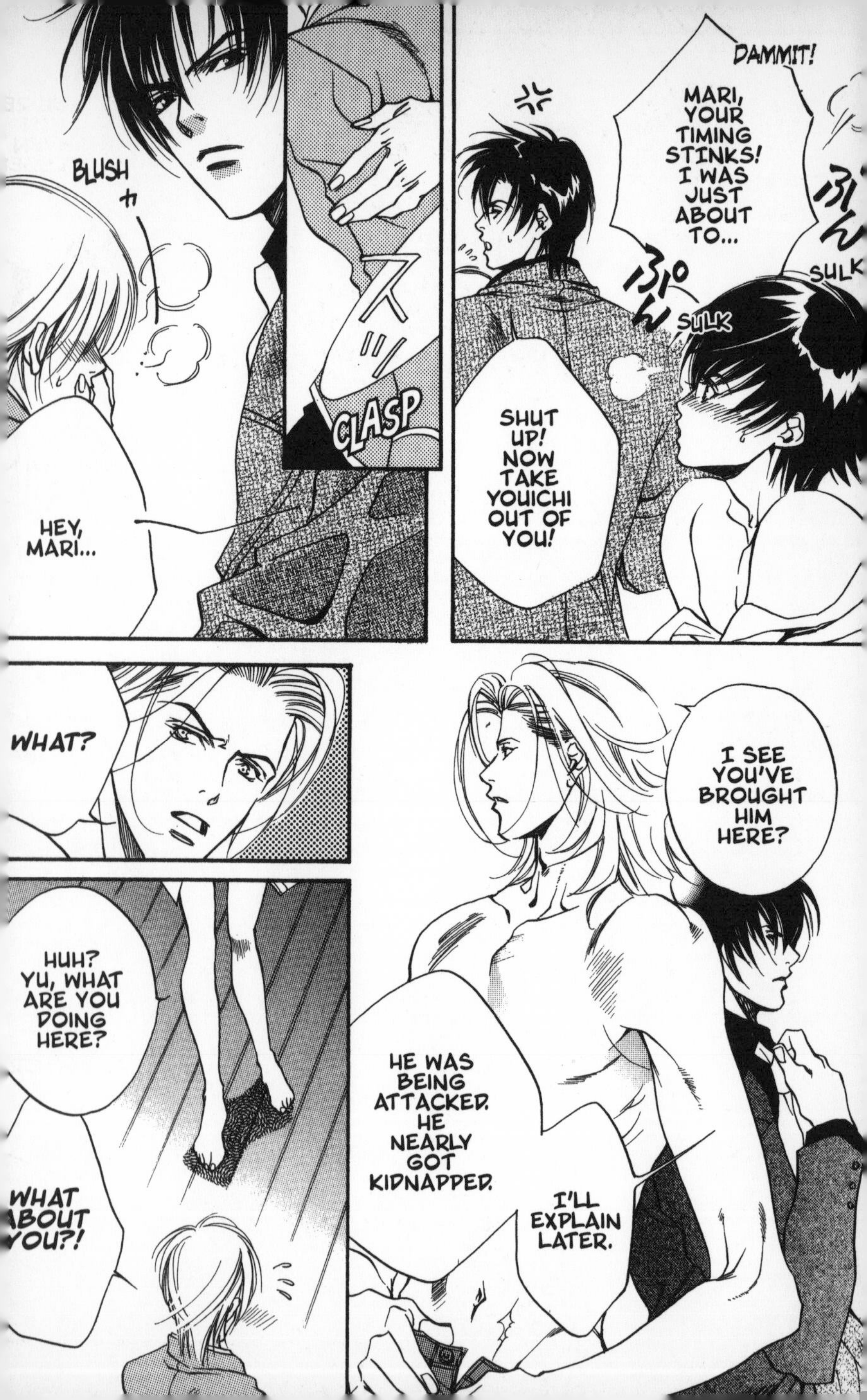
DAMMIT!
MARI, YOUR TIMING STINKS! I WAS JUST ABOUT TO...
SULK
SULK
SHUT UP! NOW TAKE YOUICHI OUT OF YOU!
CLASP
BLUSH
HEY, MARI...
I SEE YOU'VE BROUGHT HIM HERE?
HE WAS BEING ATTACKED. HE NEARLY GOT KIDNAPPED.
I'LL EXPLAIN LATER.
WHAT?
HUH? YU, WHAT ARE YOU DOING HERE?
WHAT ABOUT YOU?!

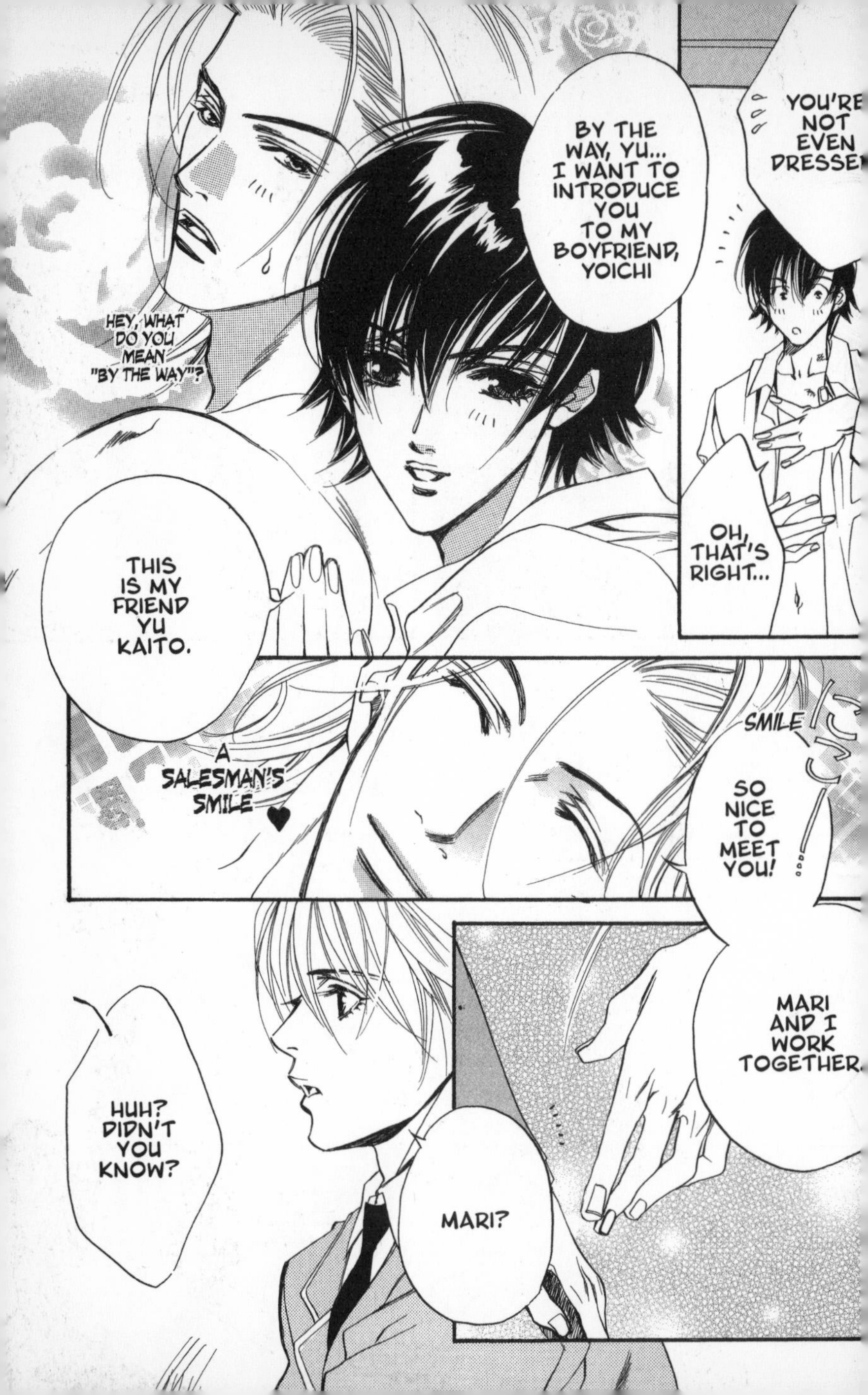

YOU'RE NOT EVEN DRESSE
OH, THAT'S RIGHT...
BY THE WAY, YU... I WANT TO INTRODUCE YOU TO MY BOYFRIEND, YOICHI
HEY, WHAT DO YOU MEAN "BY THE WAY"?
THIS IS MY FRIEND YU KAITO.
SMILE
SO NICE TO MEET YOU!
A SALESMAN'S SMILE ♥
MARI AND I WORK TOGETHER.
MARI?
HUH? DIDN'T YOU KNOW?

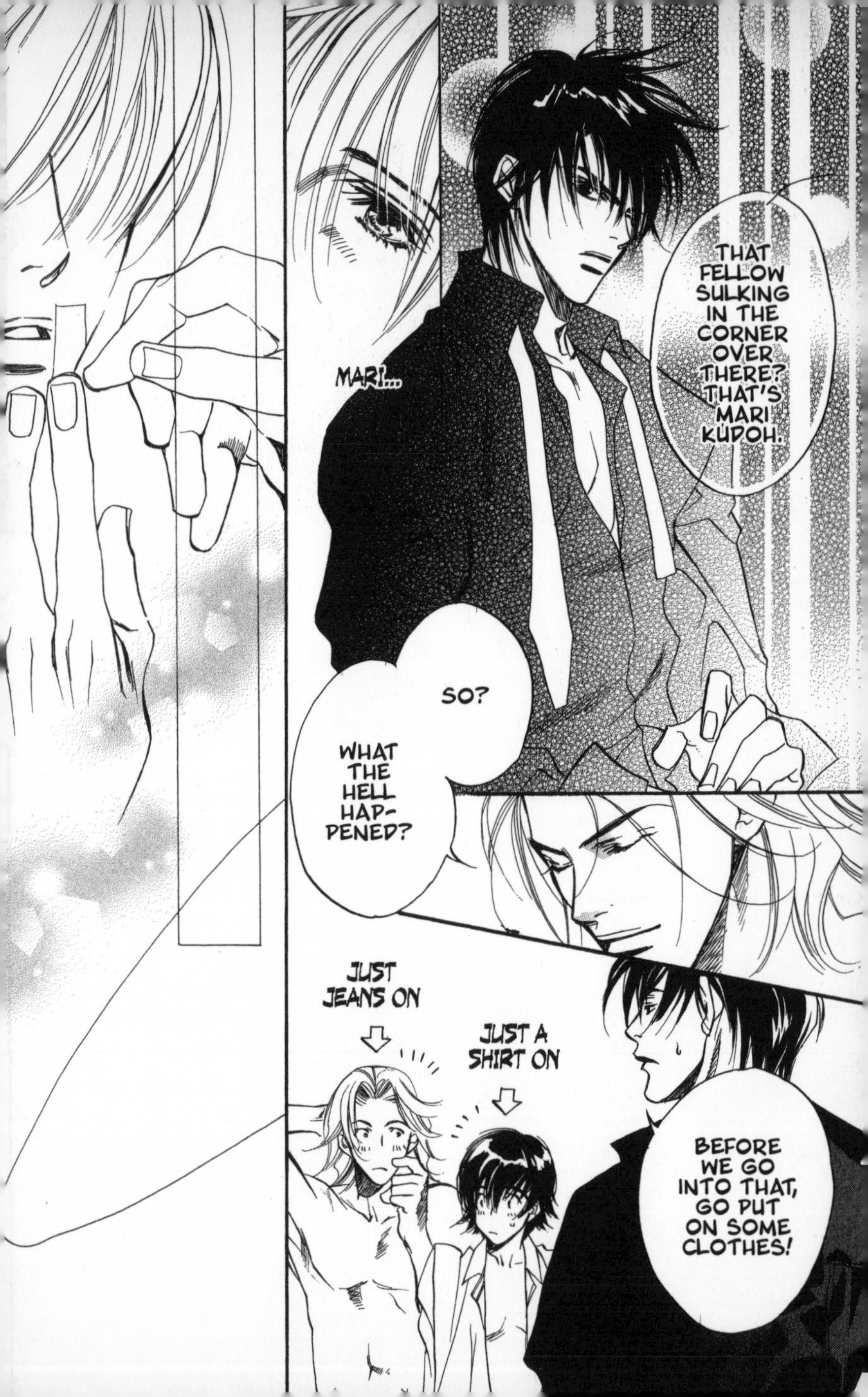
THAT FELLOW SULKING IN THE CORNER OVER THERE? THAT'S MARI KUDOH.
MARI...
SO?
WHAT THE HELL HAPPENED?
BEFORE WE GO INTO THAT, GO PUT ON SOME CLOTHES!
JUST A SHIRT ON
JUST JEANS ON

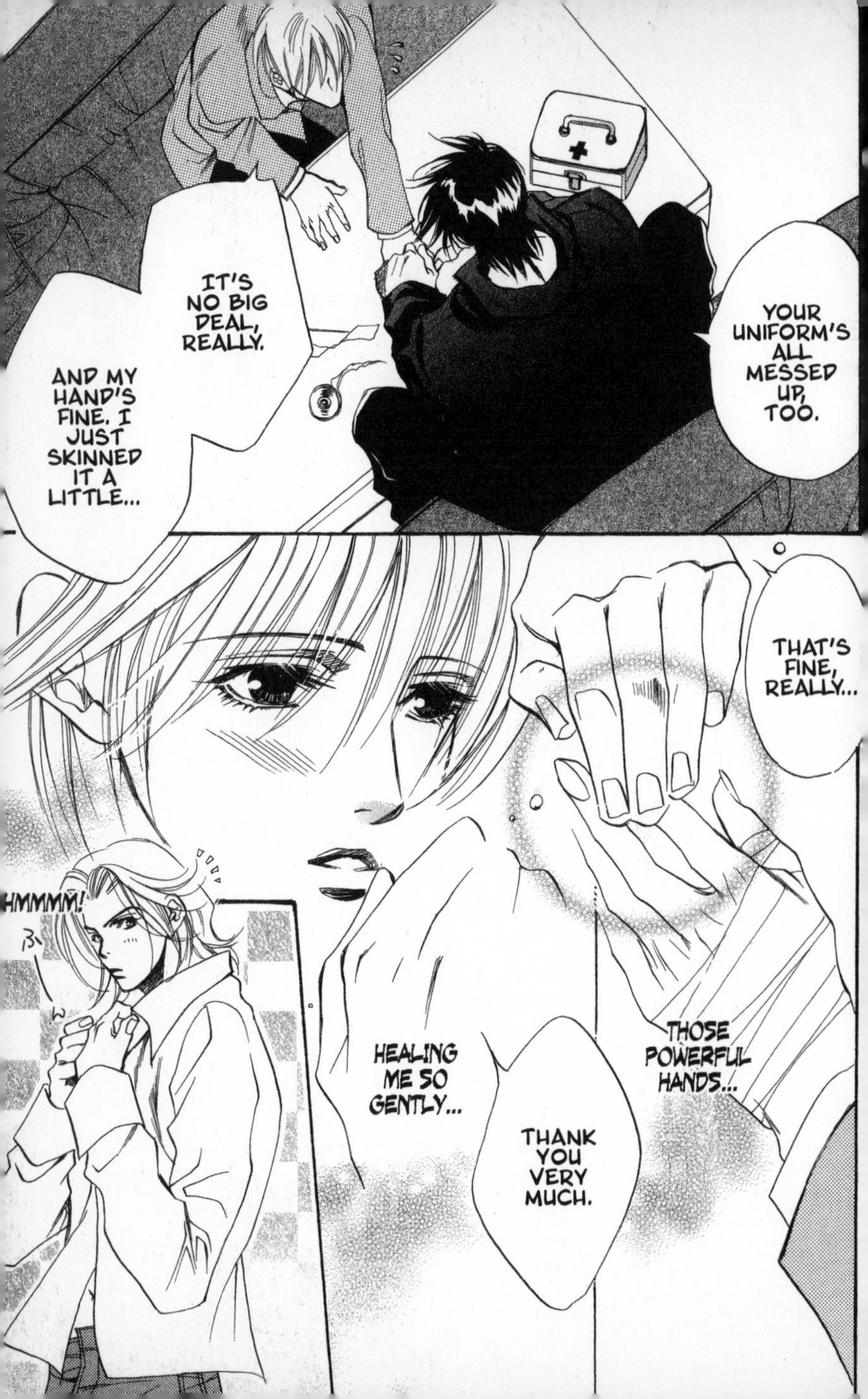
YOUR UNIFORM'S ALL MESSED UP, TOO.
IT'S NO BIG DEAL, REALLY.
AND MY HAND'S FINE. I JUST SKINNED IT A LITTLE...
THAT'S FINE, REALLY...
THOSE POWERFUL HANDS...
THANK YOU VERY MUCH.
HEALING ME SO GENTLY...
HMMMM!
ふ

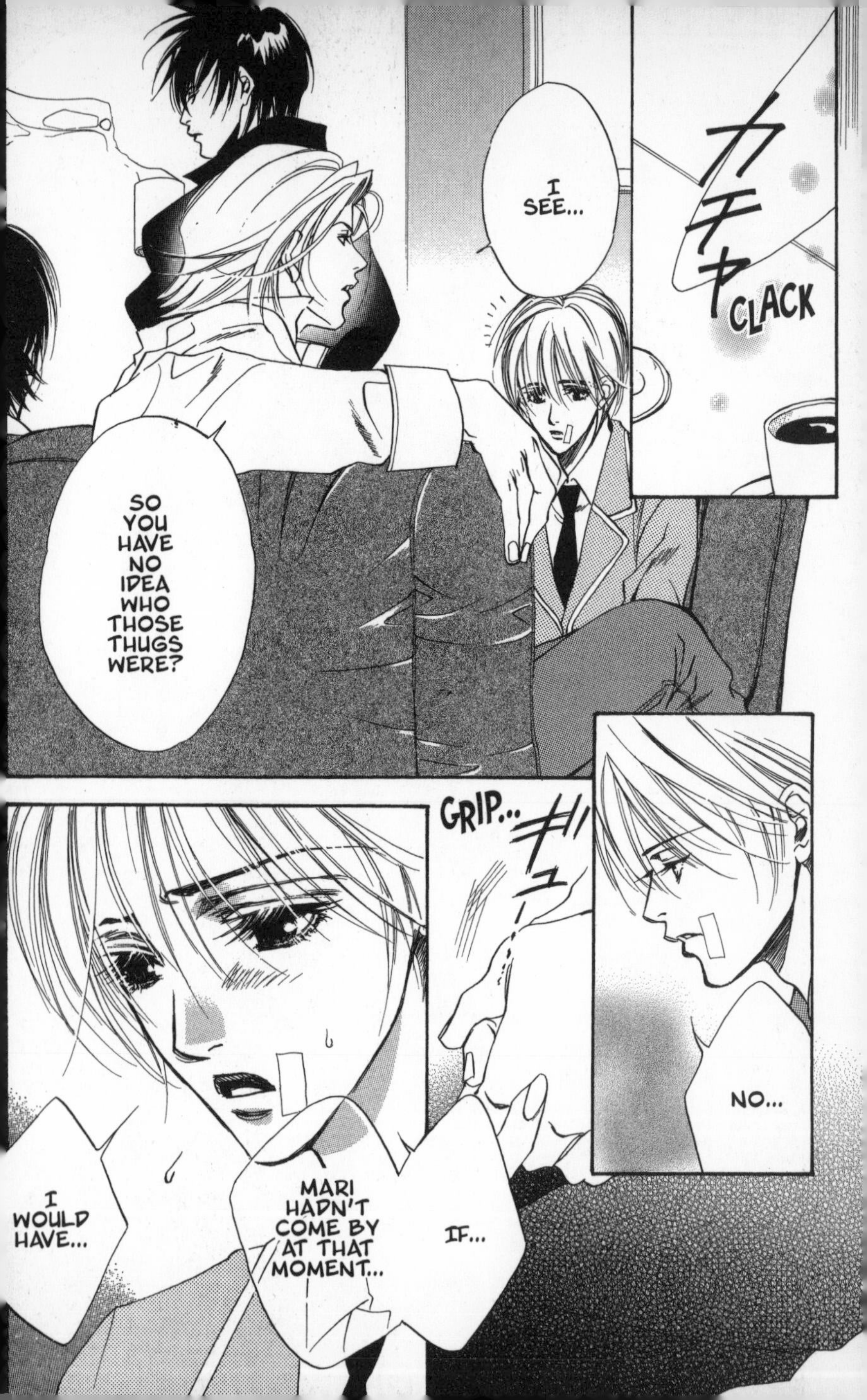
カチャ
CLACK
I SEE...
SO YOU HAVE NO IDEA WHO THOSE THUGS WERE?
NO...
GRIP...
ギュ
IF...
MARI HADN'T COME BY AT THAT MOMENT...
I WOULD HAVE...

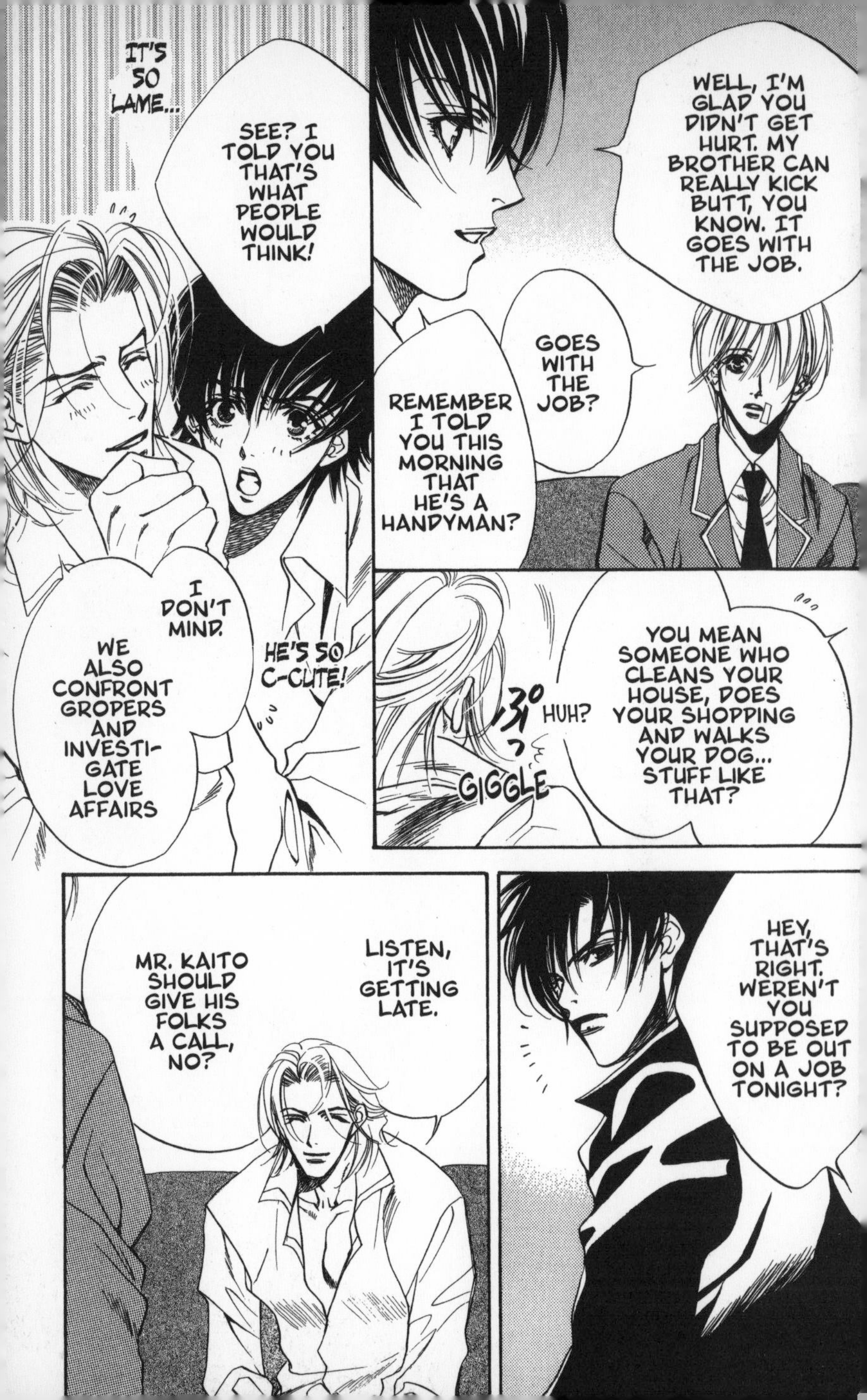
WELL, I'M GLAD YOU DIDN'T GET HURT. MY BROTHER CAN REALLY KICK BUTT, YOU KNOW. IT GOES WITH THE JOB.
GOES WITH THE JOB?
REMEMBER I TOLD YOU THIS MORNING THAT HE'S A HANDYMAN?
YOU MEAN SOMEONE WHO CLEANS YOUR HOUSE, DOES YOUR SHOPPING AND WALKS YOUR DOG... STUFF LIKE THAT?
HUH?
GIGGLE
SEE? I TOLD YOU THAT'S WHAT PEOPLE WOULD THINK!
IT'S SO LAME...
HE'S SO C-CUTE!
I DON'T MIND.
WE ALSO CONFRONT GROPERS AND INVESTI-GATE LOVE AFFAIRS
HEY, THAT'S RIGHT. WEREN'T YOU SUPPOSED TO BE OUT ON A JOB TONIGHT?
LISTEN, IT'S GETTING LATE.
MR. KAITO SHOULD GIVE HIS FOLKS A CALL, NO?

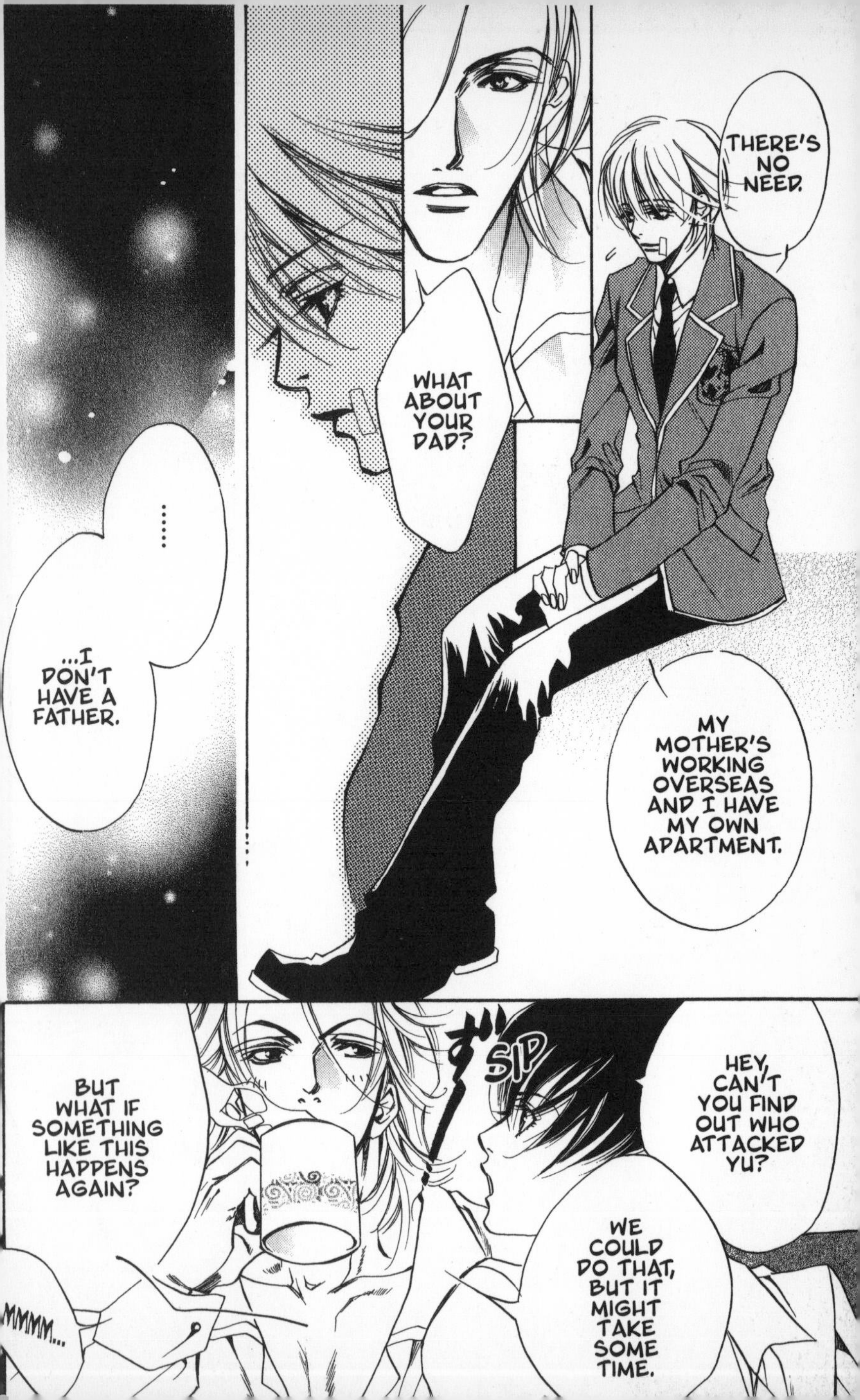
THERE'S NO NEED.
MY MOTHER'S WORKING OVERSEAS AND I HAVE MY OWN APARTMENT.
WHAT ABOUT YOUR DAD?
......
...I DON'T HAVE A FATHER.
HEY, CAN'T YOU FIND OUT WHO ATTACKED YU?
SIP
WE COULD DO THAT, BUT IT MIGHT TAKE SOME TIME.
BUT WHAT IF SOMETHING LIKE THIS HAPPENS AGAIN?
MMMM...

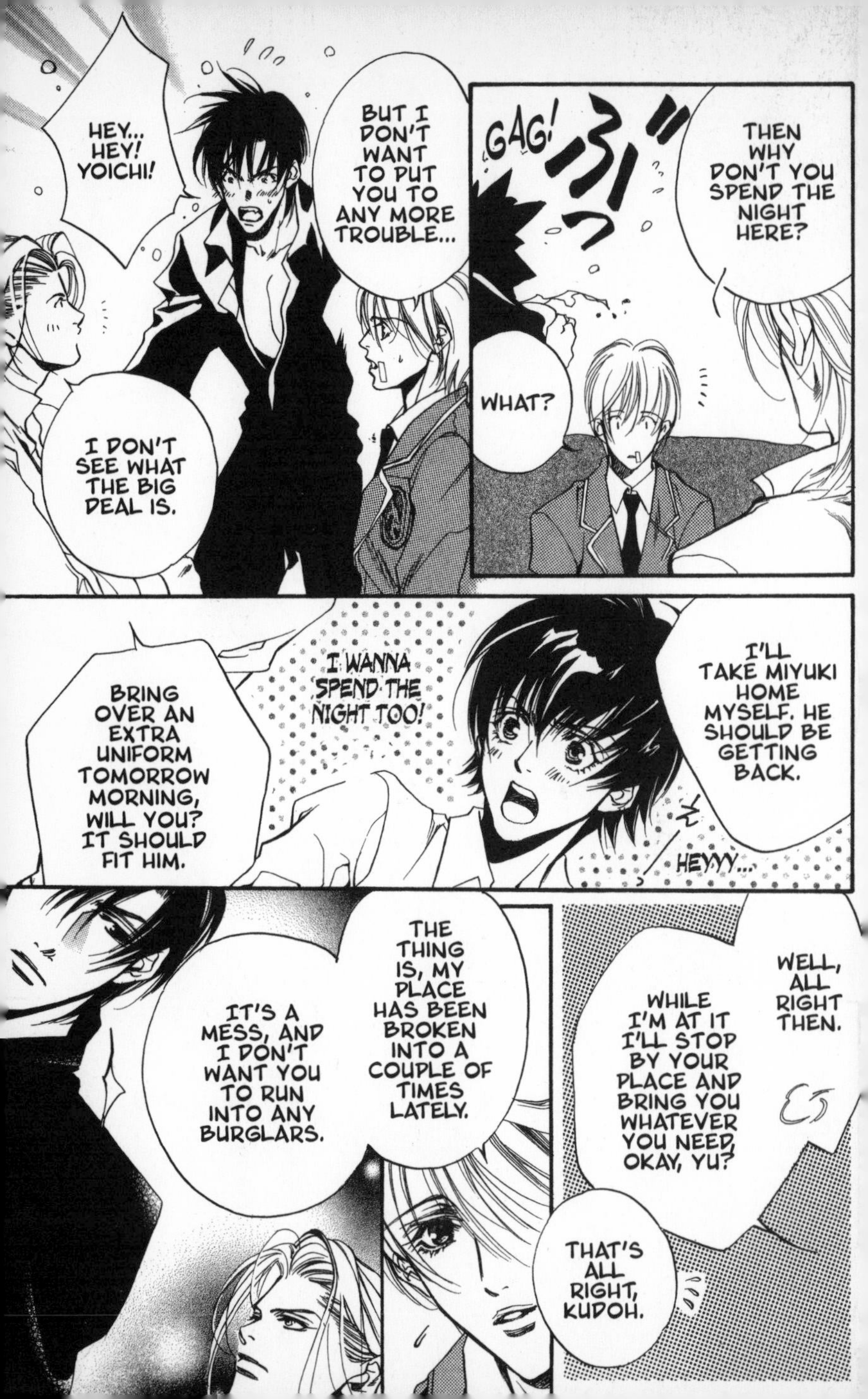
THEN WHY DON'T YOU SPEND THE NIGHT HERE?
GAG!
WHAT?
BUT I DON'T WANT TO PUT YOU TO ANY MORE TROUBLE...
HEY... HEY! YOICHI!
I DON'T SEE WHAT THE BIG DEAL IS.
I'LL TAKE MIYUKI HOME MYSELF. HE SHOULD BE GETTING BACK.
HEYYY...
I WANNA SPEND THE NIGHT TOO!
BRING OVER AN EXTRA UNIFORM TOMORROW MORNING, WILL YOU? IT SHOULD FIT HIM.
WELL, ALL RIGHT THEN.
WHILE I'M AT IT I'LL STOP BY YOUR PLACE AND BRING YOU WHATEVER YOU NEED, OKAY, YU?
THAT'S ALL RIGHT, KUDOH.
THE THING IS, MY PLACE HAS BEEN BROKEN INTO A COUPLE OF TIMES LATELY.
IT'S A MESS, AND I DON'T WANT YOU TO RUN INTO ANY BURGLARS.

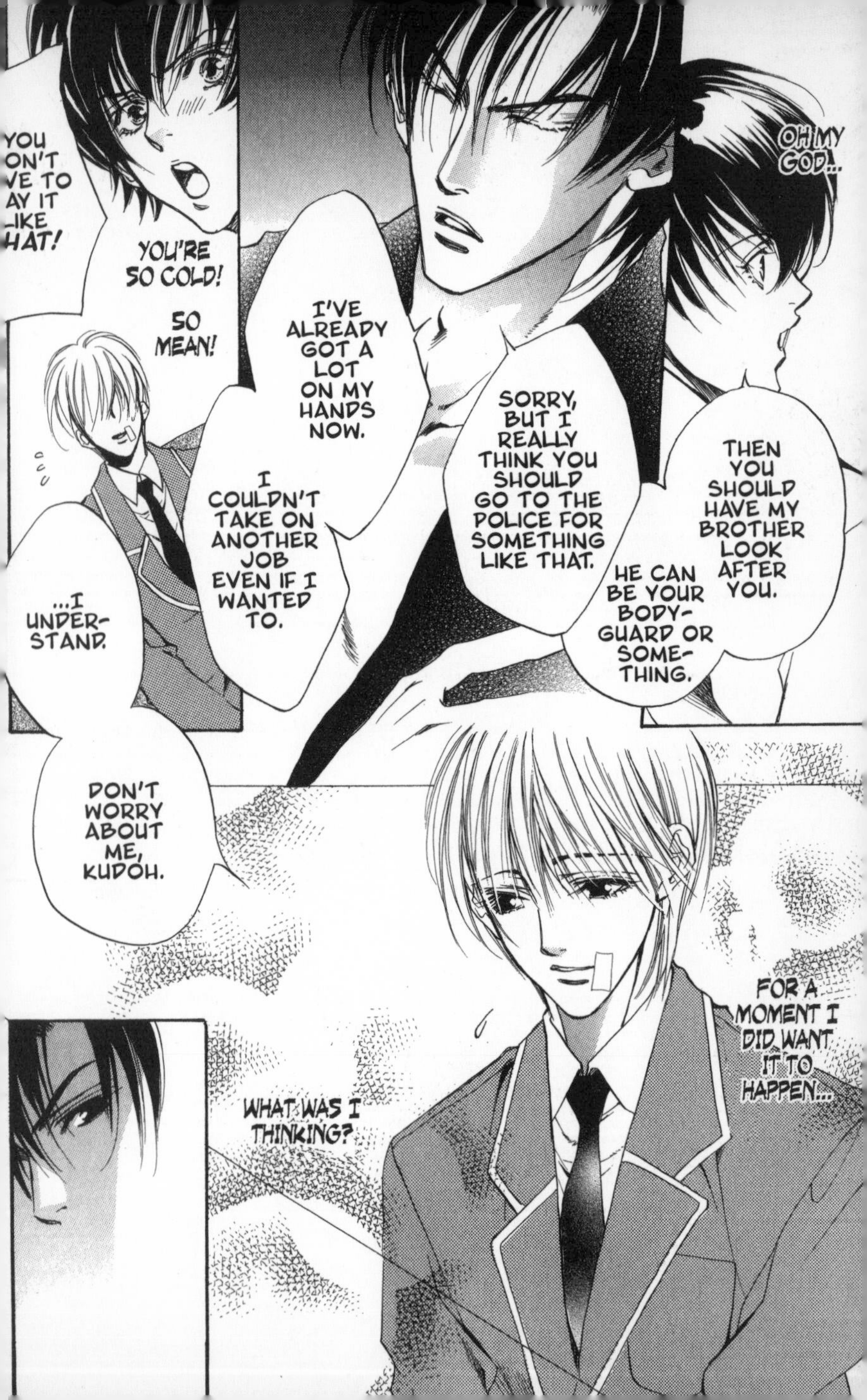
OH MY GOD...
THEN YOU SHOULD HAVE MY BROTHER LOOK AFTER YOU.
HE CAN BE YOUR BODY-GUARD OR SOME-THING.
SORRY, BUT I REALLY THINK YOU SHOULD GO TO THE POLICE FOR SOMETHING LIKE THAT.
I'VE ALREADY GOT A LOT ON MY HANDS NOW.
I COULDN'T TAKE ON ANOTHER JOB EVEN IF I WANTED TO.
YOU ON'T VE TO AY IT LIKE HAT!
YOU'RE SO COLD!
SO MEAN!
...I UNDER-STAND.
DON'T WORRY ABOUT ME, KUDOH.
FOR A MOMENT I DID WANT IT TO HAPPEN...
WHAT WAS I THINKING?

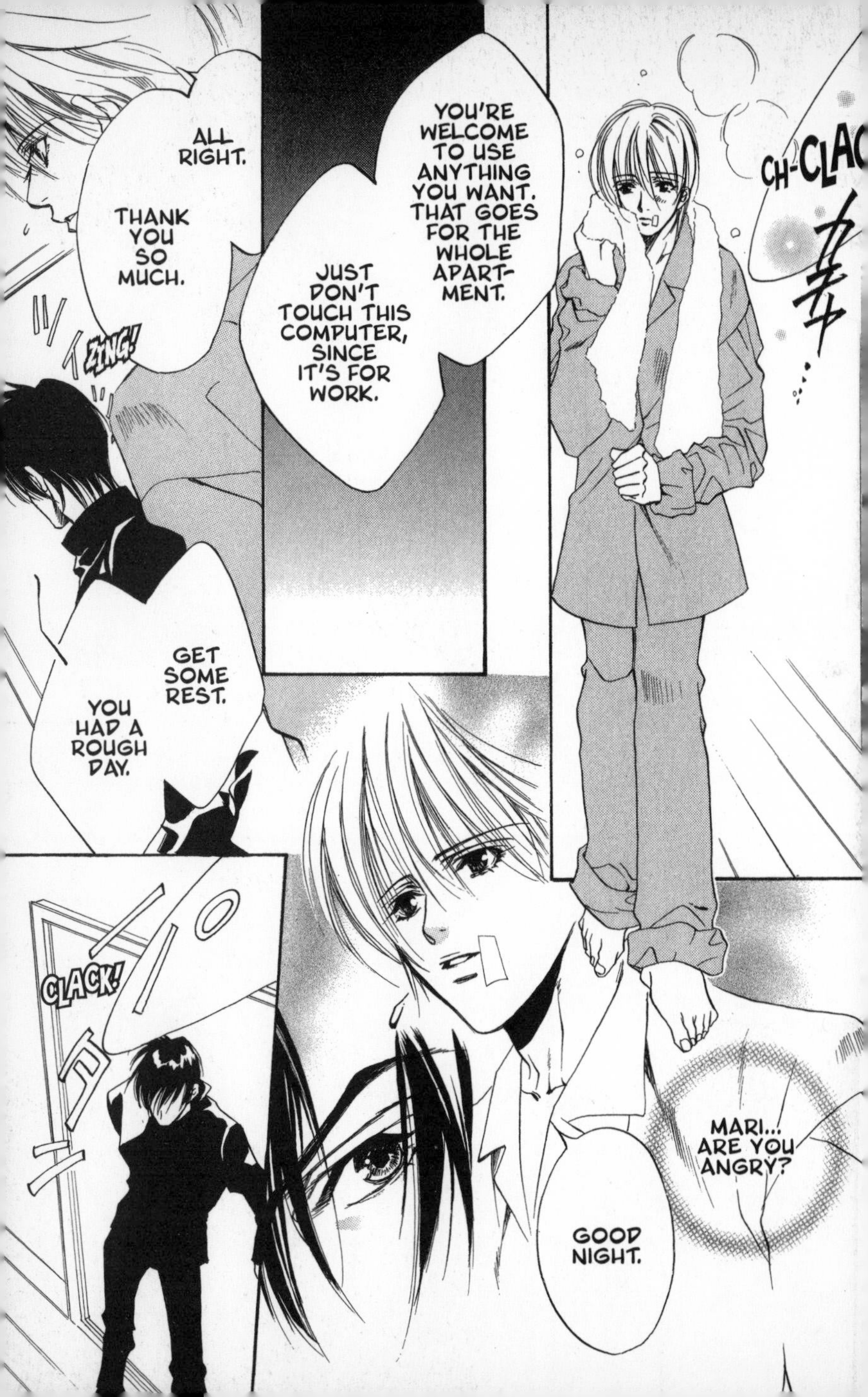
CH-CLAC
YOU'RE WELCOME TO USE ANYTHING YOU WANT. THAT GOES FOR THE WHOLE APARTMENT.
JUST DON'T TOUCH THIS COMPUTER, SINCE IT'S FOR WORK.
ALL RIGHT.
THANK YOU SO MUCH.
ZING!
GET SOME REST.
YOU HAD A ROUGH DAY.
MARI... ARE YOU ANGRY?
GOOD NIGHT.
CLACK!

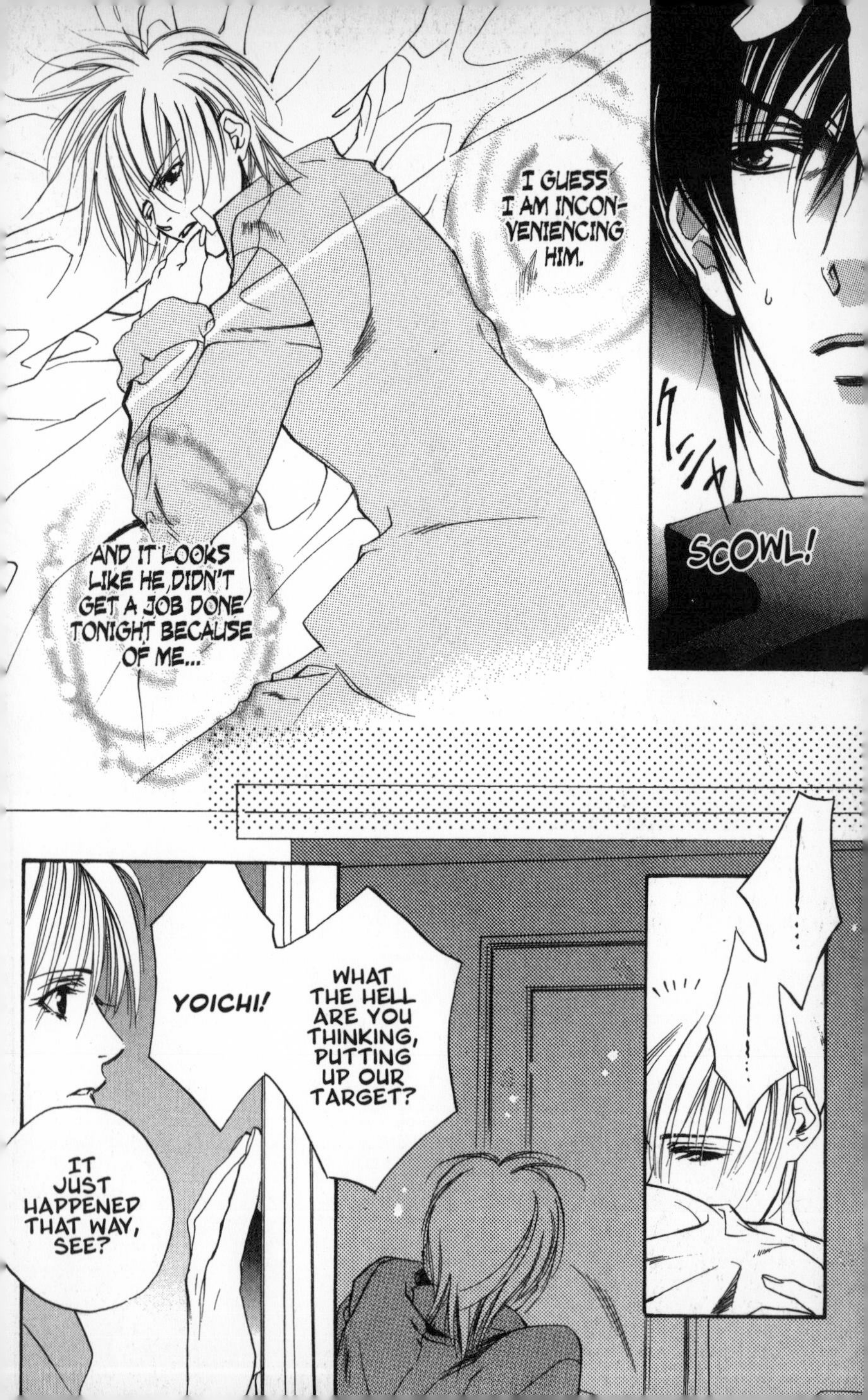
SCOWL!
I GUESS I AM INCON-VENIENCING HIM.
AND IT LOOKS LIKE HE DIDN'T GET A JOB DONE TONIGHT BECAUSE OF ME...
...
YOICHI!
WHAT THE HELL ARE YOU THINKING, PUTTING UP OUR TARGET?
IT JUST HAPPENED THAT WAY, SEE?

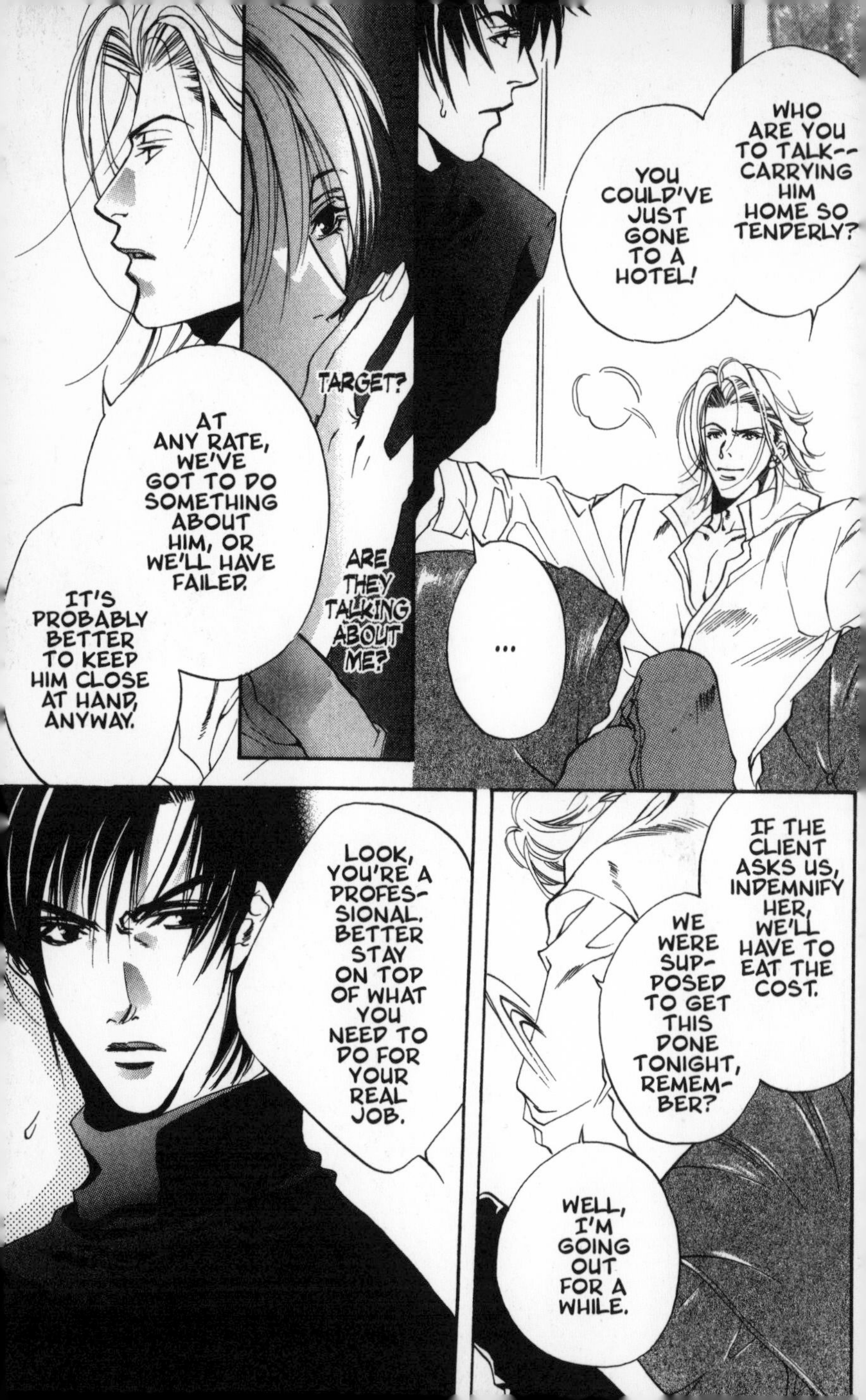
WHO ARE YOU TO TALK--CARRYING HIM HOME SO TENDERLY?
YOU COULD'VE JUST GONE TO A HOTEL!
...
TARGET?
ARE THEY TALKING ABOUT ME?
AT ANY RATE, WE'VE GOT TO DO SOMETHING ABOUT HIM, OR WE'LL HAVE FAILED.
IT'S PROBABLY BETTER TO KEEP HIM CLOSE AT HAND, ANYWAY.
IF THE CLIENT ASKS US, INDEMNIFY HER, WE'LL HAVE TO EAT THE COST.
WE WERE SUP-POSED TO GET THIS DONE TONIGHT, REMEM-BER?
WELL, I'M GOING OUT FOR A WHILE.
LOOK, YOU'RE A PROFES-SIONAL. BETTER STAY ON TOP OF WHAT YOU NEED TO DO FOR YOUR REAL JOB.

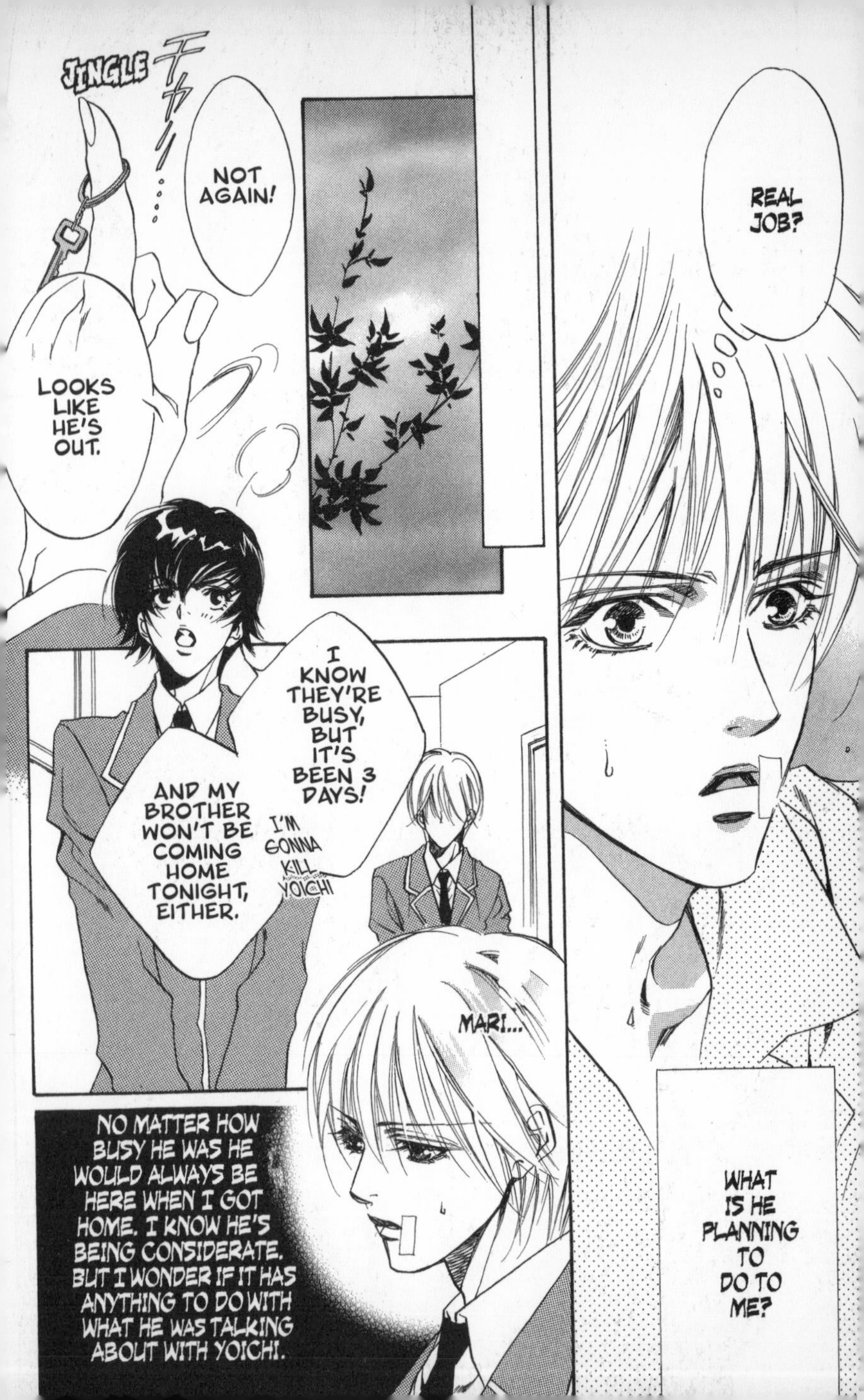
REAL JOB?
WHAT IS HE PLANNING TO DO TO ME?
NOT AGAIN!
JINGLE
チャリ…
LOOKS LIKE HE'S OUT.
I KNOW THEY'RE BUSY, BUT IT'S BEEN 3 DAYS!
AND MY BROTHER WON'T BE COMING HOME TONIGHT, EITHER.
I'M GONNA KILL YOICHI
MARI...
NO MATTER HOW BUSY HE WAS HE WOULD ALWAYS BE HERE WHEN I GOT HOME. I KNOW HE'S BEING CONSIDERATE, BUT I WONDER IF IT HAS ANYTHING TO DO WITH WHAT HE WAS TALKING ABOUT WITH YOICHI.

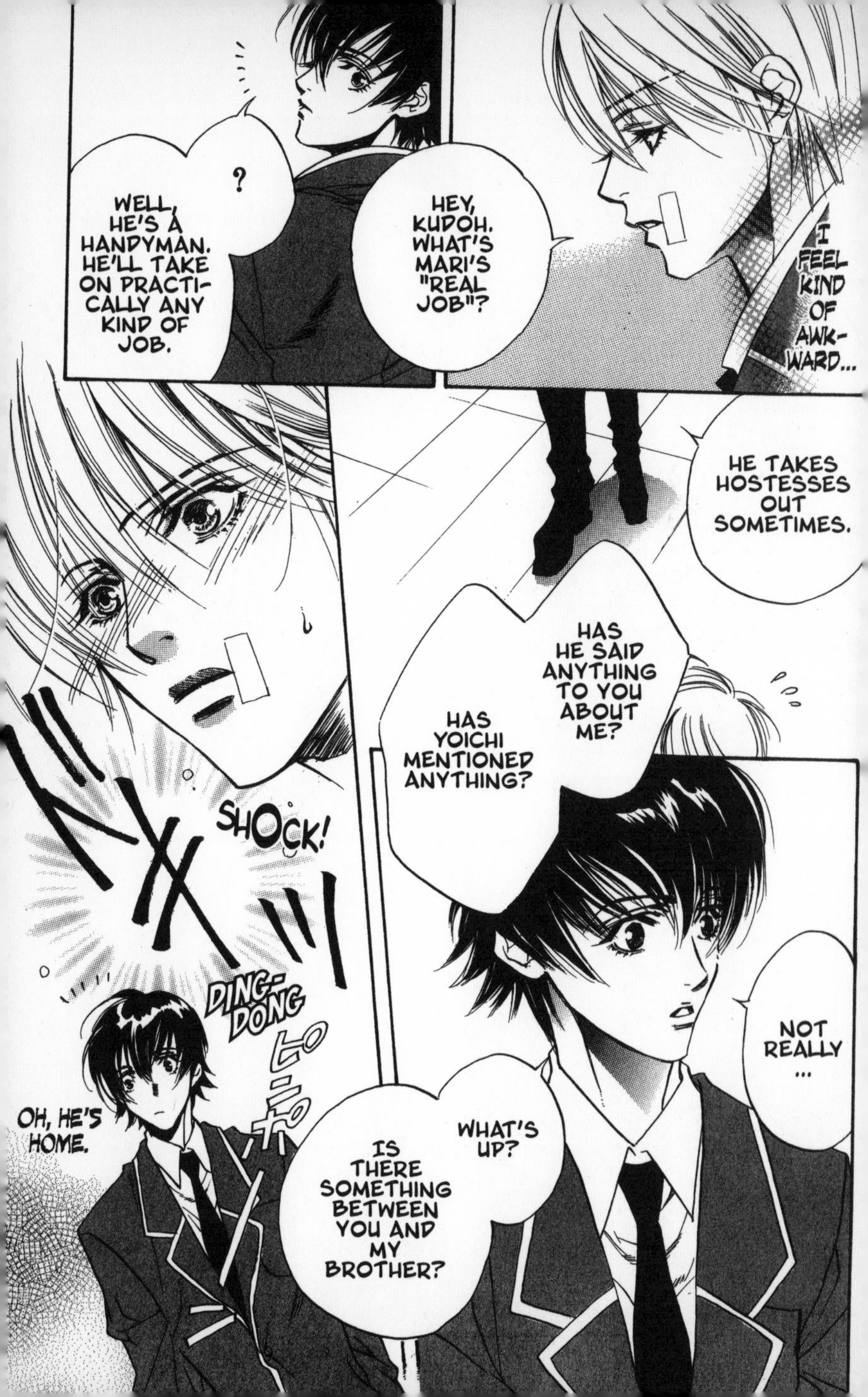
I FEEL KIND OF AWKWARD...
HEY, KUDOH. WHAT'S MARI'S "REAL JOB"?
?
WELL, HE'S A HANDYMAN. HE'LL TAKE ON PRACTICALLY ANY KIND OF JOB.
HE TAKES HOSTESSES OUT SOMETIMES.
SHOCK!
HAS HE SAID ANYTHING TO YOU ABOUT ME?
HAS YOICHI MENTIONED ANYTHING?
NOT REALLY ...
WHAT'S UP?
IS THERE SOMETHING BETWEEN YOU AND MY BROTHER?
DING-DONG
OH, HE'S HOME.

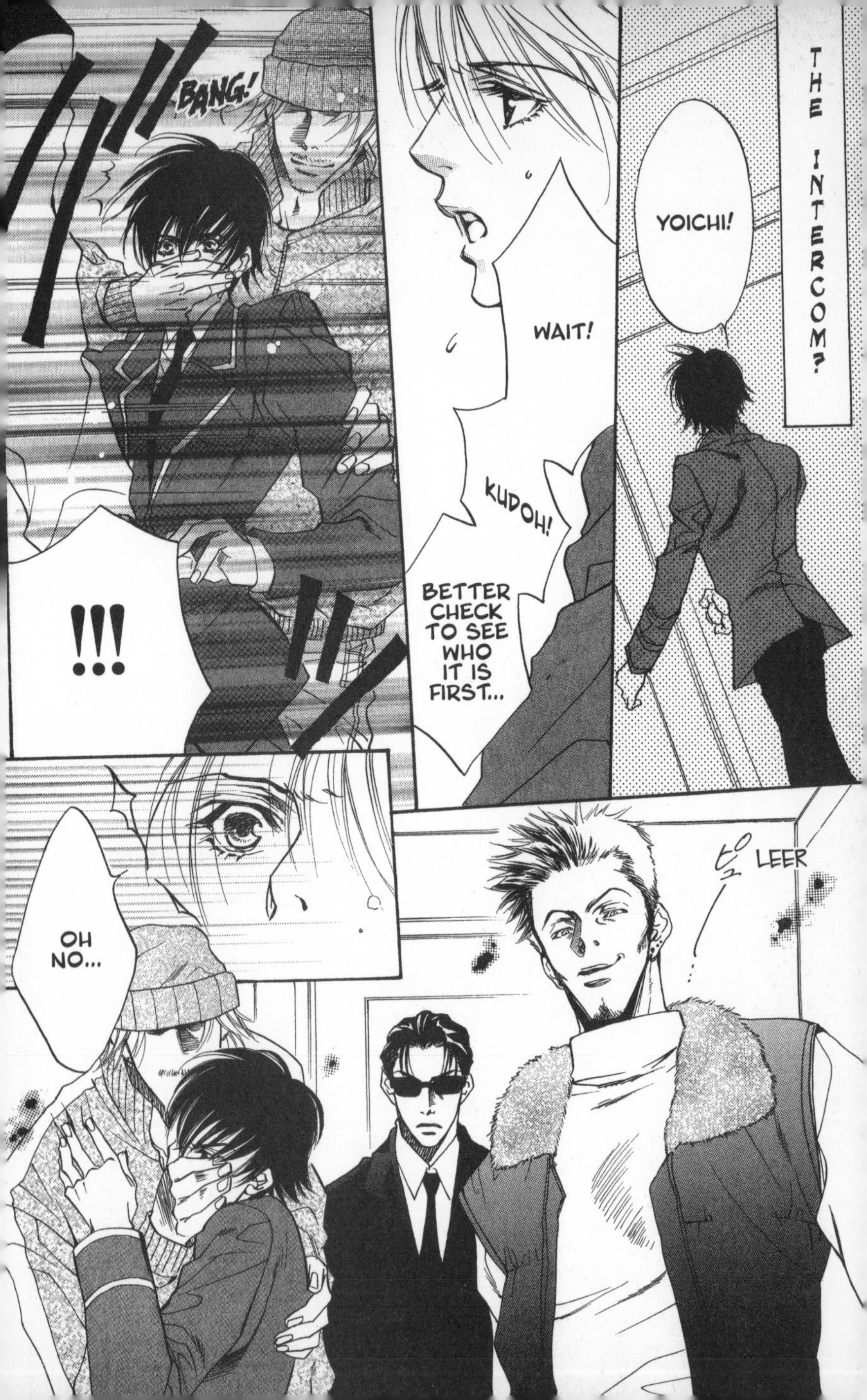
THE INTERCOM?
YOICHI!
WAIT!
KUDOH!
BETTER CHECK TO SEE WHO IT IS FIRST...
BANG!
!!!
LEER
OH NO...

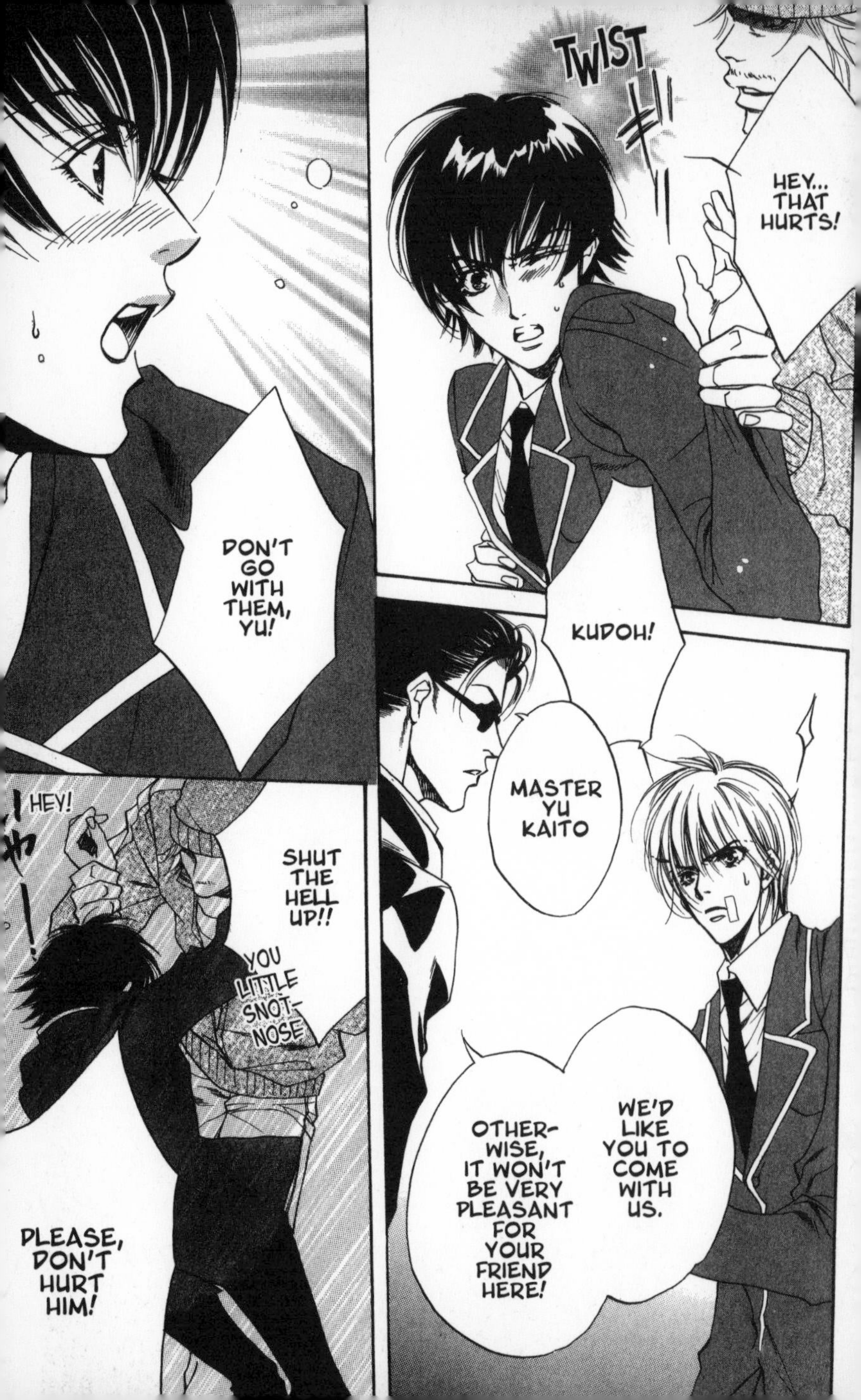

TWIST
HEY... THAT HURTS!
DON'T GO WITH THEM, YU!
KUDOH!
MASTER YU KAITO
WE'D LIKE YOU TO COME WITH US.
OTHER-WISE, IT WON'T BE VERY PLEASANT FOR YOUR FRIEND HERE!
HEY!
SHUT THE HELL UP!!
YOU LITTLE SNOT-NOSE
PLEASE, DON'T HURT HIM!

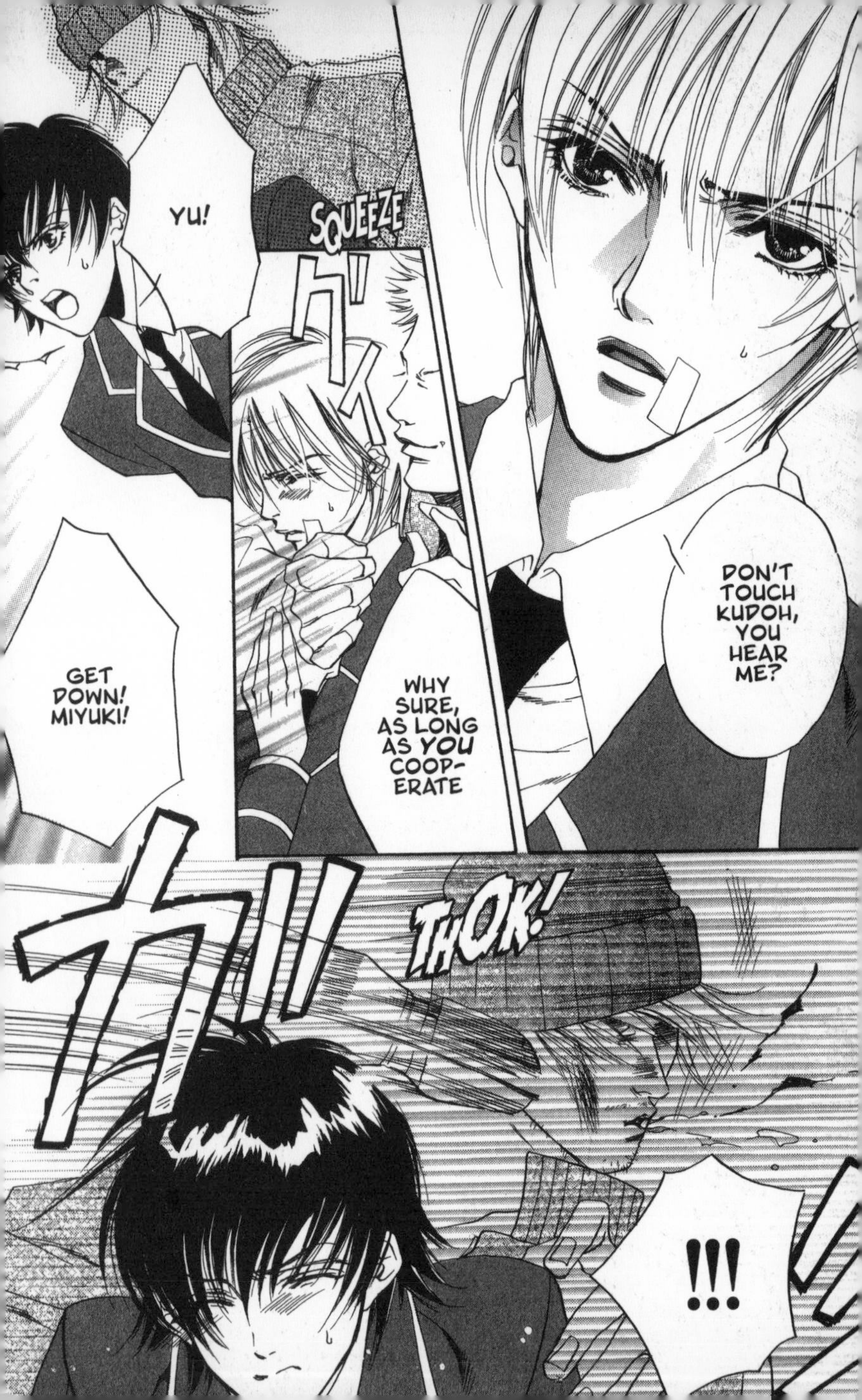
DON'T TOUCH KUDOH, YOU HEAR ME?
SQUEEZE
WHY SURE, AS LONG AS YOU COOPERATE
YU!
GET DOWN! MIYUKI!
THOK!
!!!

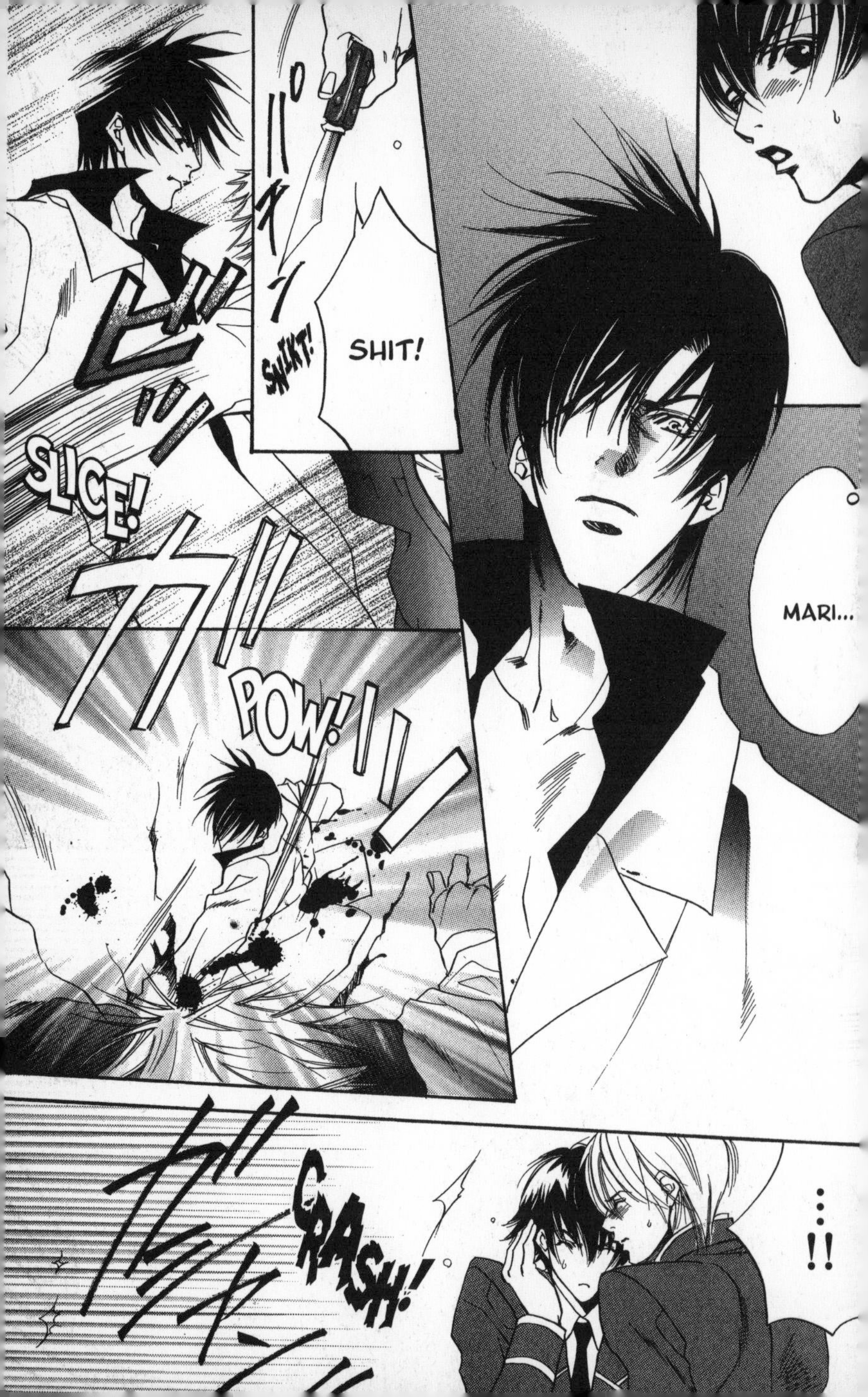
MARI...
SNIKT!
SHIT!
SLICE!
POW!
...!!
CRASH!

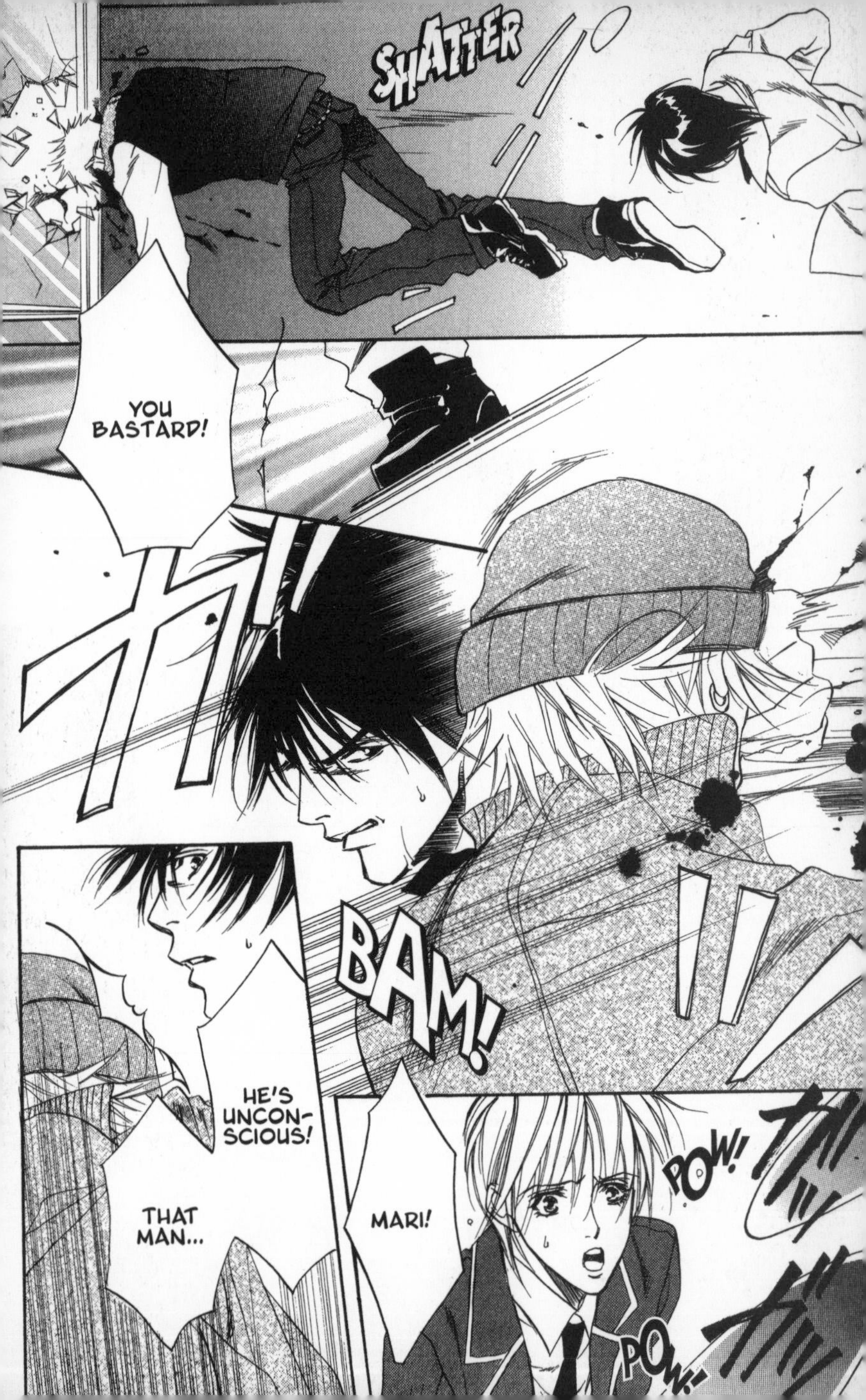
SHATTER
YOU BASTARD!
BAM!
POW!
POW!
MARI!
HE'S UNCON-SCIOUS!
THAT MAN...

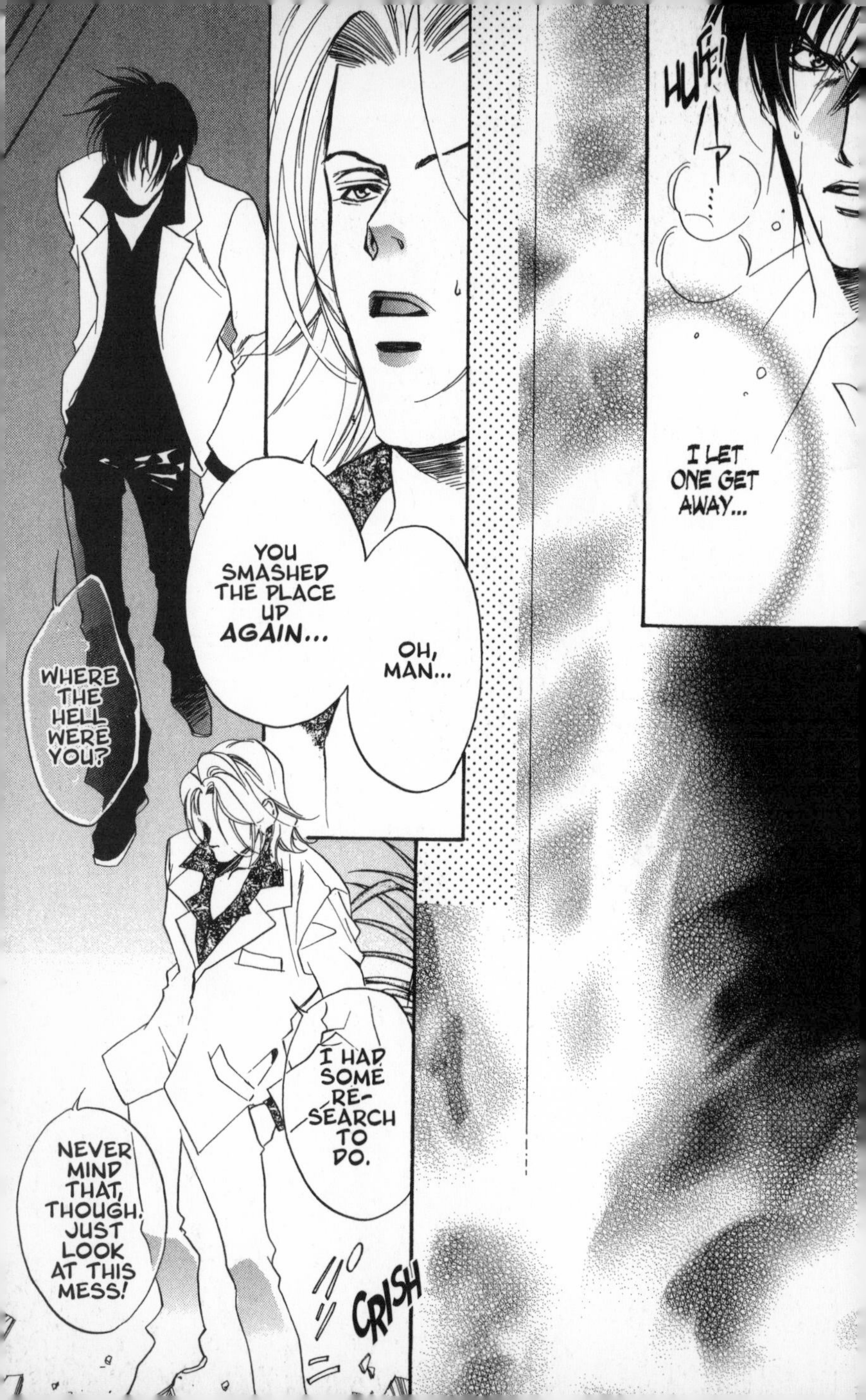
HUFF!
I LET ONE GET AWAY...
YOU SMASHED THE PLACE UP AGAIN...
OH, MAN...
WHERE THE HELL WERE YOU?
I HAD SOME RE-SEARCH TO DO.
NEVER MIND THAT, THOUGH. JUST LOOK AT THIS MESS!
CRISH

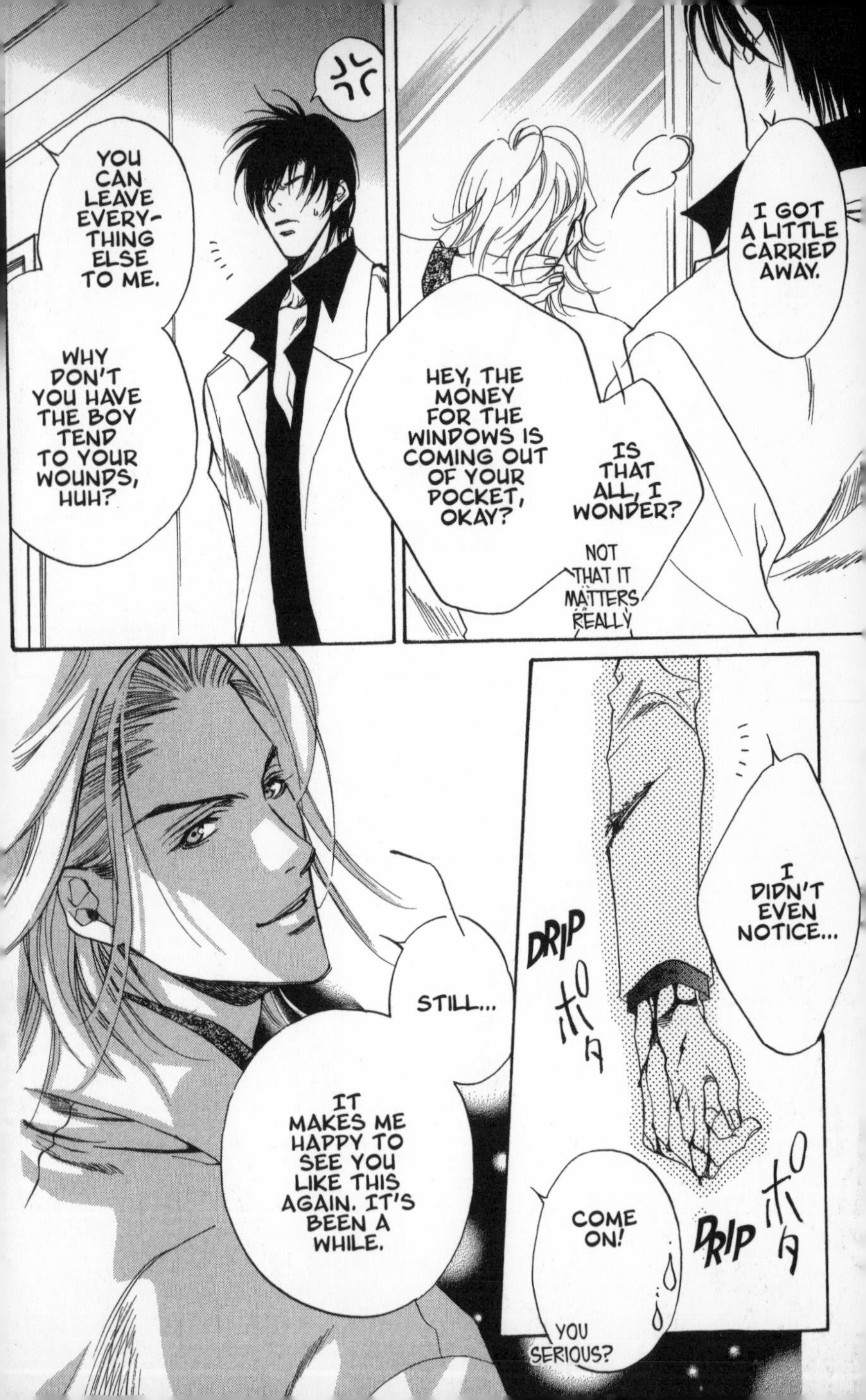
I GOT A LITTLE CARRIED AWAY.
HEY, THE MONEY FOR THE WINDOWS IS COMING OUT OF YOUR POCKET, OKAY?
IS THAT ALL, I WONDER?
NOT THAT IT MATTERS REALLY
YOU CAN LEAVE EVERY-THING ELSE TO ME.
WHY DON'T YOU HAVE THE BOY TEND TO YOUR WOUNDS, HUH?
I DIDN'T EVEN NOTICE...
DRIP
ポタ
ポタ
DRIP
COME ON!
YOU SERIOUS?
STILL...
IT MAKES ME HAPPY TO SEE YOU LIKE THIS AGAIN. IT'S BEEN A WHILE.

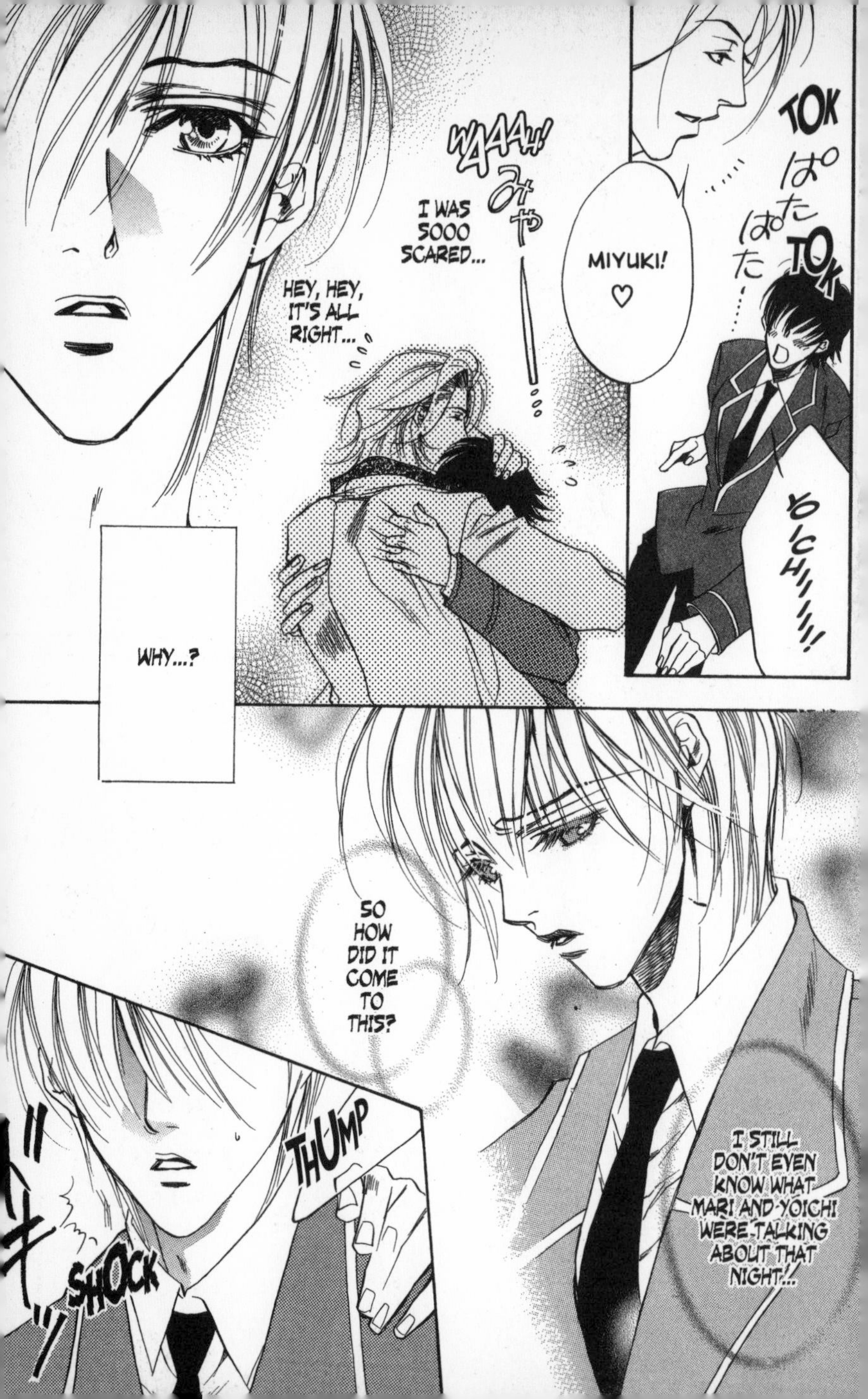

TOK
ぱたぱた
TOK
MIYUKI! ♡
YOCHI!!!!
WAAAH!
みゃ
I WAS SOOO SCARED...
HEY, HEY, IT'S ALL RIGHT...
WHY...?
SO HOW DID IT COME TO THIS?
I STILL DON'T EVEN KNOW WHAT MARI AND YOICHI WERE TALKING ABOUT THAT NIGHT!..
THUMP
SHOCK

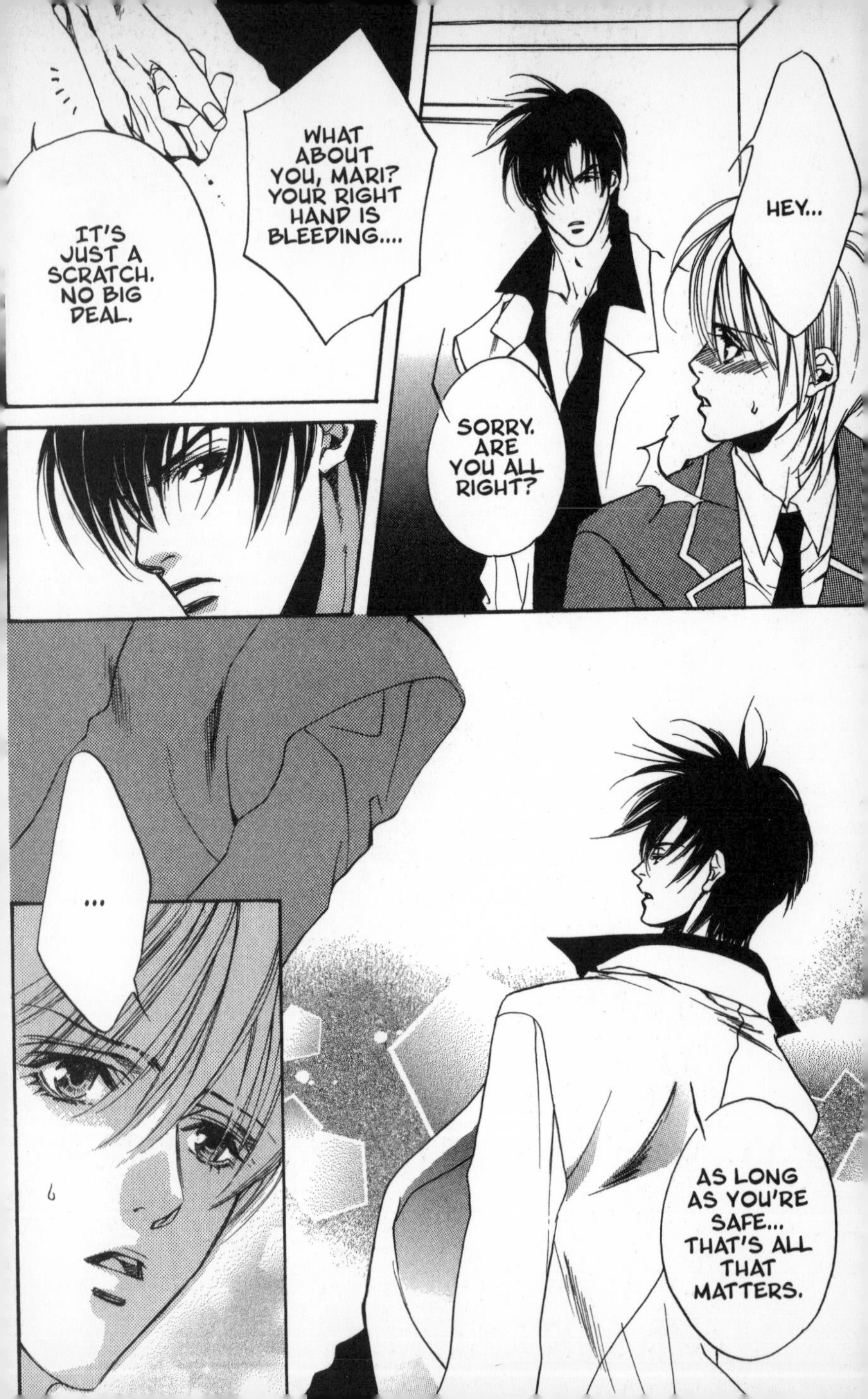
HEY...
SORRY. ARE YOU ALL RIGHT?
WHAT ABOUT YOU, MARI? YOUR RIGHT HAND IS BLEEDING....
IT'S JUST A SCRATCH. NO BIG DEAL.
AS LONG AS YOU'RE SAFE... THAT'S ALL THAT MATTERS.
...

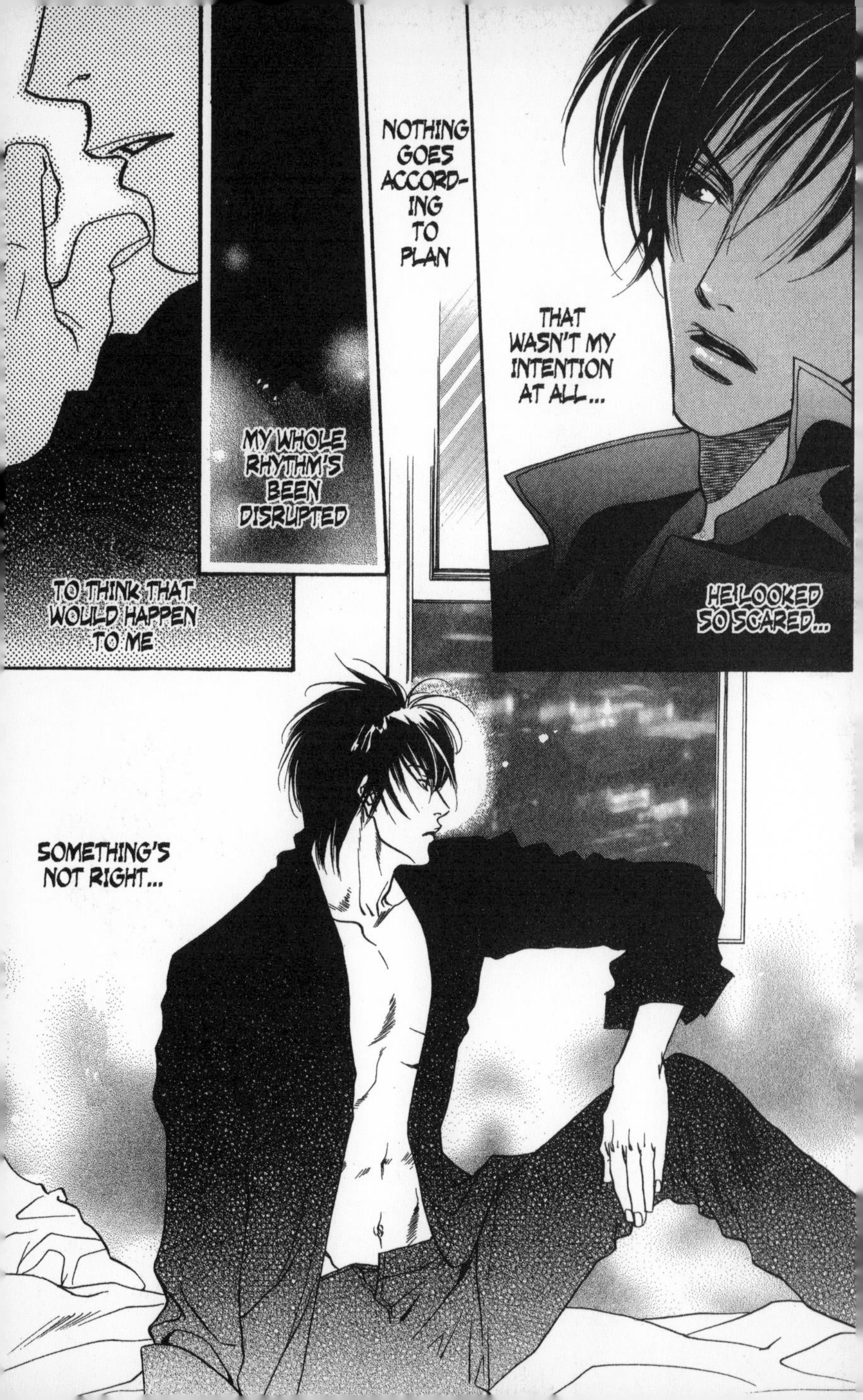
THAT WASN'T MY INTENTION AT ALL...
HE LOOKED SO SCARED...
NOTHING GOES ACCORDING TO PLAN
MY WHOLE RHYTHM'S BEEN DISRUPTED
TO THINK THAT WOULD HAPPEN TO ME
SOMETHING'S NOT RIGHT...

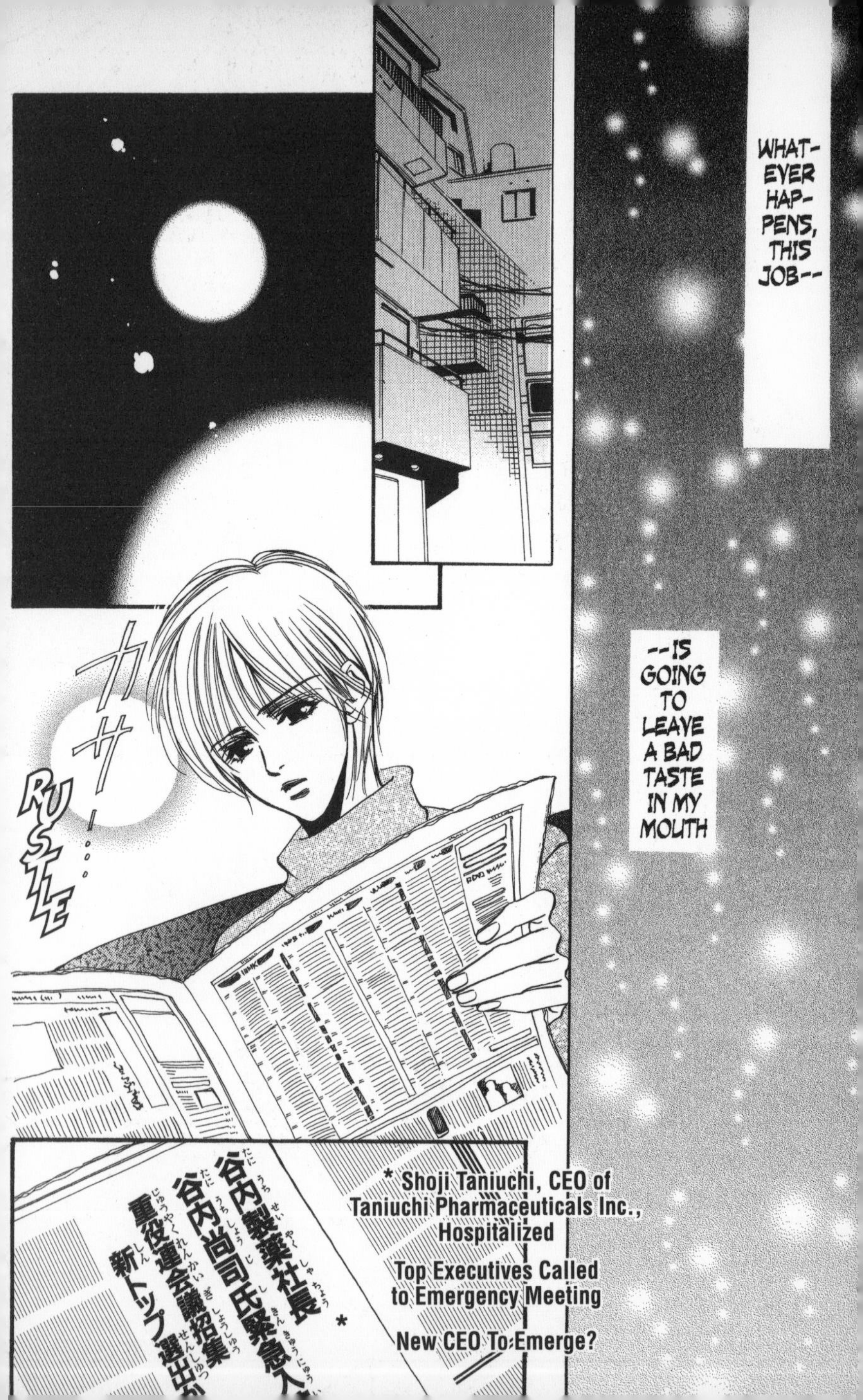
WHAT-EVER HAP-PENS, THIS JOB--
--IS GOING TO LEAVE A BAD TASTE IN MY MOUTH
カサー…
RUSTLE
谷内製薬社長
谷内尚司氏緊急入院
重役連会議招集
新トップ選出か
* Shoji Taniuchi, CEO of Taniuchi Pharmaceuticals Inc., Hospitalized
Top Executives Called to Emergency Meeting
New CEO To Emerge?

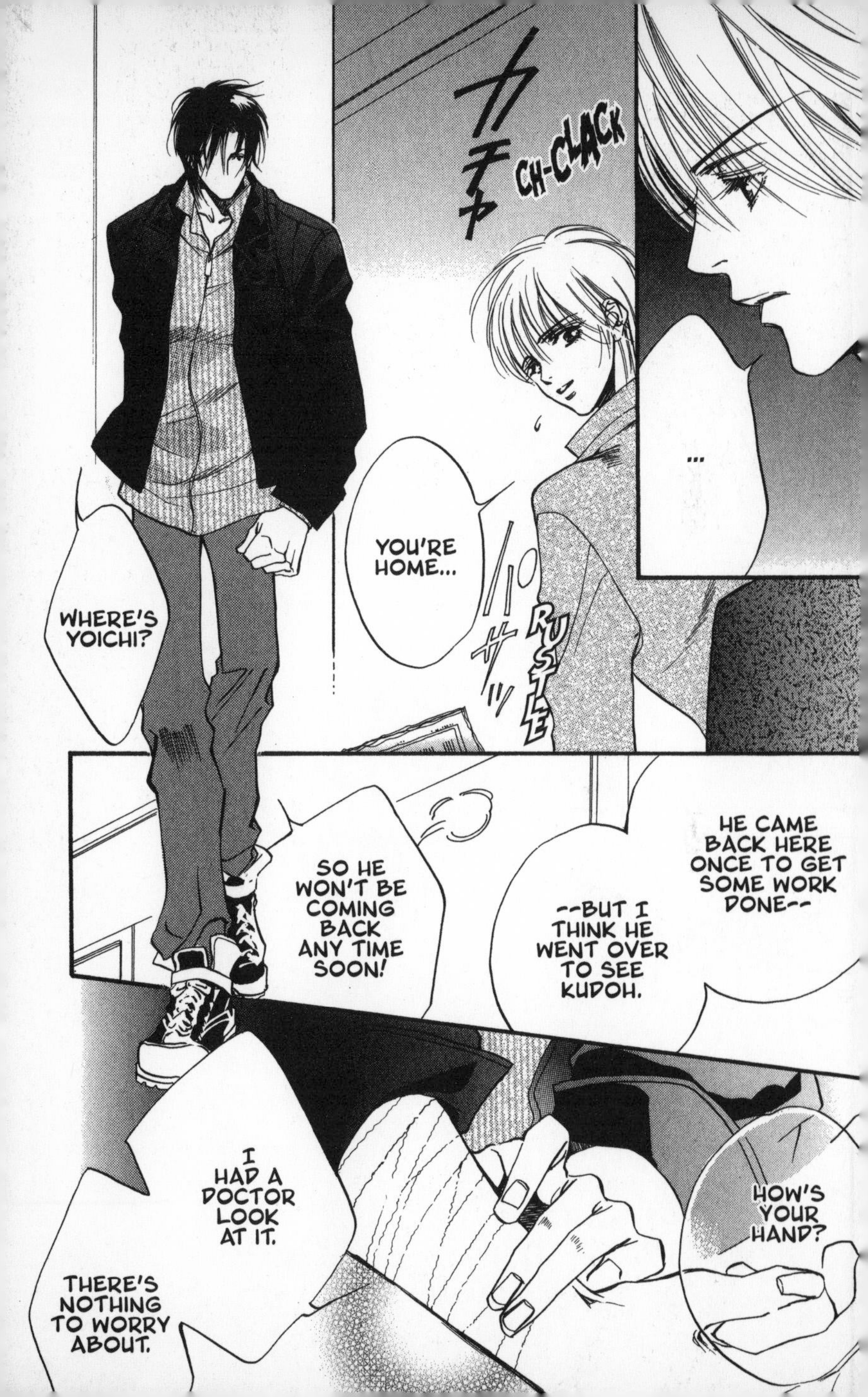

...
カチャ
CH-CLACK
YOU'RE HOME...
RUSTLE
WHERE'S YOICHI?
HE CAME BACK HERE ONCE TO GET SOME WORK DONE--
--BUT I THINK HE WENT OVER TO SEE KUDOH.
SO HE WON'T BE COMING BACK ANY TIME SOON!
HOW'S YOUR HAND?
I HAD A DOCTOR LOOK AT IT.
THERE'S NOTHING TO WORRY ABOUT.

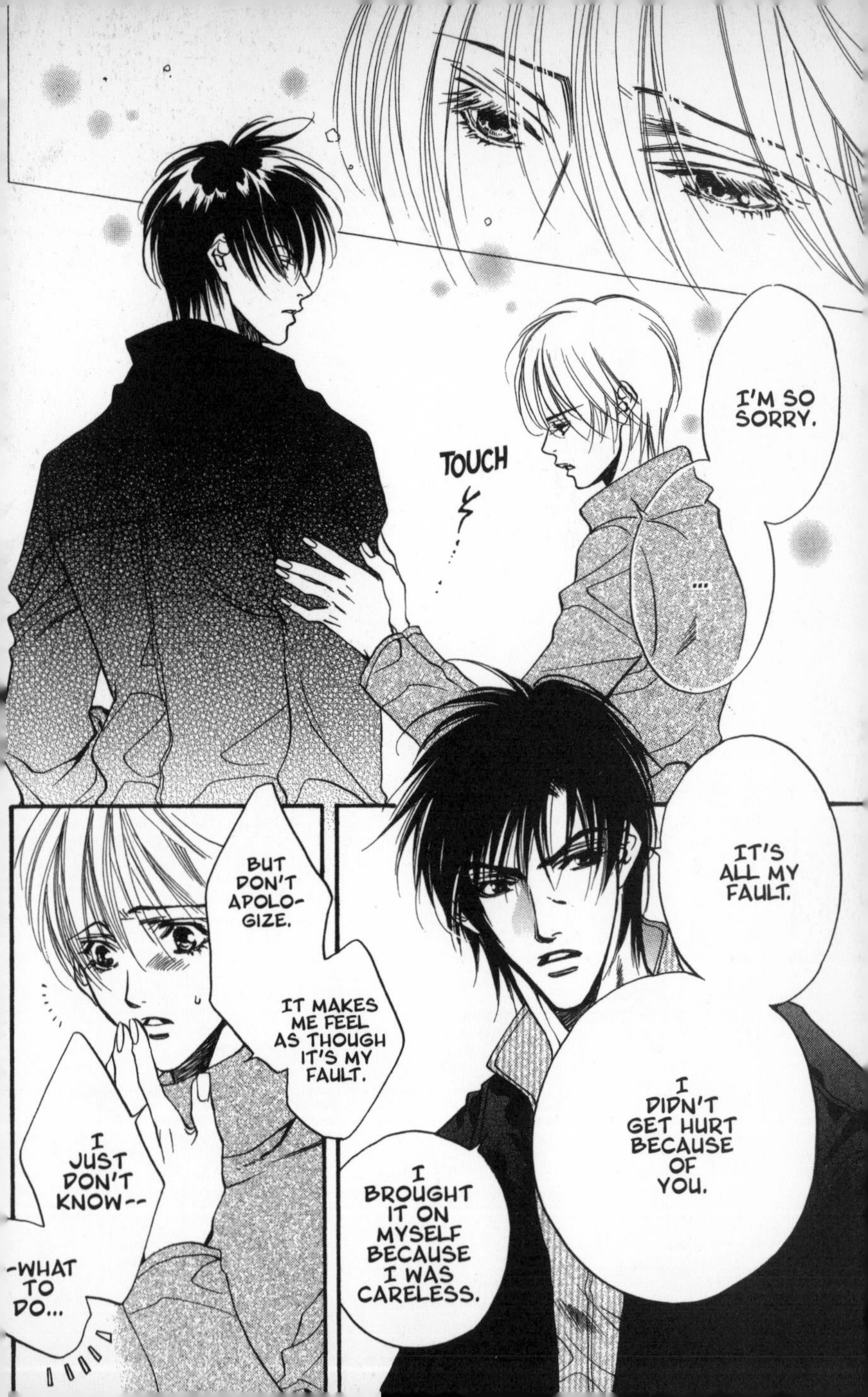

I'M SO SORRY.
TOUCH
...
IT'S ALL MY FAULT.
I DIDN'T GET HURT BECAUSE OF YOU.
I BROUGHT IT ON MYSELF BECAUSE I WAS CARELESS.
BUT DON'T APOLOGIZE.
IT MAKES ME FEEL AS THOUGH IT'S MY FAULT.
I JUST DON'T KNOW--
-WHAT TO DO...

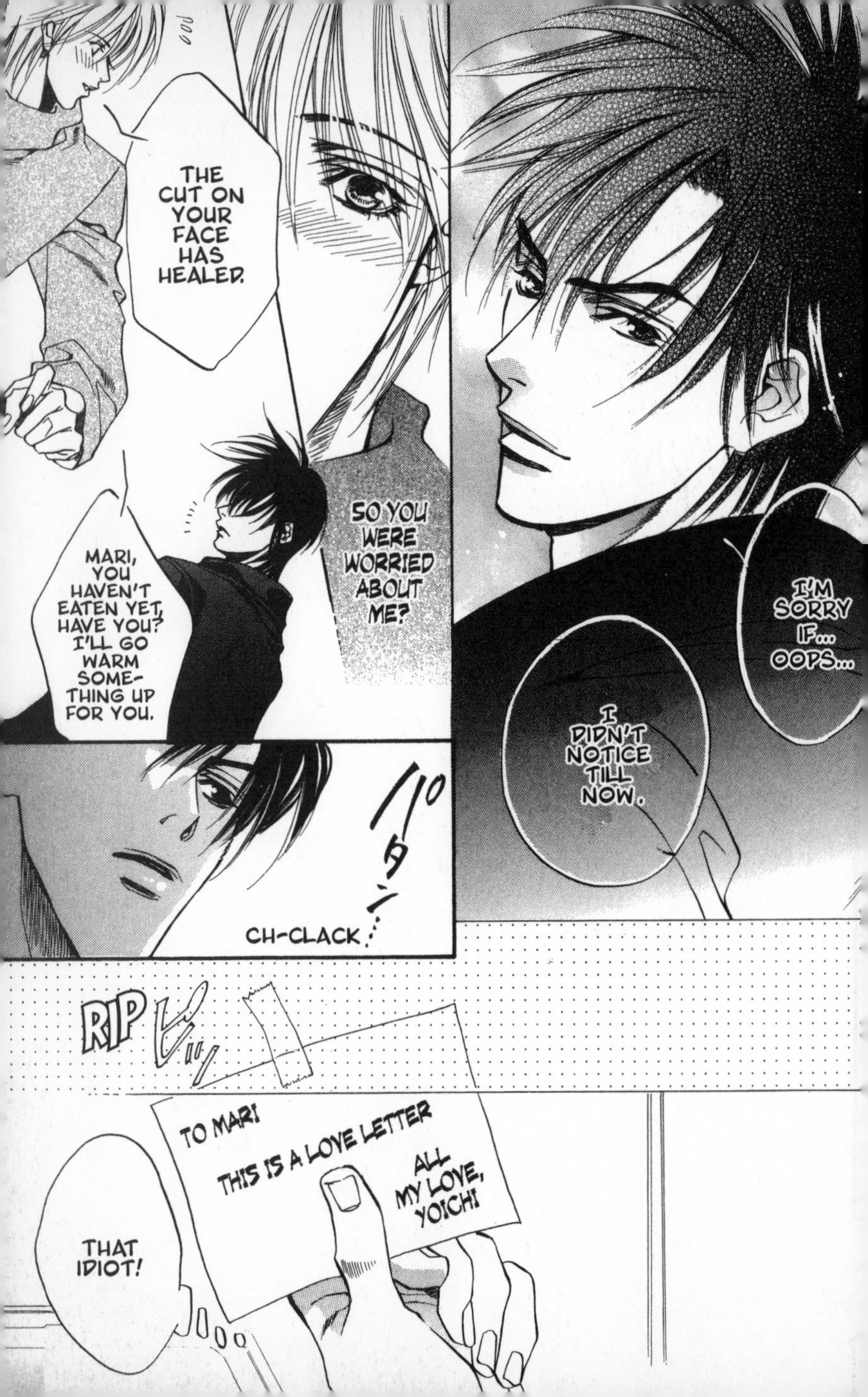
I'M SORRY IF... OOPS...
I DIDN'T NOTICE TILL NOW.
THE CUT ON YOUR FACE HAS HEALED.
SO YOU WERE WORRIED ABOUT ME?
MARI, YOU HAVEN'T EATEN YET, HAVE YOU? I'LL GO WARM SOME-THING UP FOR YOU.
CH-CLACK
RIP
TO MARI
THIS IS A LOVE LETTER
ALL MY LOVE, YOICHI
THAT IDIOT!

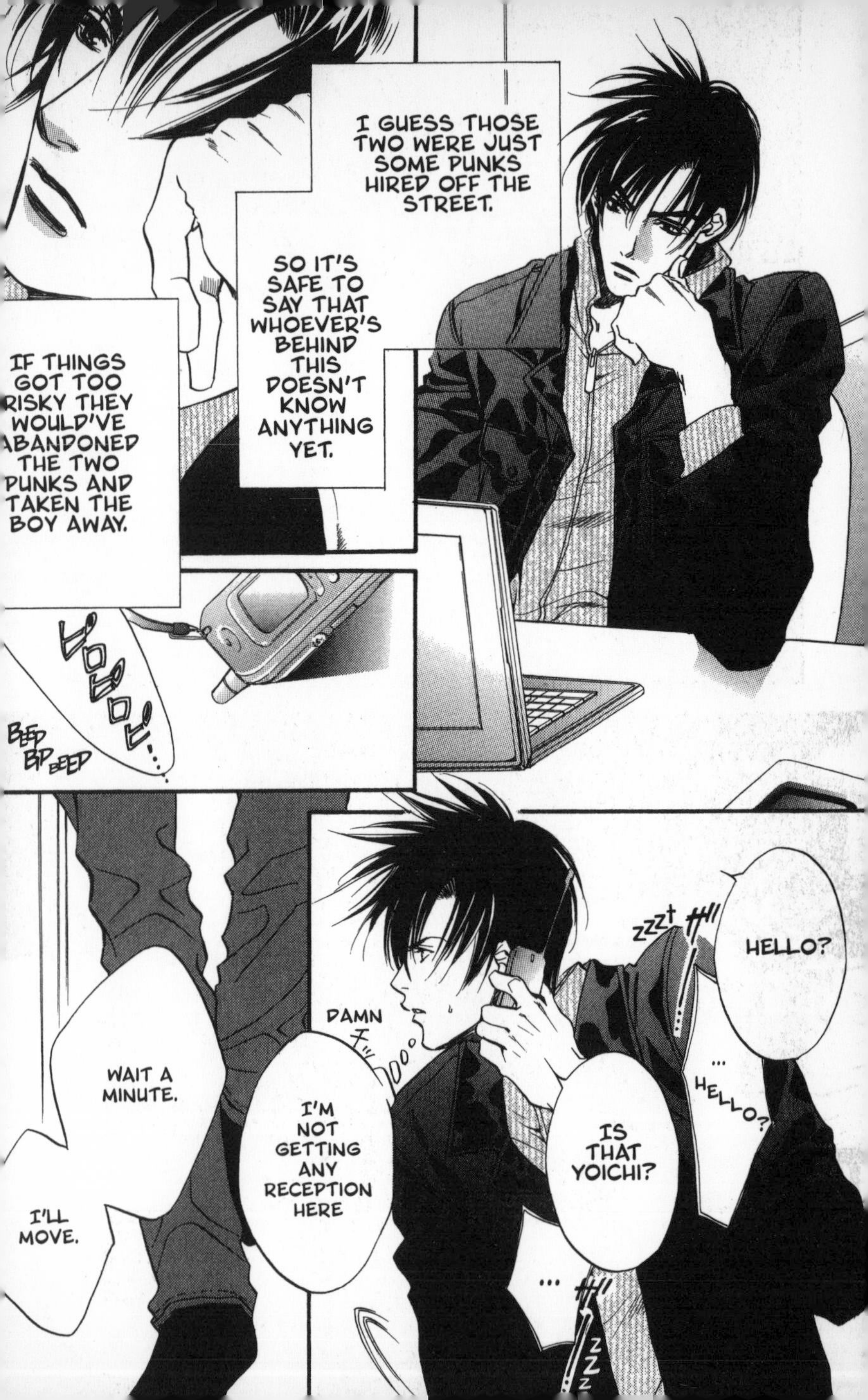
I GUESS THOSE TWO WERE JUST SOME PUNKS HIRED OFF THE STREET.
SO IT'S SAFE TO SAY THAT WHOEVER'S BEHIND THIS DOESN'T KNOW ANYTHING YET.
IF THINGS GOT TOO RISKY THEY WOULD'VE ABANDONED THE TWO PUNKS AND TAKEN THE BOY AWAY.
BEEP BIP BEEP
HELLO?
ZZZT
... HELLO?
IS THAT YOICHI?
DAMN
I'M NOT GETTING ANY RECEPTION HERE
...
ZZZ
WAIT A MINUTE.
I'LL MOVE.

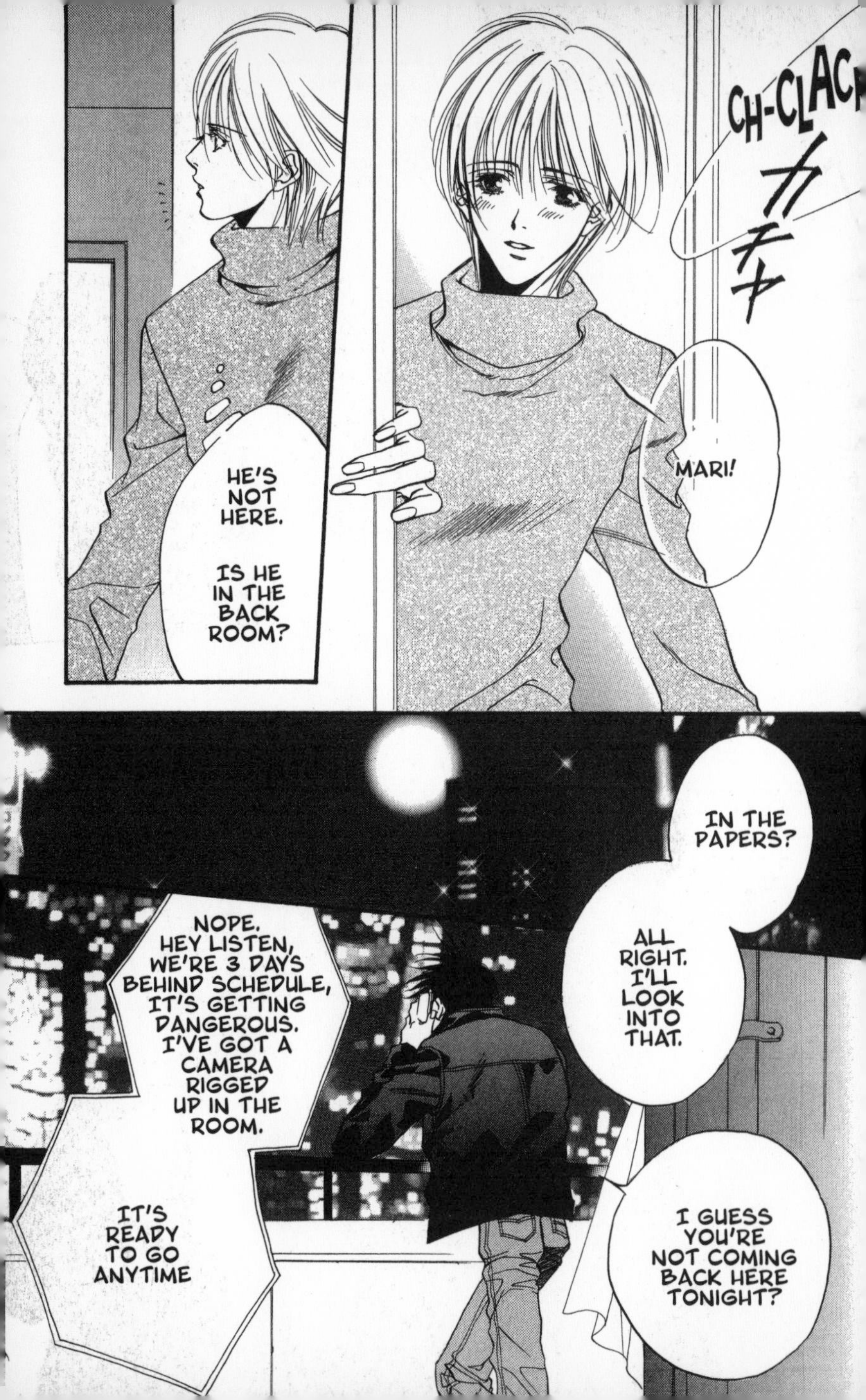
CH-CLAC
カチャ
MARI!
HE'S NOT HERE.
IS HE IN THE BACK ROOM?
IN THE PAPERS?
ALL RIGHT. I'LL LOOK INTO THAT.
NOPE. HEY LISTEN, WE'RE 3 DAYS BEHIND SCHEDULE, IT'S GETTING DANGEROUS. I'VE GOT A CAMERA RIGGED UP IN THE ROOM.
IT'S READY TO GO ANYTIME
I GUESS YOU'RE NOT COMING BACK HERE TONIGHT?

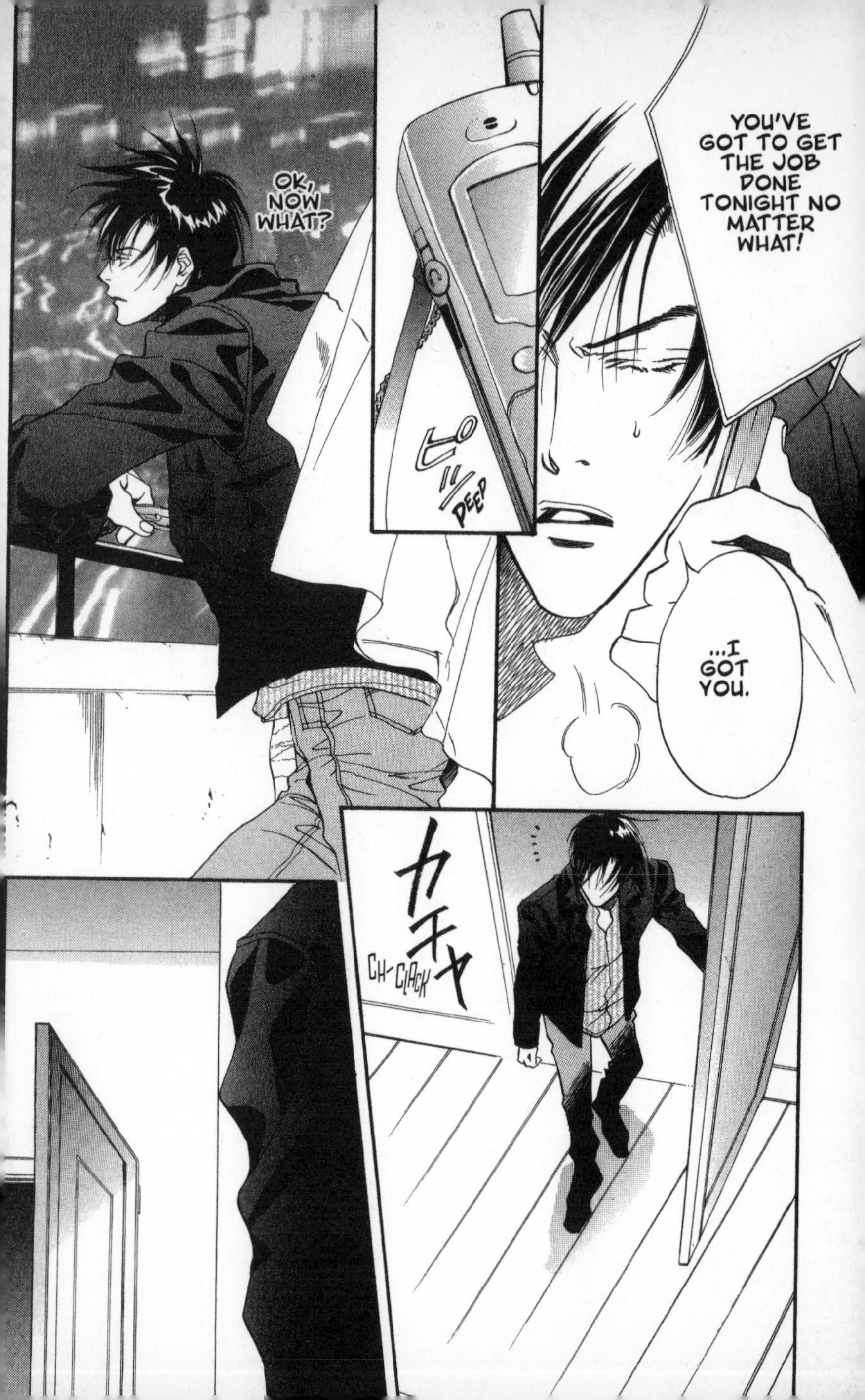
YOU'VE GOT TO GET THE JOB DONE TONIGHT NO MATTER WHAT!
...I GOT YOU.
ピッ
DEEP
OK, NOW WHAT?
カチャ
CH-CLACK
...

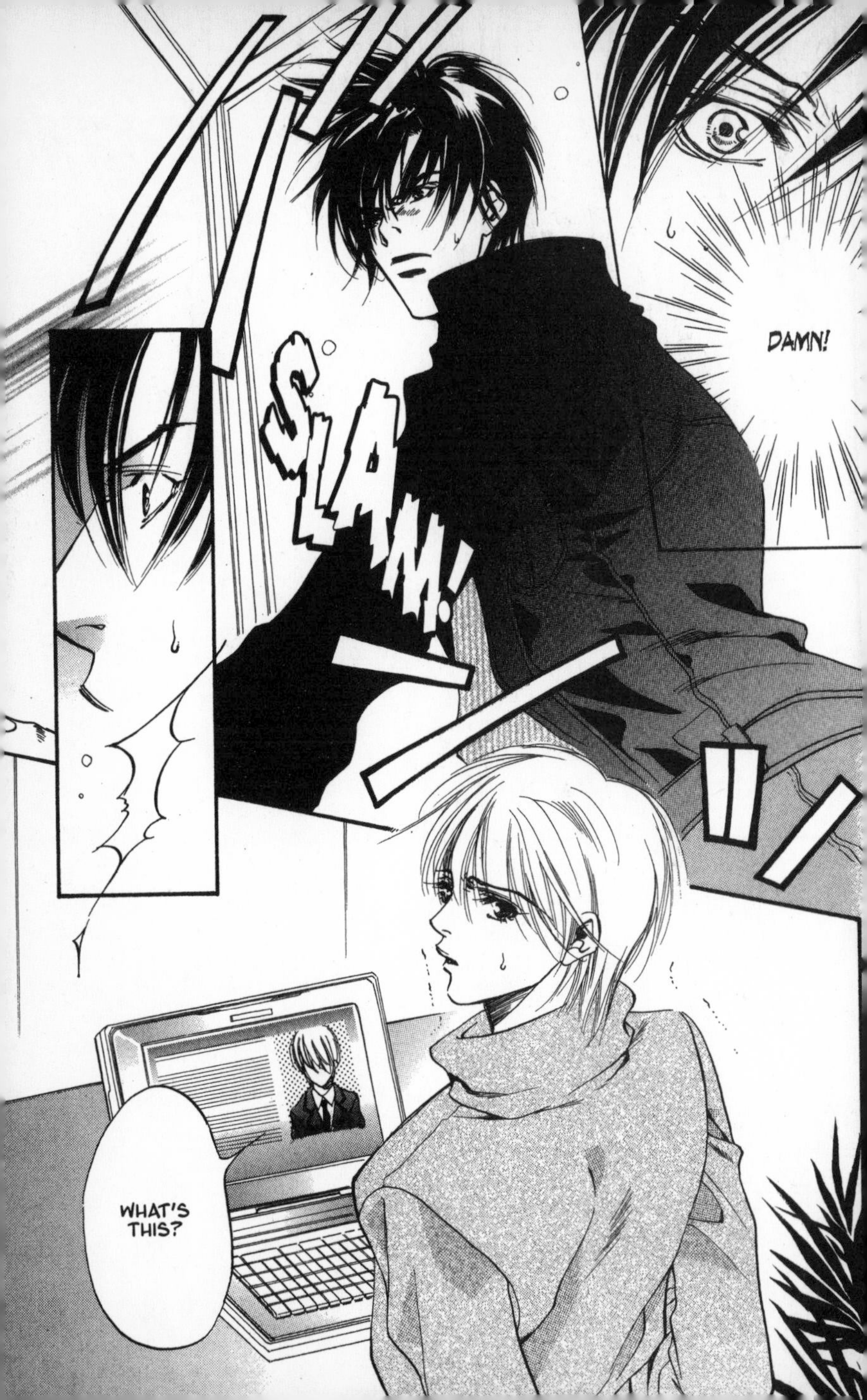
DAMN!
SLAM!
WHAT'S THIS?

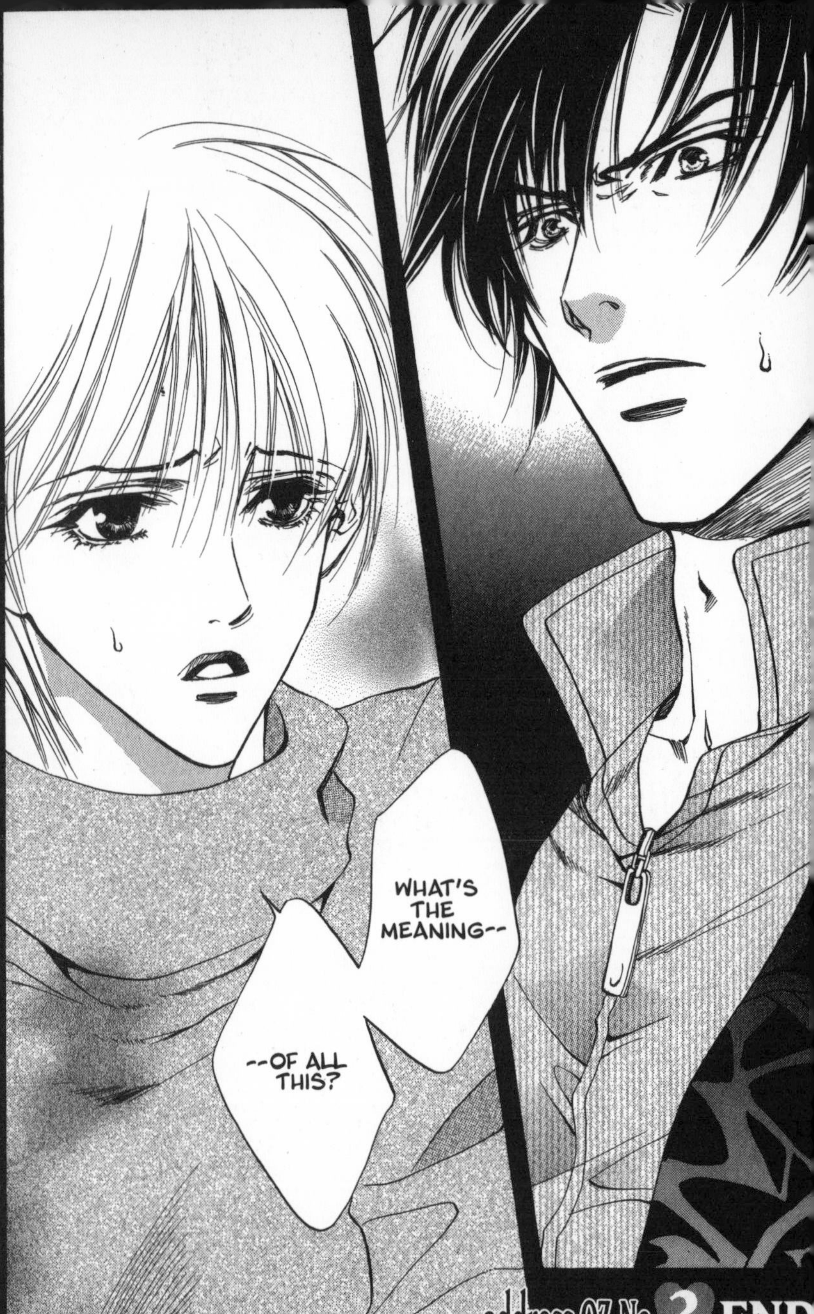
WHAT'S THE MEANING--
--OF ALL THIS?
address.OZ No. 2 END

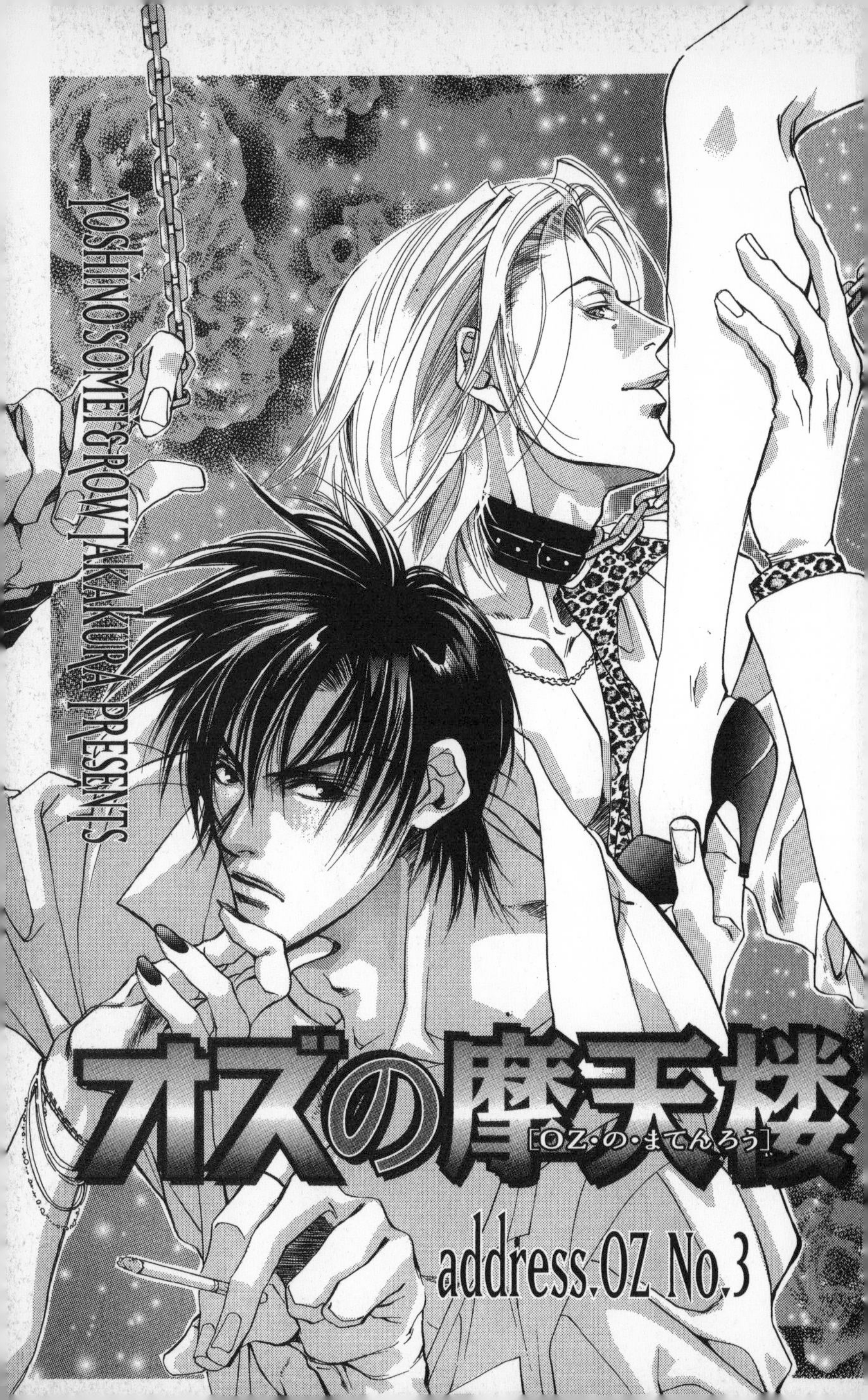
YOSHINO SOMEI & ROW TAKAKURA PRESENTS
オズの摩天楼
[O.Z.・の・まてんろう]
address.OZ No.3

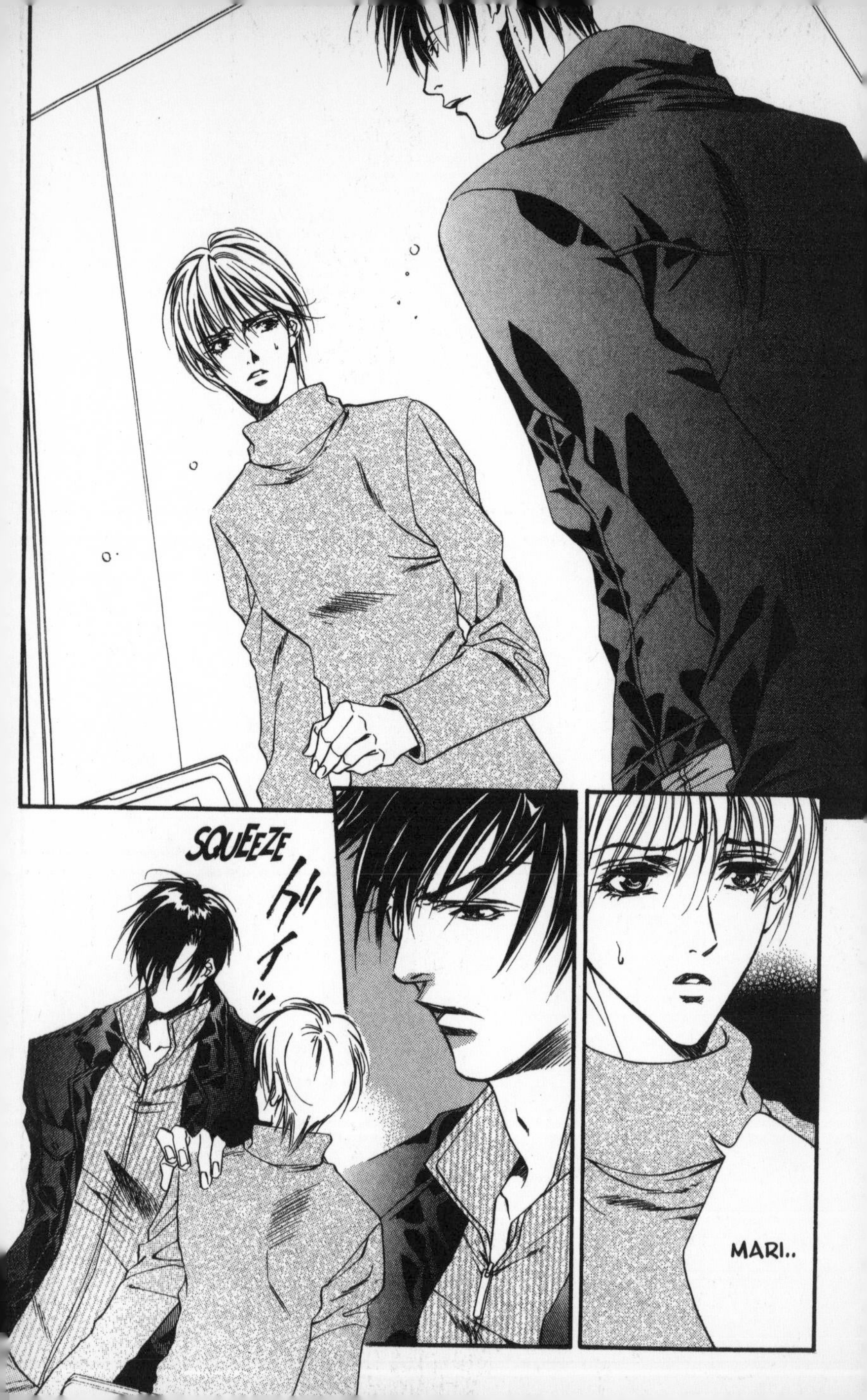
MARI..
SQUEEZE
グイッ

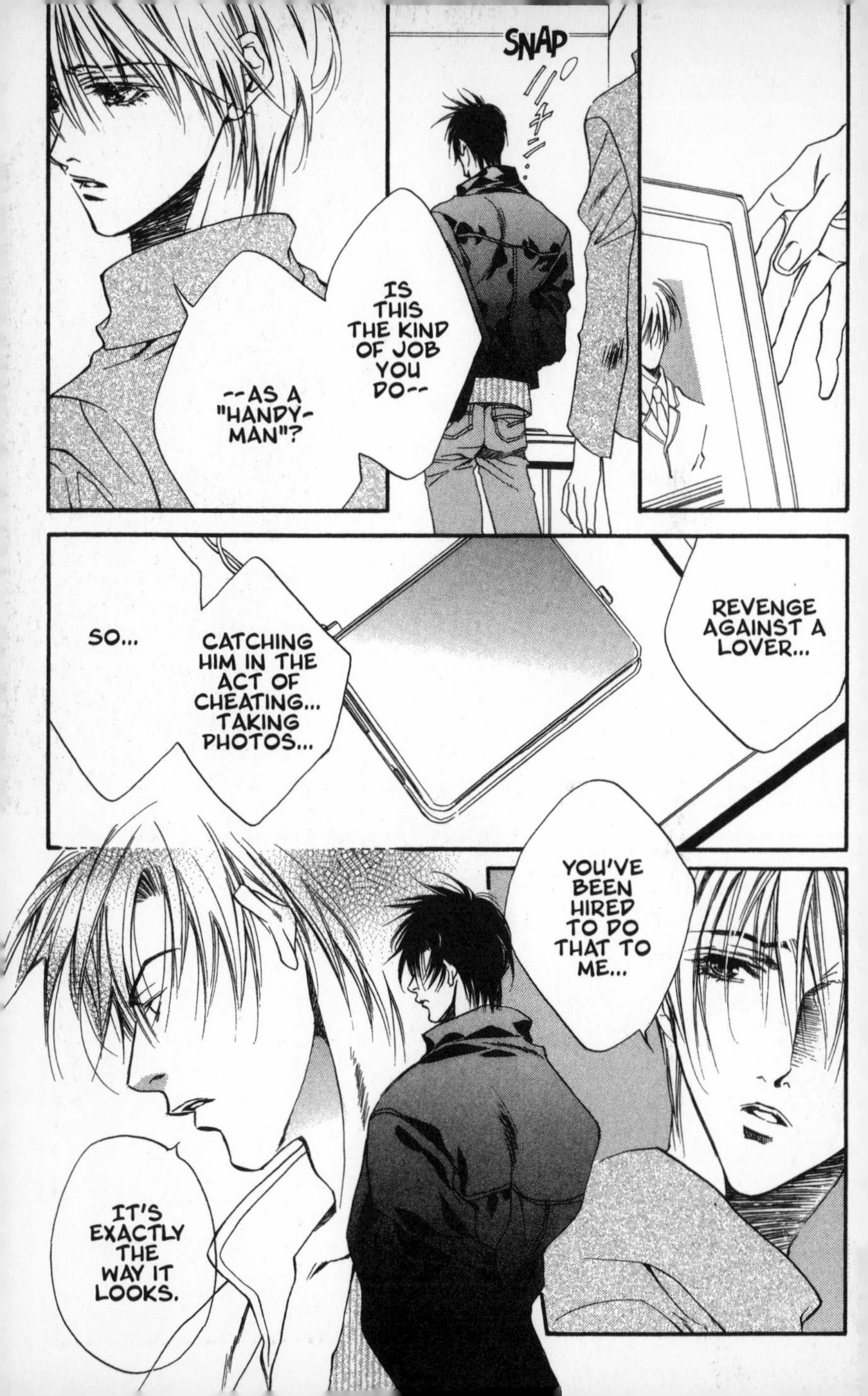
SNAP
IS THIS THE KIND OF JOB YOU DO--
--AS A "HANDY-MAN"?
REVENGE AGAINST A LOVER...
CATCHING HIM IN THE ACT OF CHEATING... TAKING PHOTOS...
SO...
YOU'VE BEEN HIRED TO DO THAT TO ME...
IT'S EXACTLY THE WAY IT LOOKS.

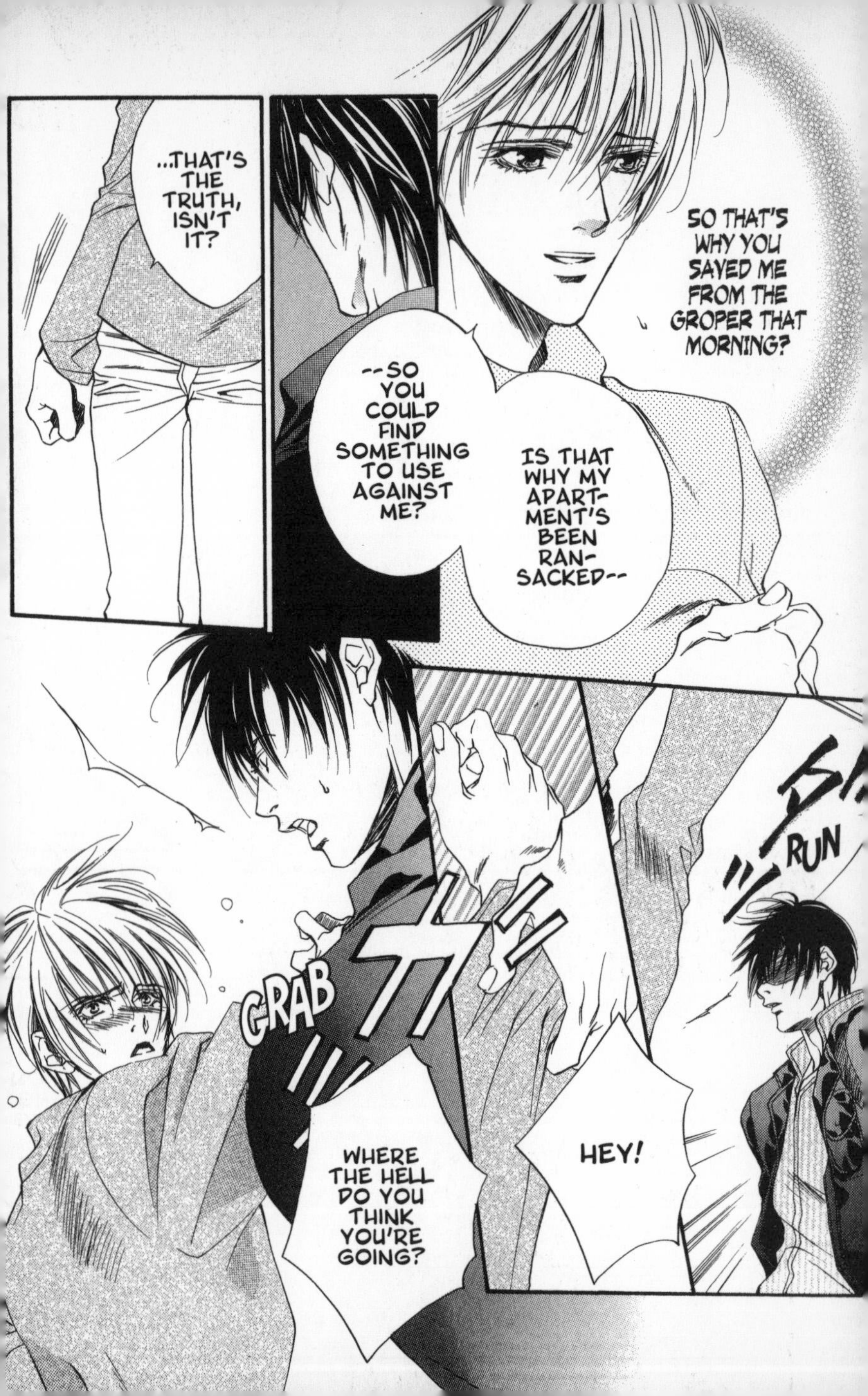
SO THAT'S WHY YOU SAVED ME FROM THE GROPER THAT MORNING?
IS THAT WHY MY APART-MENT'S BEEN RAN-SACKED--
--SO YOU COULD FIND SOMETHING TO USE AGAINST ME?
...THAT'S THE TRUTH, ISN'T IT?
RUN
HEY!
GRAB
WHERE THE HELL DO YOU THINK YOU'RE GOING?

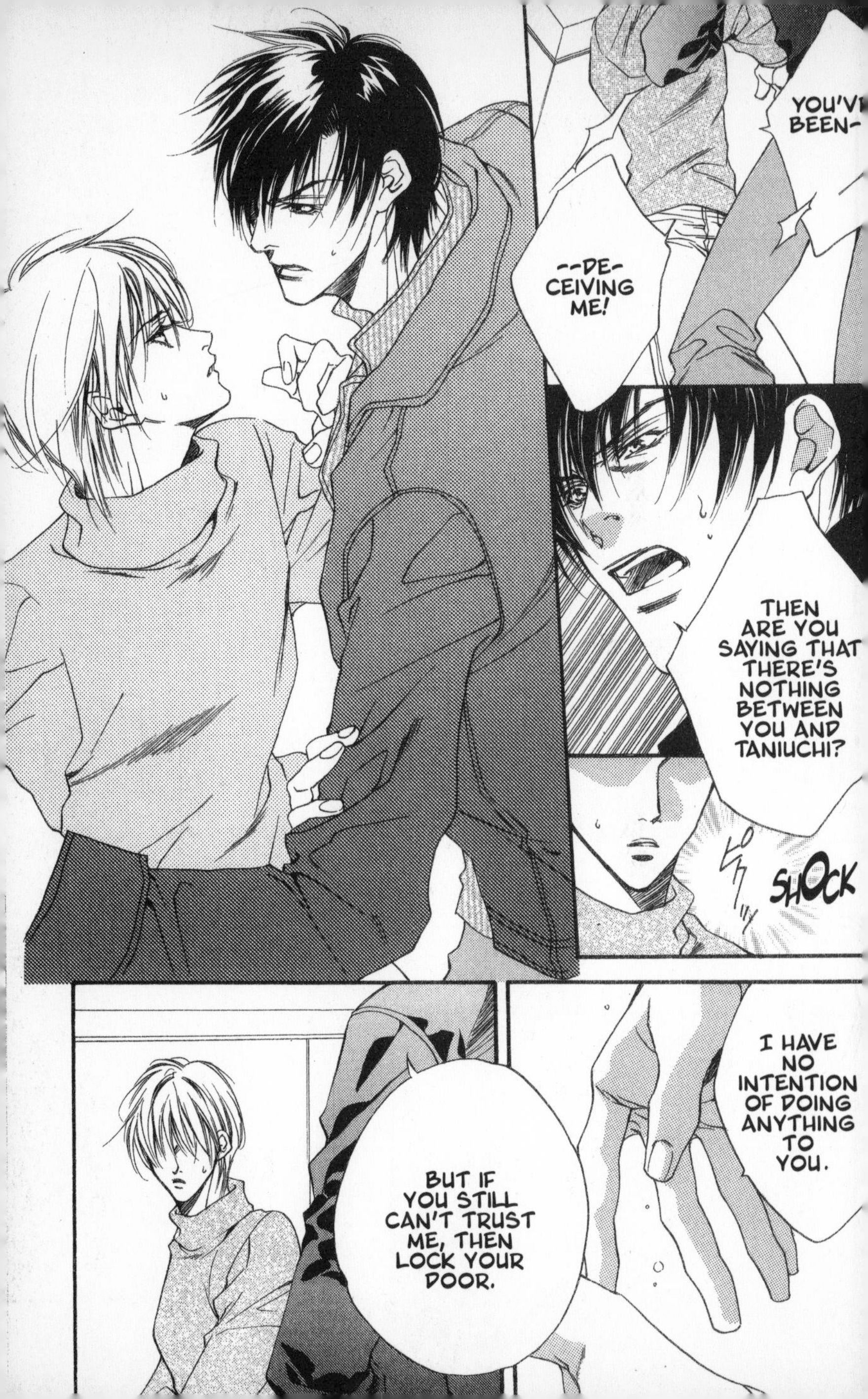
YOU'VE BEEN-
--DE-CEIVING ME!
THEN ARE YOU SAYING THAT THERE'S NOTHING BETWEEN YOU AND TANIUCHI?
SHOCK
I HAVE NO INTENTION OF DOING ANYTHING TO YOU.
BUT IF YOU STILL CAN'T TRUST ME, THEN LOCK YOUR DOOR.

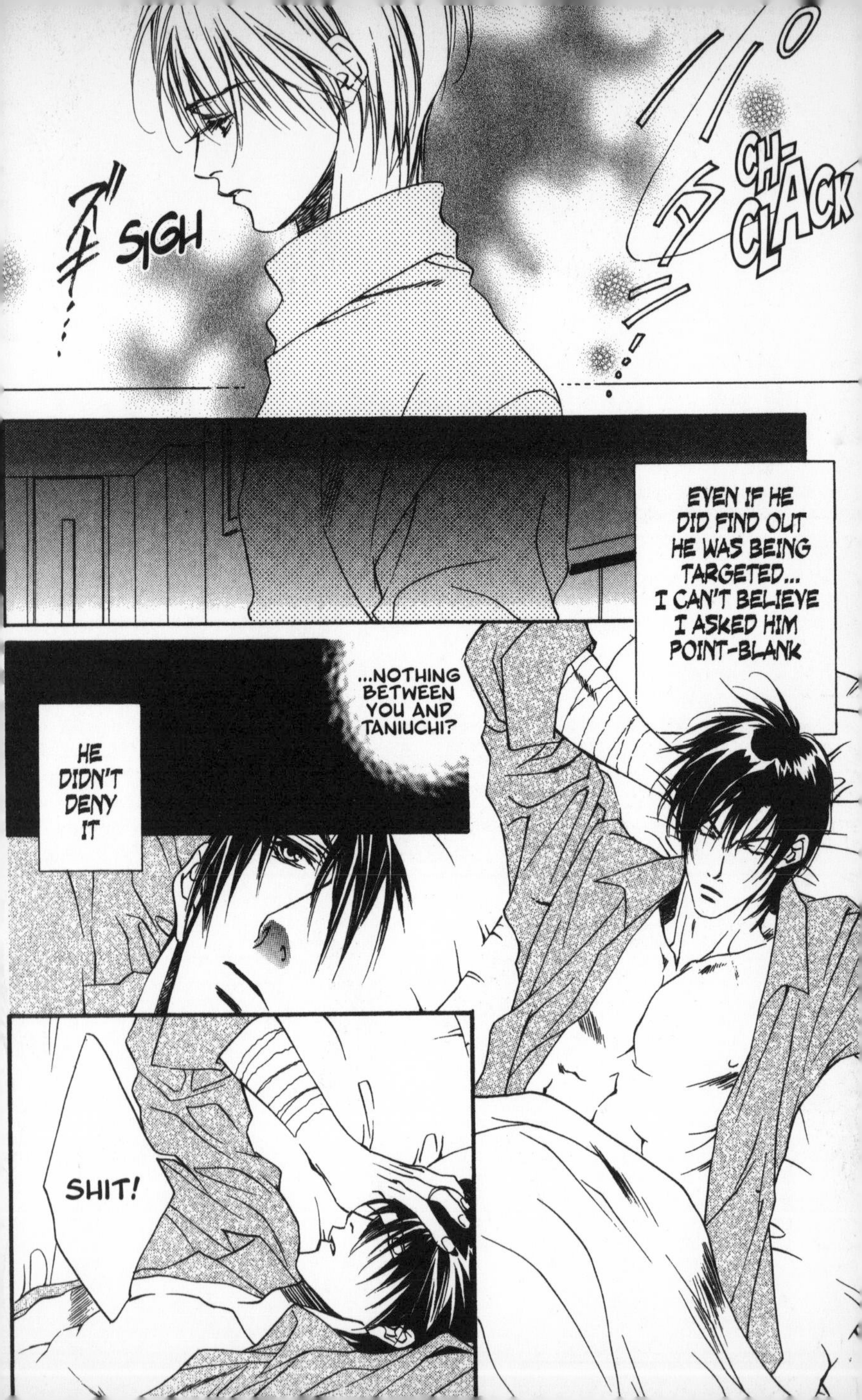
CH-CLACK
SIGH
EVEN IF HE DID FIND OUT HE WAS BEING TARGETED... I CAN'T BELIEVE I ASKED HIM POINT-BLANK
...NOTHING BETWEEN YOU AND TANIUCHI?
HE DIDN'T DENY IT
SHIT!

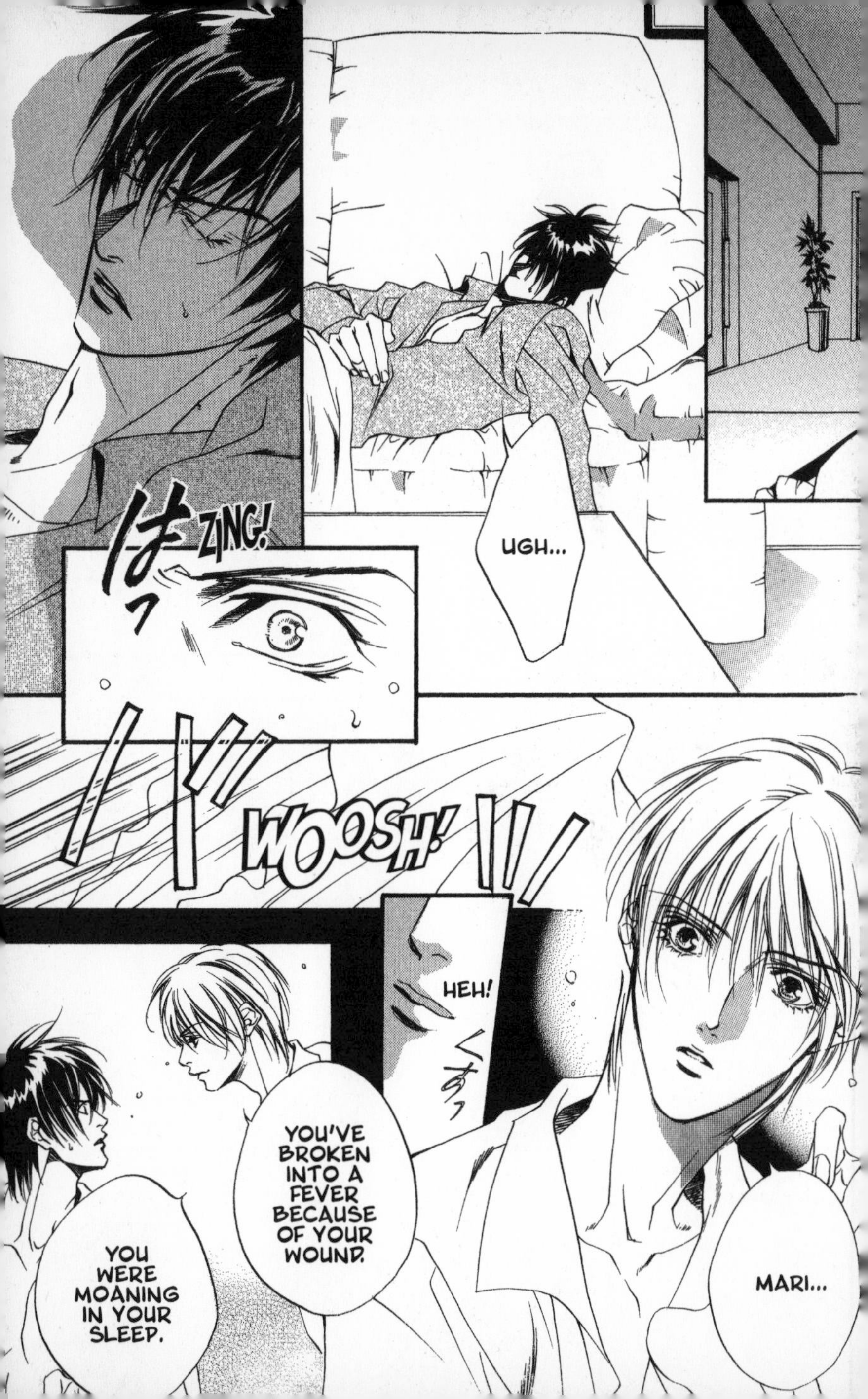

UGH...
はっ
ZING!
WOOSH!
MARI...
HEH!
くすっ
YOU'VE BROKEN INTO A FEVER BECAUSE OF YOUR WOUND.
YOU WERE MOANING IN YOUR SLEEP.

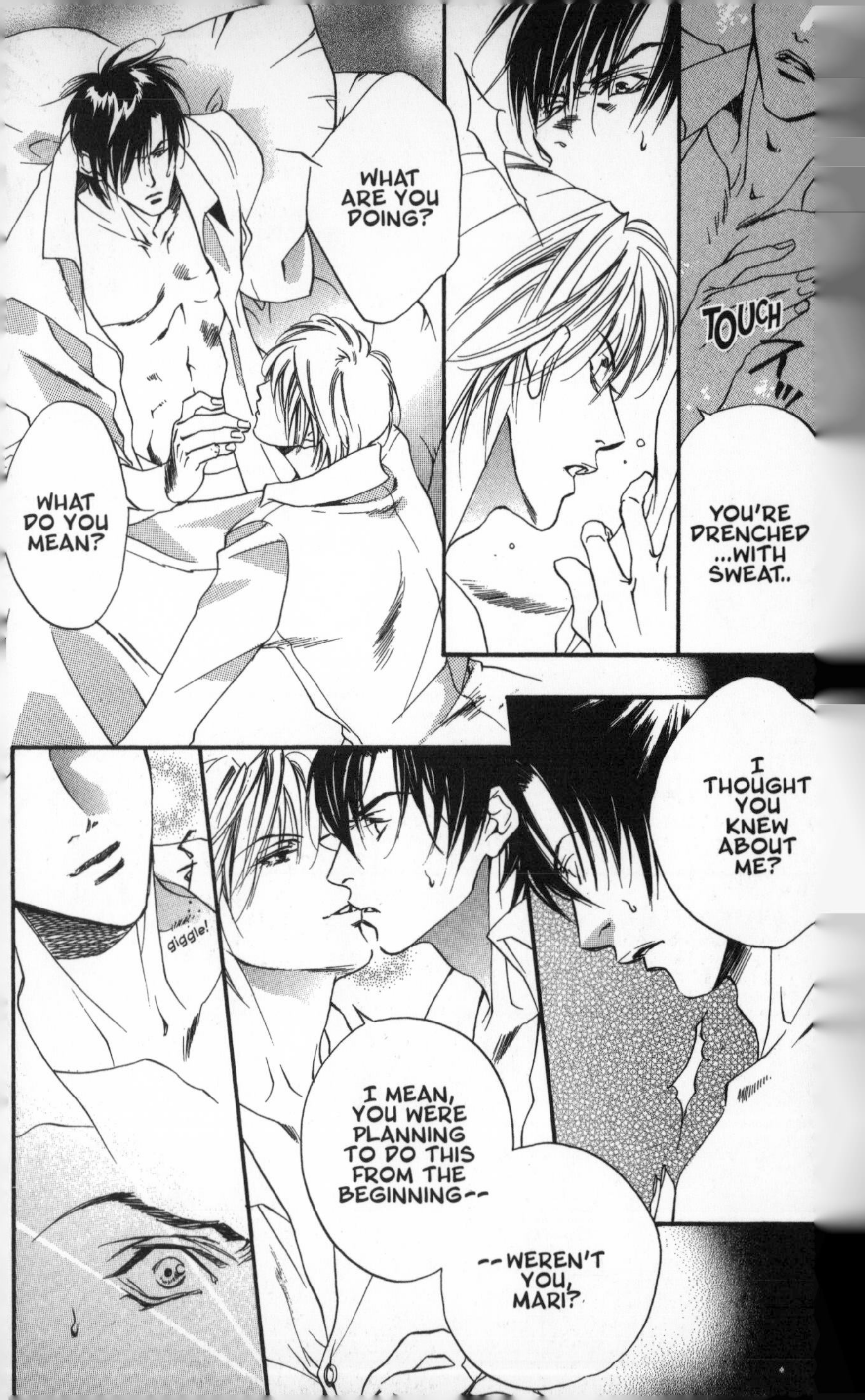
TOUCH
YOU'RE DRENCHED ...WITH SWEAT..
WHAT ARE YOU DOING?
WHAT DO YOU MEAN?
I THOUGHT YOU KNEW ABOUT ME?
I MEAN, YOU WERE PLANNING TO DO THIS FROM THE BEGINNING--
--WEREN'T YOU, MARI?
giggle!

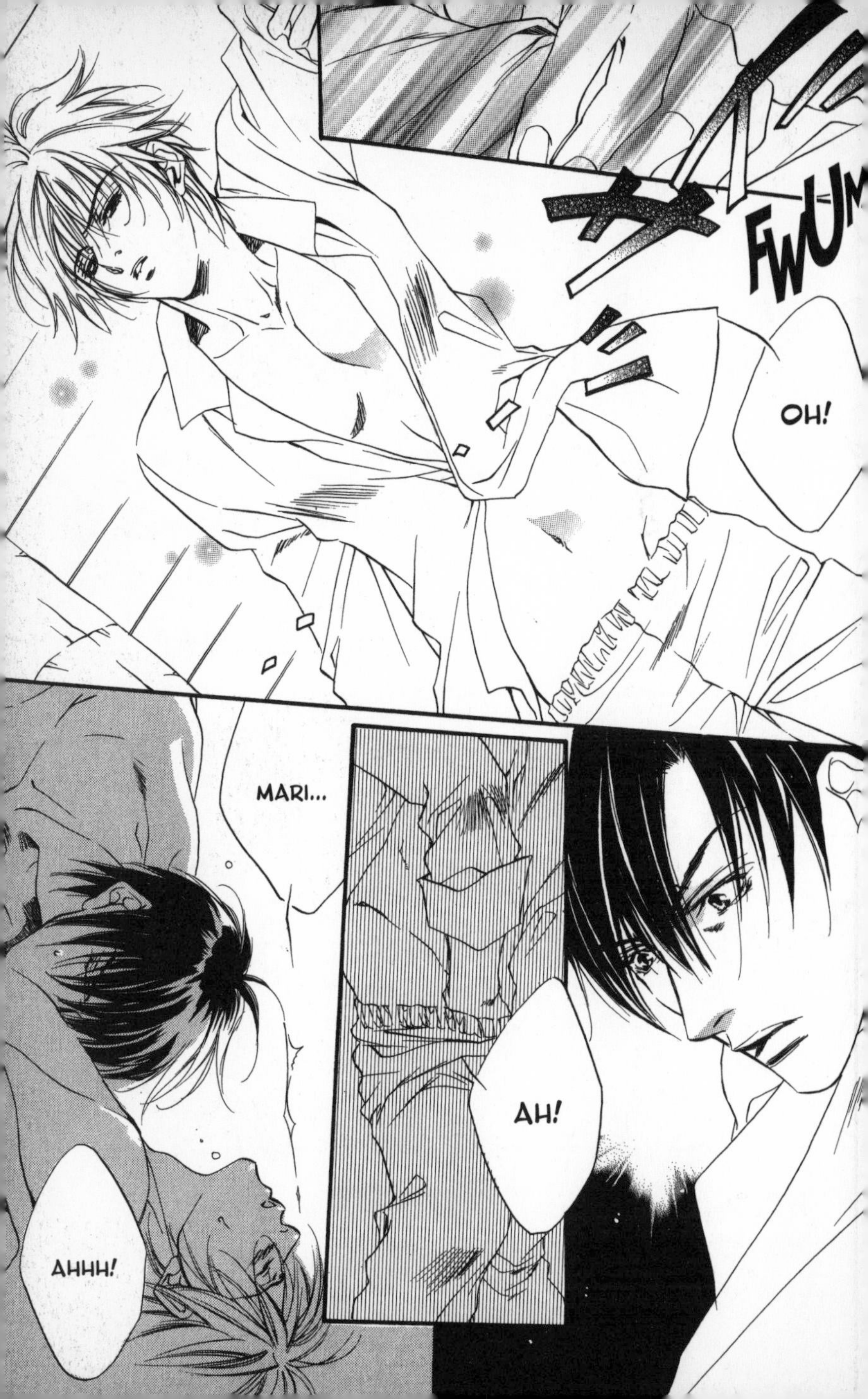
FWUM
OH!
AH!
MARI...
AHHH!

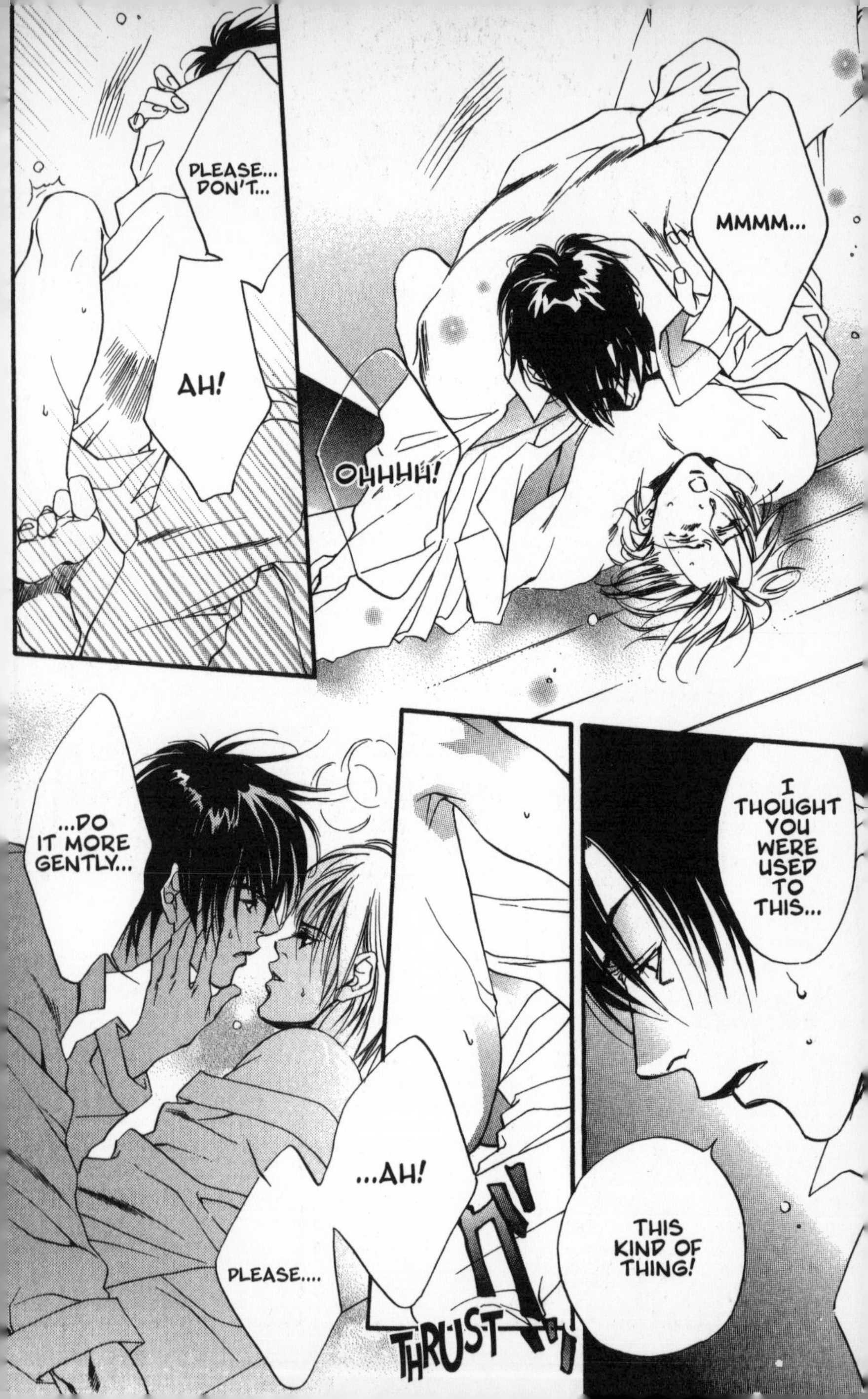
MMMM...
OHHHH!
PLEASE... DON'T...
AH!
I THOUGHT YOU WERE USED TO THIS...
THIS KIND OF THING!
...AH!
PLEASE....
THRUST
...DO IT MORE GENTLY...

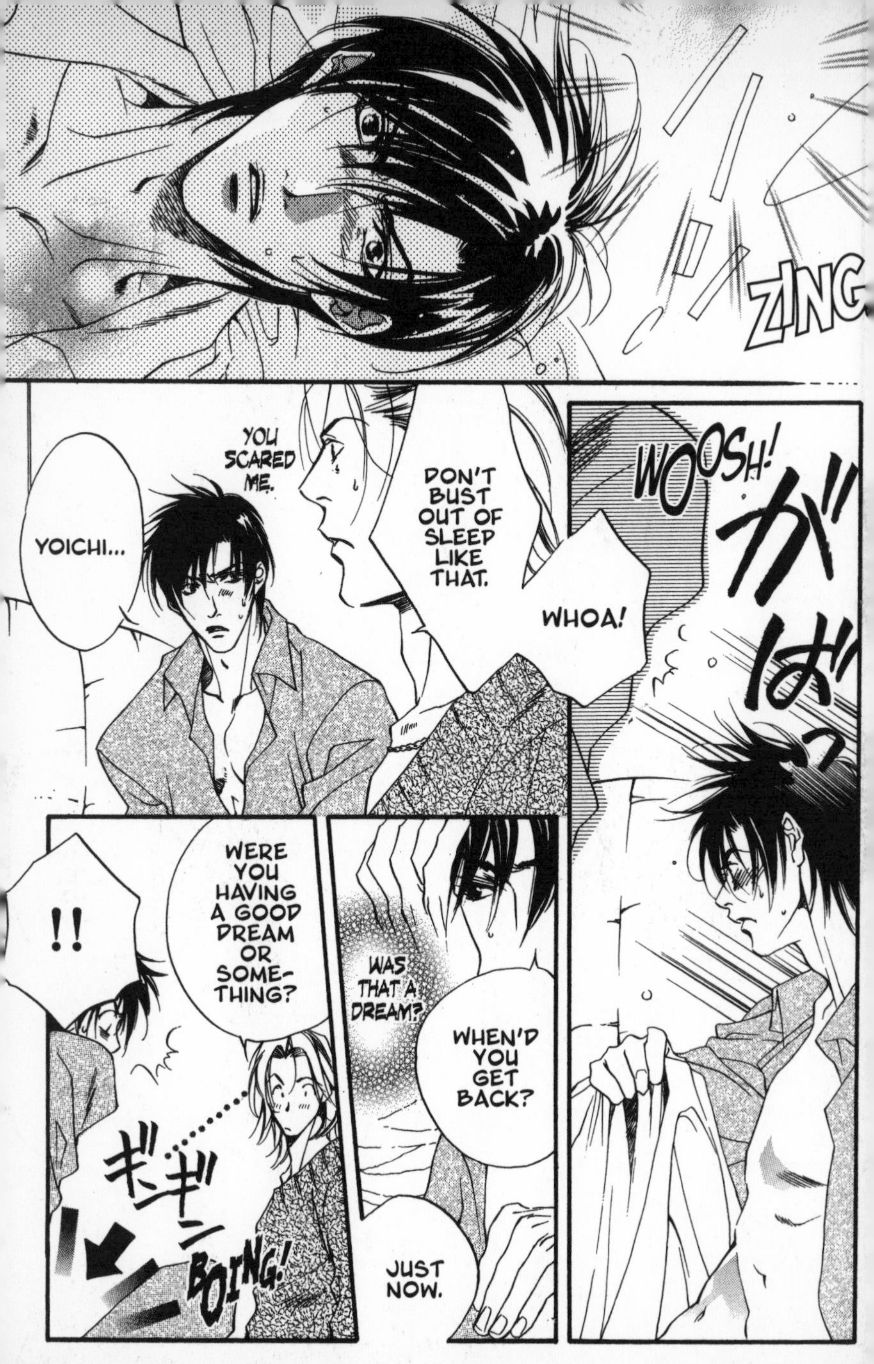
ZING
WOOSH!
がばっ
WHOA!
DON'T BUST OUT OF SLEEP LIKE THAT.
YOU SCARED ME.
YOICHI...
WAS THAT A DREAM?
WHEN'D YOU GET BACK?
JUST NOW.
WERE YOU HAVING A GOOD DREAM OR SOMETHING?
!!
ギギン
BOING!

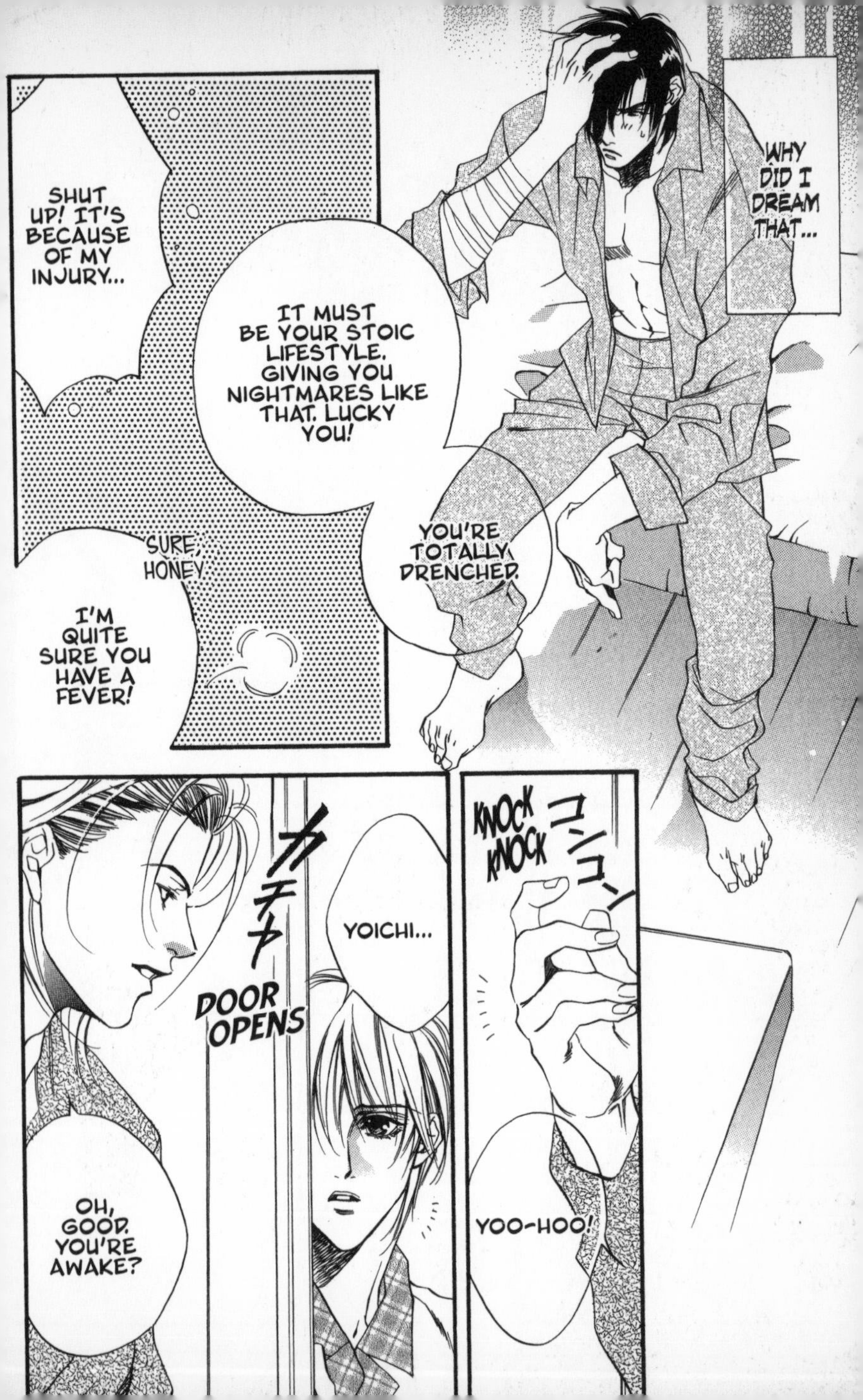
WHY DID I DREAM THAT...
YOU'RE TOTALLY DRENCHED.
IT MUST BE YOUR STOIC LIFESTYLE. GIVING YOU NIGHTMARES LIKE THAT. LUCKY YOU!
SHUT UP! IT'S BECAUSE OF MY INJURY...
SURE, HONEY
I'M QUITE SURE YOU HAVE A FEVER!
コンコン
KNOCK KNOCK
YOO-HOO!
カチャ
DOOR OPENS
YOICHI...
OH, GOOD. YOU'RE AWAKE?

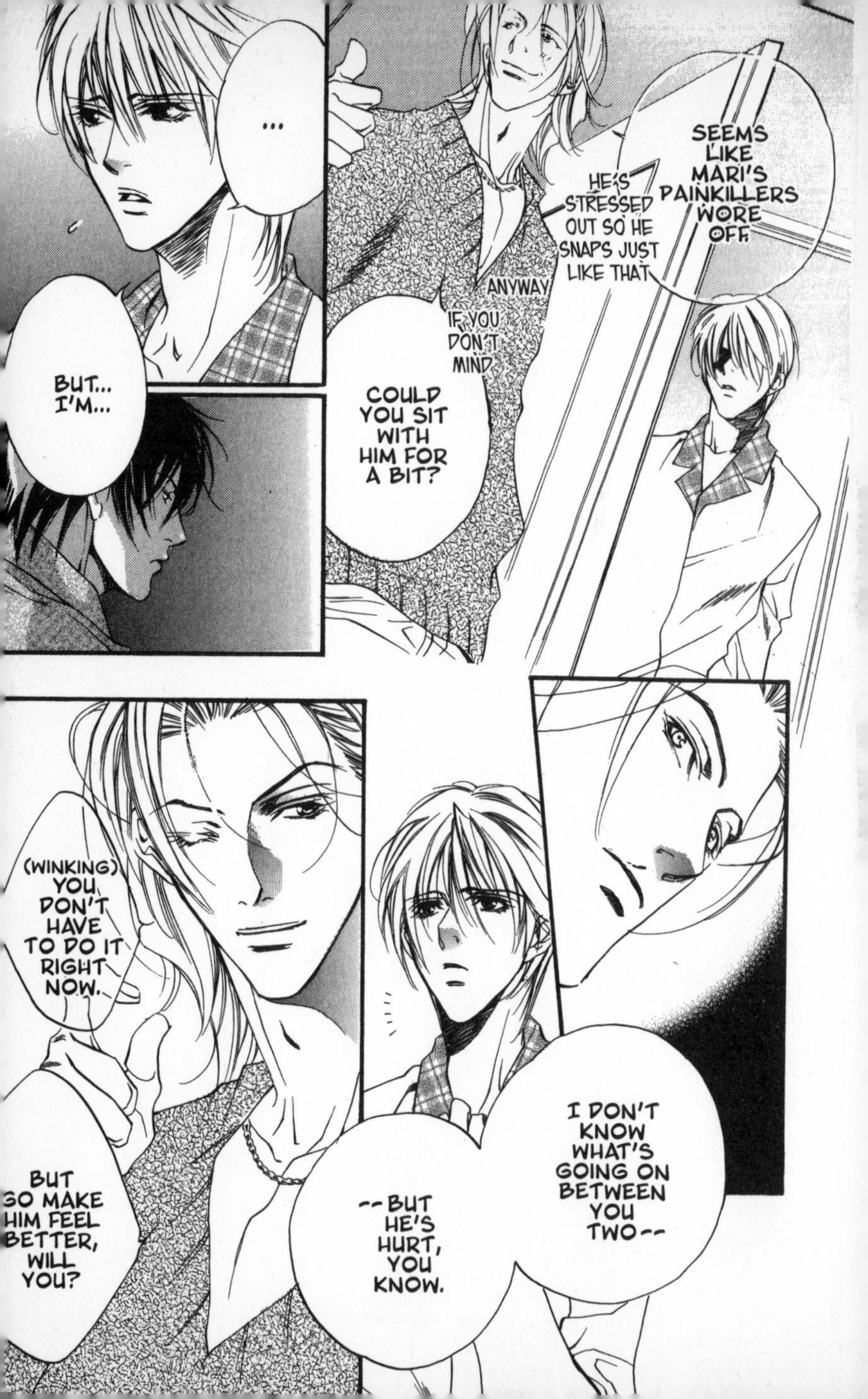
SEEMS LIKE MARI'S PAINKILLERS WORE OFF.
HE'S STRESSED OUT SO HE SNAPS JUST LIKE THAT
ANYWAY
IF YOU DON'T MIND
COULD YOU SIT WITH HIM FOR A BIT?
...
BUT... I'M...
I DON'T KNOW WHAT'S GOING ON BETWEEN YOU TWO--
--BUT HE'S HURT, YOU KNOW.
(WINKING) YOU DON'T HAVE TO DO IT RIGHT NOW.
BUT GO MAKE HIM FEEL BETTER, WILL YOU?

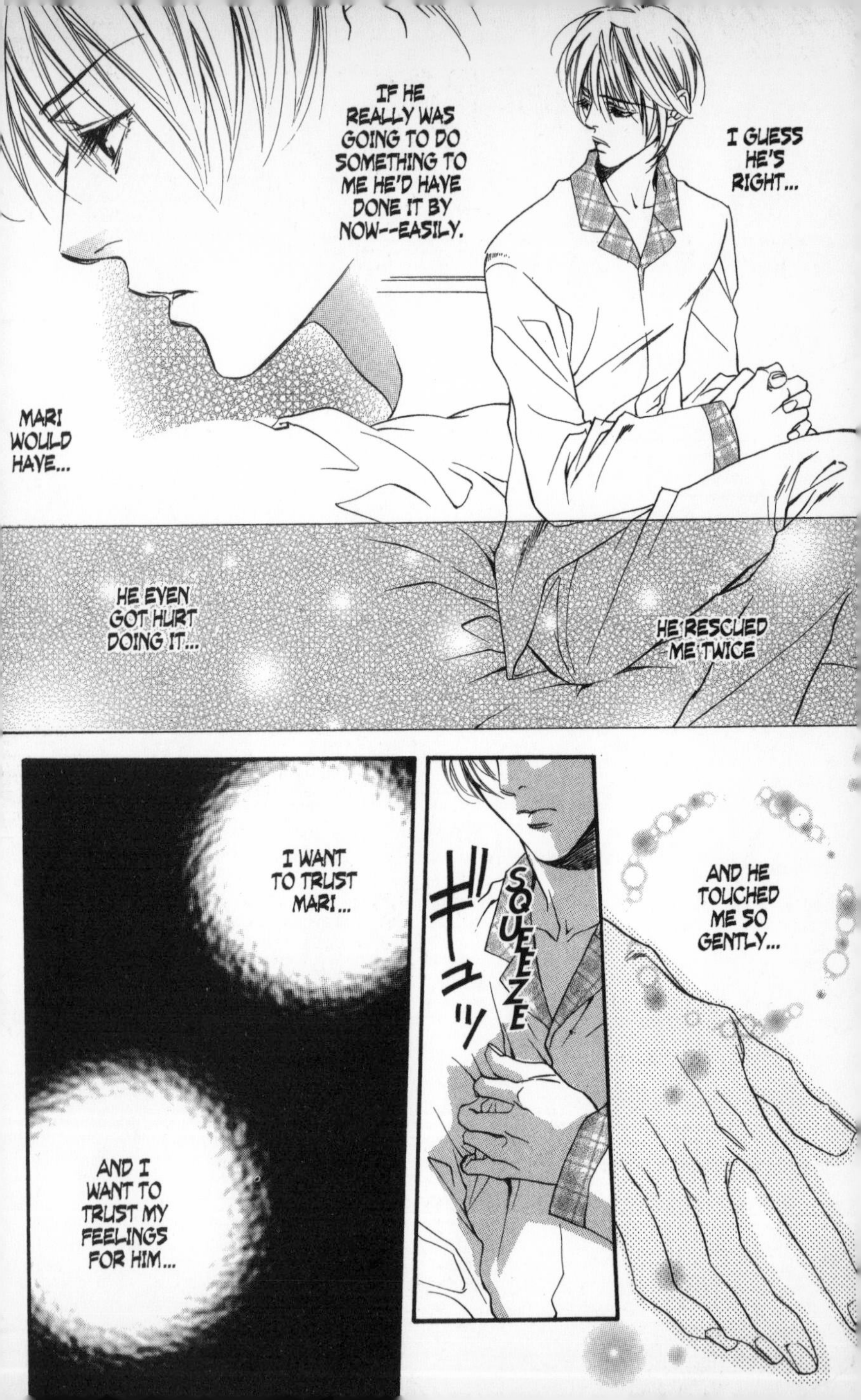
I GUESS HE'S RIGHT...
IF HE REALLY WAS GOING TO DO SOMETHING TO ME HE'D HAVE DONE IT BY NOW--EASILY.
MARI WOULD HAVE...
HE RESCUED ME TWICE
HE EVEN GOT HURT DOING IT...
AND HE TOUCHED ME SO GENTLY...
SQUEEZE
ギュッ
I WANT TO TRUST MARI...
AND I WANT TO TRUST MY FEELINGS FOR HIM...

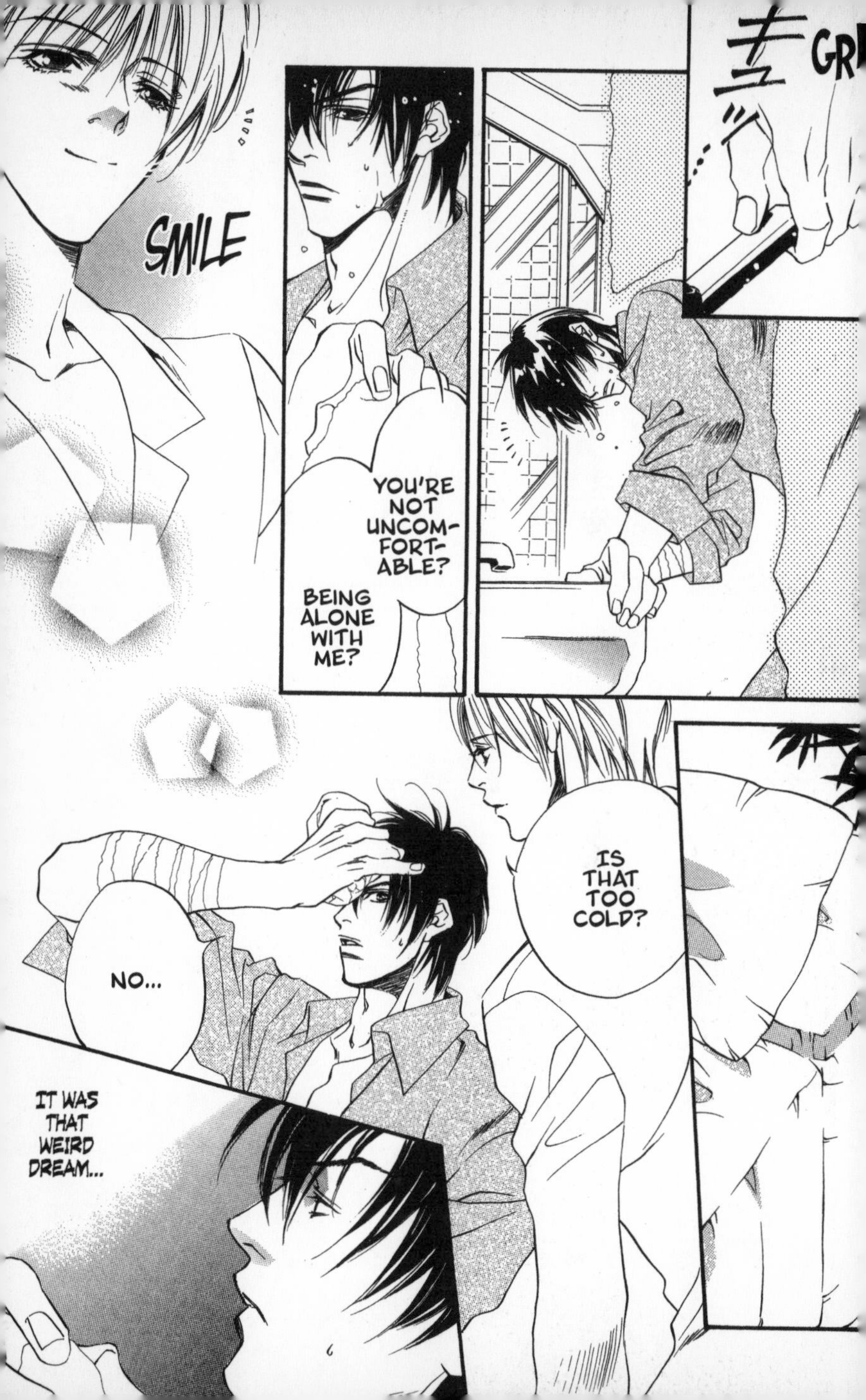
ギュッ
GR
YOU'RE NOT UNCOMFORTABLE?
BEING ALONE WITH ME?
SMILE
IS THAT TOO COLD?
NO...
IT WAS THAT WEIRD DREAM...

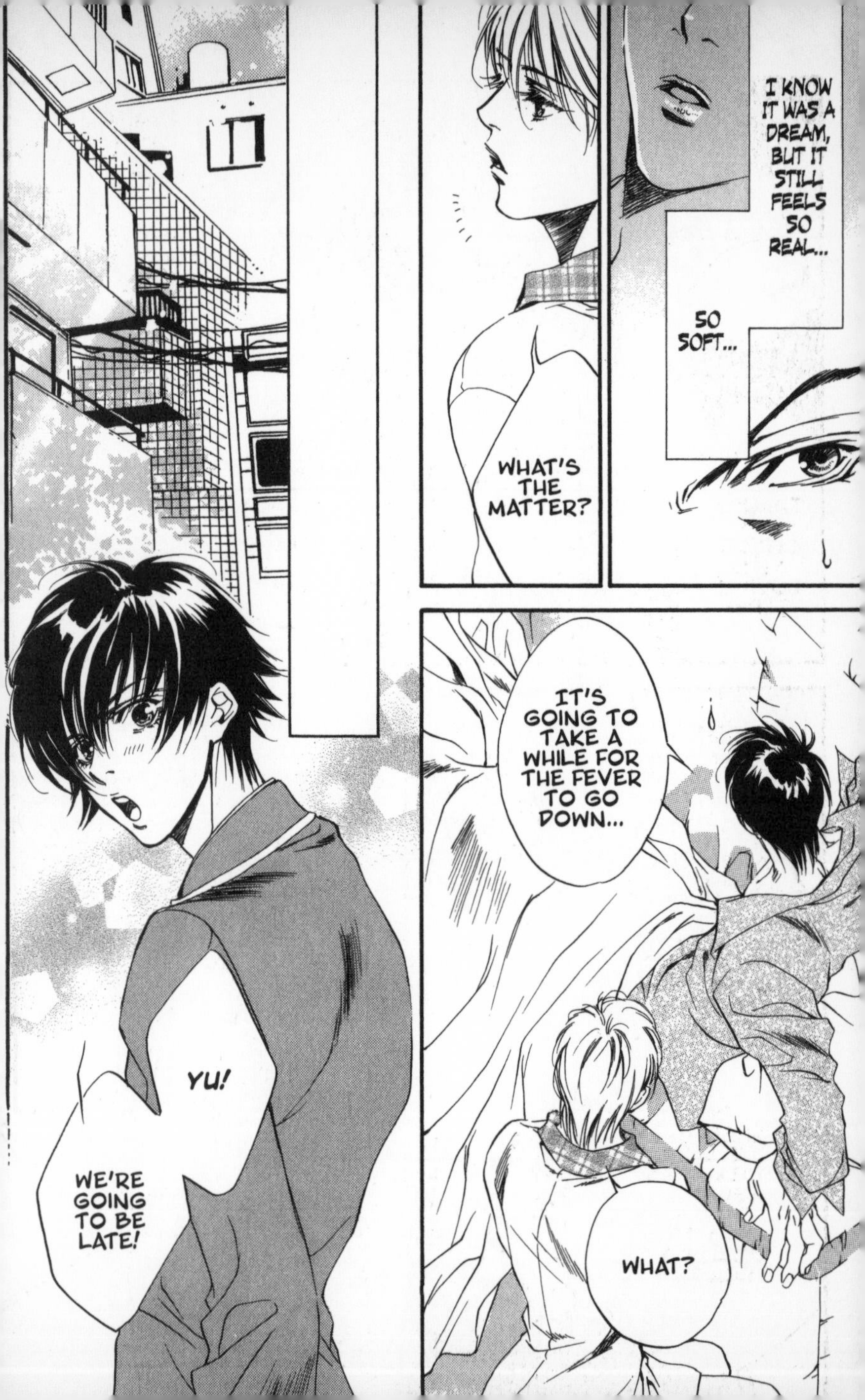
I KNOW IT WAS A DREAM, BUT IT STILL FEELS SO REAL...
SO SOFT...
WHAT'S THE MATTER?
IT'S GOING TO TAKE A WHILE FOR THE FEVER TO GO DOWN...
WHAT?
YU!
WE'RE GOING TO BE LATE!

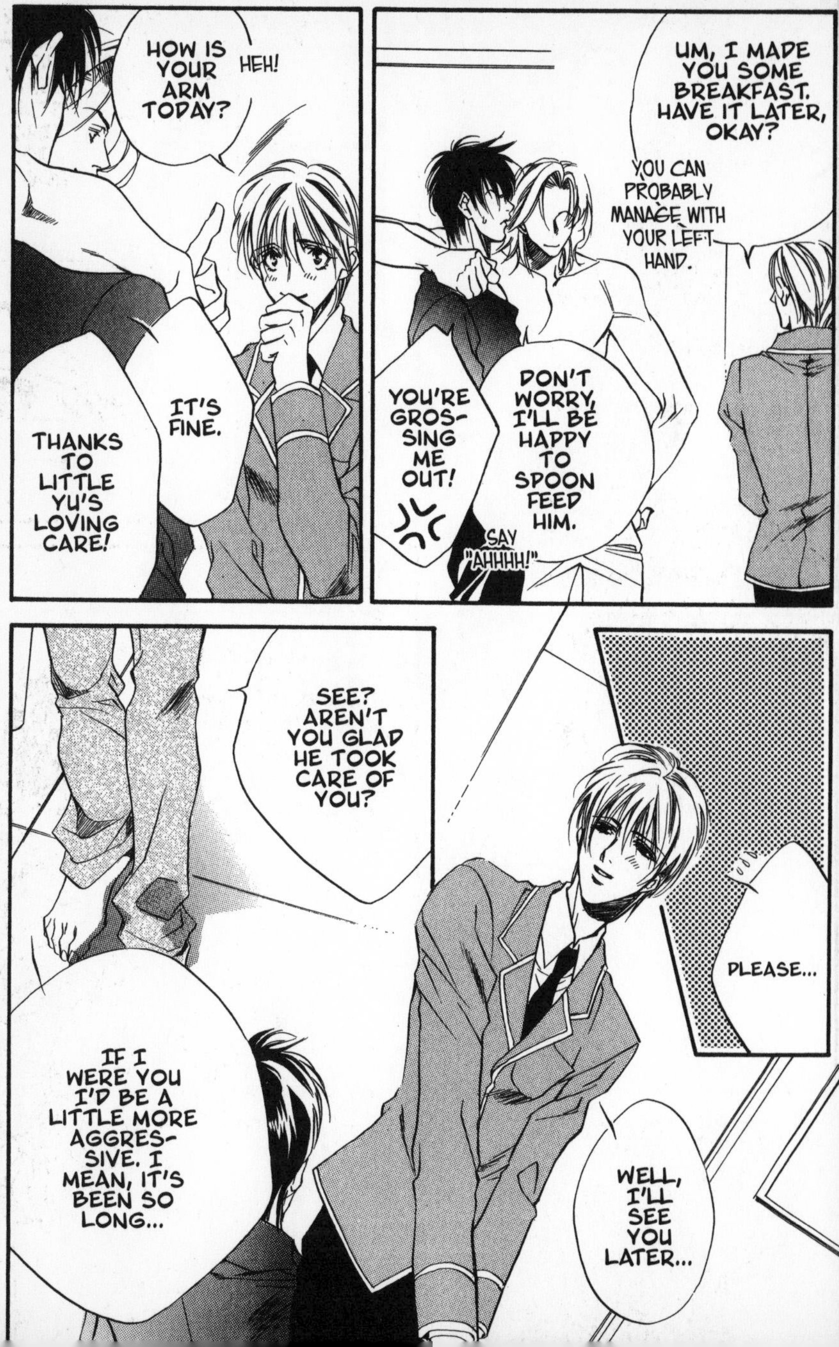
UM, I MADE YOU SOME BREAKFAST. HAVE IT LATER, OKAY?
YOU CAN PROBABLY MANAGE WITH YOUR LEFT HAND.
DON'T WORRY, I'LL BE HAPPY TO SPOON FEED HIM.
SAY "AHHHH!"
YOU'RE GROS-SING ME OUT!
HOW IS YOUR ARM TODAY?
HEH!
IT'S FINE.
THANKS TO LITTLE YU'S LOVING CARE!
PLEASE...
SEE? AREN'T YOU GLAD HE TOOK CARE OF YOU?
IF I WERE YOU I'D BE A LITTLE MORE AGGRES-SIVE. I MEAN, IT'S BEEN SO LONG...
WELL, I'LL SEE YOU LATER...

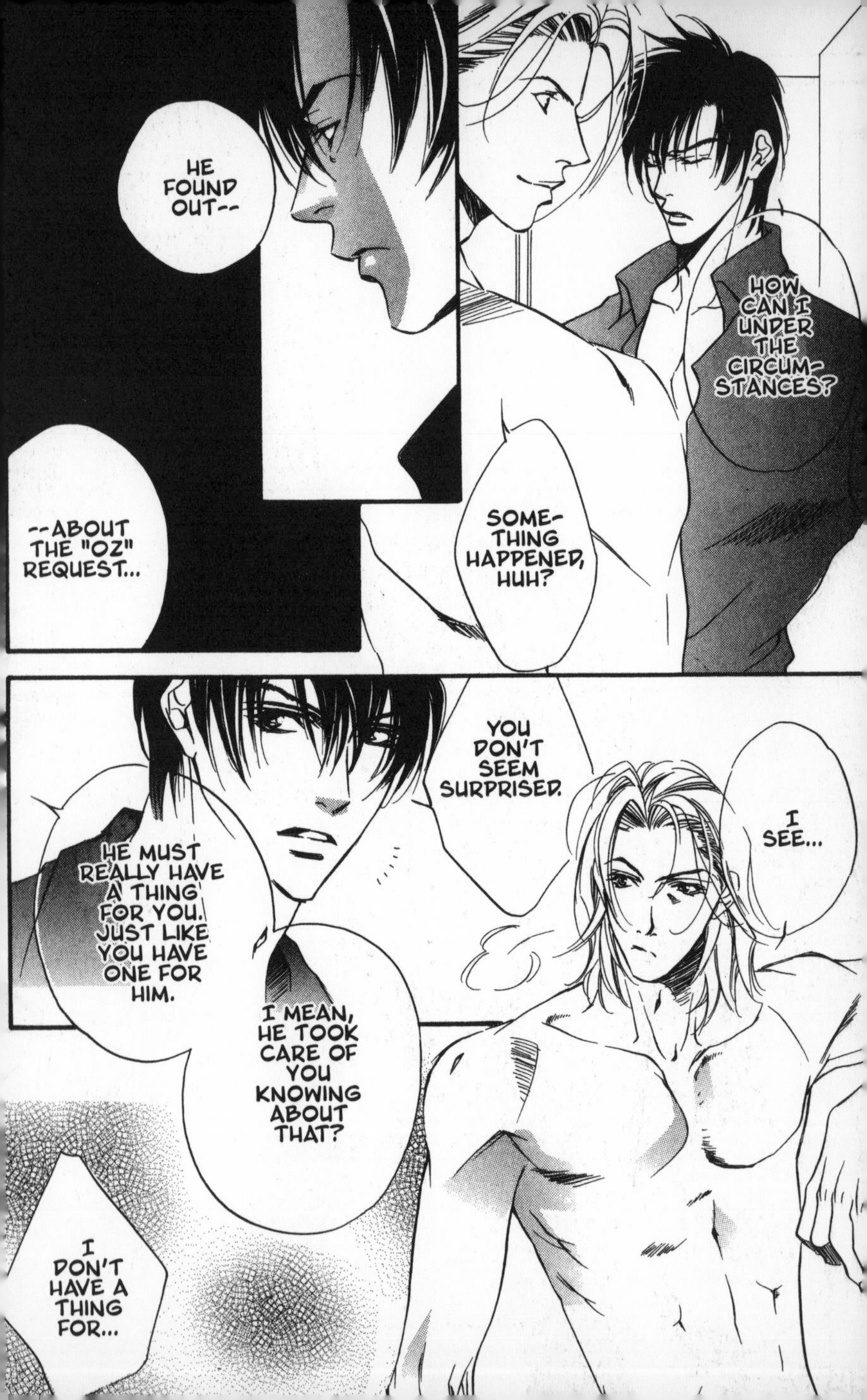
HOW CAN I UNDER THE CIRCUM-STANCES?
SOME-THING HAPPENED, HUH?
HE FOUND OUT--
--ABOUT THE "OZ" REQUEST...
I SEE...
YOU DON'T SEEM SURPRISED.
HE MUST REALLY HAVE A THING FOR YOU. JUST LIKE YOU HAVE ONE FOR HIM.
I MEAN, HE TOOK CARE OF YOU KNOWING ABOUT THAT?
I DON'T HAVE A THING FOR...

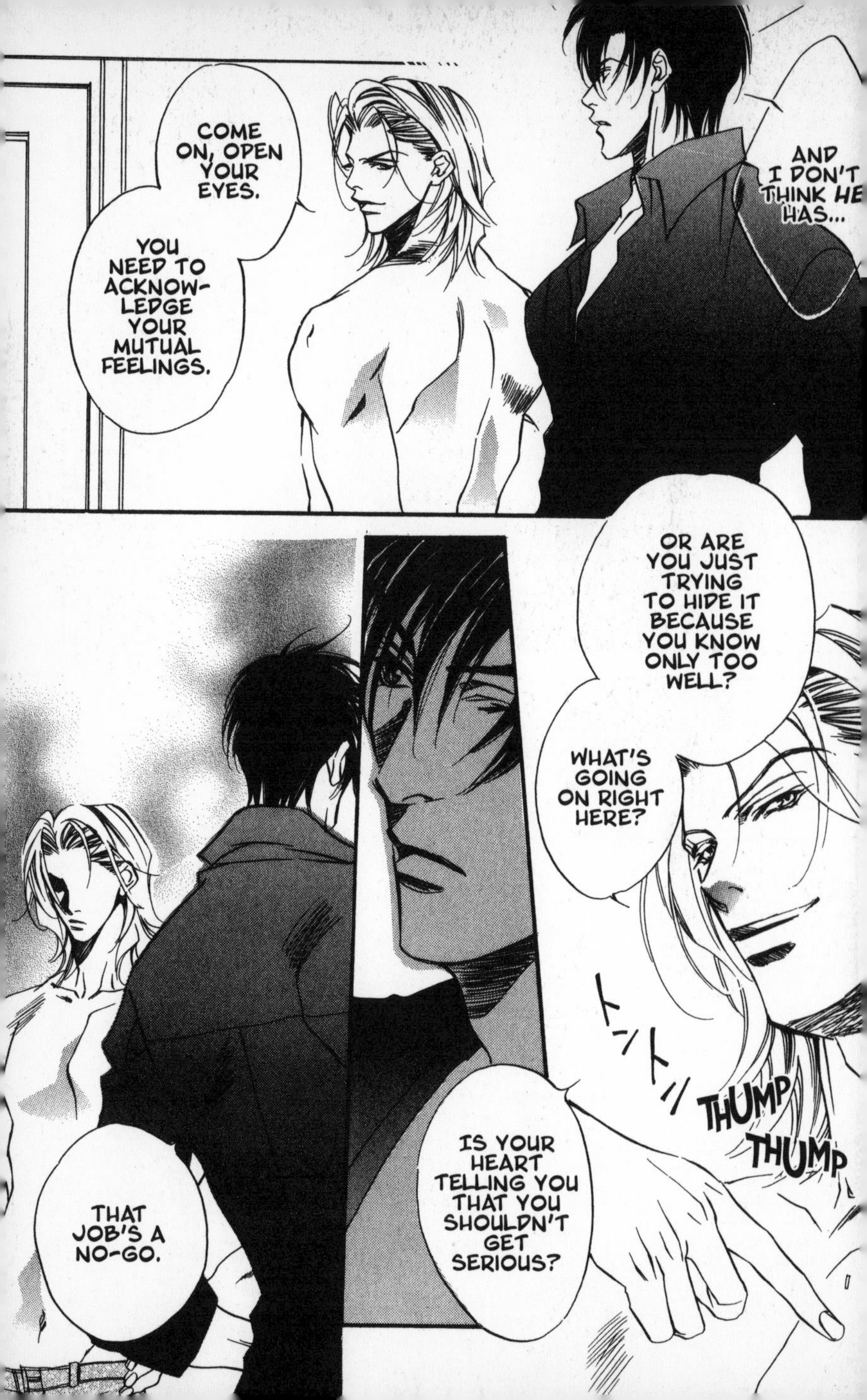
AND I DON'T THINK HE HAS...
COME ON, OPEN YOUR EYES.
YOU NEED TO ACKNOW-LEDGE YOUR MUTUAL FEELINGS.
OR ARE YOU JUST TRYING TO HIDE IT BECAUSE YOU KNOW ONLY TOO WELL?
WHAT'S GOING ON RIGHT HERE?
THUMP THUMP
IS YOUR HEART TELLING YOU THAT YOU SHOULDN'T GET SERIOUS?
THAT JOB'S A NO-GO.

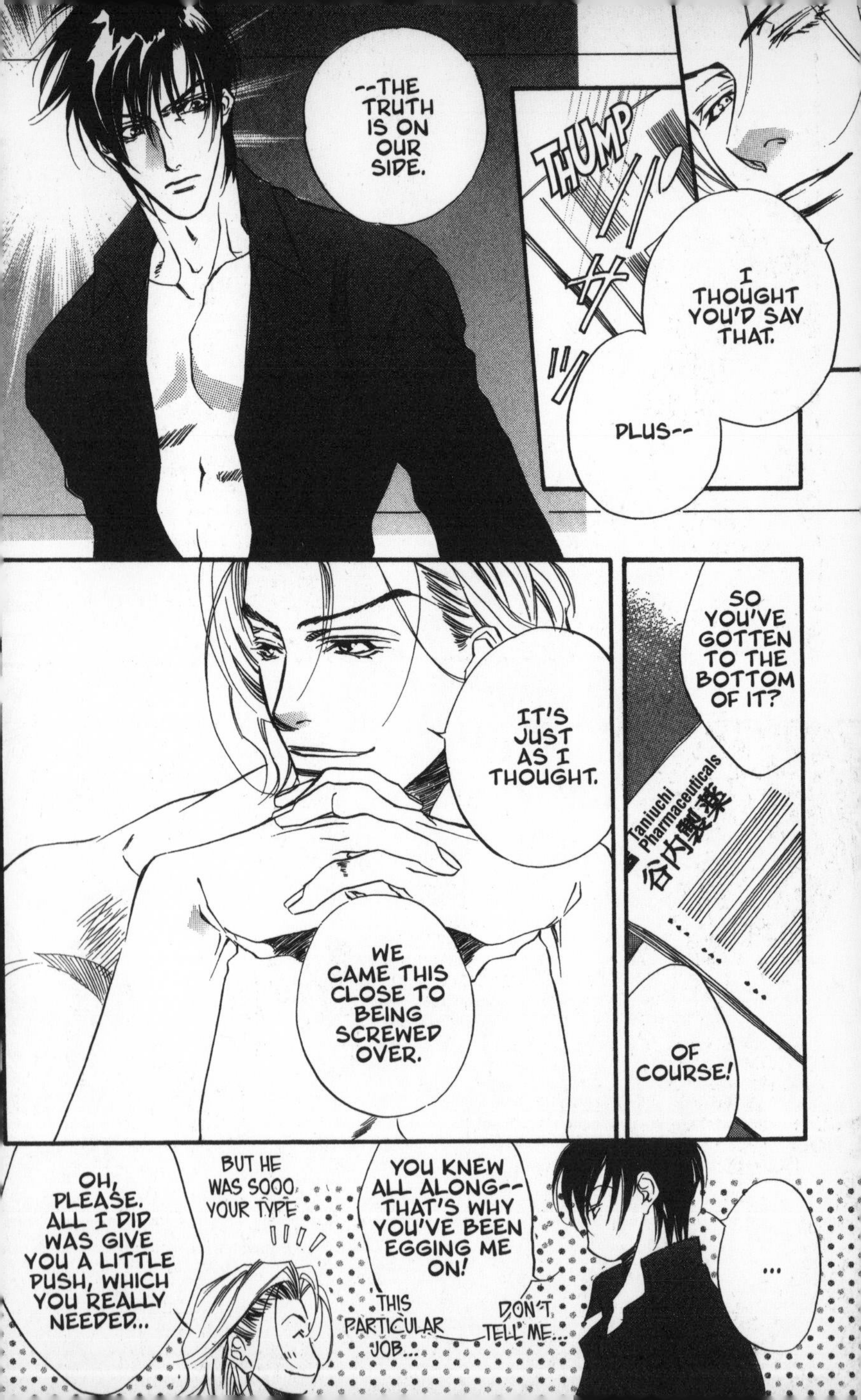
THUMP
I THOUGHT YOU'D SAY THAT.
PLUS--
--THE TRUTH IS ON OUR SIDE.
SO YOU'VE GOTTEN TO THE BOTTOM OF IT?
Taniuchi Pharmaceuticals
谷内製薬
...
...
...
OF COURSE!
IT'S JUST AS I THOUGHT.
WE CAME THIS CLOSE TO BEING SCREWED OVER.
...
DON'T TELL ME...
THIS PARTICULAR JOB...
YOU KNEW ALL ALONG--THAT'S WHY YOU'VE BEEN EGGING ME ON!
BUT HE WAS SOOO YOUR TYPE
OH, PLEASE. ALL I DID WAS GIVE YOU A LITTLE PUSH, WHICH YOU REALLY NEEDED...

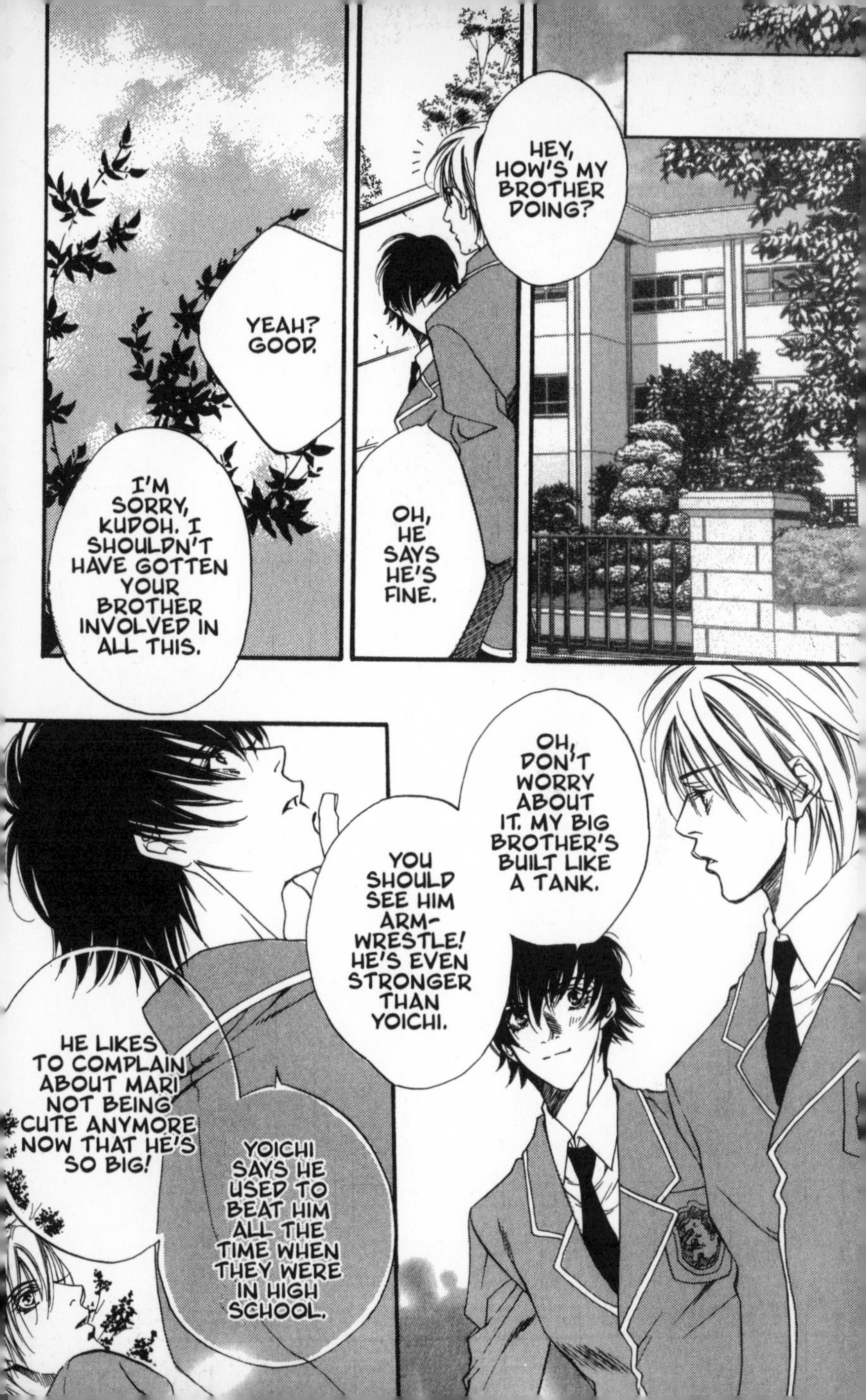
HEY, HOW'S MY BROTHER DOING?
OH, HE SAYS HE'S FINE.
YEAH? GOOD.
I'M SORRY, KUDOH. I SHOULDN'T HAVE GOTTEN YOUR BROTHER INVOLVED IN ALL THIS.
OH, DON'T WORRY ABOUT IT. MY BIG BROTHER'S BUILT LIKE A TANK.
YOU SHOULD SEE HIM ARM-WRESTLE! HE'S EVEN STRONGER THAN YOICHI.
YOICHI SAYS HE USED TO BEAT HIM ALL THE TIME WHEN THEY WERE IN HIGH SCHOOL.
HE LIKES TO COMPLAIN ABOUT MARI NOT BEING CUTE ANYMORE NOW THAT HE'S SO BIG!

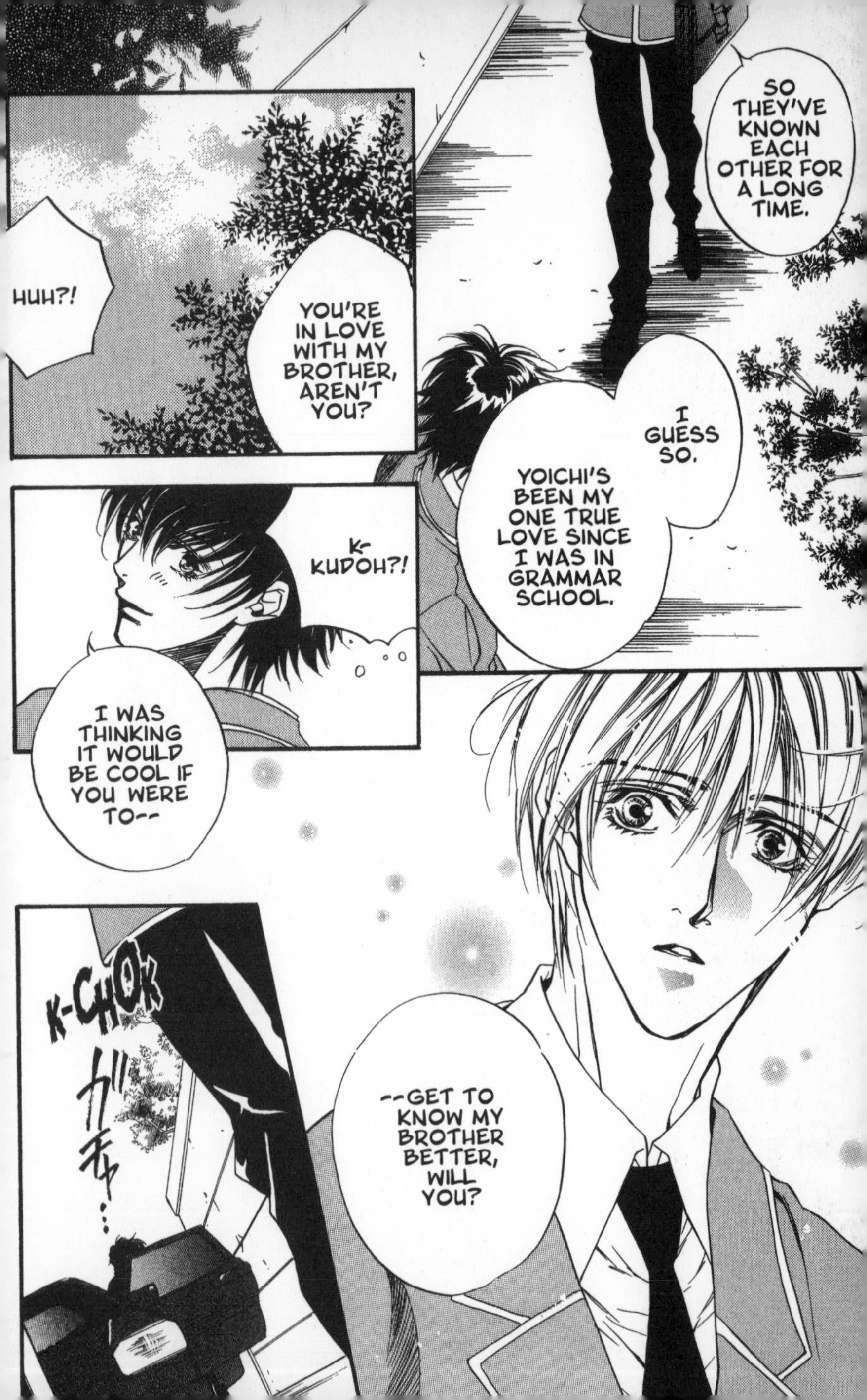
SO THEY'VE KNOWN EACH OTHER FOR A LONG TIME.
YOU'RE IN LOVE WITH MY BROTHER, AREN'T YOU?
HUH?!
I GUESS SO.
YOICHI'S BEEN MY ONE TRUE LOVE SINCE I WAS IN GRAMMAR SCHOOL.
K-KUDOH?!
I WAS THINKING IT WOULD BE COOL IF YOU WERE TO--
--GET TO KNOW MY BROTHER BETTER, WILL YOU?
K-CHOK

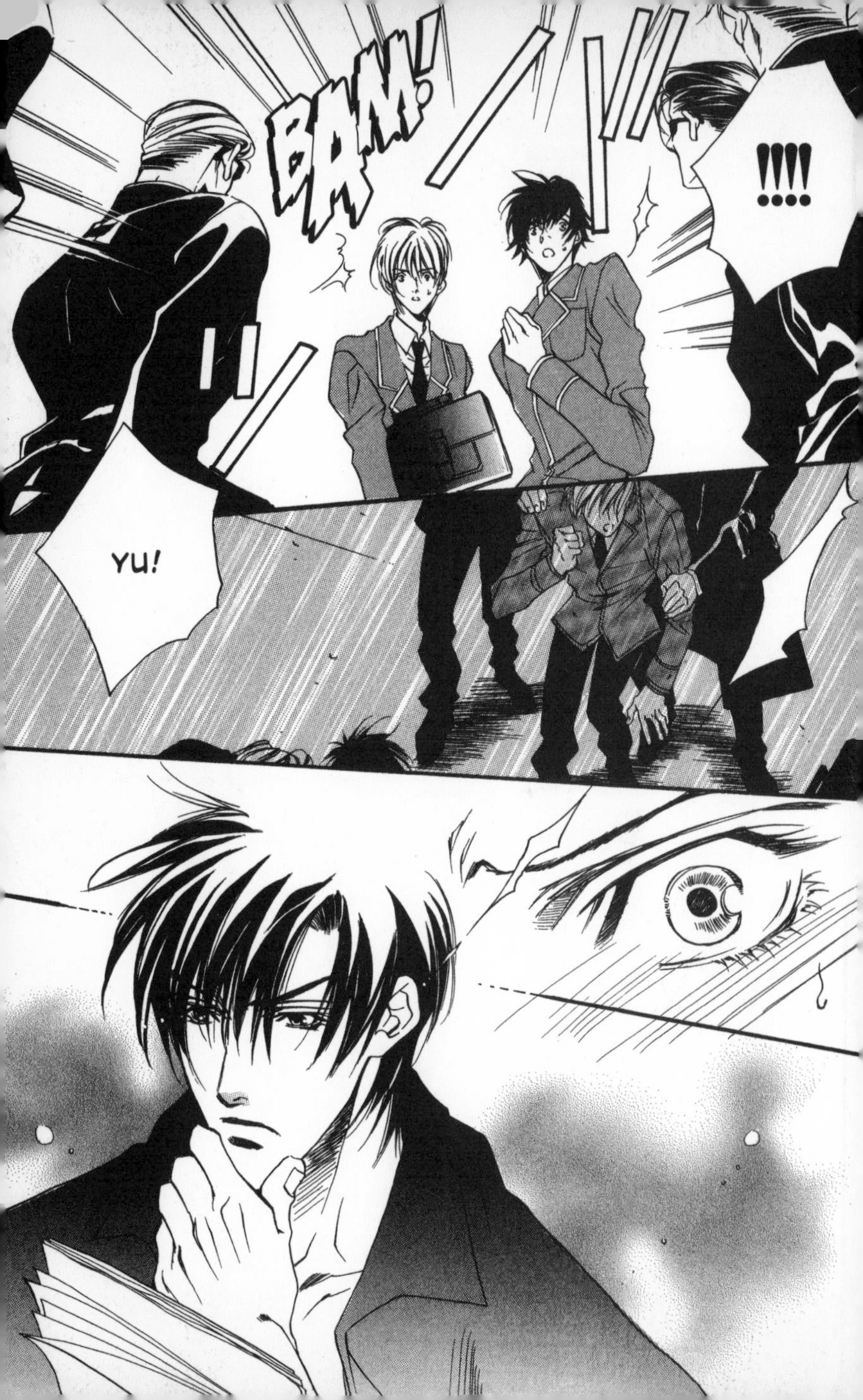
!!!!
BAM!
YU!

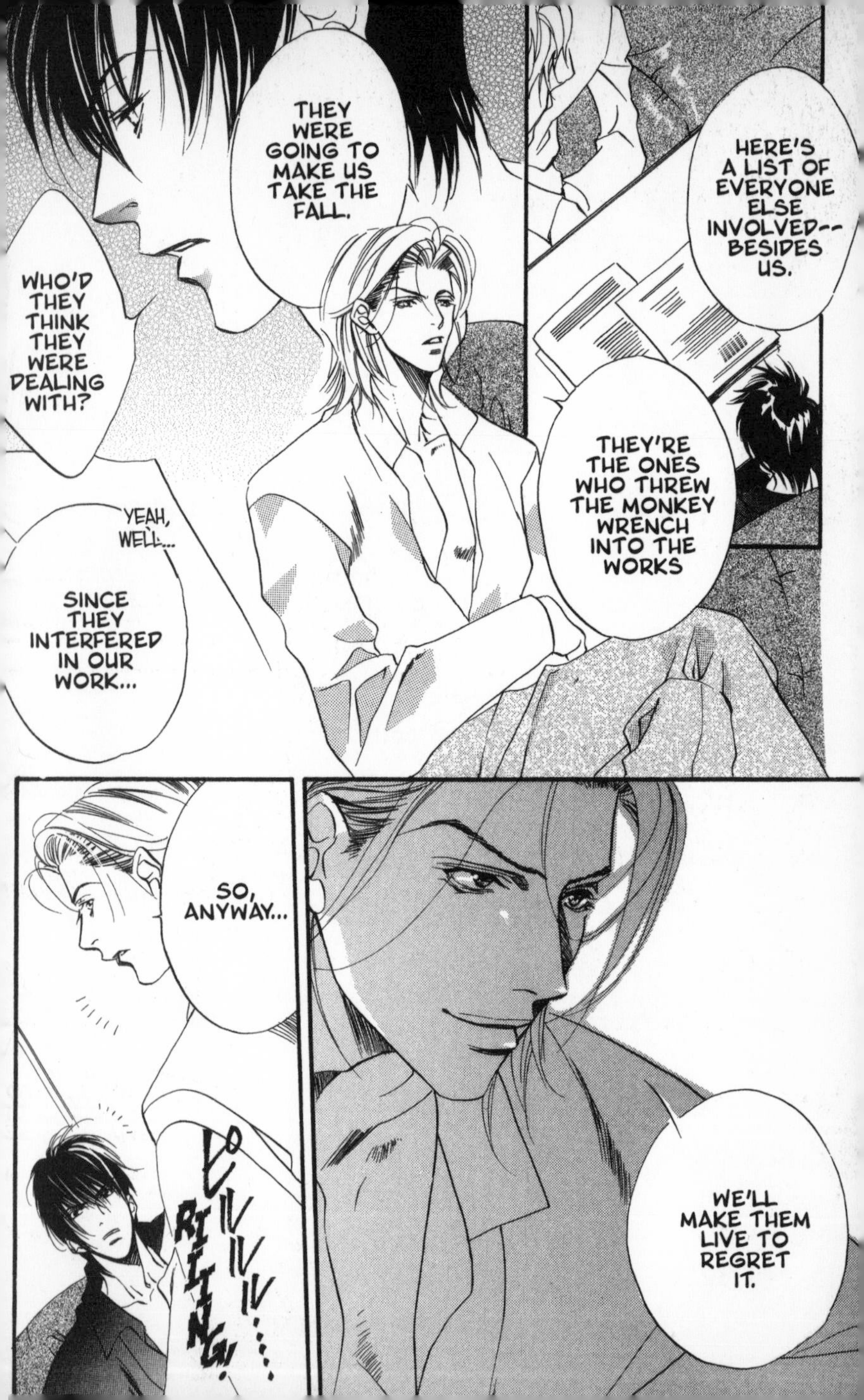
HERE'S A LIST OF EVERYONE ELSE INVOLVED-- BESIDES US.
THEY'RE THE ONES WHO THREW THE MONKEY WRENCH INTO THE WORKS
THEY WERE GOING TO MAKE US TAKE THE FALL.
WHO'D THEY THINK THEY WERE DEALING WITH?
YEAH, WELL...
SINCE THEY INTERFERED IN OUR WORK...
WE'LL MAKE THEM LIVE TO REGRET IT.
SO, ANYWAY...
RIIING!

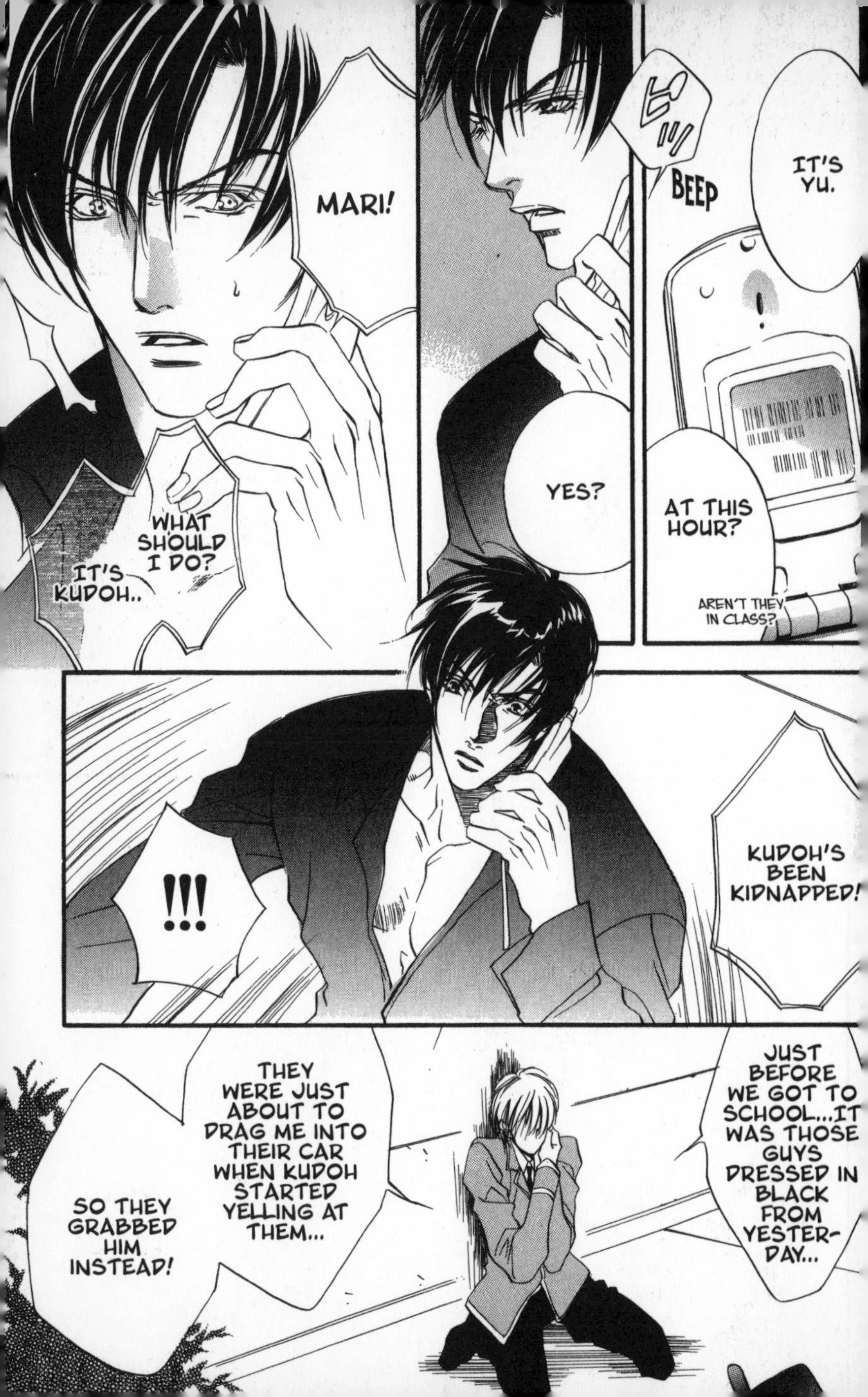
ピッ
BEEP
IT'S YU.
AT THIS HOUR?
AREN'T THEY IN CLASS?
YES?
MARI!
WHAT SHOULD I DO?
IT'S KUDOH..
KUDOH'S BEEN KIDNAPPED!
!!!
JUST BEFORE WE GOT TO SCHOOL...IT WAS THOSE GUYS DRESSED IN BLACK FROM YESTER-DAY...
THEY WERE JUST ABOUT TO DRAG ME INTO THEIR CAR WHEN KUDOH STARTED YELLING AT THEM...
SO THEY GRABBED HIM INSTEAD!

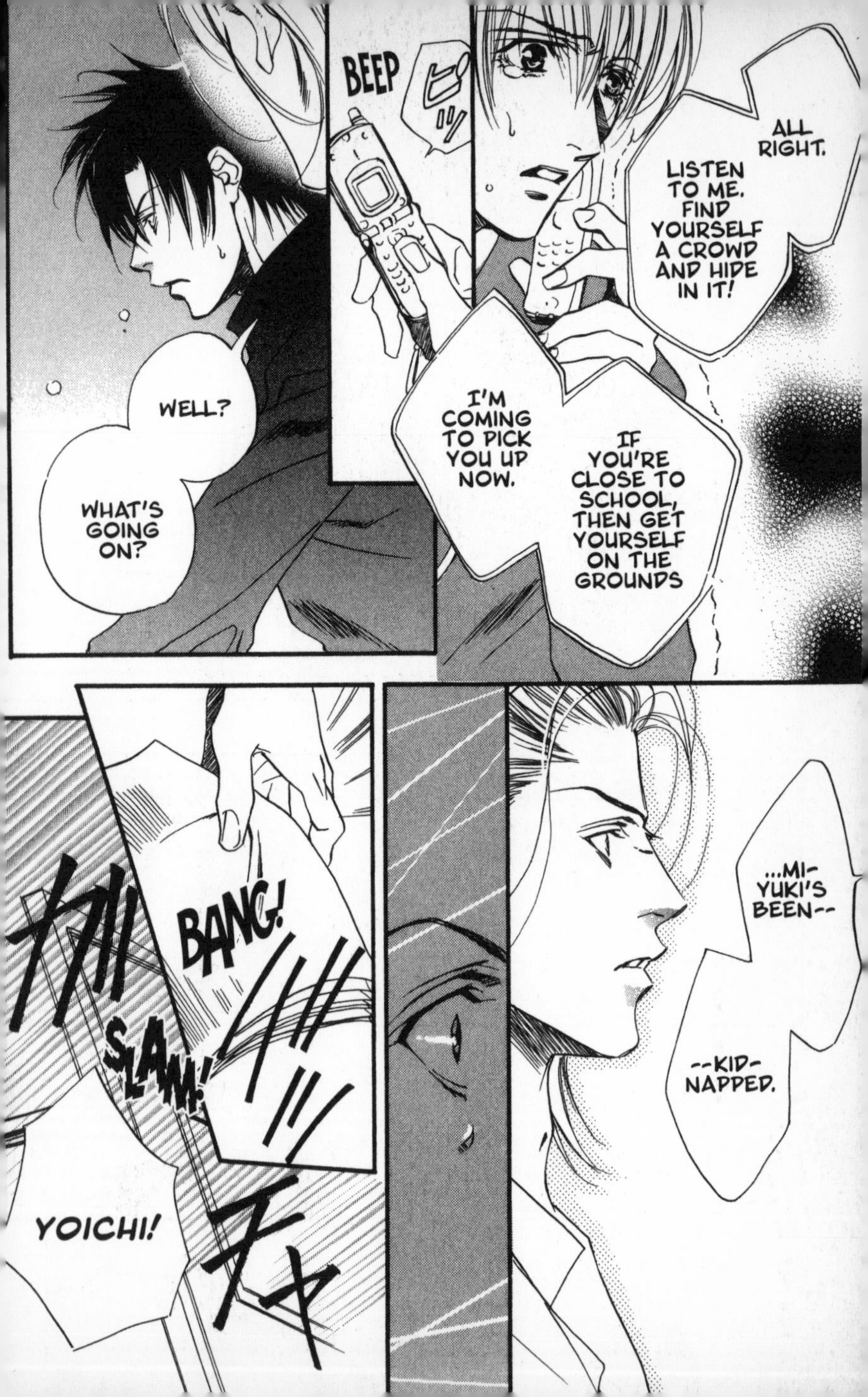
ALL RIGHT.
LISTEN TO ME. FIND YOURSELF A CROWD AND HIDE IN IT!
I'M COMING TO PICK YOU UP NOW.
IF YOU'RE CLOSE TO SCHOOL, THEN GET YOURSELF ON THE GROUNDS
BEEP
ピッ
WELL?
WHAT'S GOING ON?
...MI-YUKI'S BEEN--
--KID-NAPPED.
BANG!
SLAM!
YOICHI!

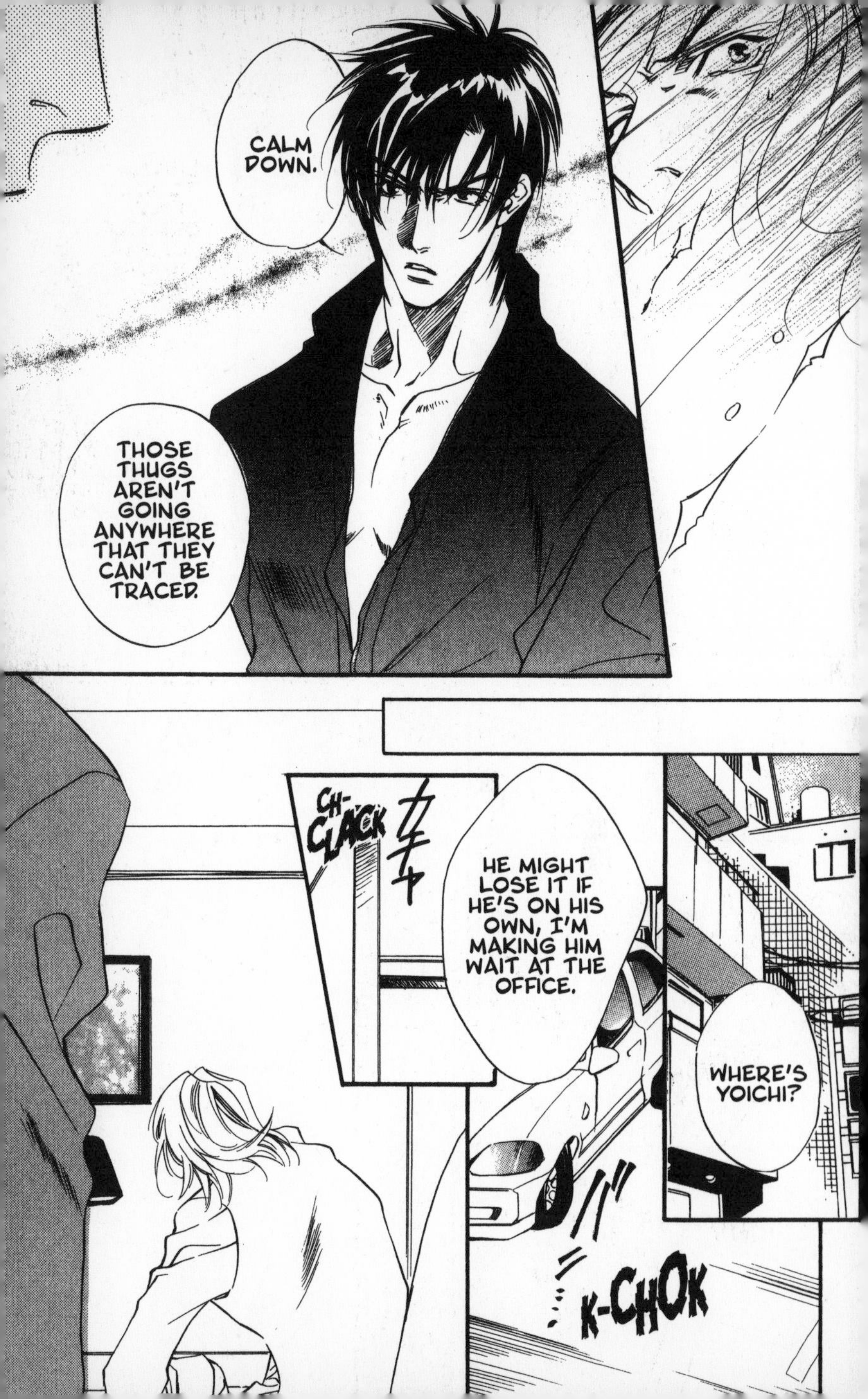
CALM DOWN.
THOSE THUGS AREN'T GOING ANYWHERE THAT THEY CAN'T BE TRACED.
WHERE'S YOICHI?
K-CHOK
CH-CLACK
HE MIGHT LOSE IT IF HE'S ON HIS OWN, I'M MAKING HIM WAIT AT THE OFFICE.

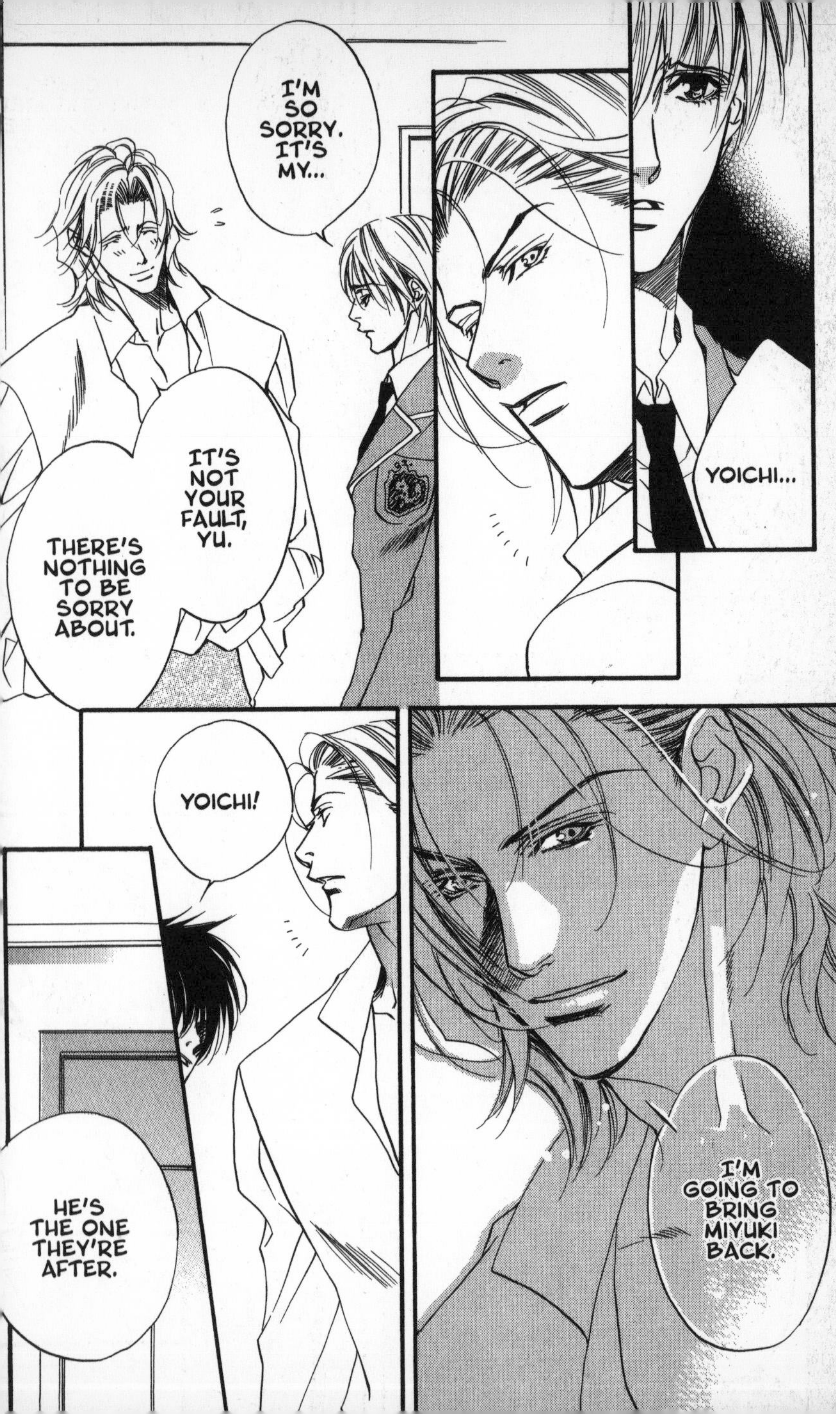
YOICHI...
I'M SO SORRY. IT'S MY...
IT'S NOT YOUR FAULT, YU.
THERE'S NOTHING TO BE SORRY ABOUT.
I'M GOING TO BRING MIYUKI BACK.
YOICHI!
HE'S THE ONE THEY'RE AFTER.

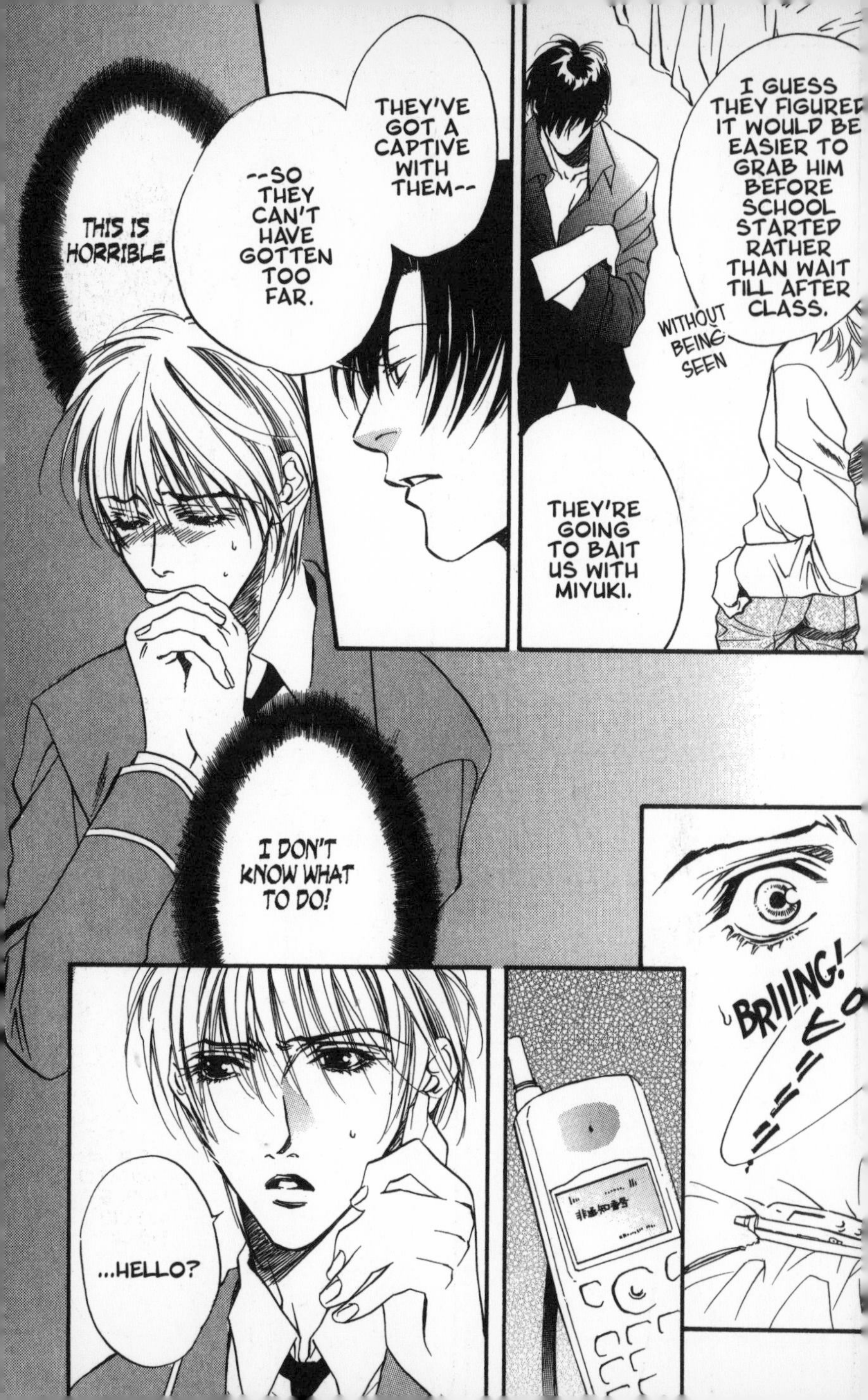
I GUESS THEY FIGURED IT WOULD BE EASIER TO GRAB HIM BEFORE SCHOOL STARTED RATHER THAN WAIT TILL AFTER CLASS.
WITHOUT BEING SEEN
THEY'RE GOING TO BAIT US WITH MIYUKI.
THEY'VE GOT A CAPTIVE WITH THEM--
--SO THEY CAN'T HAVE GOTTEN TOO FAR.
THIS IS HORRIBLE
I DON'T KNOW WHAT TO DO!
BRIIING!
...HELLO?

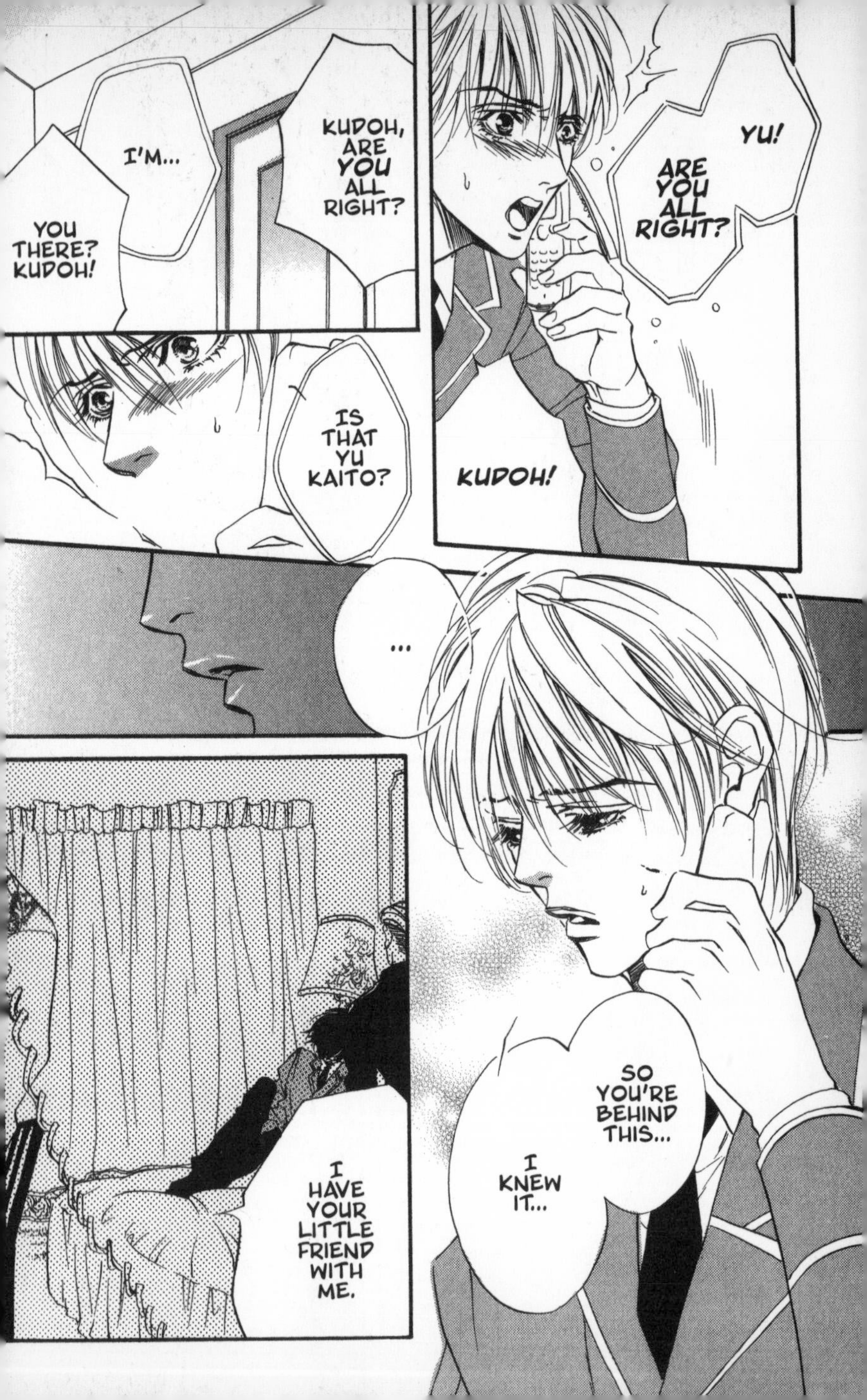
YU!
ARE YOU ALL RIGHT?
KUDOH!
KUDOH, ARE YOU ALL RIGHT?
I'M...
YOU THERE? KUDOH!
IS THAT YU KAITO?
...
SO YOU'RE BEHIND THIS...
I KNEW IT...
I HAVE YOUR LITTLE FRIEND WITH ME.

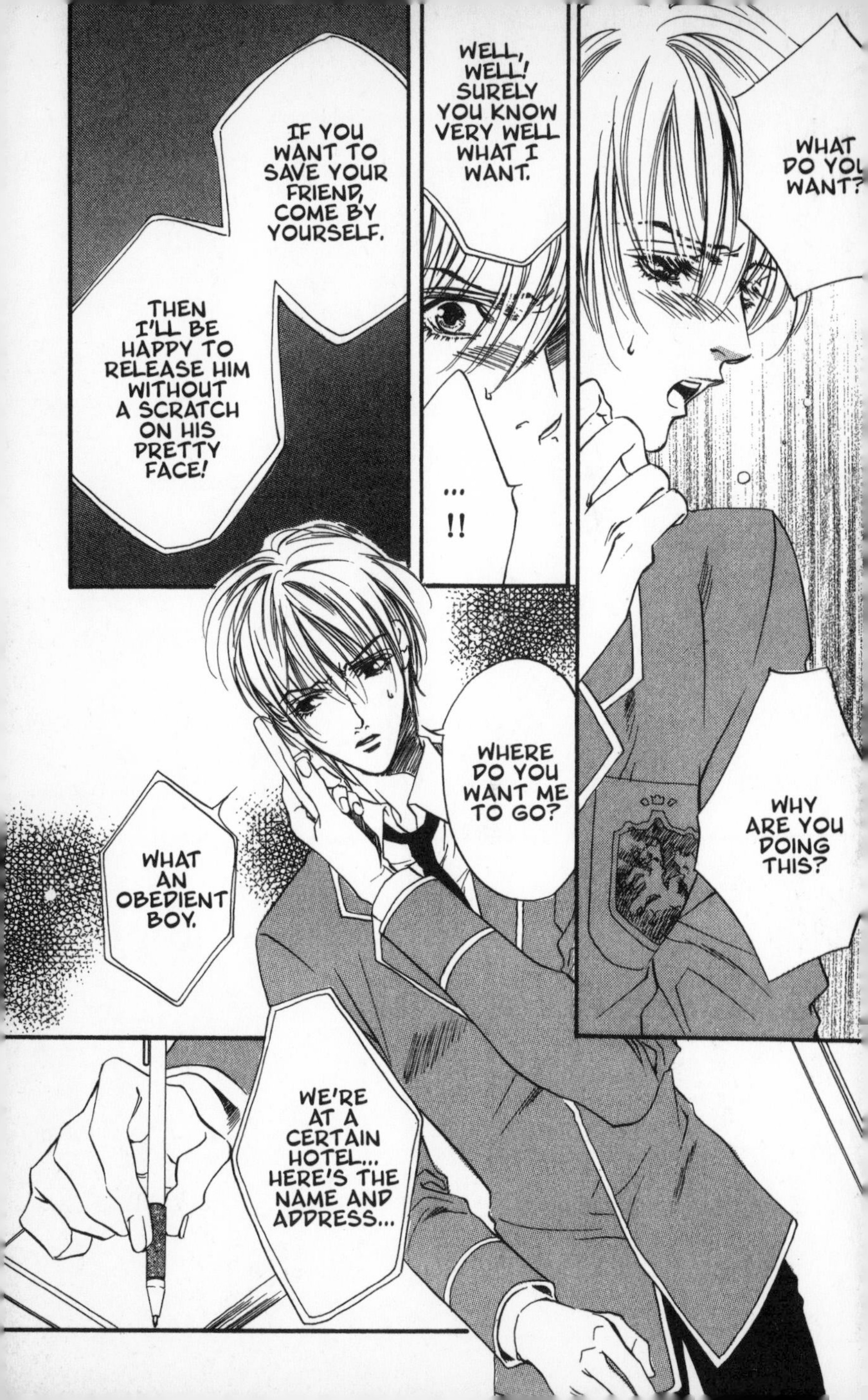
WHAT DO YOU WANT?
WHY ARE YOU DOING THIS?
WELL, WELL! SURELY YOU KNOW VERY WELL WHAT I WANT.
...!!
IF YOU WANT TO SAVE YOUR FRIEND, COME BY YOURSELF.
THEN I'LL BE HAPPY TO RELEASE HIM WITHOUT A SCRATCH ON HIS PRETTY FACE!
WHERE DO YOU WANT ME TO GO?
WHAT AN OBEDIENT BOY.
WE'RE AT A CERTAIN HOTEL... HERE'S THE NAME AND ADDRESS...

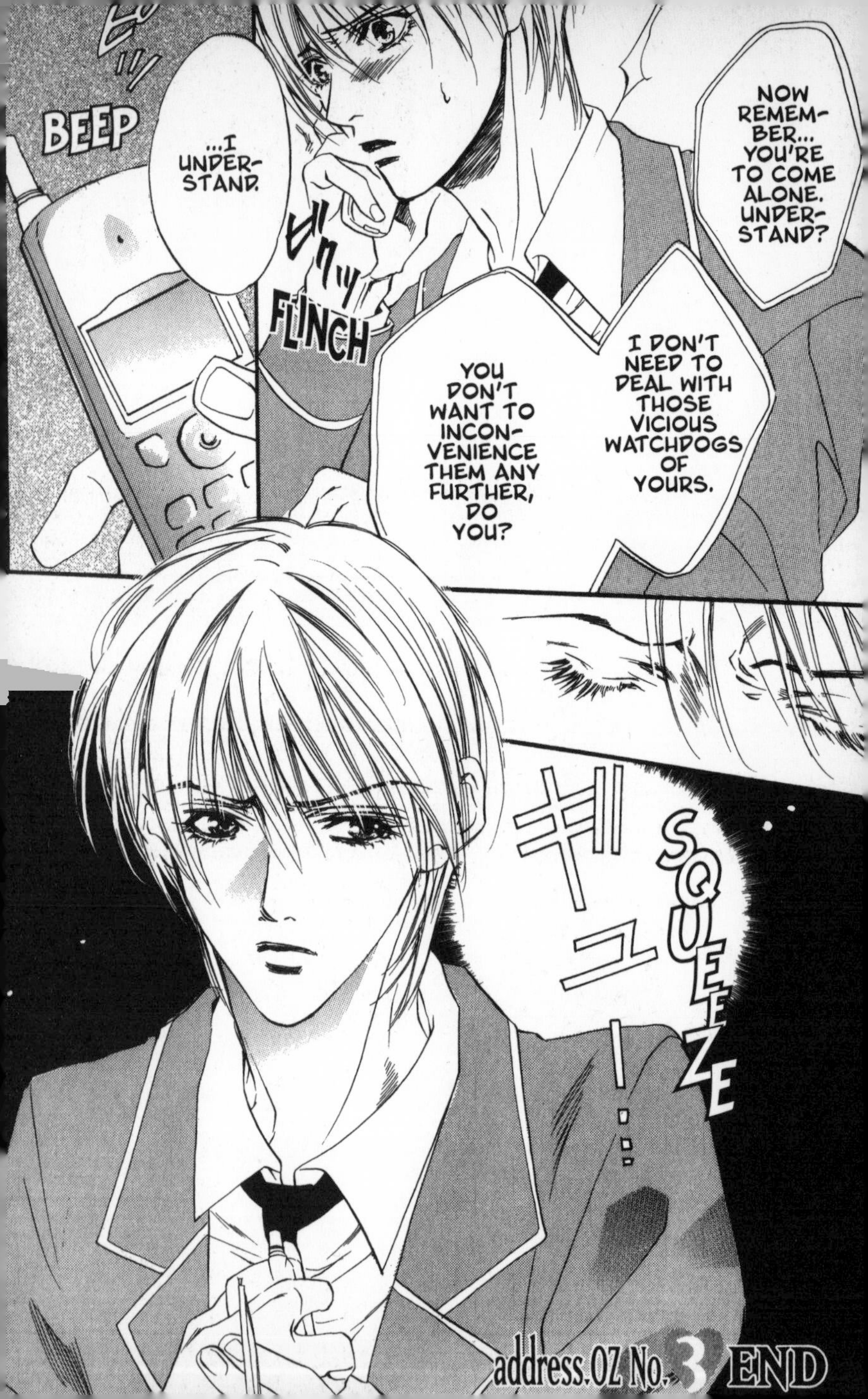
NOW REMEMBER... YOU'RE TO COME ALONE. UNDERSTAND?
I DON'T NEED TO DEAL WITH THOSE VICIOUS WATCHDOGS OF YOURS.
YOU DON'T WANT TO INCONVENIENCE THEM ANY FURTHER, DO YOU?
FLINCH
...I UNDERSTAND.
BEEP
SQUEEZE
address.OZ No. 3 END

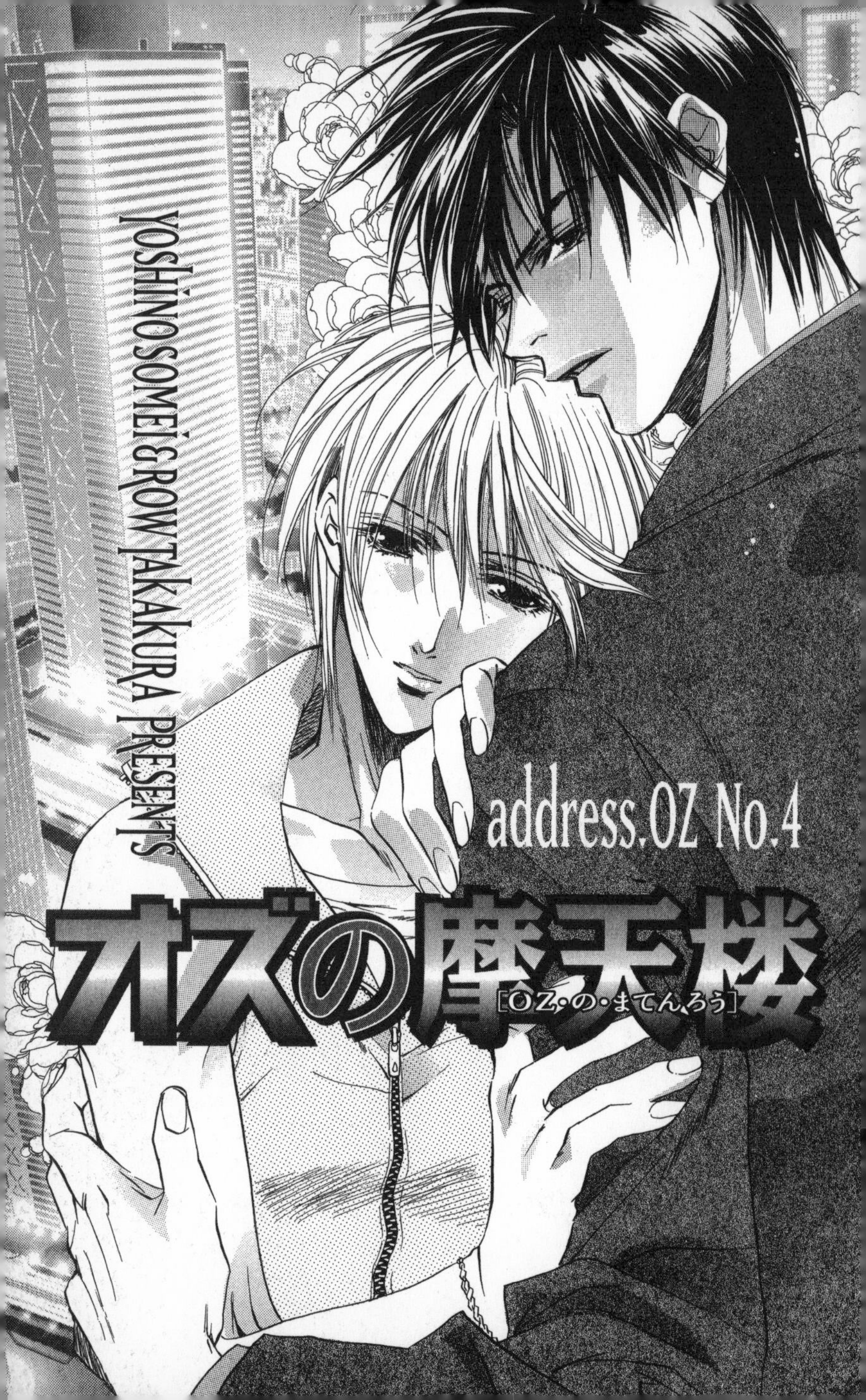
YOSHINO SOMEI & ROW TAKAKURA PRESENTS
address.OZ No.4
オズの摩天楼
[OZ・の・まてんろう]

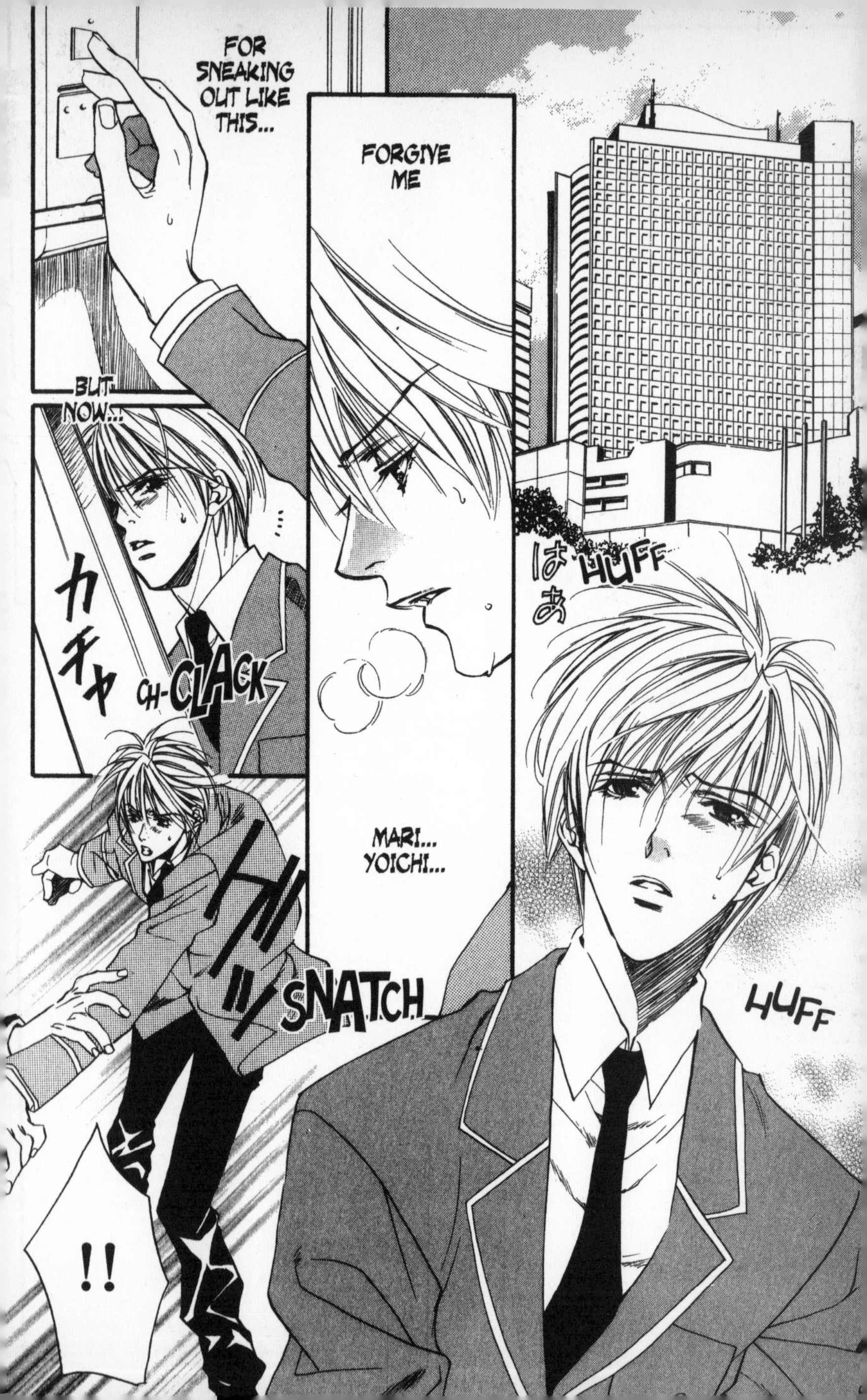
はあ HUFF
HUFF
FORGIVE ME
MARI... YOICHI...
FOR SNEAKING OUT LIKE THIS...
BUT NOW...
...
カチャ CH-CLACK
トッ SNATCH
!!

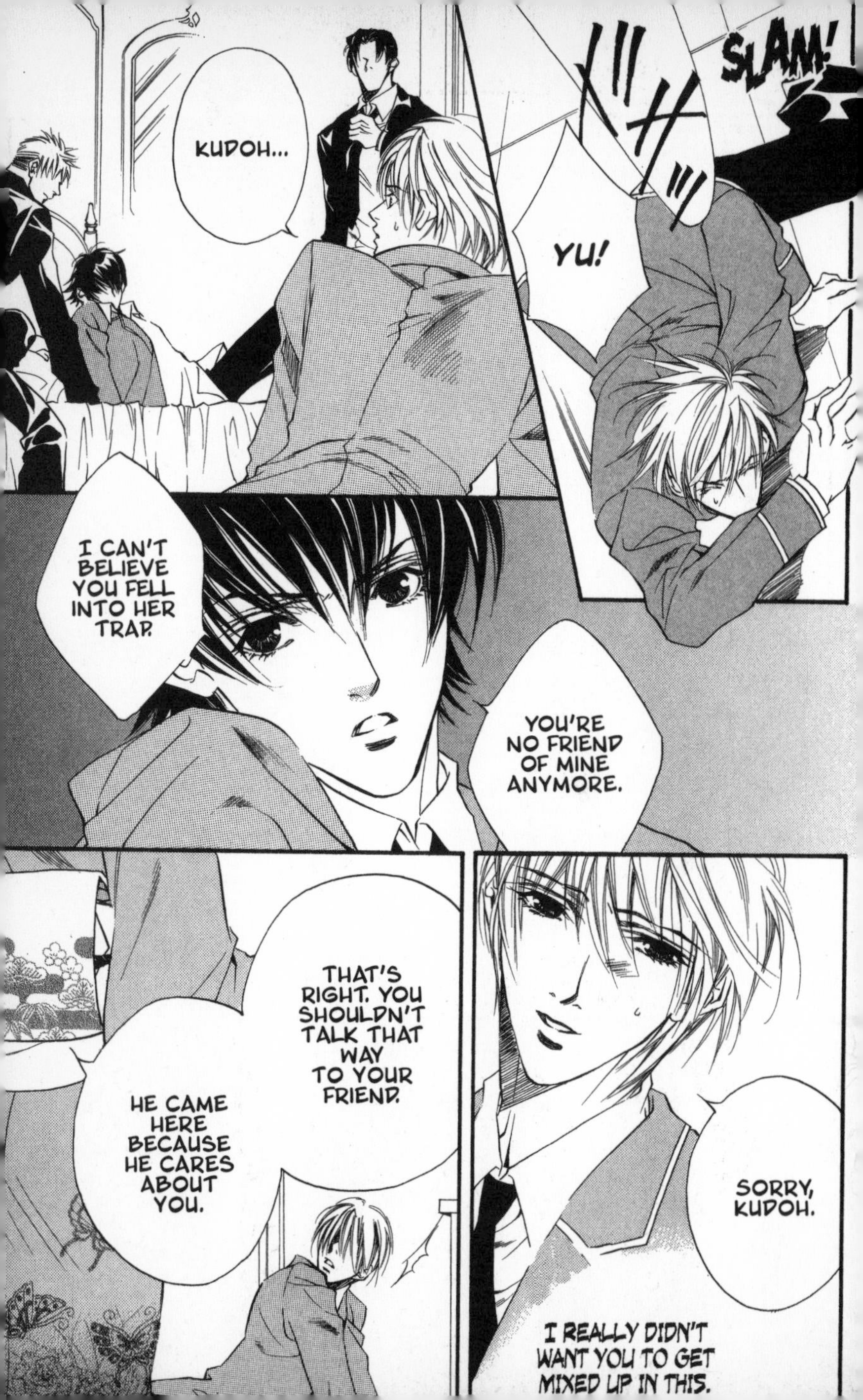
SLAM!
YU!
KUDOH...
I CAN'T BELIEVE YOU FELL INTO HER TRAP.
YOU'RE NO FRIEND OF MINE ANYMORE.
SORRY, KUDOH.
I REALLY DIDN'T WANT YOU TO GET MIXED UP IN THIS.
THAT'S RIGHT. YOU SHOULDN'T TALK THAT WAY TO YOUR FRIEND.
HE CAME HERE BECAUSE HE CARES ABOUT YOU.

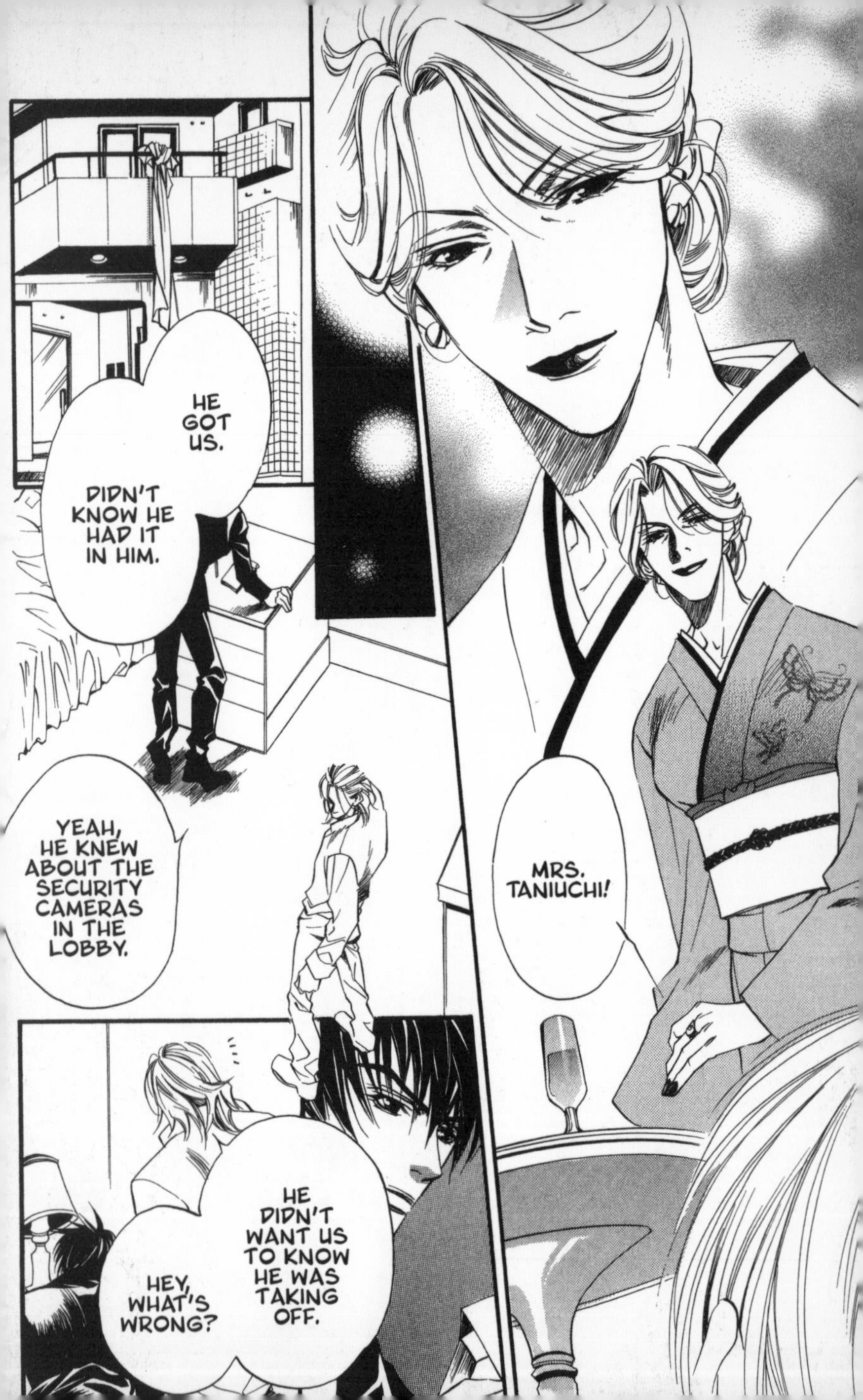
MRS. TANIUCHI!
HE GOT US.
DIDN'T KNOW HE HAD IT IN HIM.
YEAH, HE KNEW ABOUT THE SECURITY CAMERAS IN THE LOBBY.
HE DIDN'T WANT US TO KNOW HE WAS TAKING OFF.
HEY, WHAT'S WRONG?

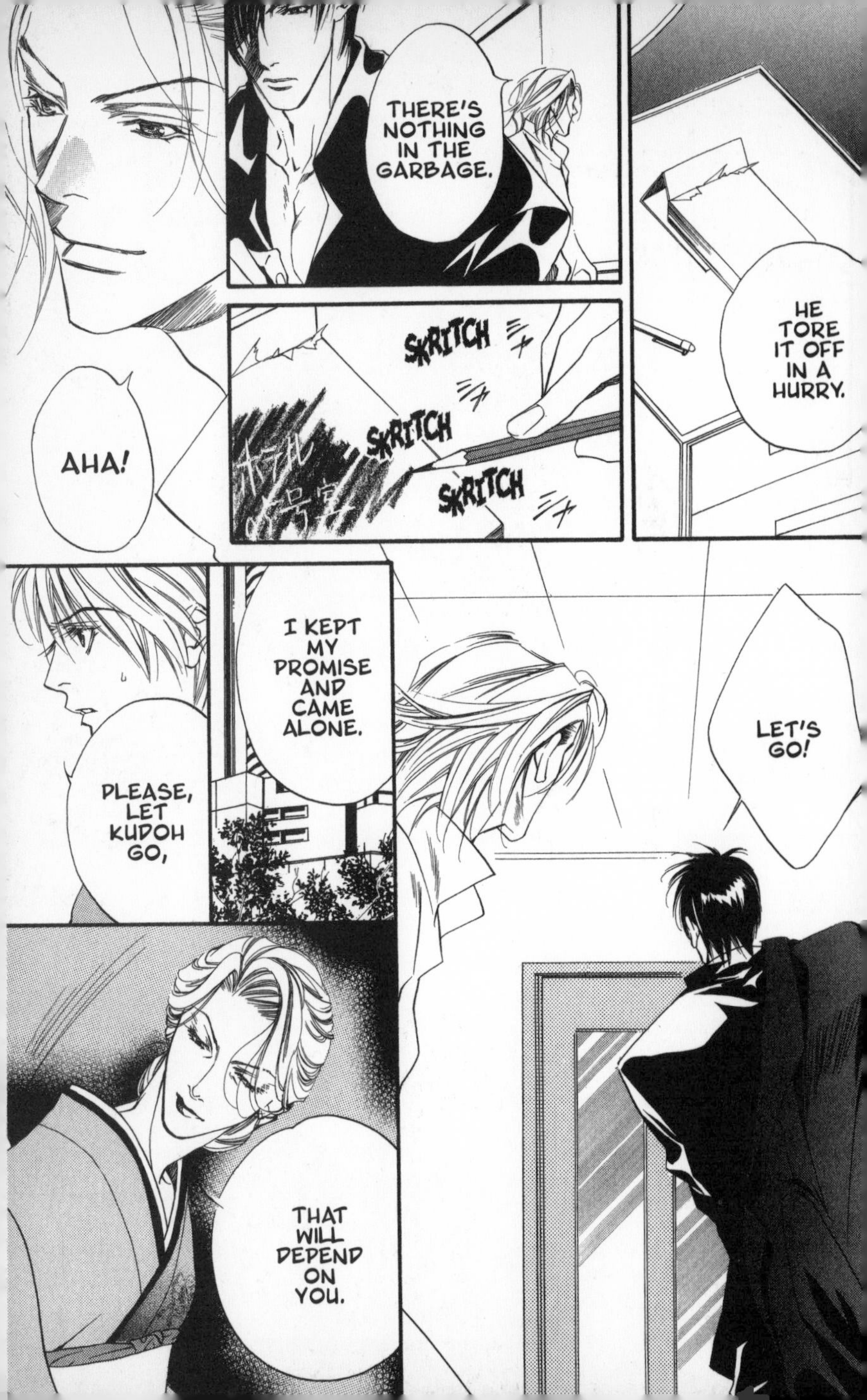
HE TORE IT OFF IN A HURRY.
THERE'S NOTHING IN THE GARBAGE.
SKRITCH
SKRITCH
SKRITCH
AHA!
LET'S GO!
I KEPT MY PROMISE AND CAME ALONE.
PLEASE, LET KUDOH GO,
THAT WILL DEPEND ON YOU.

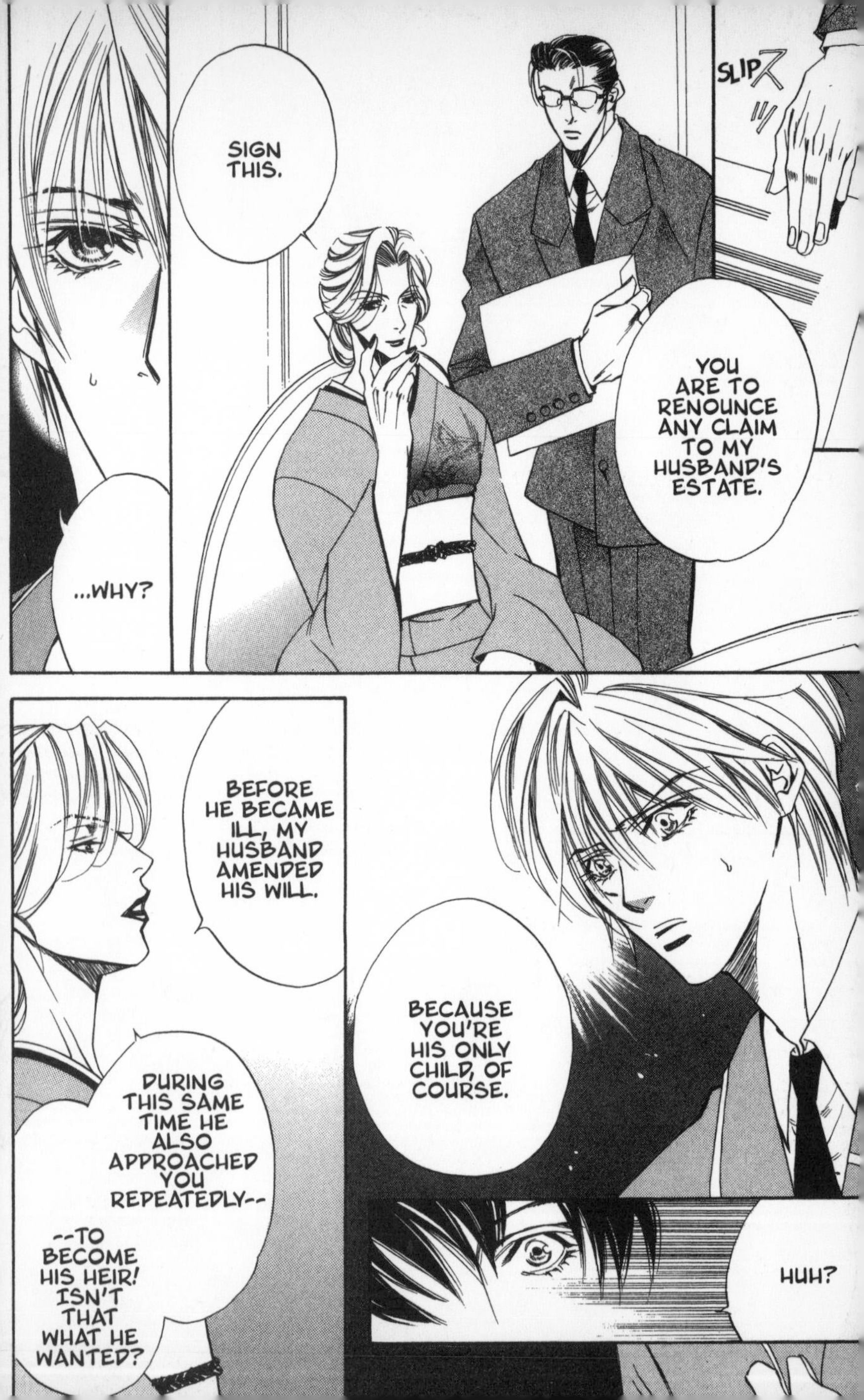
SLIP
SIGN THIS.
YOU ARE TO RENOUNCE ANY CLAIM TO MY HUSBAND'S ESTATE.
...WHY?
BECAUSE YOU'RE HIS ONLY CHILD, OF COURSE.
HUH?
BEFORE HE BECAME ILL, MY HUSBAND AMENDED HIS WILL.
DURING THIS SAME TIME HE ALSO APPROACHED YOU REPEATEDLY--
--TO BECOME HIS HEIR! ISN'T THAT WHAT HE WANTED?

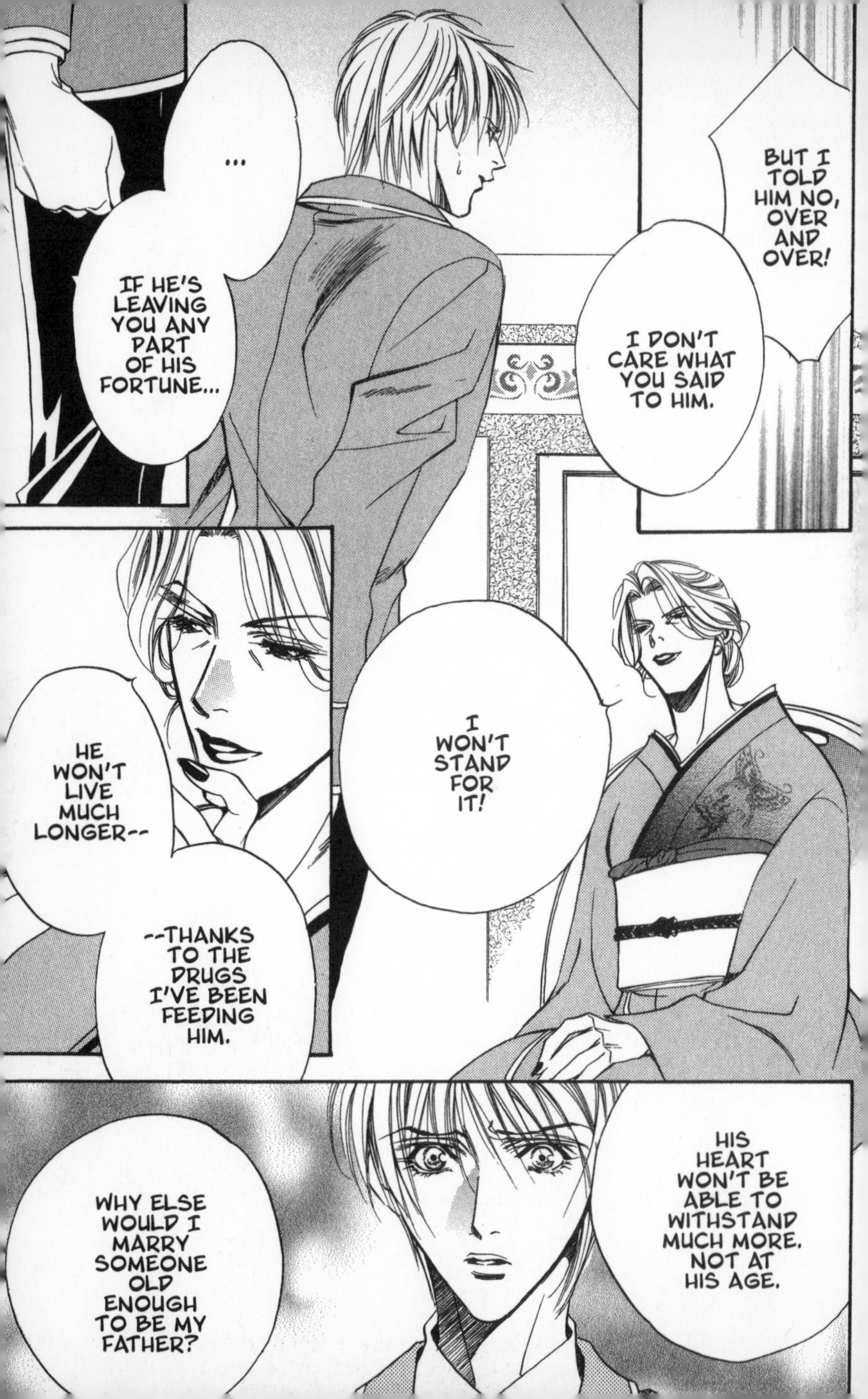
BUT I TOLD HIM NO, OVER AND OVER!
I DON'T CARE WHAT YOU SAID TO HIM.
...
IF HE'S LEAVING YOU ANY PART OF HIS FORTUNE...
I WON'T STAND FOR IT!
HE WON'T LIVE MUCH LONGER--
--THANKS TO THE DRUGS I'VE BEEN FEEDING HIM.
HIS HEART WON'T BE ABLE TO WITHSTAND MUCH MORE. NOT AT HIS AGE.
WHY ELSE WOULD I MARRY SOMEONE OLD ENOUGH TO BE MY FATHER?

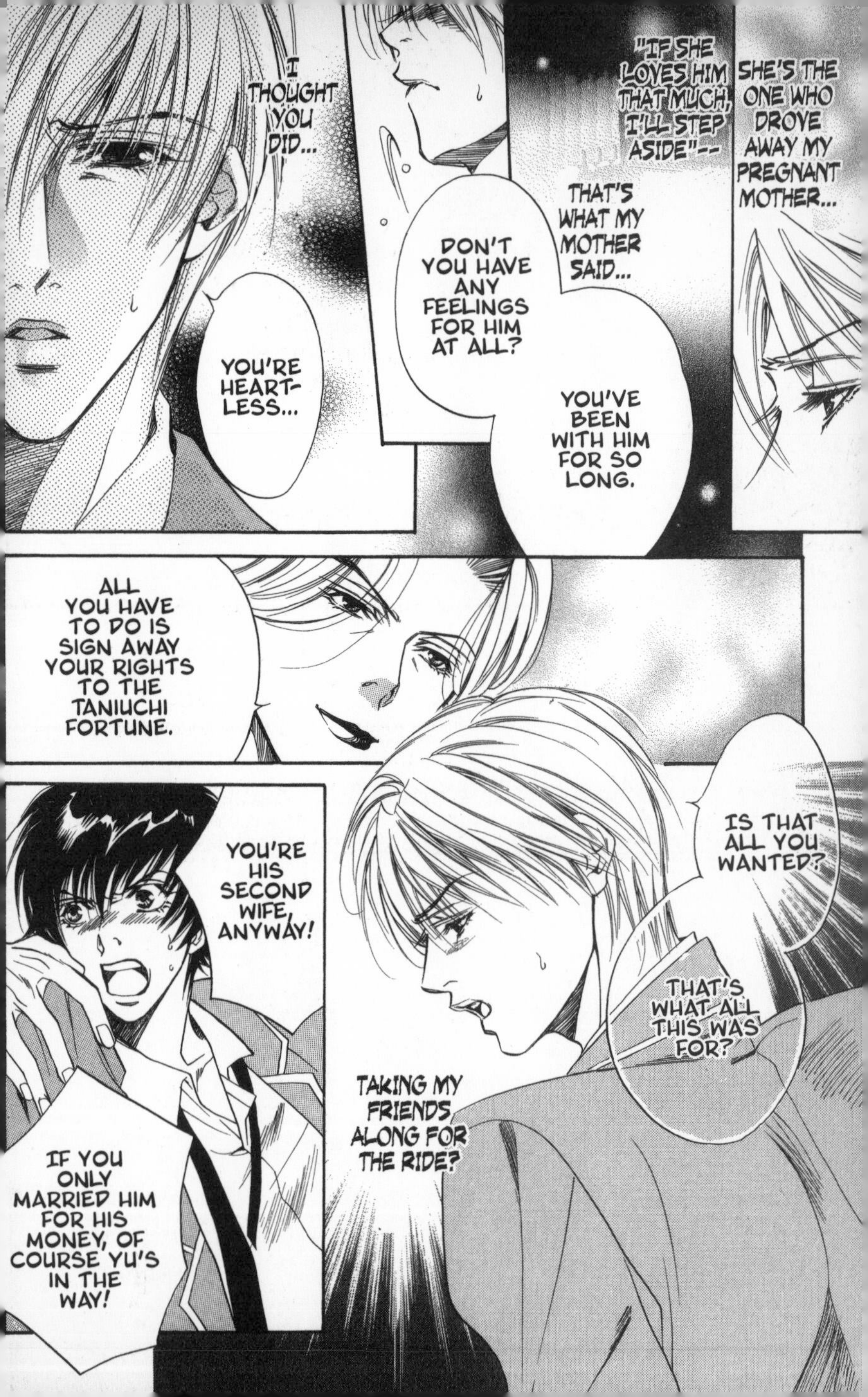
SHE'S THE ONE WHO DROVE AWAY MY PREGNANT MOTHER...
"IF SHE LOVES HIM THAT MUCH, I'LL STEP ASIDE"--
THAT'S WHAT MY MOTHER SAID...
DON'T YOU HAVE ANY FEELINGS FOR HIM AT ALL?
YOU'VE BEEN WITH HIM FOR SO LONG.
I THOUGHT YOU DID...
YOU'RE HEART-LESS...
ALL YOU HAVE TO DO IS SIGN AWAY YOUR RIGHTS TO THE TANIUCHI FORTUNE.
IS THAT ALL YOU WANTED?
THAT'S WHAT ALL THIS WAS FOR?
TAKING MY FRIENDS ALONG FOR THE RIDE?
YOU'RE HIS SECOND WIFE, ANYWAY!
IF YOU ONLY MARRIED HIM FOR HIS MONEY, OF COURSE YU'S IN THE WAY!

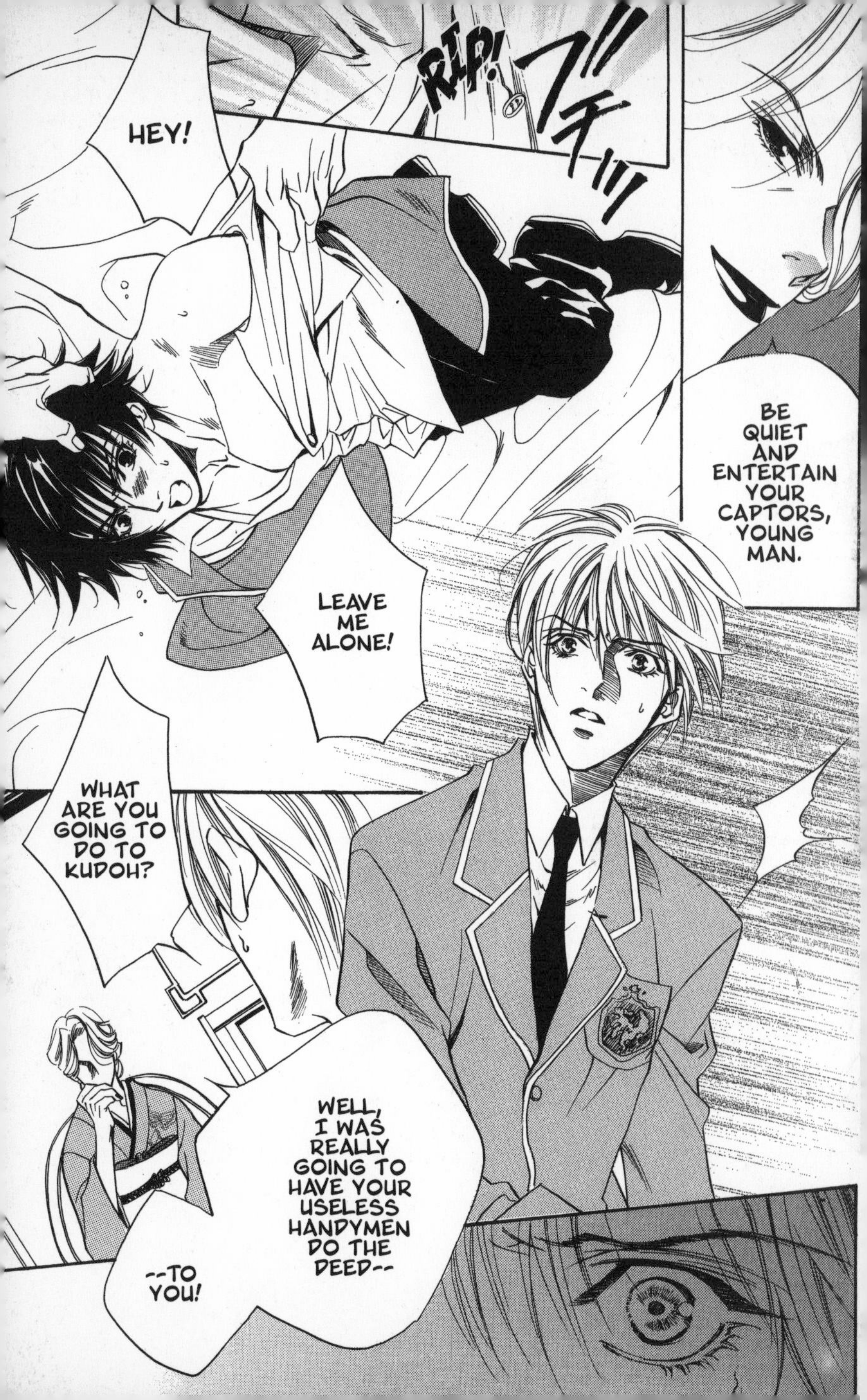
BE QUIET AND ENTERTAIN YOUR CAPTORS, YOUNG MAN.
RIP!
ブチッ
HEY!
LEAVE ME ALONE!
WHAT ARE YOU GOING TO DO TO KUDOH?
WELL, I WAS REALLY GOING TO HAVE YOUR USELESS HANDYMEN DO THE DEED--
--TO YOU!

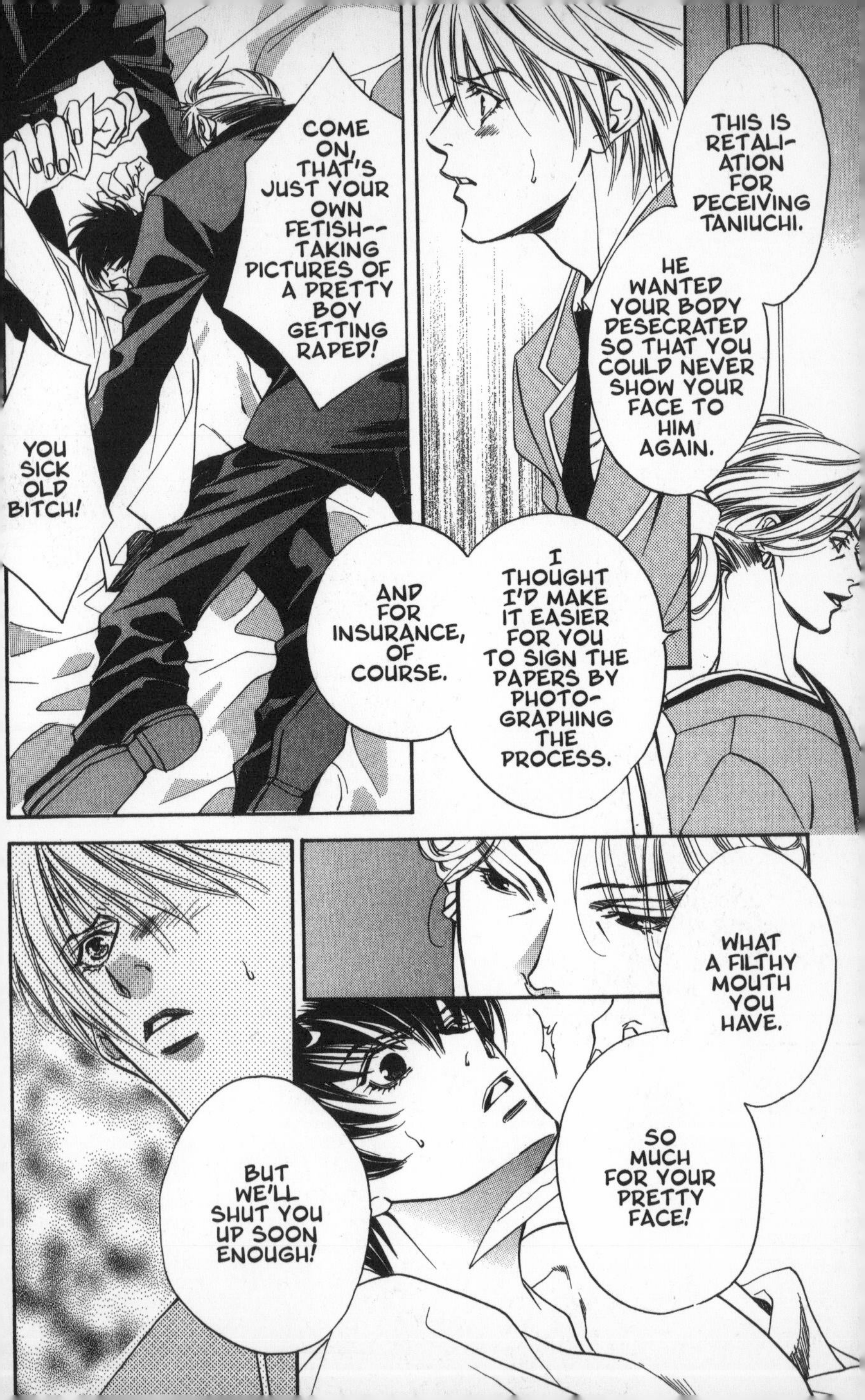
THIS IS RETALI- ATION FOR DECEIVING TANIUCHI.
HE WANTED YOUR BODY DESECRATED SO THAT YOU COULD NEVER SHOW YOUR FACE TO HIM AGAIN.
I THOUGHT I'D MAKE IT EASIER FOR YOU TO SIGN THE PAPERS BY PHOTO- GRAPHING THE PROCESS.
AND FOR INSURANCE, OF COURSE.
COME ON, THAT'S JUST YOUR OWN FETISH-- TAKING PICTURES OF A PRETTY BOY GETTING RAPED!
YOU SICK OLD BITCH!
WHAT A FILTHY MOUTH YOU HAVE.
SO MUCH FOR YOUR PRETTY FACE!
BUT WE'LL SHUT YOU UP SOON ENOUGH!

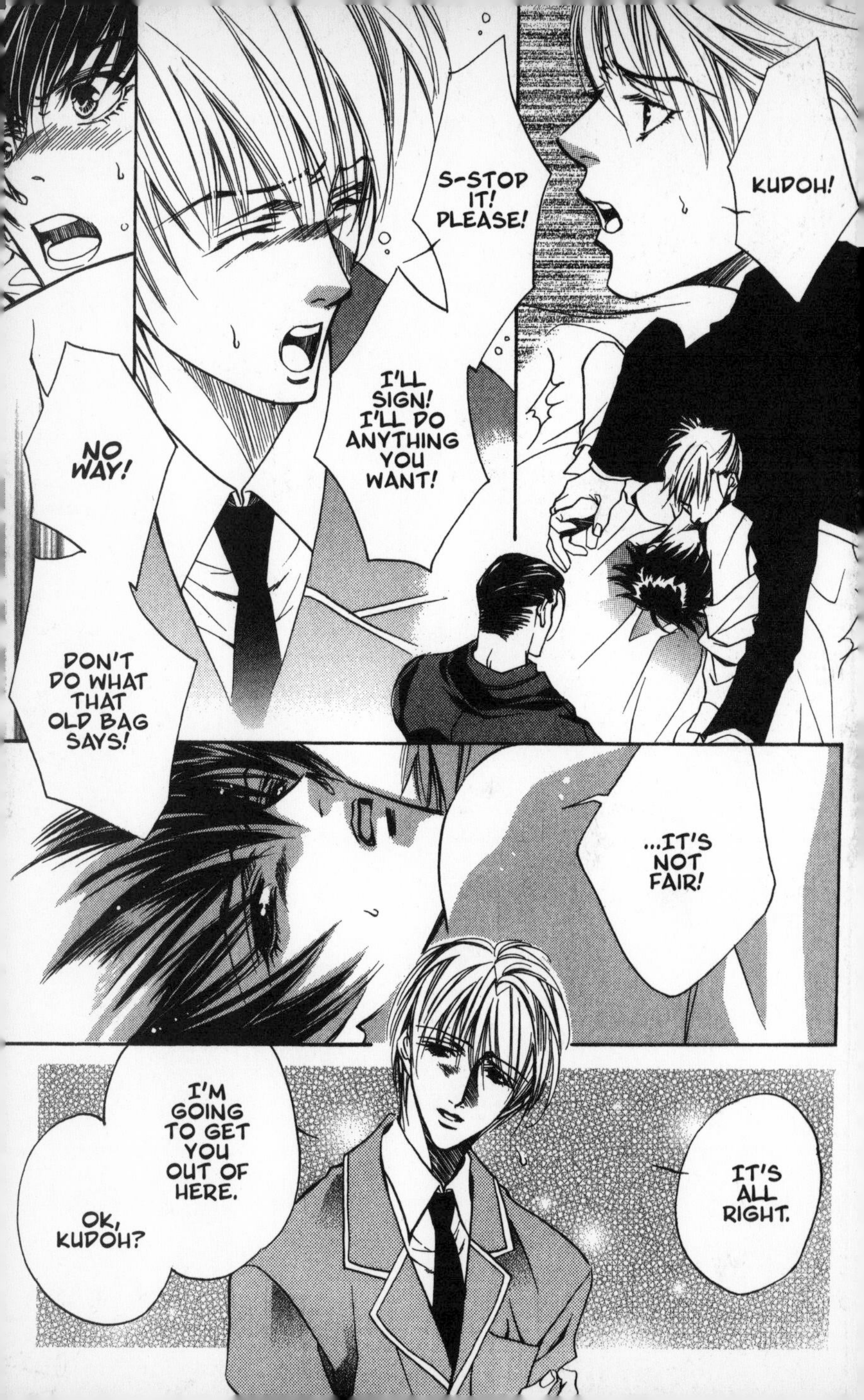
KUDOH!
S-STOP IT! PLEASE!
I'LL SIGN! I'LL DO ANYTHING YOU WANT!
NO WAY!
DON'T DO WHAT THAT OLD BAG SAYS!
...IT'S NOT FAIR!
IT'S ALL RIGHT.
I'M GOING TO GET YOU OUT OF HERE.
OK, KUDOH?

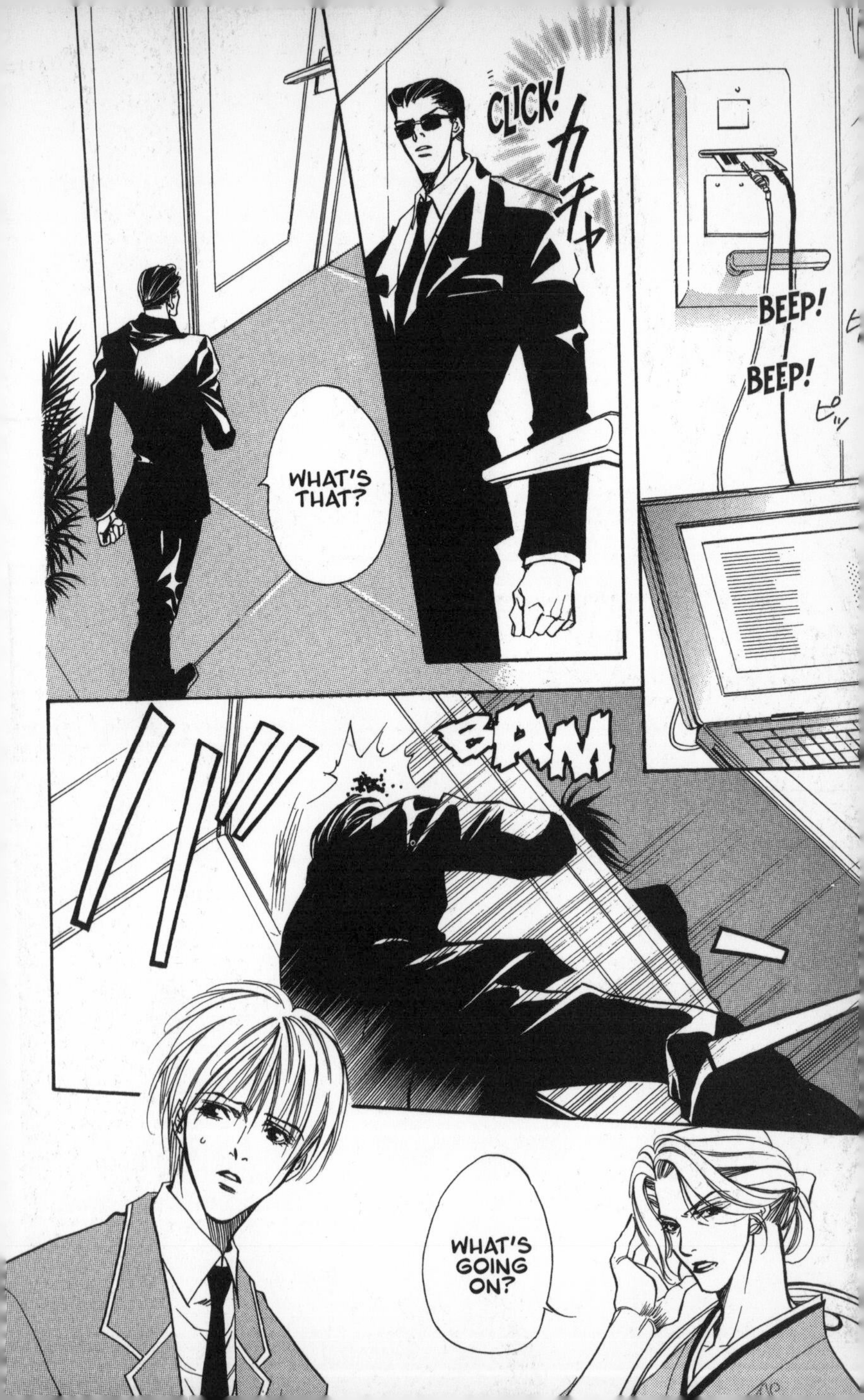
BEEP!
BEEP!
ピッ
CLICK!
カチャ
WHAT'S THAT?
BAM
WHAT'S GOING ON?

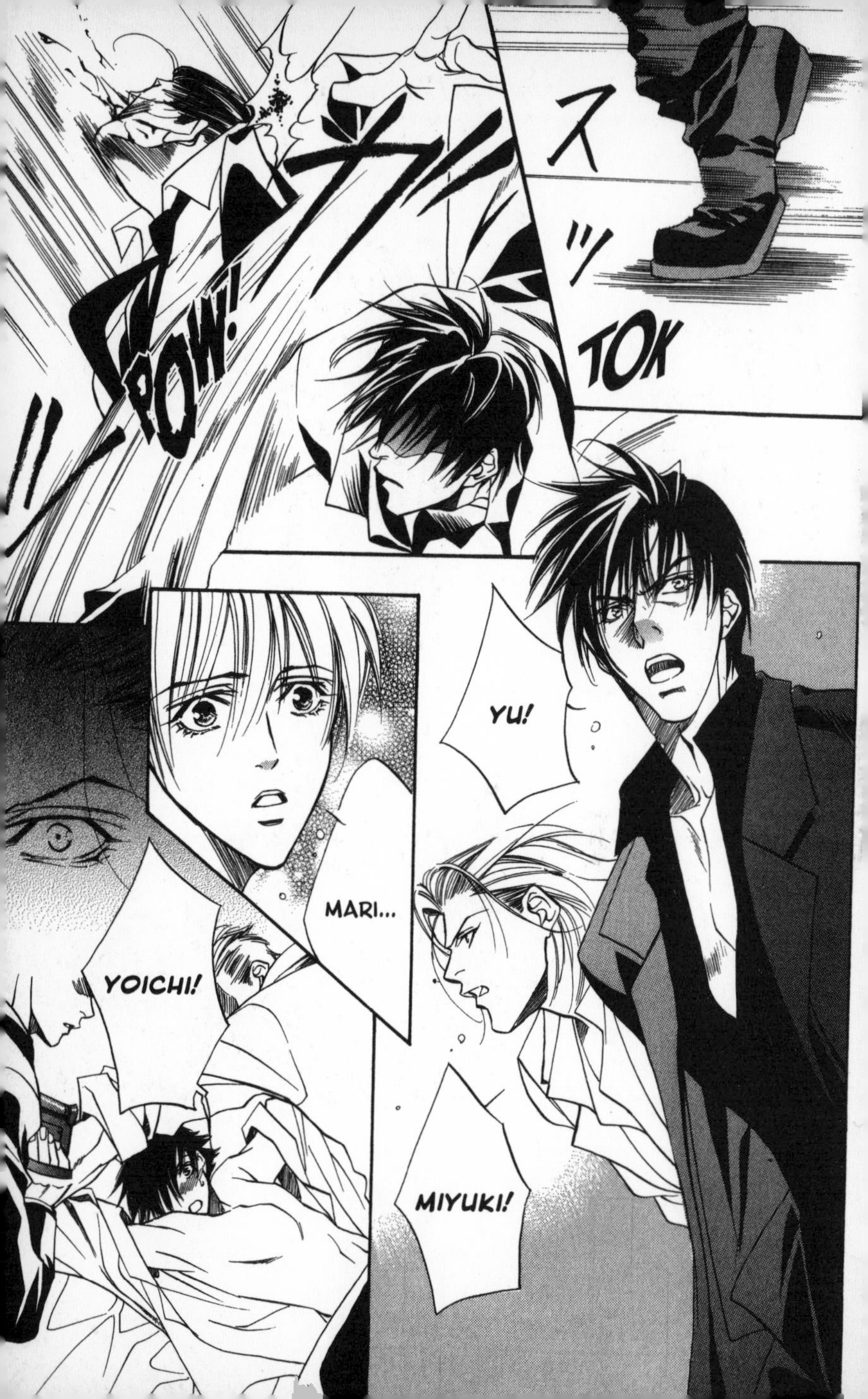
スッ
TOK
POW!
YU!
MIYUKI!
MARI...
YOICHI!

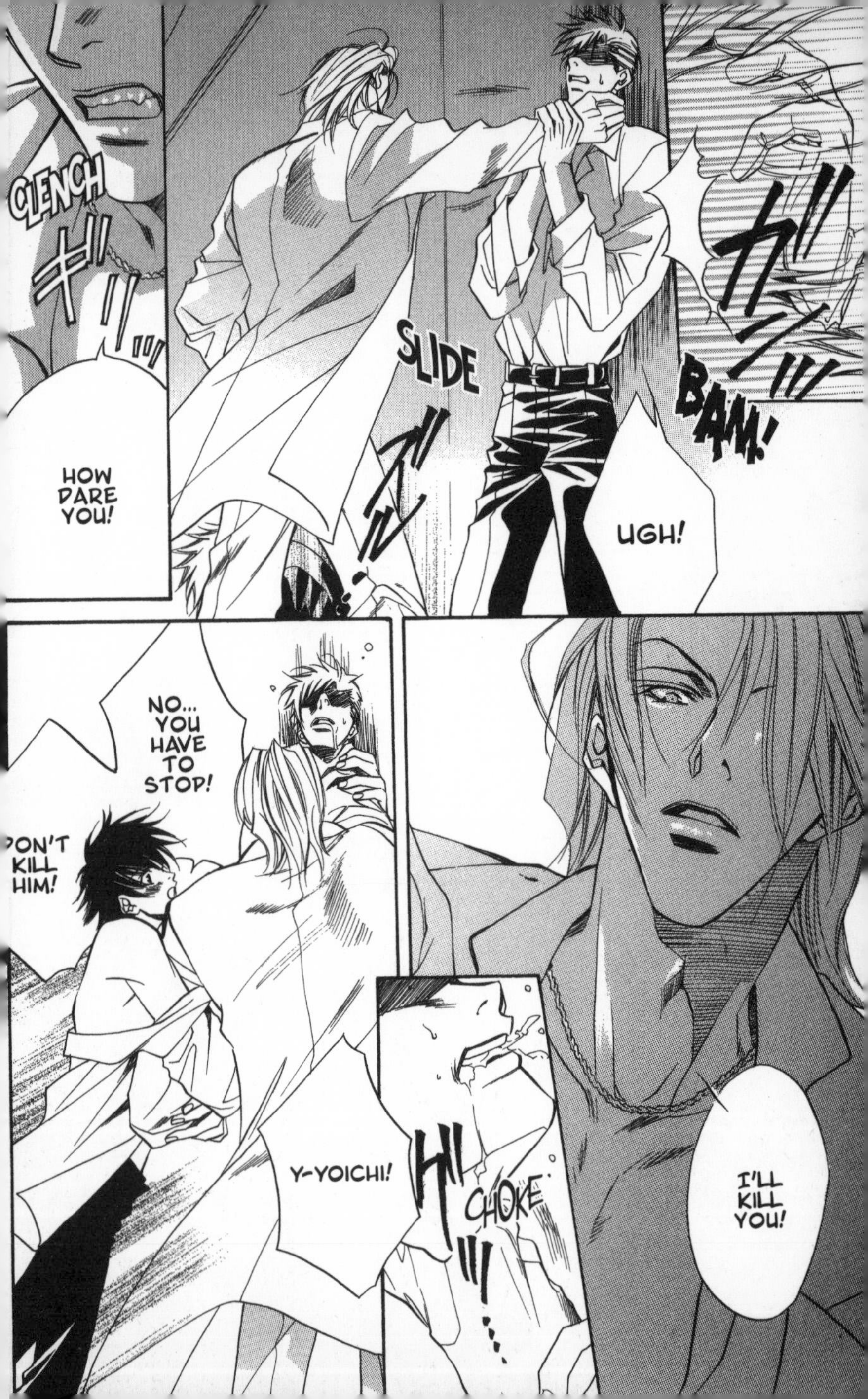
BAM!
SLIDE
UGH!
CLENCH
HOW DARE YOU!
I'LL KILL YOU!
CHOKE
NO... YOU HAVE TO STOP!
ON'T KILL HIM!
Y-YOICHI!

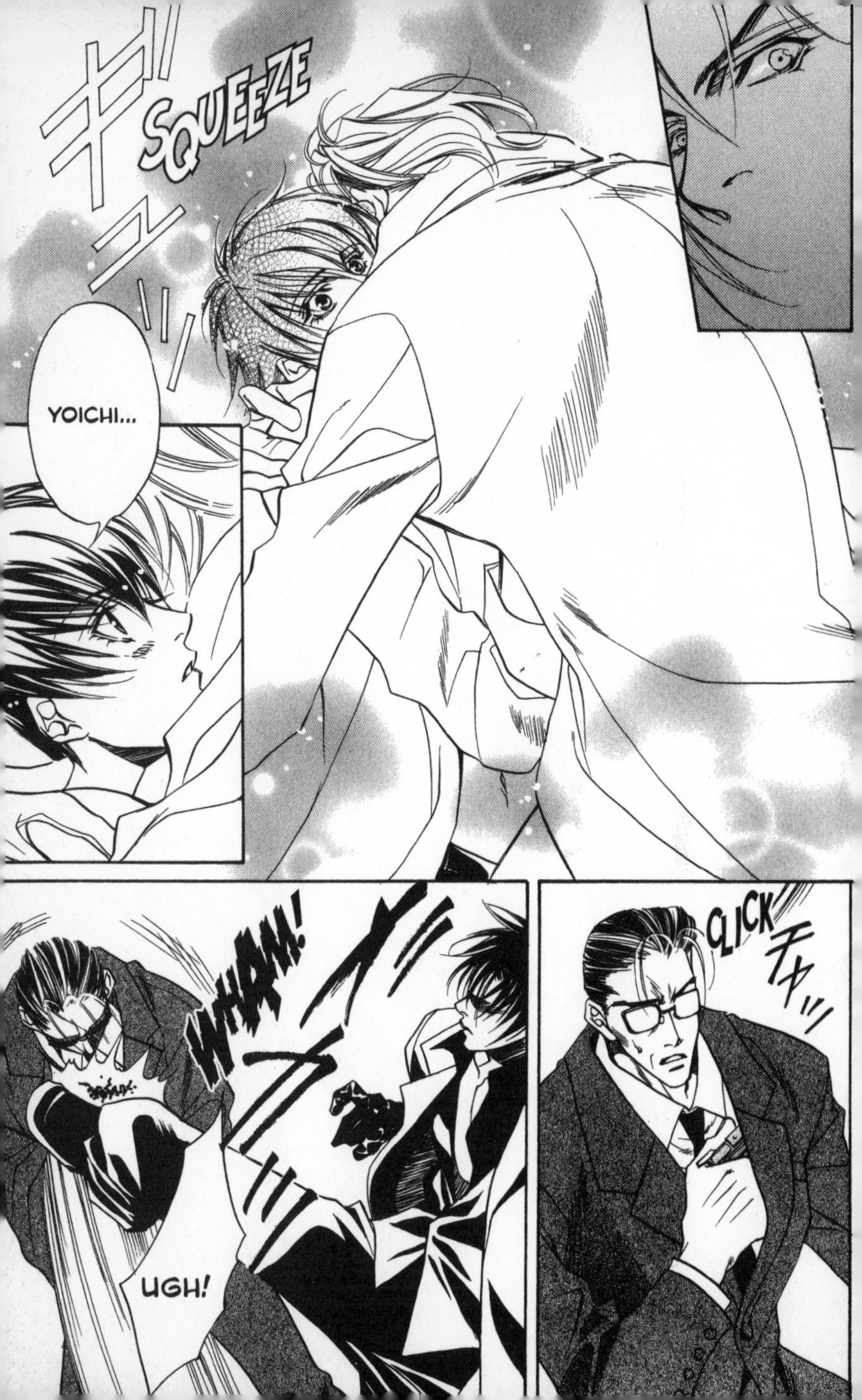
SQUEEZE
YOICHI...
CLICK
WHAM!
UGH!

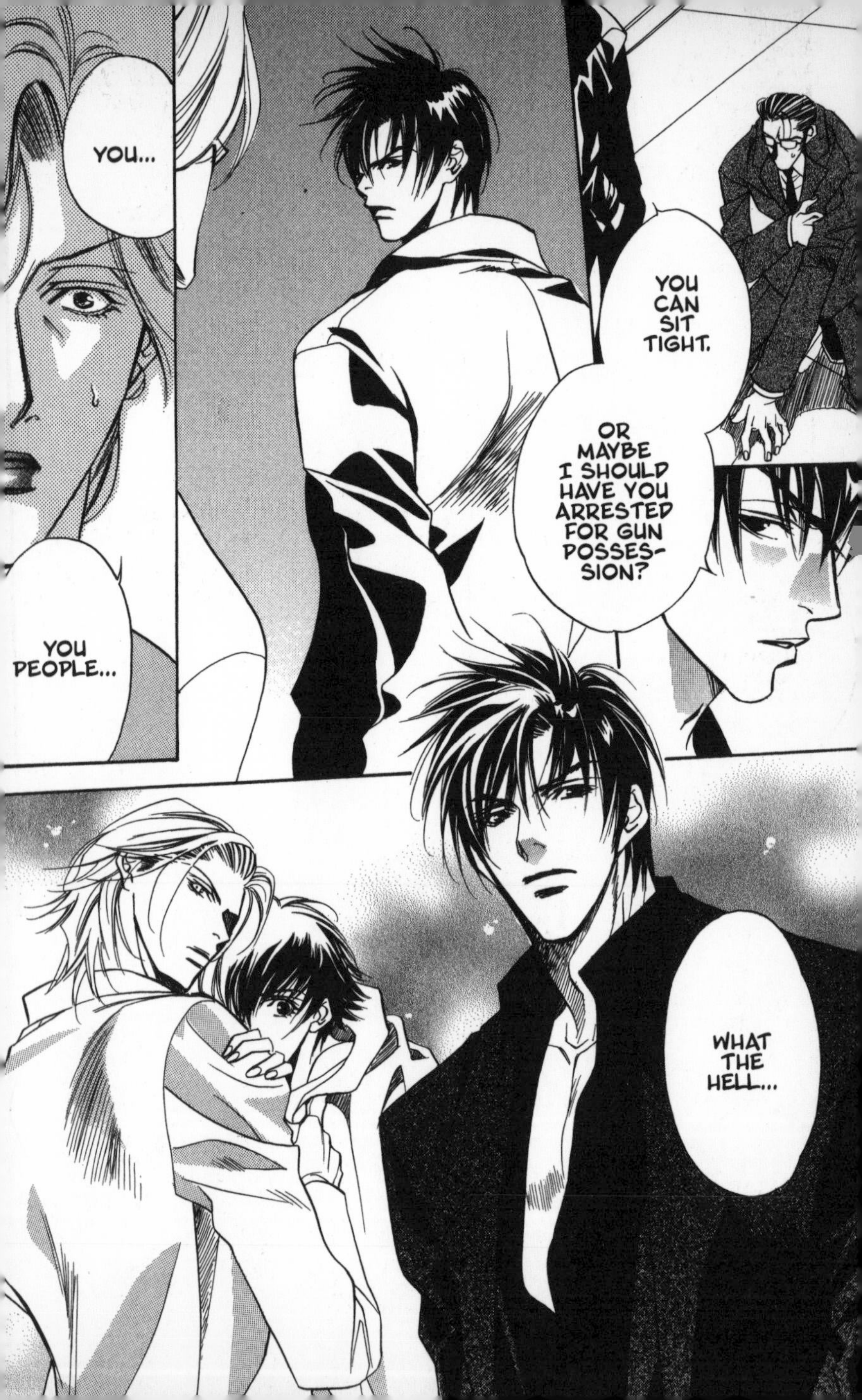
YOU CAN SIT TIGHT.
OR MAYBE I SHOULD HAVE YOU ARRESTED FOR GUN POSSESSION?
YOU...
YOU PEOPLE...
WHAT THE HELL...

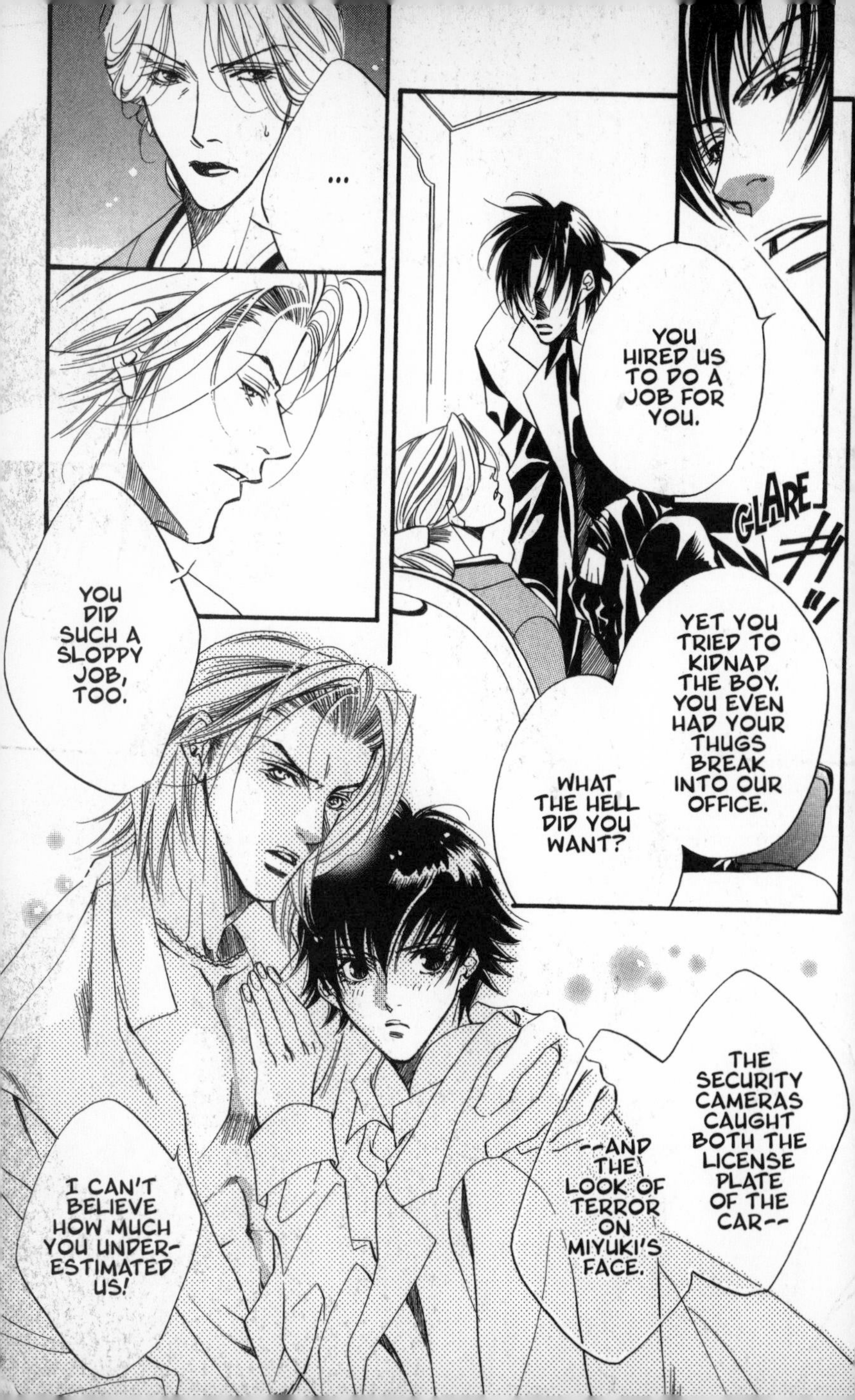
YOU HIRED US TO DO A JOB FOR YOU.
GLARE
YET YOU TRIED TO KIDNAP THE BOY. YOU EVEN HAD YOUR THUGS BREAK INTO OUR OFFICE.
WHAT THE HELL DID YOU WANT?
...
YOU DID SUCH A SLOPPY JOB, TOO.
THE SECURITY CAMERAS CAUGHT BOTH THE LICENSE PLATE OF THE CAR--
--AND THE LOOK OF TERROR ON MIYUKI'S FACE.
I CAN'T BELIEVE HOW MUCH YOU UNDER-ESTIMATED US!

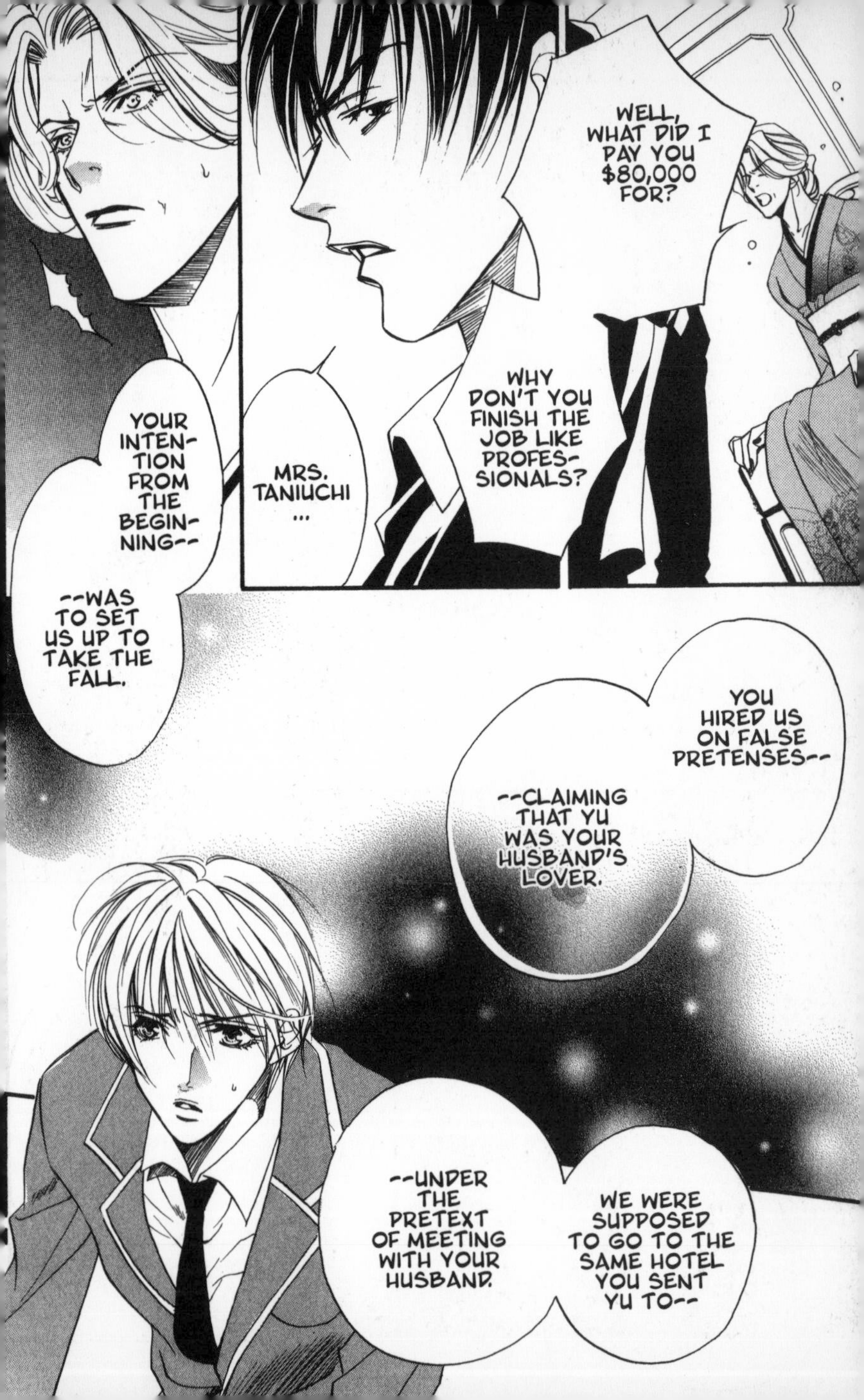
WELL, WHAT DID I PAY YOU $80,000 FOR?
WHY DON'T YOU FINISH THE JOB LIKE PROFESSIONALS?
MRS. TANIUCHI ...
YOUR INTENTION FROM THE BEGINNING--
--WAS TO SET US UP TO TAKE THE FALL.
YOU HIRED US ON FALSE PRETENSES--
--CLAIMING THAT YU WAS YOUR HUSBAND'S LOVER.
WE WERE SUPPOSED TO GO TO THE SAME HOTEL YOU SENT YU TO--
--UNDER THE PRETEXT OF MEETING WITH YOUR HUSBAND.

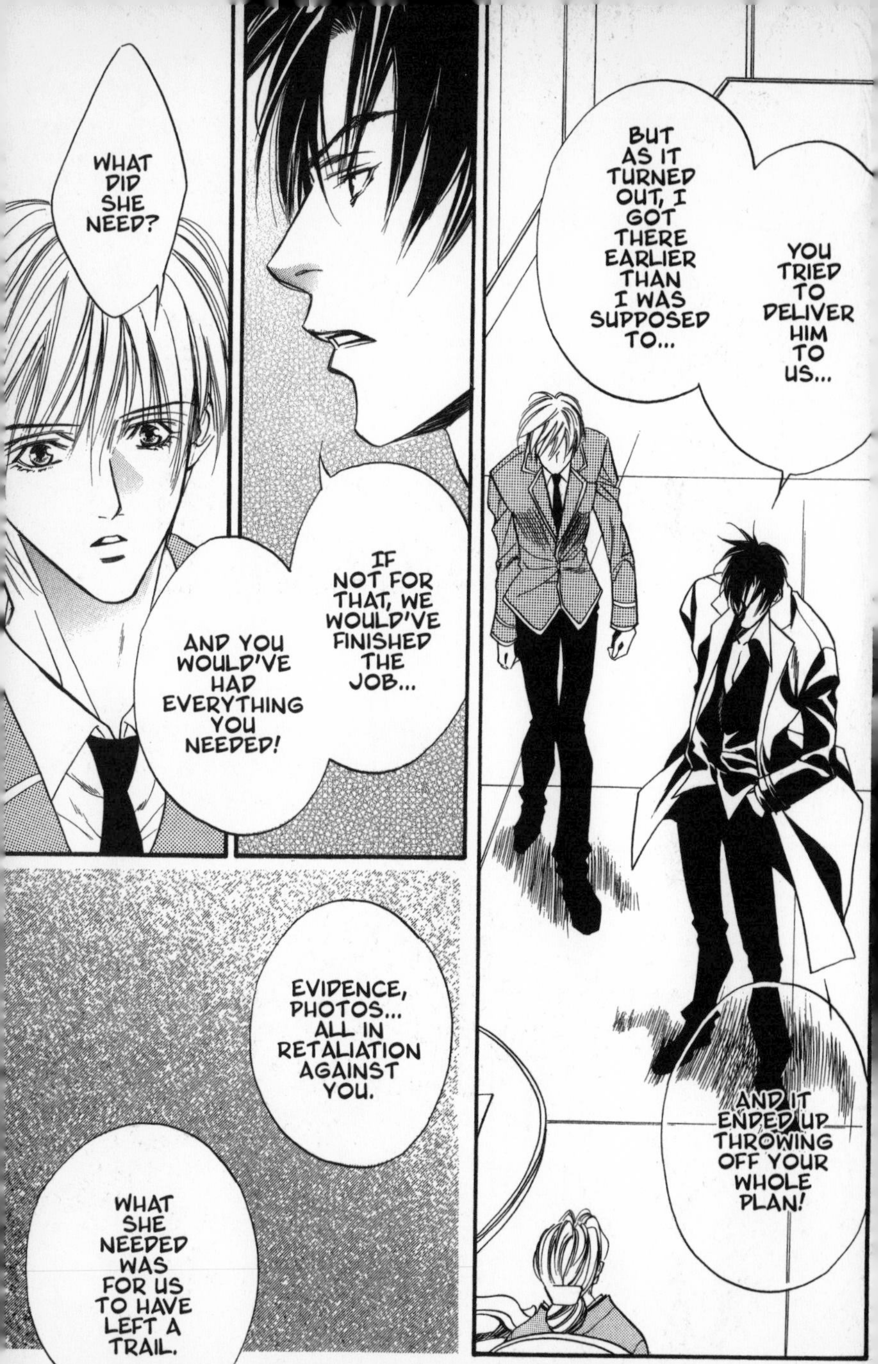
YOU TRIED TO DELIVER HIM TO US...
BUT AS IT TURNED OUT, I GOT THERE EARLIER THAN I WAS SUPPOSED TO...
AND IT ENDED UP THROWING OFF YOUR WHOLE PLAN!
IF NOT FOR THAT, WE WOULD'VE FINISHED THE JOB...
AND YOU WOULD'VE HAD EVERYTHING YOU NEEDED!
WHAT DID SHE NEED?
EVIDENCE, PHOTOS... ALL IN RETALIATION AGAINST YOU.
WHAT SHE NEEDED WAS FOR US TO HAVE LEFT A TRAIL.

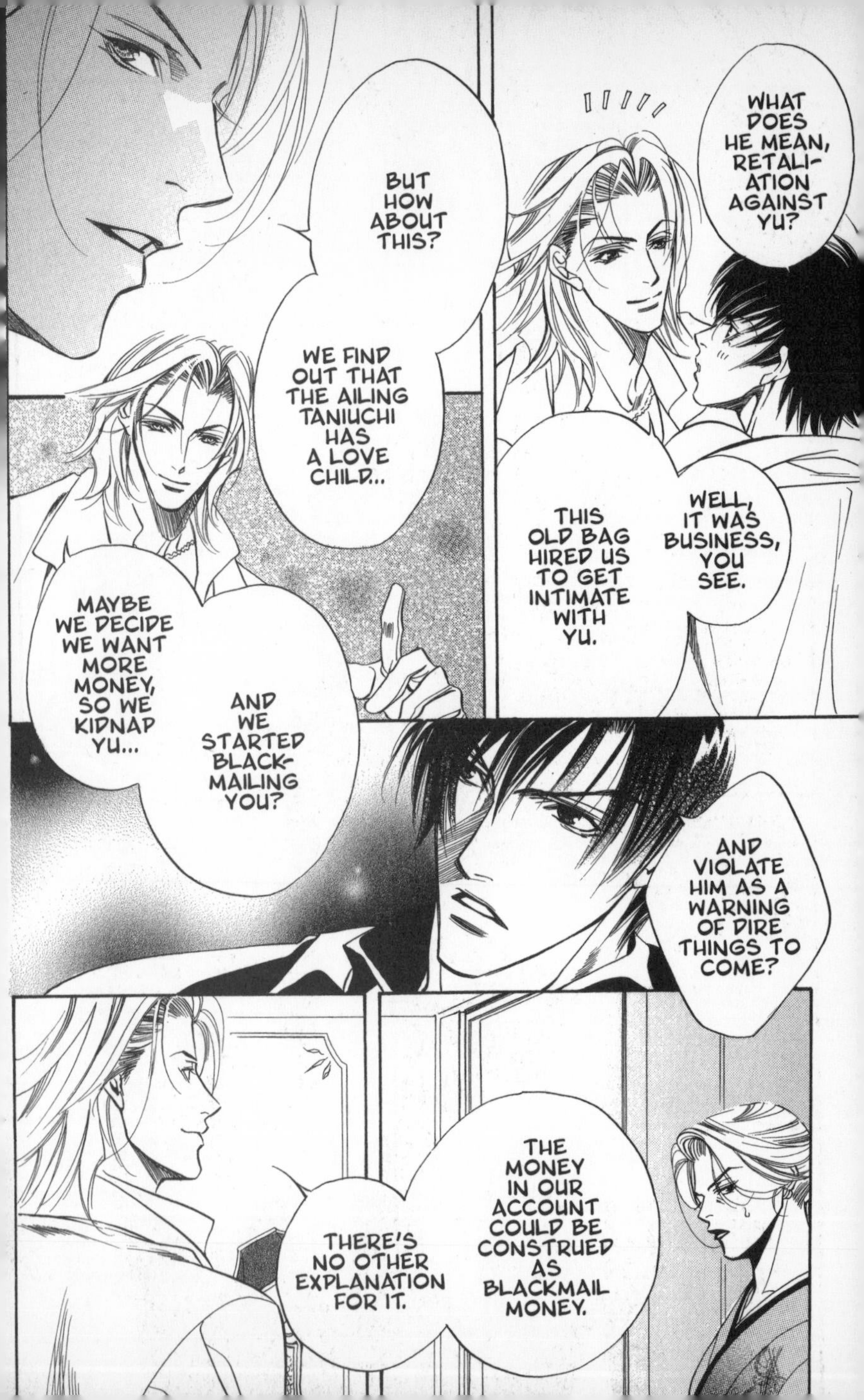
WHAT DOES HE MEAN, RETALI-ATION AGAINST YU?
WELL, IT WAS BUSINESS, YOU SEE.
THIS OLD BAG HIRED US TO GET INTIMATE WITH YU.
BUT HOW ABOUT THIS?
WE FIND OUT THAT THE AILING TANIUCHI HAS A LOVE CHILD...
MAYBE WE DECIDE WE WANT MORE MONEY, SO WE KIDNAP YU...
AND WE STARTED BLACK-MAILING YOU?
AND VIOLATE HIM AS A WARNING OF DIRE THINGS TO COME?
THE MONEY IN OUR ACCOUNT COULD BE CONSTRUED AS BLACKMAIL MONEY.
THERE'S NO OTHER EXPLANATION FOR IT.

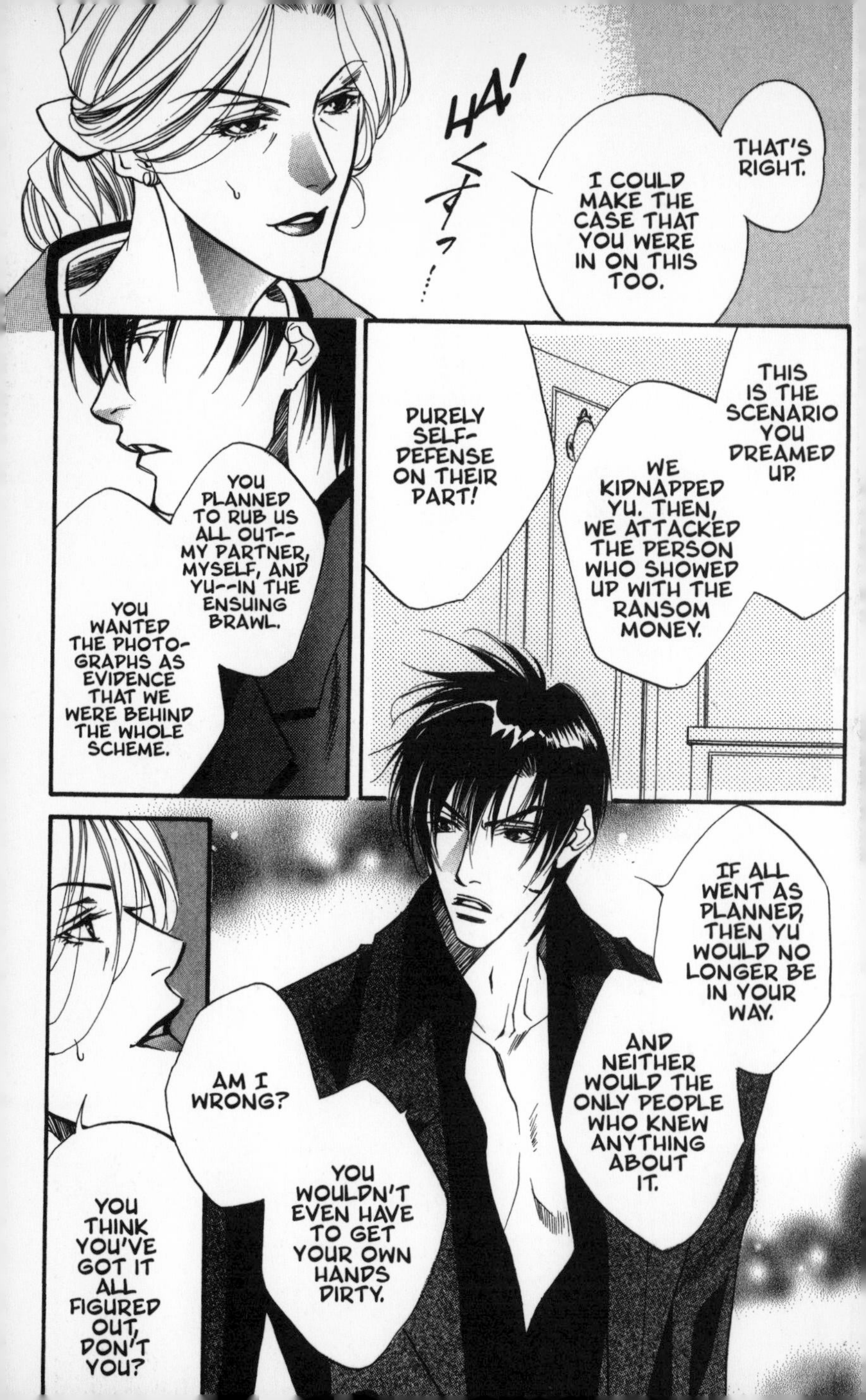
THAT'S RIGHT.
I COULD MAKE THE CASE THAT YOU WERE IN ON THIS TOO.
HA!
THIS IS THE SCENARIO YOU DREAMED UP.
WE KIDNAPPED YU. THEN, WE ATTACKED THE PERSON WHO SHOWED UP WITH THE RANSOM MONEY.
PURELY SELF-DEFENSE ON THEIR PART!
YOU PLANNED TO RUB US ALL OUT--MY PARTNER, MYSELF, AND YU--IN THE ENSUING BRAWL.
YOU WANTED THE PHOTOGRAPHS AS EVIDENCE THAT WE WERE BEHIND THE WHOLE SCHEME.
IF ALL WENT AS PLANNED, THEN YU WOULD NO LONGER BE IN YOUR WAY.
AND NEITHER WOULD THE ONLY PEOPLE WHO KNEW ANYTHING ABOUT IT.
AM I WRONG?
YOU WOULDN'T EVEN HAVE TO GET YOUR OWN HANDS DIRTY.
YOU THINK YOU'VE GOT IT ALL FIGURED OUT, DON'T YOU?

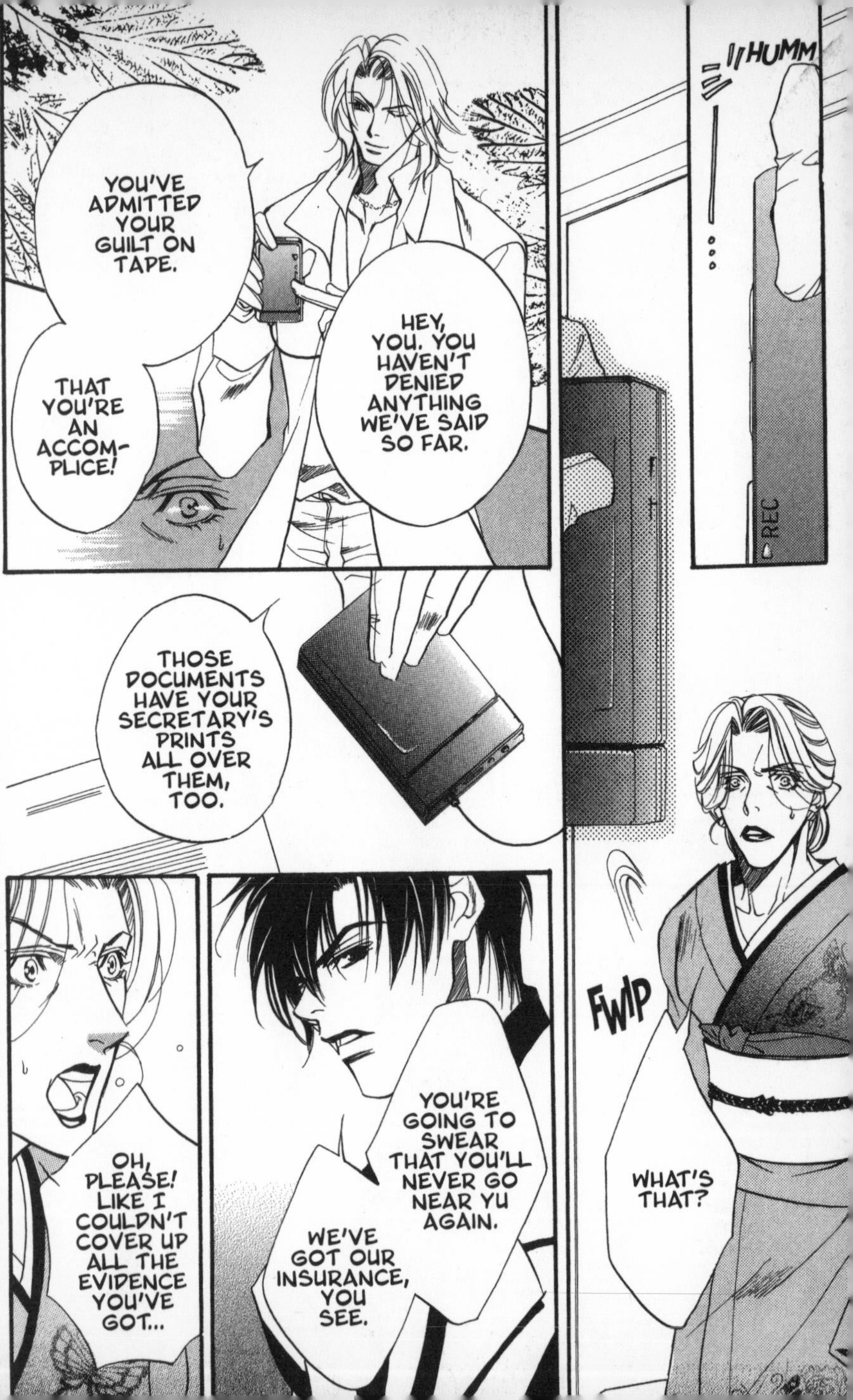
HUMM
...
REC
HEY, YOU. YOU HAVEN'T DENIED ANYTHING WE'VE SAID SO FAR.
YOU'VE ADMITTED YOUR GUILT ON TAPE.
THAT YOU'RE AN ACCOM-PLICE!
FWIP
WHAT'S THAT?
THOSE DOCUMENTS HAVE YOUR SECRETARY'S PRINTS ALL OVER THEM, TOO.
YOU'RE GOING TO SWEAR THAT YOU'LL NEVER GO NEAR YU AGAIN.
WE'VE GOT OUR INSURANCE, YOU SEE.
OH, PLEASE! LIKE I COULDN'T COVER UP ALL THE EVIDENCE YOU'VE GOT...

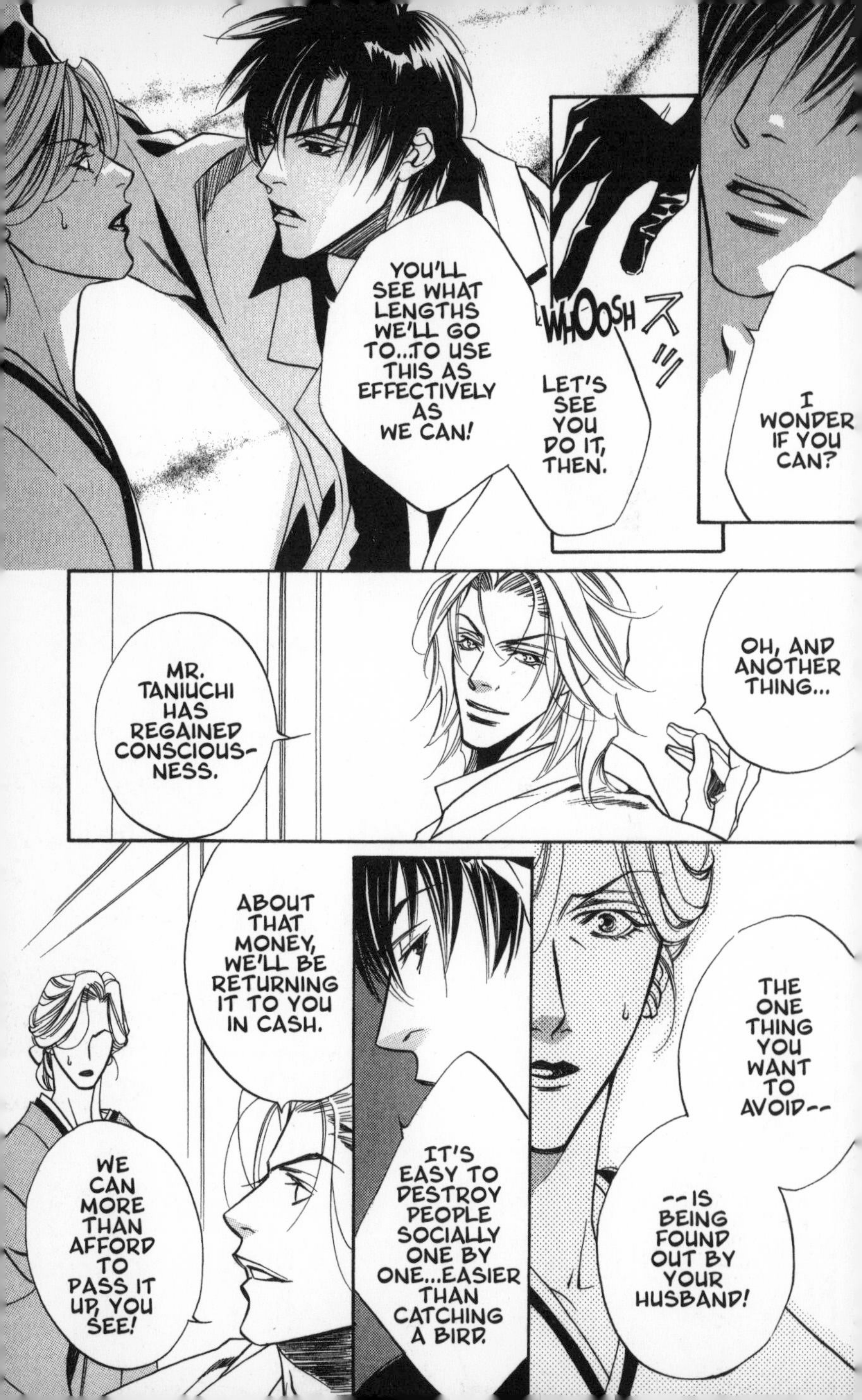
I WONDER IF YOU CAN?
WHOOSH スッ
LET'S SEE YOU DO IT, THEN.
YOU'LL SEE WHAT LENGTHS WE'LL GO TO...TO USE THIS AS EFFECTIVELY AS WE CAN!
OH, AND ANOTHER THING...
MR. TANIUCHI HAS REGAINED CONSCIOUS-NESS.
THE ONE THING YOU WANT TO AVOID--
--IS BEING FOUND OUT BY YOUR HUSBAND!
IT'S EASY TO DESTROY PEOPLE SOCIALLY ONE BY ONE...EASIER THAN CATCHING A BIRD.
ABOUT THAT MONEY, WE'LL BE RETURNING IT TO YOU IN CASH.
WE CAN MORE THAN AFFORD TO PASS IT UP, YOU SEE!

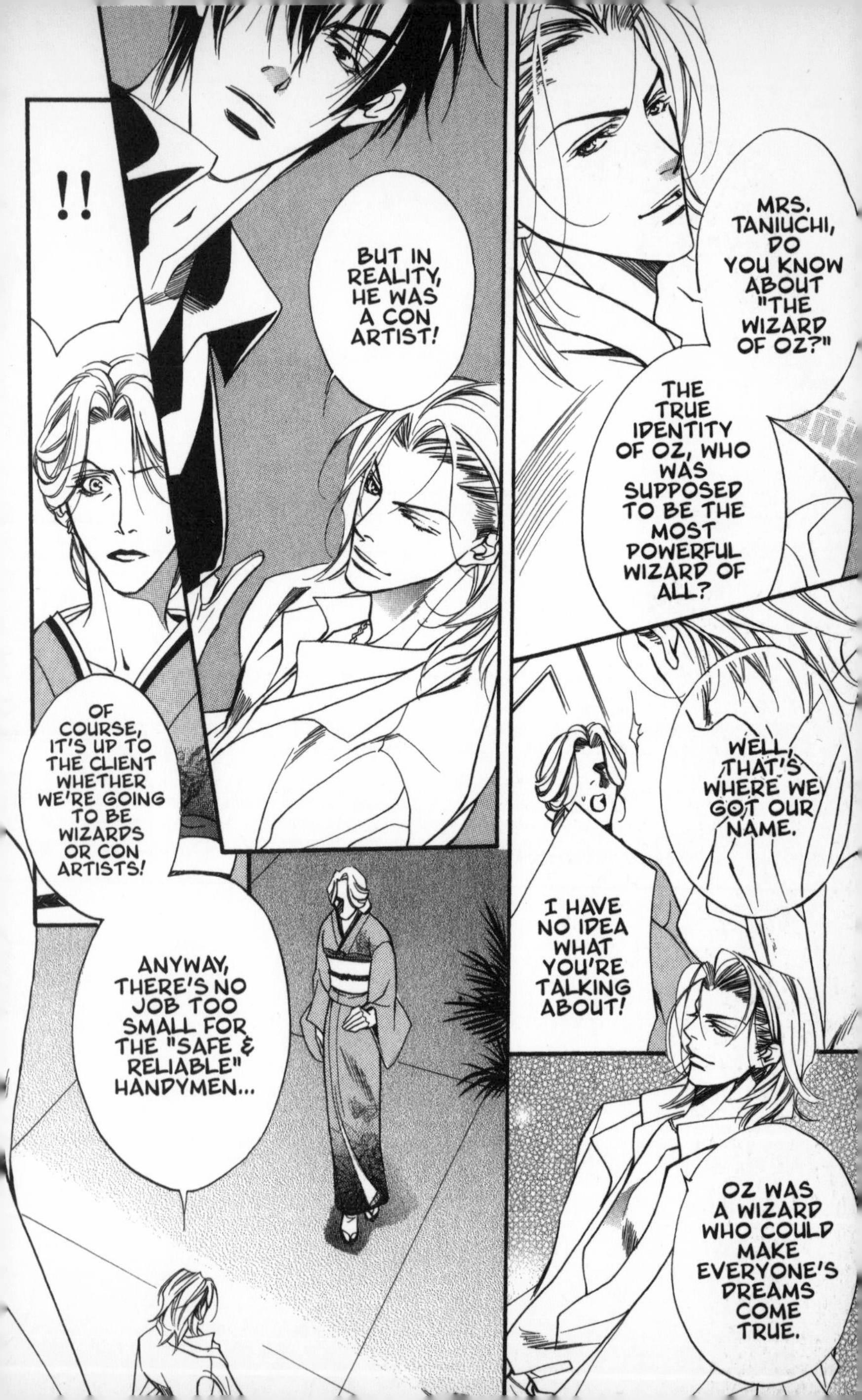
MRS. TANIUCHI, DO YOU KNOW ABOUT "THE WIZARD OF OZ?"
THE TRUE IDENTITY OF OZ, WHO WAS SUPPOSED TO BE THE MOST POWERFUL WIZARD OF ALL?
WELL, THAT'S WHERE WE GOT OUR NAME.
I HAVE NO IDEA WHAT YOU'RE TALKING ABOUT!
OZ WAS A WIZARD WHO COULD MAKE EVERYONE'S DREAMS COME TRUE.
BUT IN REALITY, HE WAS A CON ARTIST!
!!
OF COURSE, IT'S UP TO THE CLIENT WHETHER WE'RE GOING TO BE WIZARDS OR CON ARTISTS!
ANYWAY, THERE'S NO JOB TOO SMALL FOR THE "SAFE & RELIABLE" HANDYMEN...

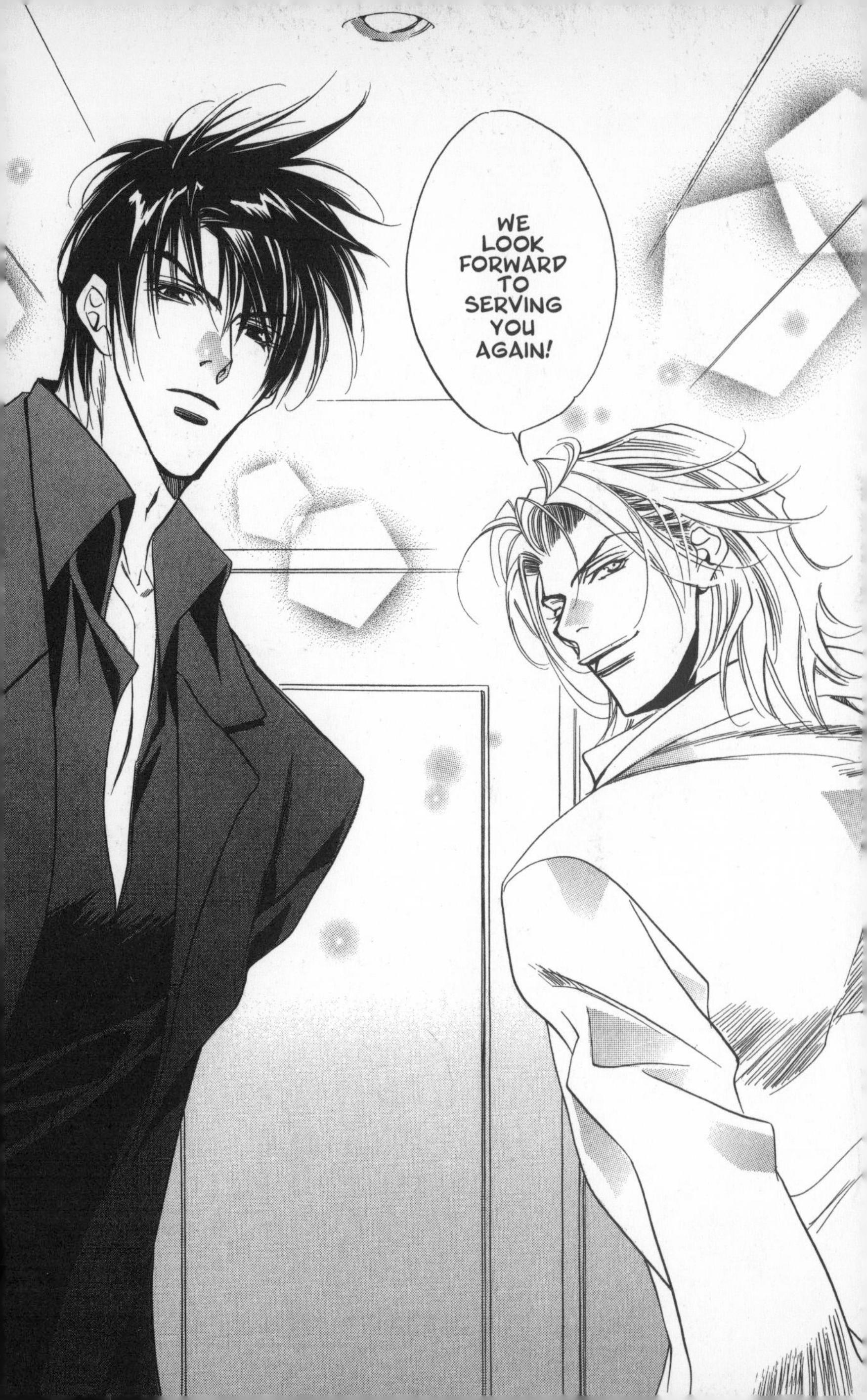
WE LOOK FORWARD TO SERVING YOU AGAIN!

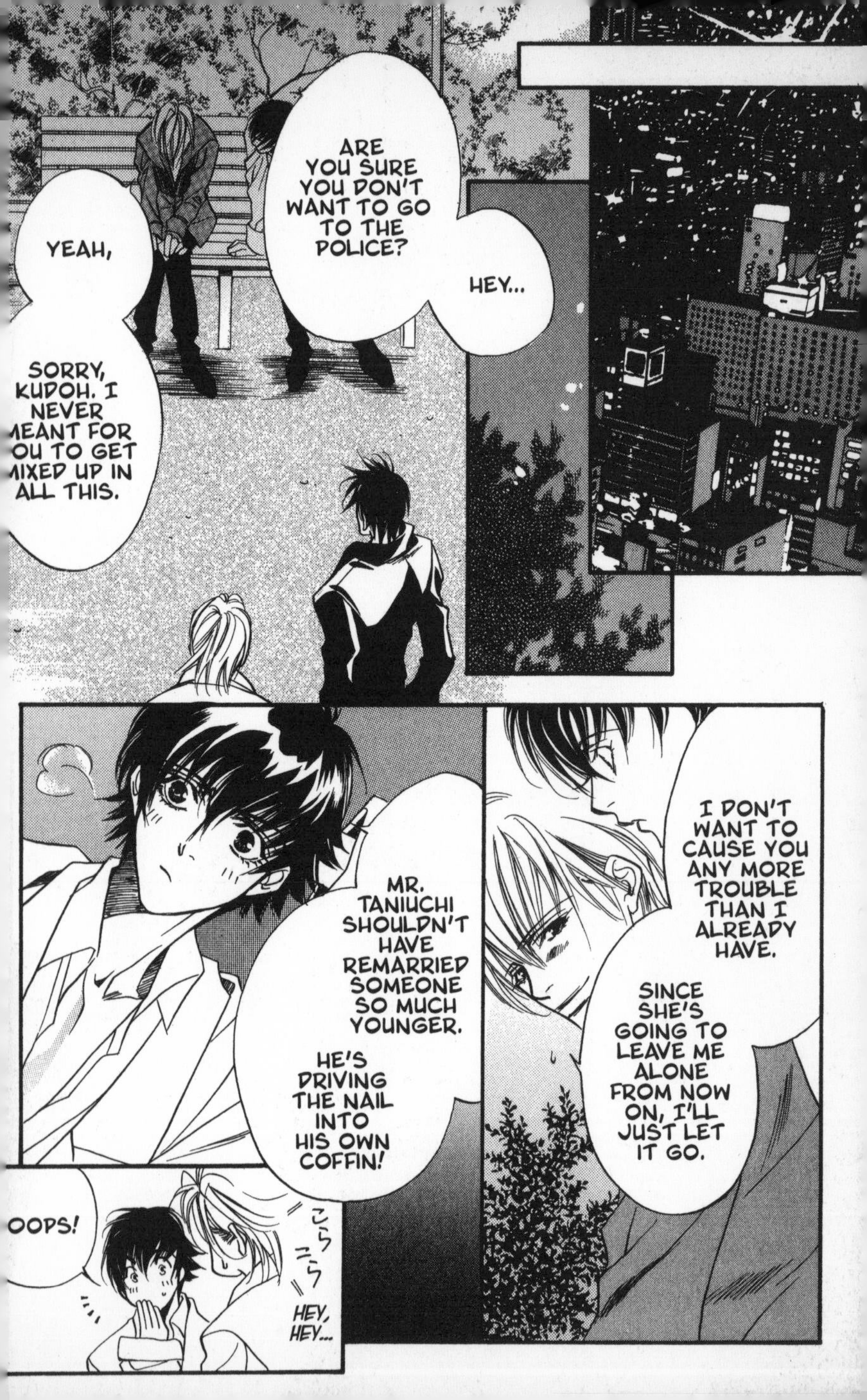
HEY...
ARE YOU SURE YOU DON'T WANT TO GO TO THE POLICE?
YEAH,
SORRY, KUDOH. I NEVER MEANT FOR OU TO GET IXED UP IN ALL THIS.
I DON'T WANT TO CAUSE YOU ANY MORE TROUBLE THAN I ALREADY HAVE.
SINCE SHE'S GOING TO LEAVE ME ALONE FROM NOW ON, I'LL JUST LET IT GO.
MR. TANIUCHI SHOULDN'T HAVE REMARRIED SOMEONE SO MUCH YOUNGER.
HE'S DRIVING THE NAIL INTO HIS OWN COFFIN!
こら こら
HEY, HEY...
OOPS!

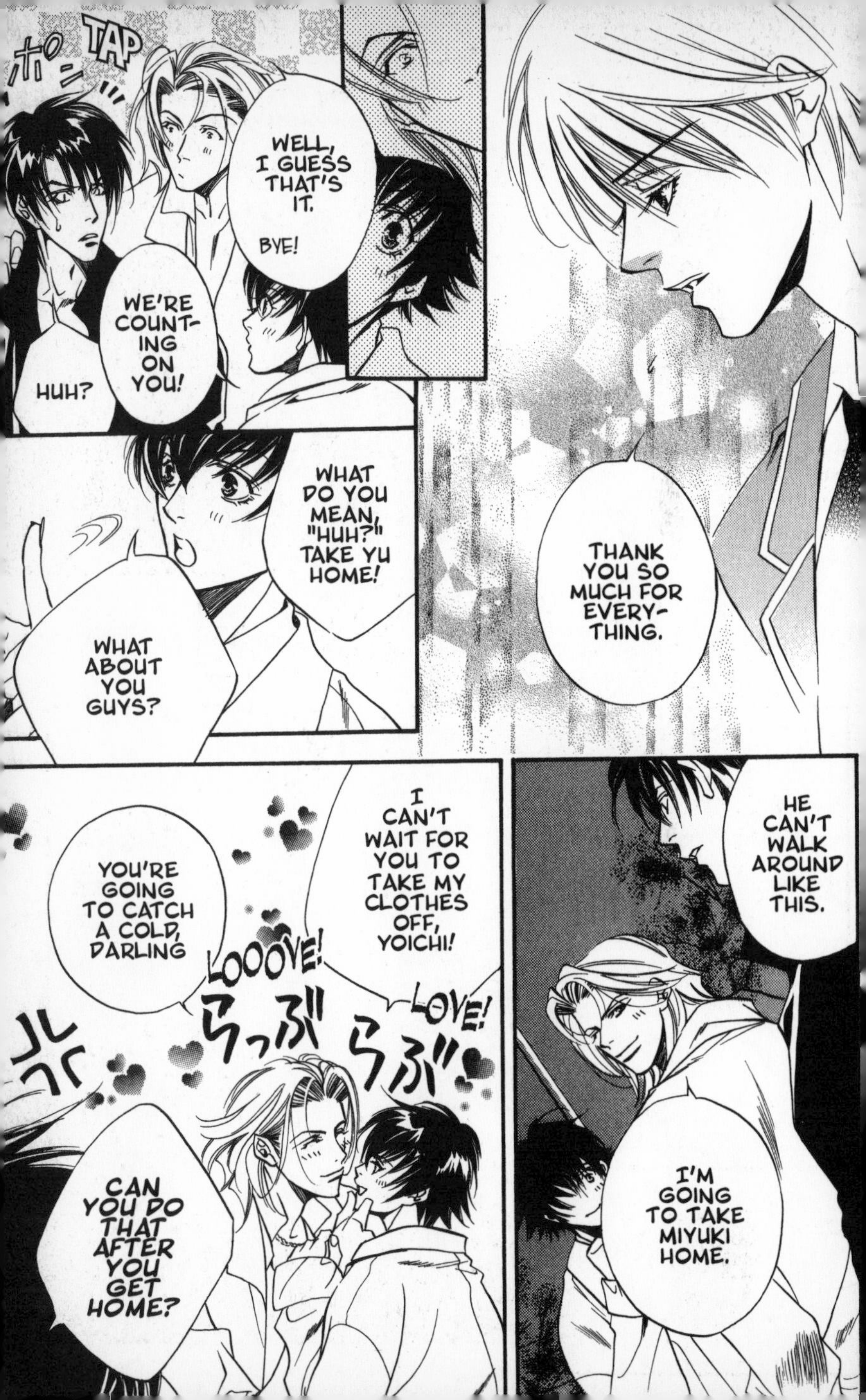
THANK YOU SO MUCH FOR EVERY-THING.
TAP
WELL, I GUESS THAT'S IT.
BYE!
WE'RE COUNT-ING ON YOU!
HUH?
WHAT DO YOU MEAN, "HUH?" TAKE YU HOME!
WHAT ABOUT YOU GUYS?
HE CAN'T WALK AROUND LIKE THIS.
I'M GOING TO TAKE MIYUKI HOME.
I CAN'T WAIT FOR YOU TO TAKE MY CLOTHES OFF, YOICHI!
YOU'RE GOING TO CATCH A COLD, DARLING
LOOOVE!
LOVE!
らっぶ らぶ
CAN YOU DO THAT AFTER YOU GET HOME?

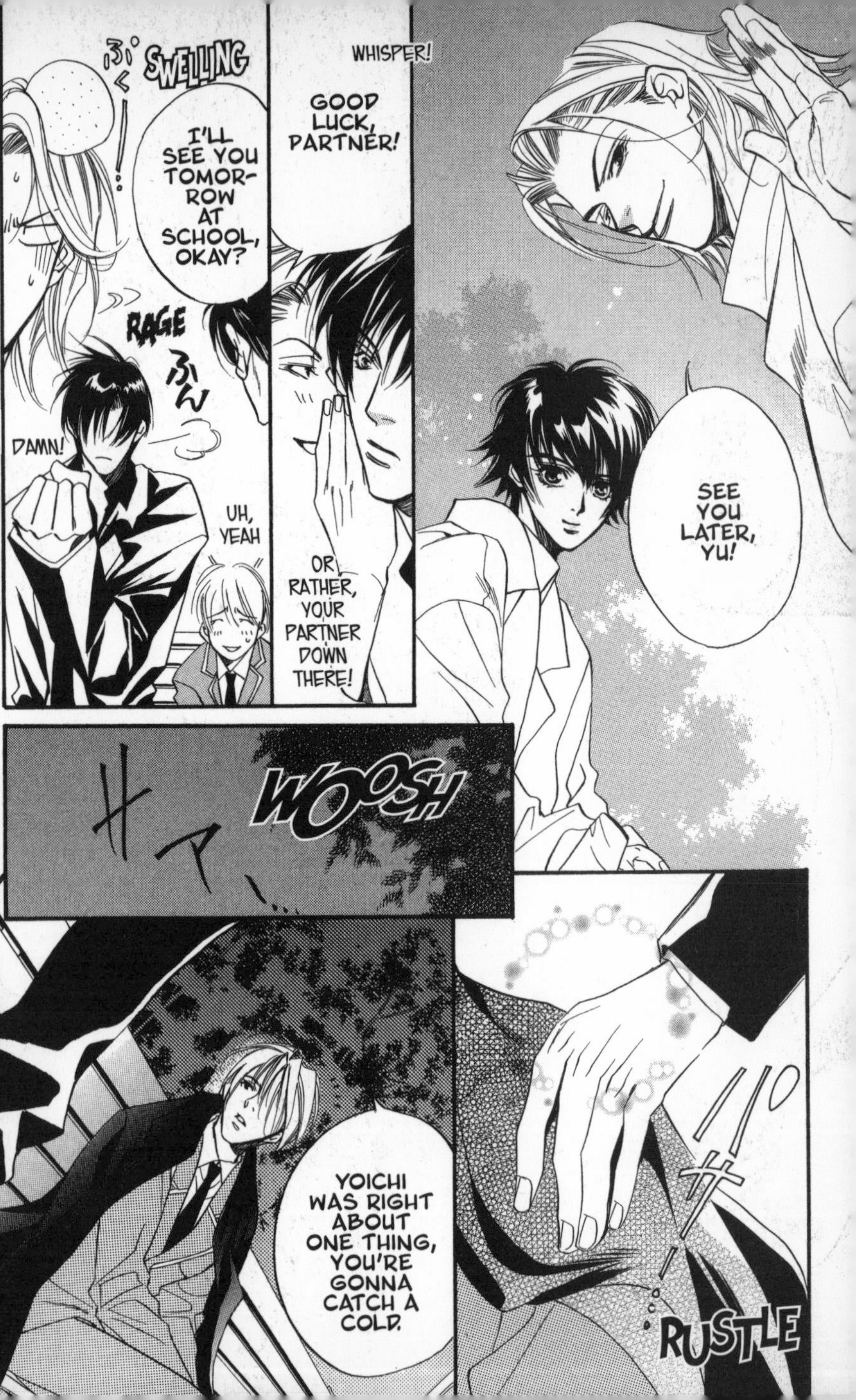
SEE YOU LATER, YU!
WHISPER!
GOOD LUCK, PARTNER!
OR RATHER, YOUR PARTNER DOWN THERE!
ふく
SWELLING
I'LL SEE YOU TOMORROW AT SCHOOL, OKAY?
RAGE
ふん
DAMN!
UH, YEAH
サァ…
WOOSH
パサ
RUSTLE
YOICHI WAS RIGHT ABOUT ONE THING, YOU'RE GONNA CATCH A COLD.

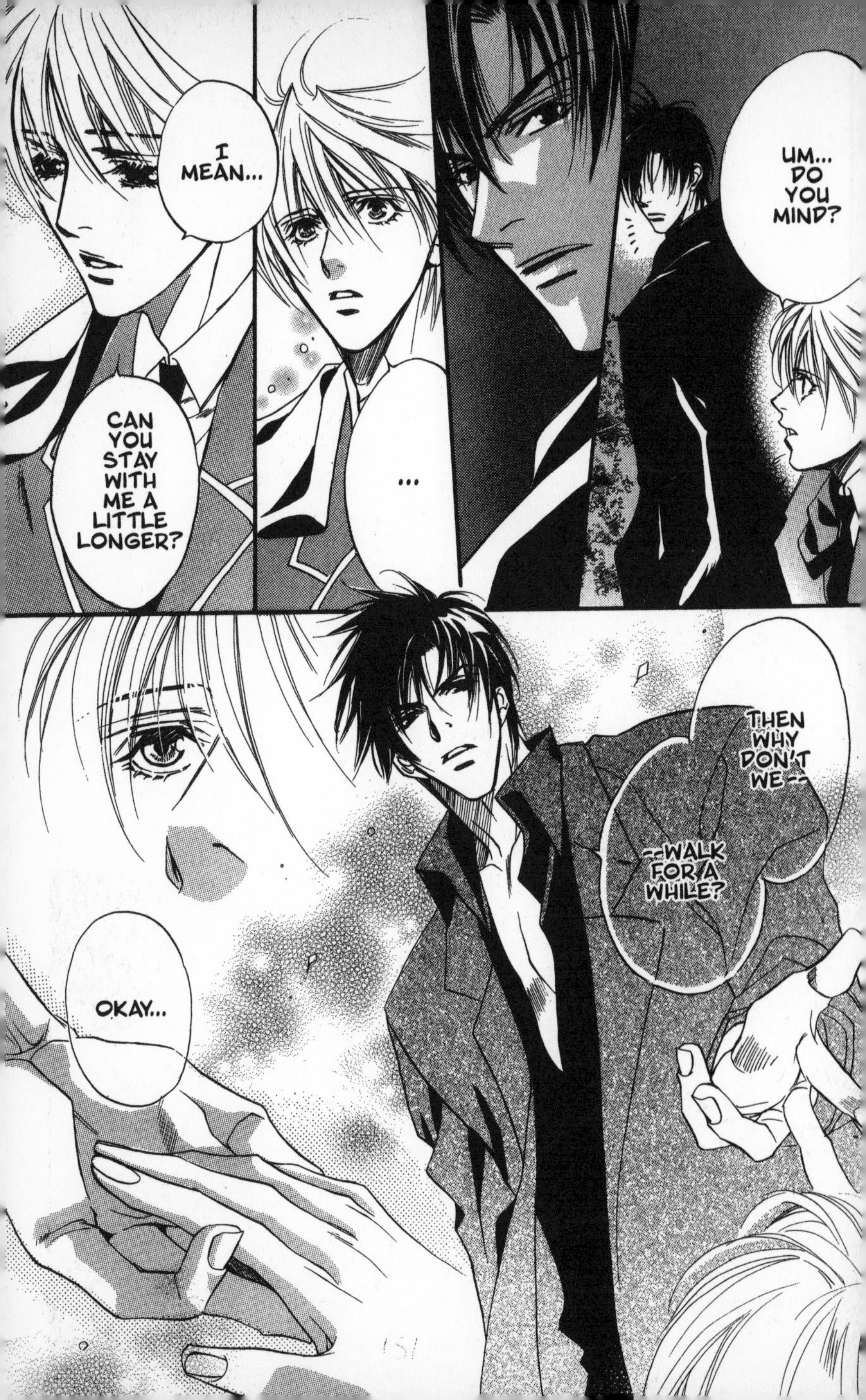
UM... DO YOU MIND?
...
I MEAN...
CAN YOU STAY WITH ME A LITTLE LONGER?
THEN WHY DON'T WE --
--WALK FOR A WHILE?
OKAY...

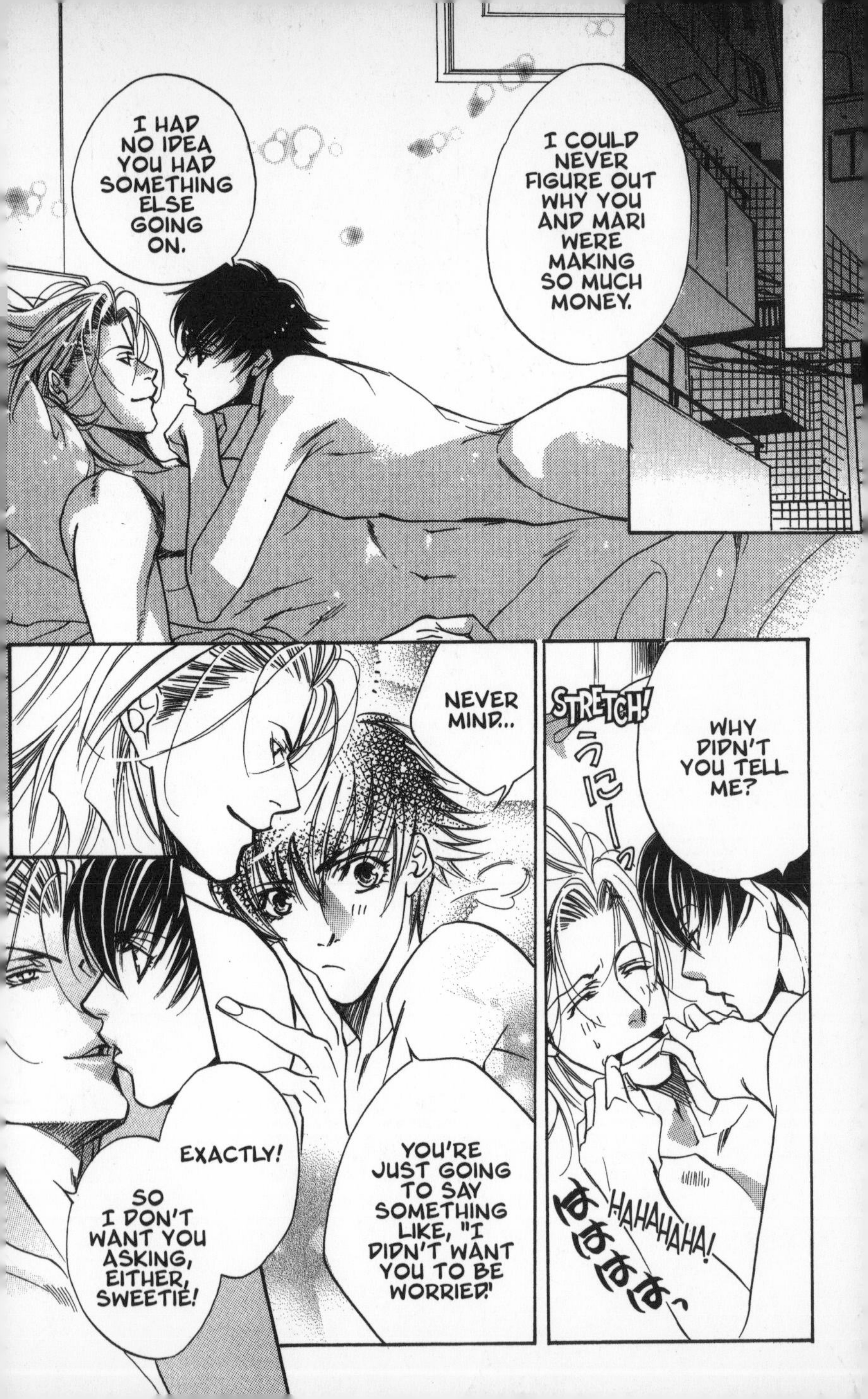
I COULD NEVER FIGURE OUT WHY YOU AND MARI WERE MAKING SO MUCH MONEY.
I HAD NO IDEA YOU HAD SOMETHING ELSE GOING ON.
WHY DIDN'T YOU TELL ME?
STRETCH!
うにー
HAHAHAHA!
ははははは〜
NEVER MIND...
YOU'RE JUST GOING TO SAY SOMETHING LIKE, "I DIDN'T WANT YOU TO BE WORRIED!'
EXACTLY!
SO I DON'T WANT YOU ASKING, EITHER, SWEETIE!

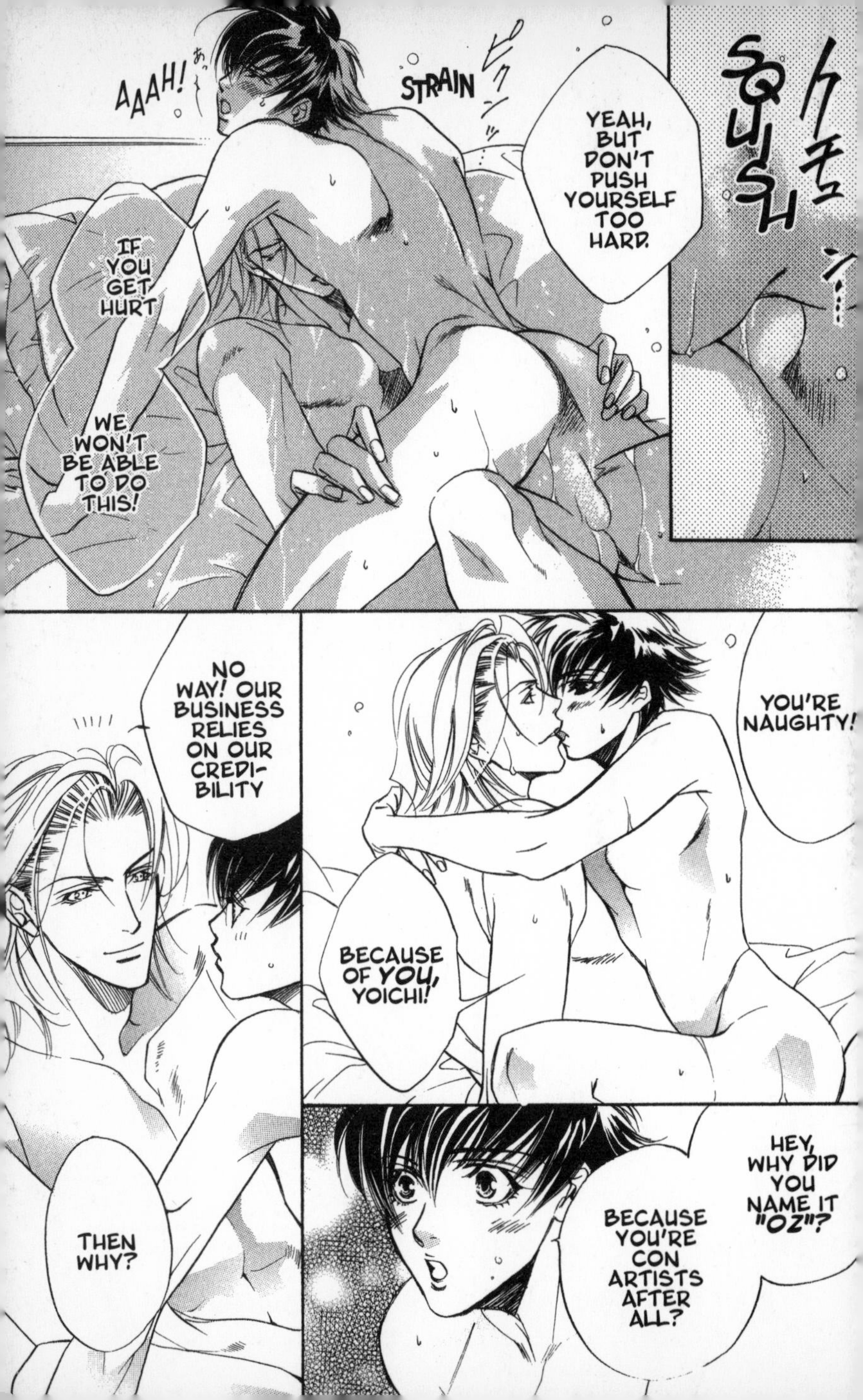
SQUISH
クチュ
STRAIN
ビクン
YEAH, BUT DON'T PUSH YOURSELF TOO HARD.
AAAH!
あっ
IF YOU GET HURT
WE WON'T BE ABLE TO DO THIS!
YOU'RE NAUGHTY!
BECAUSE OF YOU, YOICHI!
HEY, WHY DID YOU NAME IT "OZ"?
BECAUSE YOU'RE CON ARTISTS AFTER ALL?
NO WAY! OUR BUSINESS RELIES ON OUR CREDIBILITY
THEN WHY?

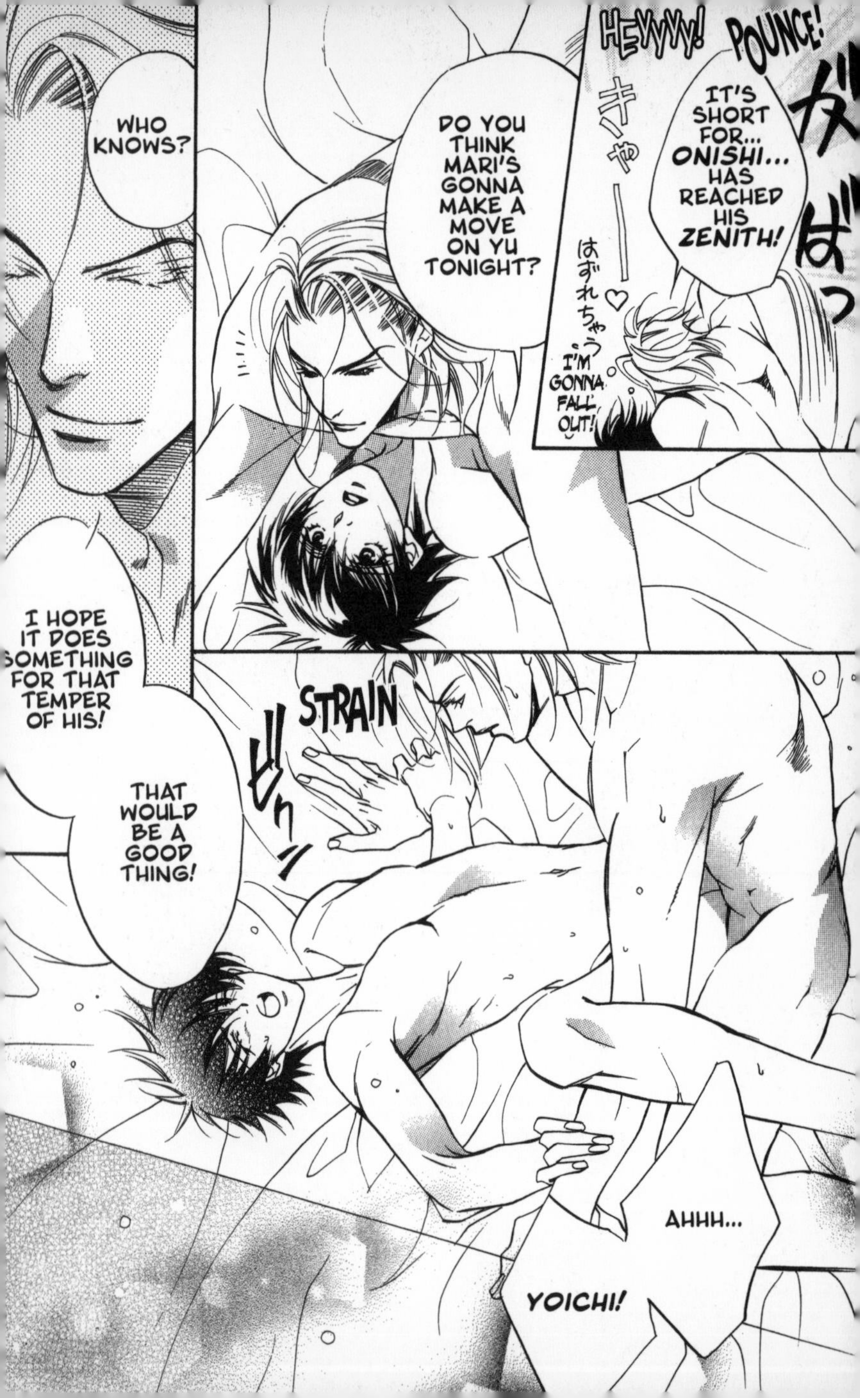
HEYYYY!
POUNCE!
がばっ
IT'S SHORT FOR... ONISHI... HAS REACHED HIS ZENITH!
キャー♡
はずれちゃう
I'M GONNA FALL OUT!
DO YOU THINK MARI'S GONNA MAKE A MOVE ON YU TONIGHT?
WHO KNOWS?
I HOPE IT DOES SOMETHING FOR THAT TEMPER OF HIS!
THAT WOULD BE A GOOD THING!
STRAIN
AHHH...
YOICHI!

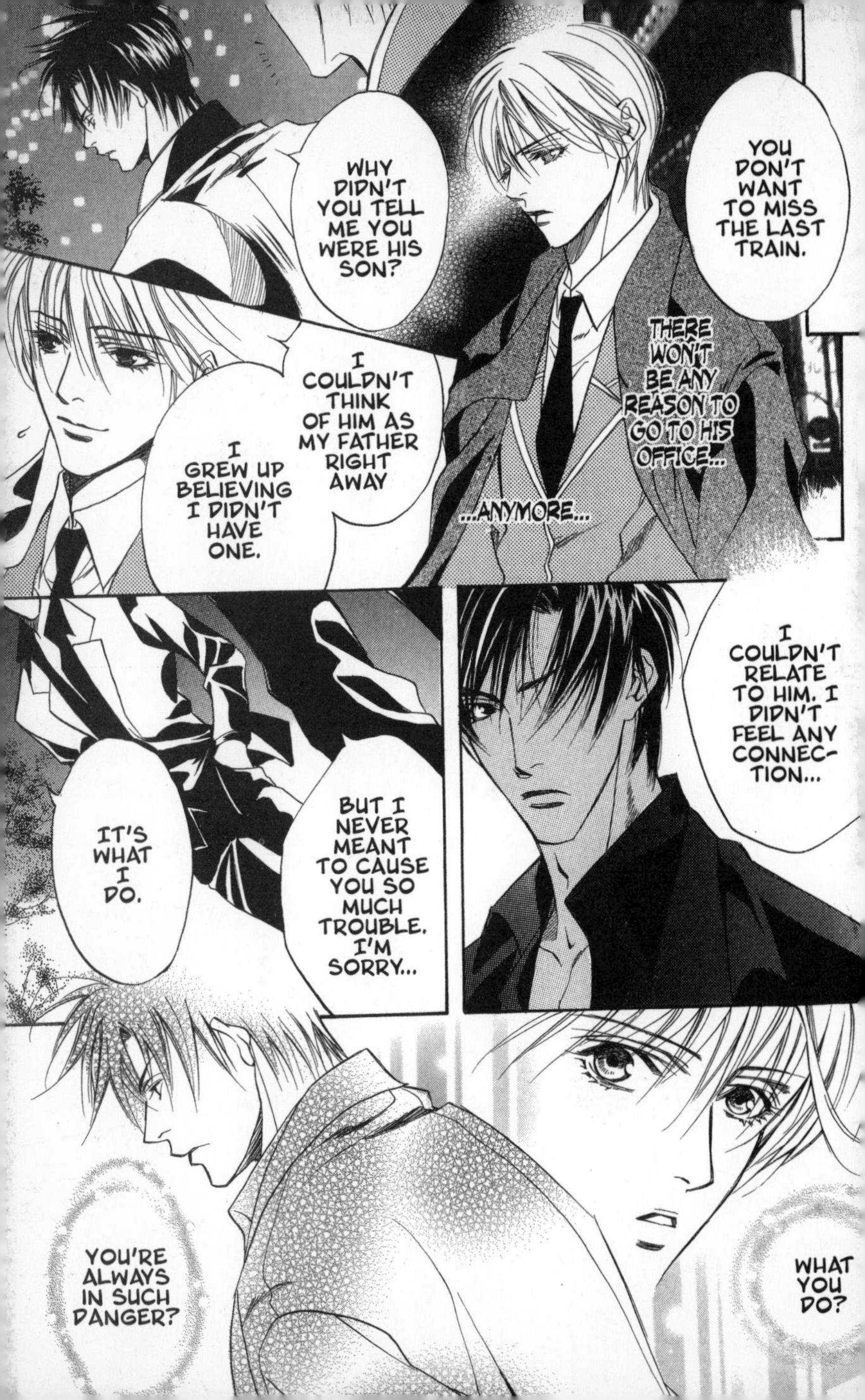
YOU DON'T WANT TO MISS THE LAST TRAIN.
THERE WON'T BE ANY REASON TO GO TO HIS OFFICE...
...ANYMORE...
WHY DIDN'T YOU TELL ME YOU WERE HIS SON?
I COULDN'T THINK OF HIM AS MY FATHER RIGHT AWAY
I GREW UP BELIEVING I DIDN'T HAVE ONE.
I COULDN'T RELATE TO HIM. I DIDN'T FEEL ANY CONNEC-TION...
BUT I NEVER MEANT TO CAUSE YOU SO MUCH TROUBLE. I'M SORRY...
IT'S WHAT I DO.
WHAT YOU DO?
YOU'RE ALWAYS IN SUCH DANGER?

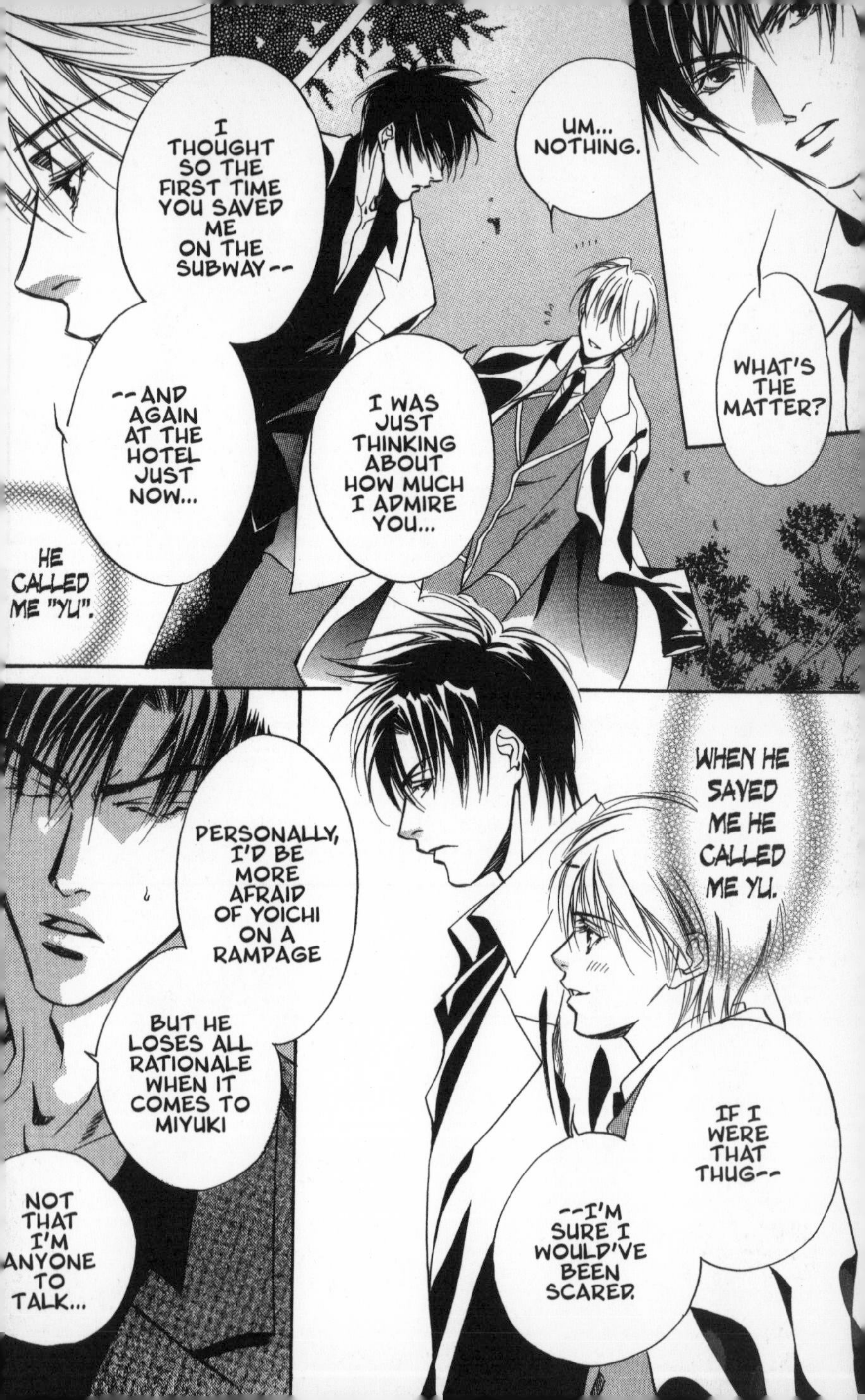

WHAT'S THE MATTER?
UM... NOTHING.
....
I WAS JUST THINKING ABOUT HOW MUCH I ADMIRE YOU...
I THOUGHT SO THE FIRST TIME YOU SAVED ME ON THE SUBWAY--
--AND AGAIN AT THE HOTEL JUST NOW...
HE CALLED ME "YU".
WHEN HE SAVED ME HE CALLED ME YU.
IF I WERE THAT THUG--
--I'M SURE I WOULD'VE BEEN SCARED.
PERSONALLY, I'D BE MORE AFRAID OF YOICHI ON A RAMPAGE
BUT HE LOSES ALL RATIONALE WHEN IT COMES TO MIYUKI
NOT THAT I'M ANYONE TO TALK...

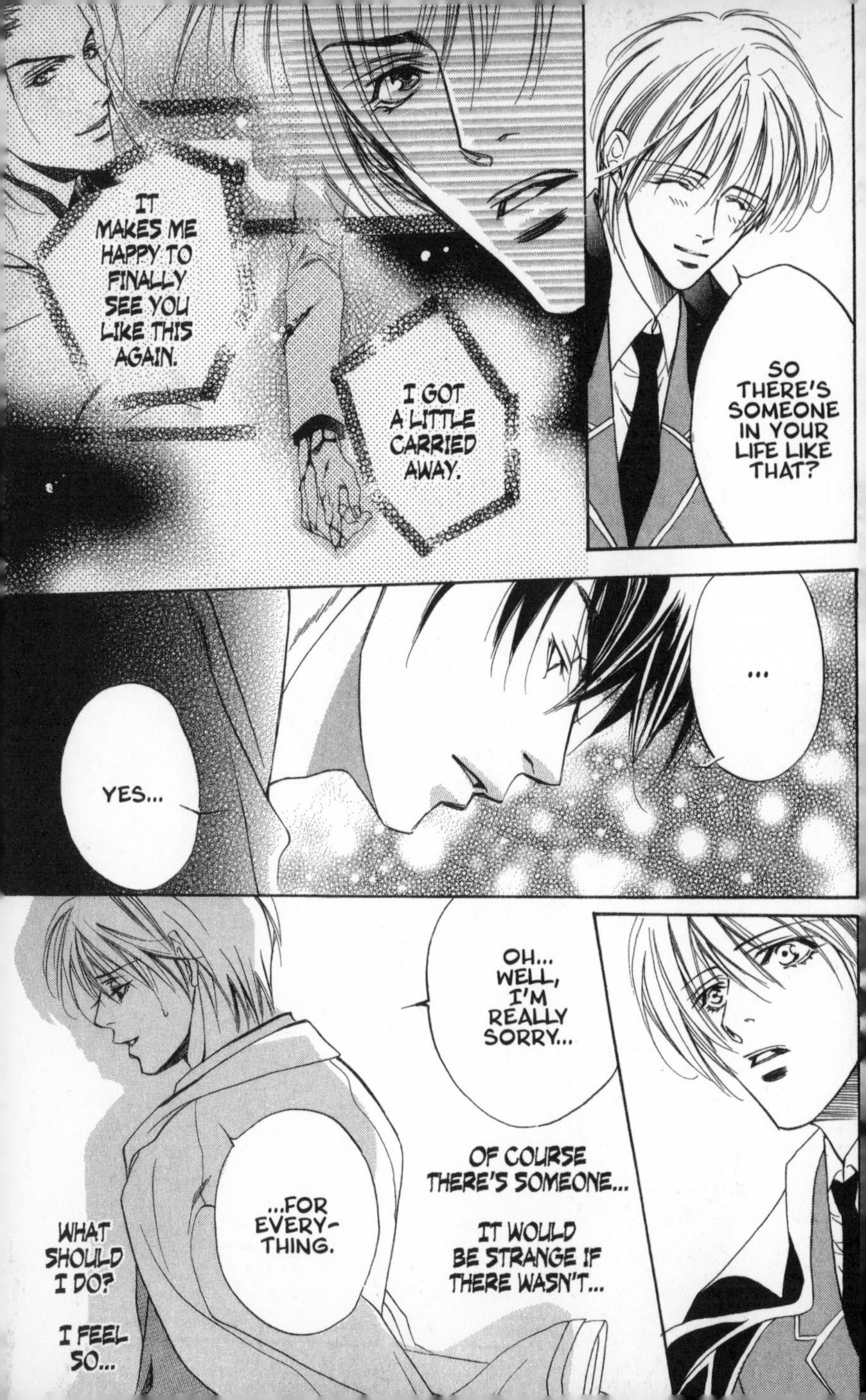
SO THERE'S SOMEONE IN YOUR LIFE LIKE THAT?
I GOT A LITTLE CARRIED AWAY.
IT MAKES ME HAPPY TO FINALLY SEE YOU LIKE THIS AGAIN.
...
YES...
OH... WELL, I'M REALLY SORRY...
...FOR EVERY-THING.
OF COURSE THERE'S SOMEONE...
IT WOULD BE STRANGE IF THERE WASN'T...
WHAT SHOULD I DO?
I FEEL SO...

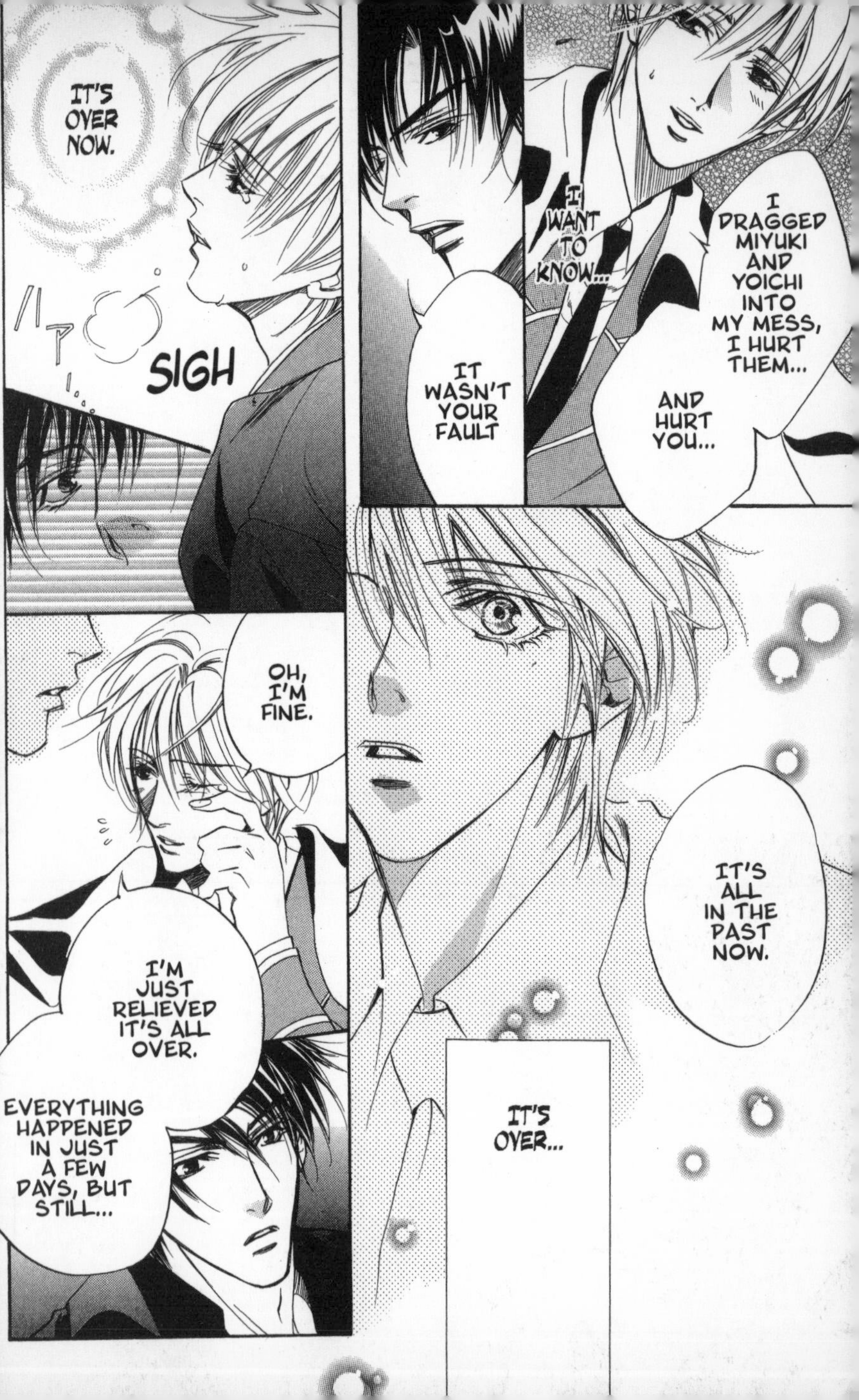
I DRAGGED MIYUKI AND YOICHI INTO MY MESS, I HURT THEM...
I WANT TO KNOW...
AND HURT YOU...
IT WASN'T YOUR FAULT
IT'S OVER NOW.
ハア
SIGH
IT'S ALL IN THE PAST NOW.
IT'S OVER...
OH, I'M FINE.
I'M JUST RELIEVED IT'S ALL OVER.
EVERYTHING HAPPENED IN JUST A FEW DAYS, BUT STILL...

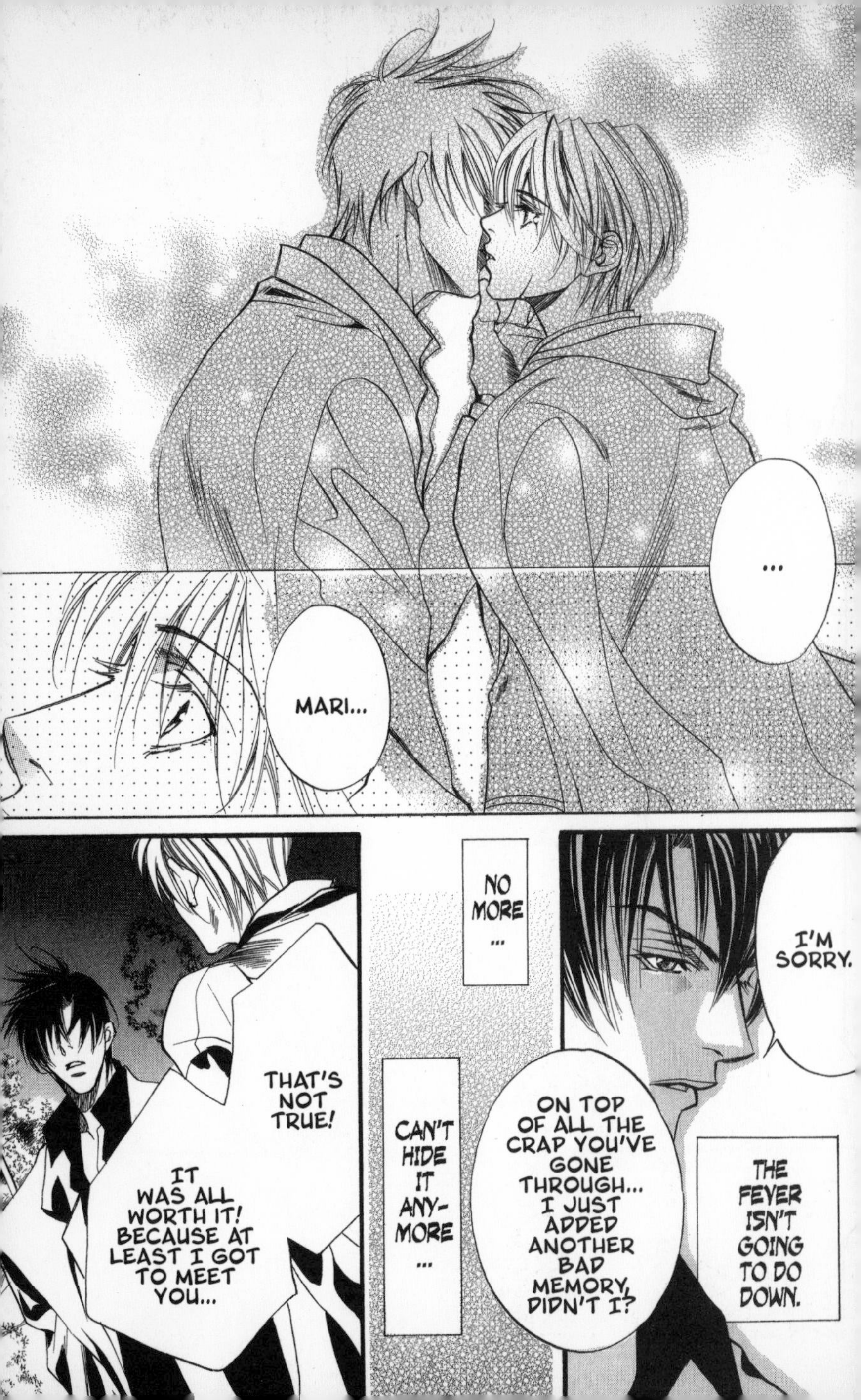
...
MARI...
I'M SORRY.
THE FEVER ISN'T GOING TO DO DOWN.
ON TOP OF ALL THE CRAP YOU'VE GONE THROUGH... I JUST ADDED ANOTHER BAD MEMORY, DIDN'T I?
NO MORE ...
CAN'T HIDE IT ANY-MORE ...
THAT'S NOT TRUE!
IT WAS ALL WORTH IT! BECAUSE AT LEAST I GOT TO MEET YOU...

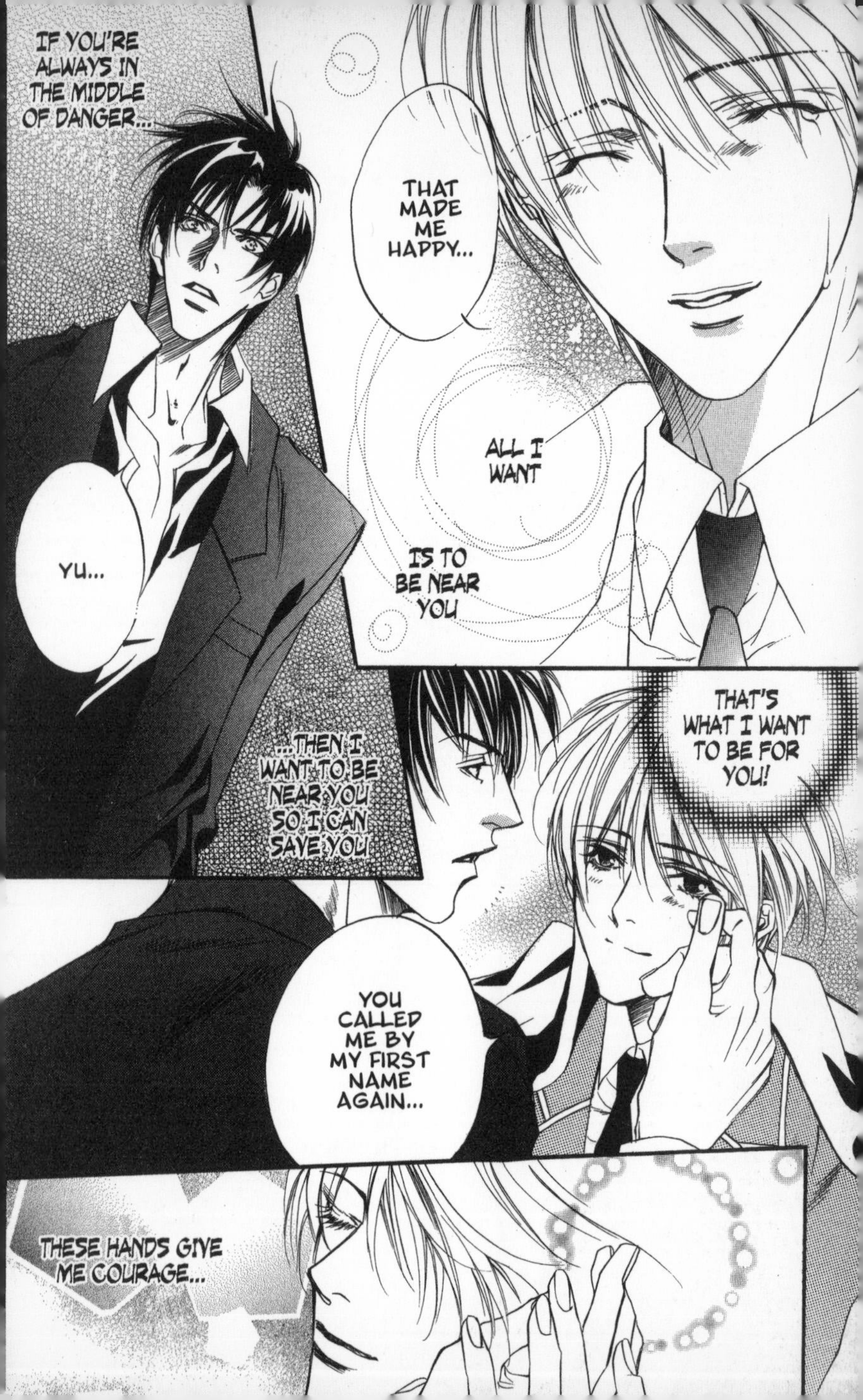
THAT MADE ME HAPPY...
ALL I WANT
IS TO BE NEAR YOU
IF YOU'RE ALWAYS IN THE MIDDLE OF DANGER...
YU...
...THEN I WANT TO BE NEAR YOU SO I CAN SAVE YOU
THAT'S WHAT I WANT TO BE FOR YOU!
YOU CALLED ME BY MY FIRST NAME AGAIN...
THESE HANDS GIVE ME COURAGE...

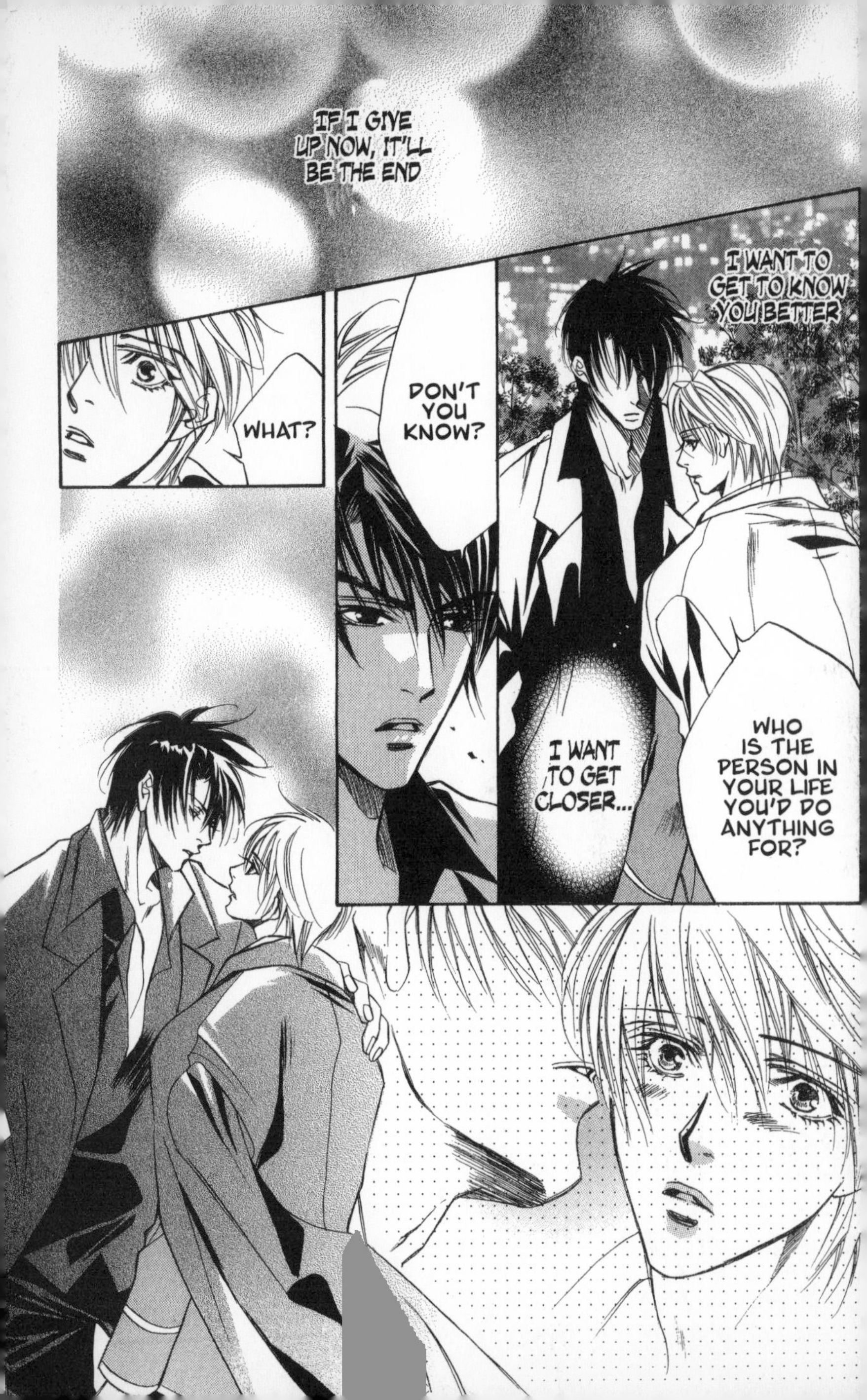
IF I GIVE UP NOW, IT'LL BE THE END
I WANT TO GET TO KNOW YOU BETTER
WHO IS THE PERSON IN YOUR LIFE YOU'D DO ANYTHING FOR?
I WANT TO GET CLOSER...
DON'T YOU KNOW?
WHAT?

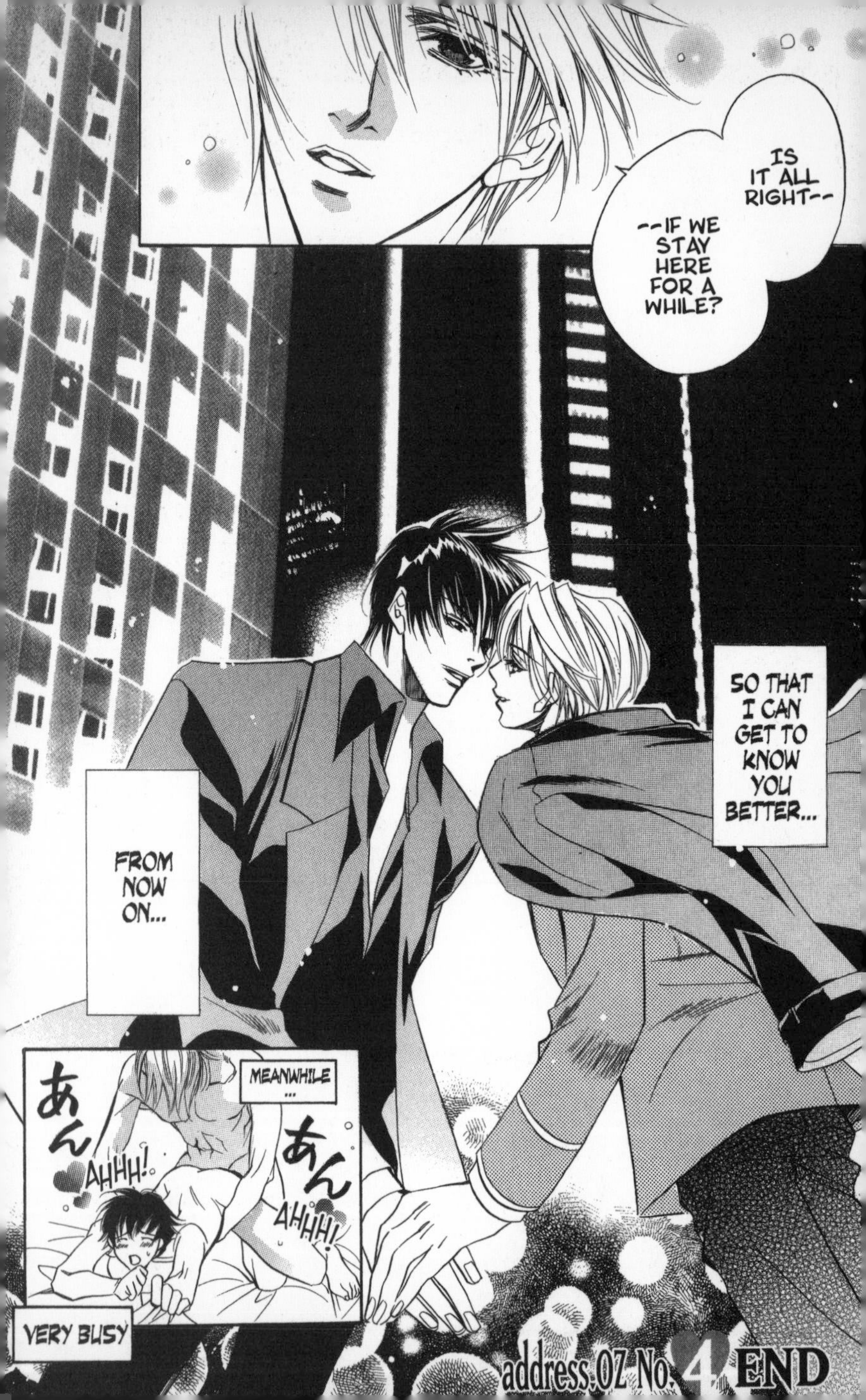
IS IT ALL RIGHT--
--IF WE STAY HERE FOR A WHILE?
SO THAT I CAN GET TO KNOW YOU BETTER...
FROM NOW ON...
MEANWHILE ...
あん
AHHH!
あん
AHHH!
VERY BUSY
address.OZ No.4 END

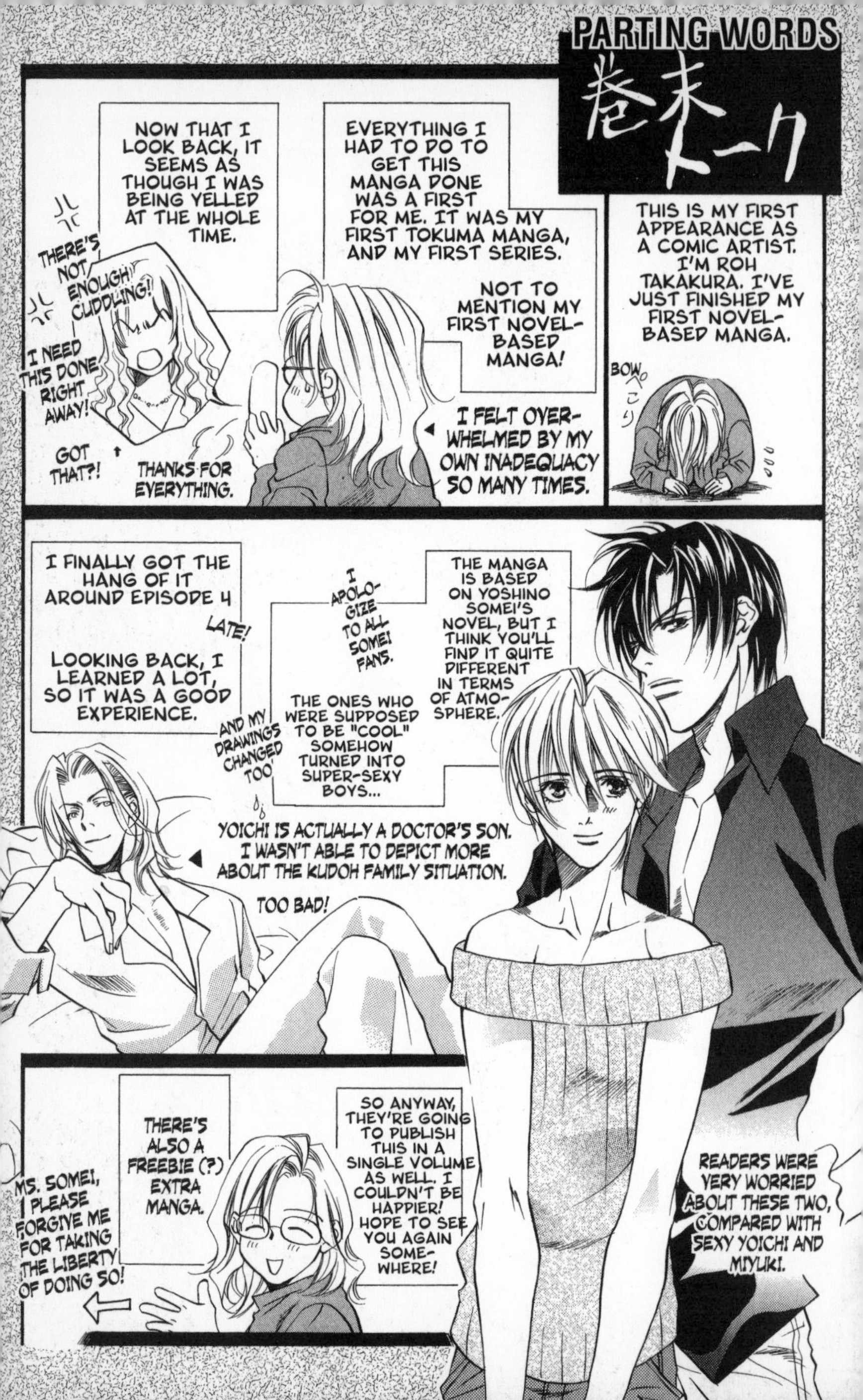
PARTING WORDS
巻末トーク
THIS IS MY FIRST APPEARANCE AS A COMIC ARTIST. I'M ROH TAKAKURA. I'VE JUST FINISHED MY FIRST NOVEL-BASED MANGA.
BOW
ペこり
EVERYTHING I HAD TO DO TO GET THIS MANGA DONE WAS A FIRST FOR ME. IT WAS MY FIRST TOKUMA MANGA, AND MY FIRST SERIES.
NOT TO MENTION MY FIRST NOVEL-BASED MANGA!
I FELT OVER-WHELMED BY MY OWN INADEQUACY SO MANY TIMES.
NOW THAT I LOOK BACK, IT SEEMS AS THOUGH I WAS BEING YELLED AT THE WHOLE TIME.
THERE'S NOT ENOUGH CUDDLING!
I NEED THIS DONE RIGHT AWAY!
GOT THAT?!
THANKS FOR EVERYTHING.
THE MANGA IS BASED ON YOSHINO SOMEI'S NOVEL, BUT I THINK YOU'LL FIND IT QUITE DIFFERENT IN TERMS OF ATMO-SPHERE.
I APOLO-GIZE TO ALL SOMEI FANS.
THE ONES WHO WERE SUPPOSED TO BE "COOL" SOMEHOW TURNED INTO SUPER-SEXY BOYS...
AND MY DRAWINGS CHANGED TOO
I FINALLY GOT THE HANG OF IT AROUND EPISODE 4
LATE!
LOOKING BACK, I LEARNED A LOT, SO IT WAS A GOOD EXPERIENCE.
YOICHI IS ACTUALLY A DOCTOR'S SON. I WASN'T ABLE TO DEPICT MORE ABOUT THE KUDOH FAMILY SITUATION.
TOO BAD!
READERS WERE VERY WORRIED ABOUT THESE TWO, COMPARED WITH SEXY YOICHI AND MIYUKI.
SO ANYWAY, THEY'RE GOING TO PUBLISH THIS IN A SINGLE VOLUME AS WELL. I COULDN'T BE HAPPIER! HOPE TO SEE YOU AGAIN SOME-WHERE!
THERE'S ALSO A FREEBIE (?) EXTRA MANGA.
MS. SOMEI, PLEASE FORGIVE ME FOR TAKING THE LIBERTY OF DOING SO!

address.OZ SPECIAL

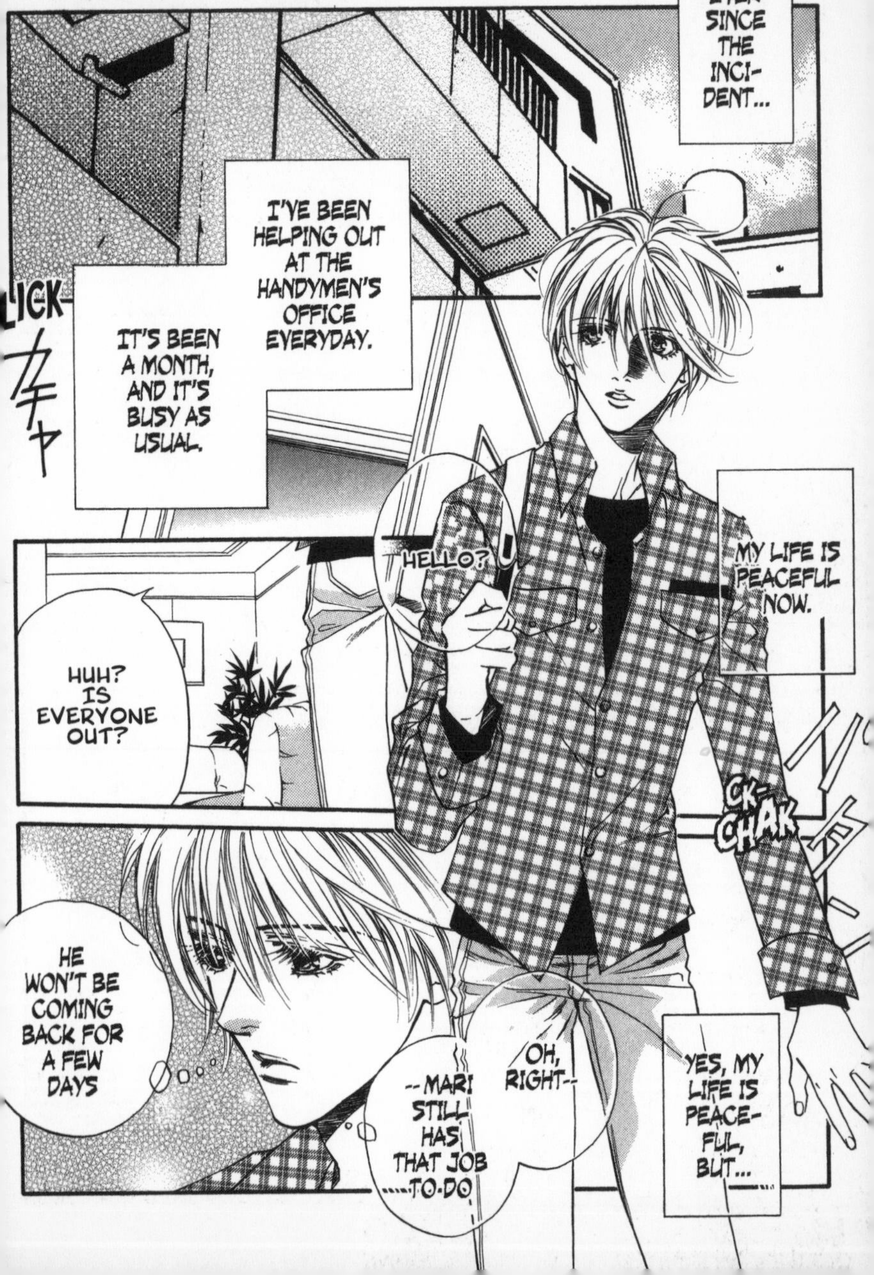
EVER SINCE THE INCI-DENT...
I'VE BEEN HELPING OUT AT THE HANDYMEN'S OFFICE EVERYDAY.
IT'S BEEN A MONTH, AND IT'S BUSY AS USUAL.
LICK-
カチャ
MY LIFE IS PEACEFUL NOW.
HELLO?
HUH? IS EVERYONE OUT?
CK-CHAK
OH, RIGHT--
--MARI STILL HAS THAT JOB TO DO
HE WON'T BE COMING BACK FOR A FEW DAYS
YES, MY LIFE IS PEACE-FUL, BUT...

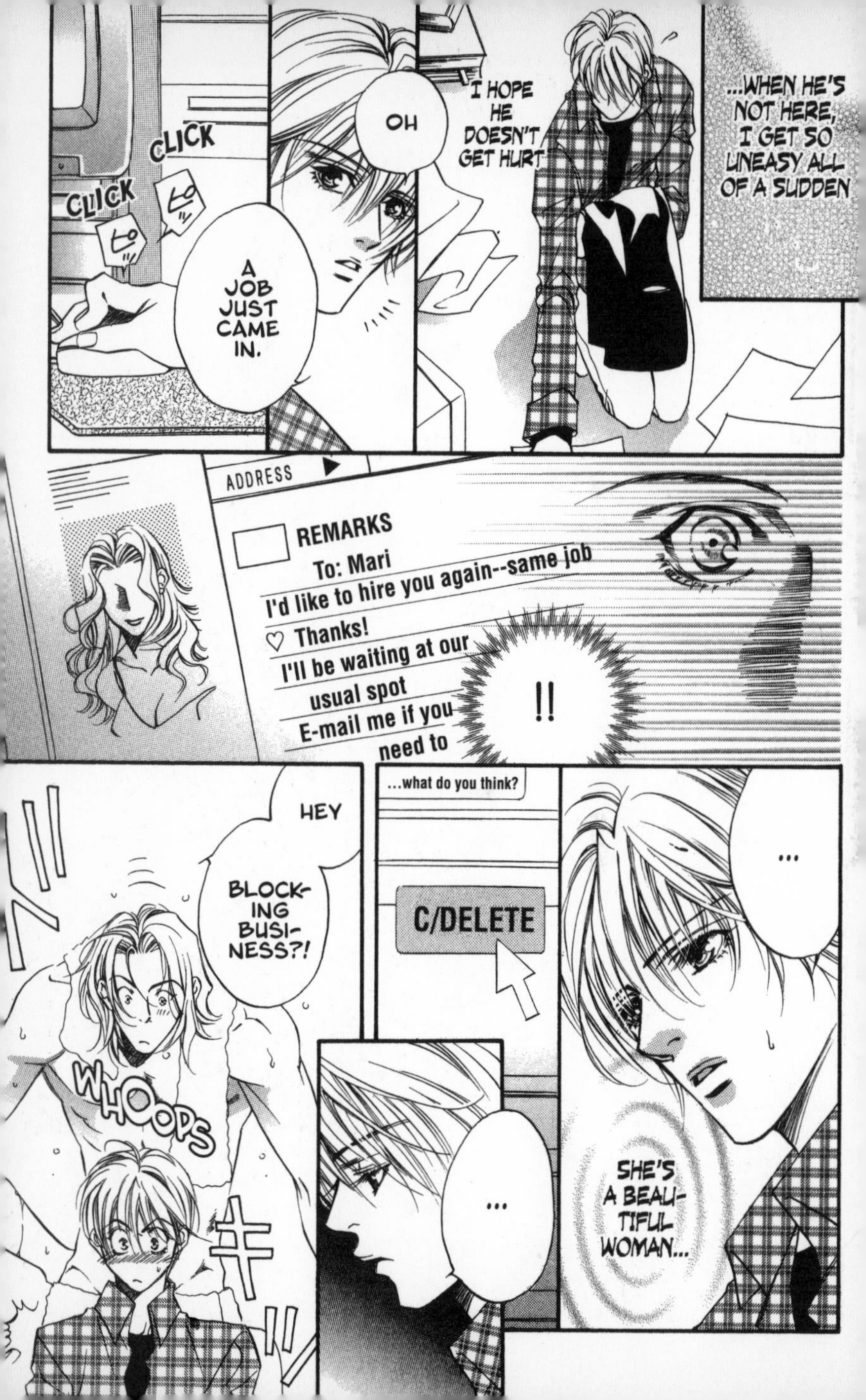

...WHEN HE'S NOT HERE, I GET SO UNEASY ALL OF A SUDDEN
I HOPE HE DOESN'T GET HURT
OH
A JOB JUST CAME IN.
CLICK
CLICK
ADDRESS
REMARKS
To: Mari
I'd like to hire you again--same job
♡ Thanks!
I'll be waiting at our usual spot
E-mail me if you need to
!!
...
SHE'S A BEAUTIFUL WOMAN...
...what do you think?
C/DELETE
...
HEY
BLOCKING BUSINESS?!
WHOOPS

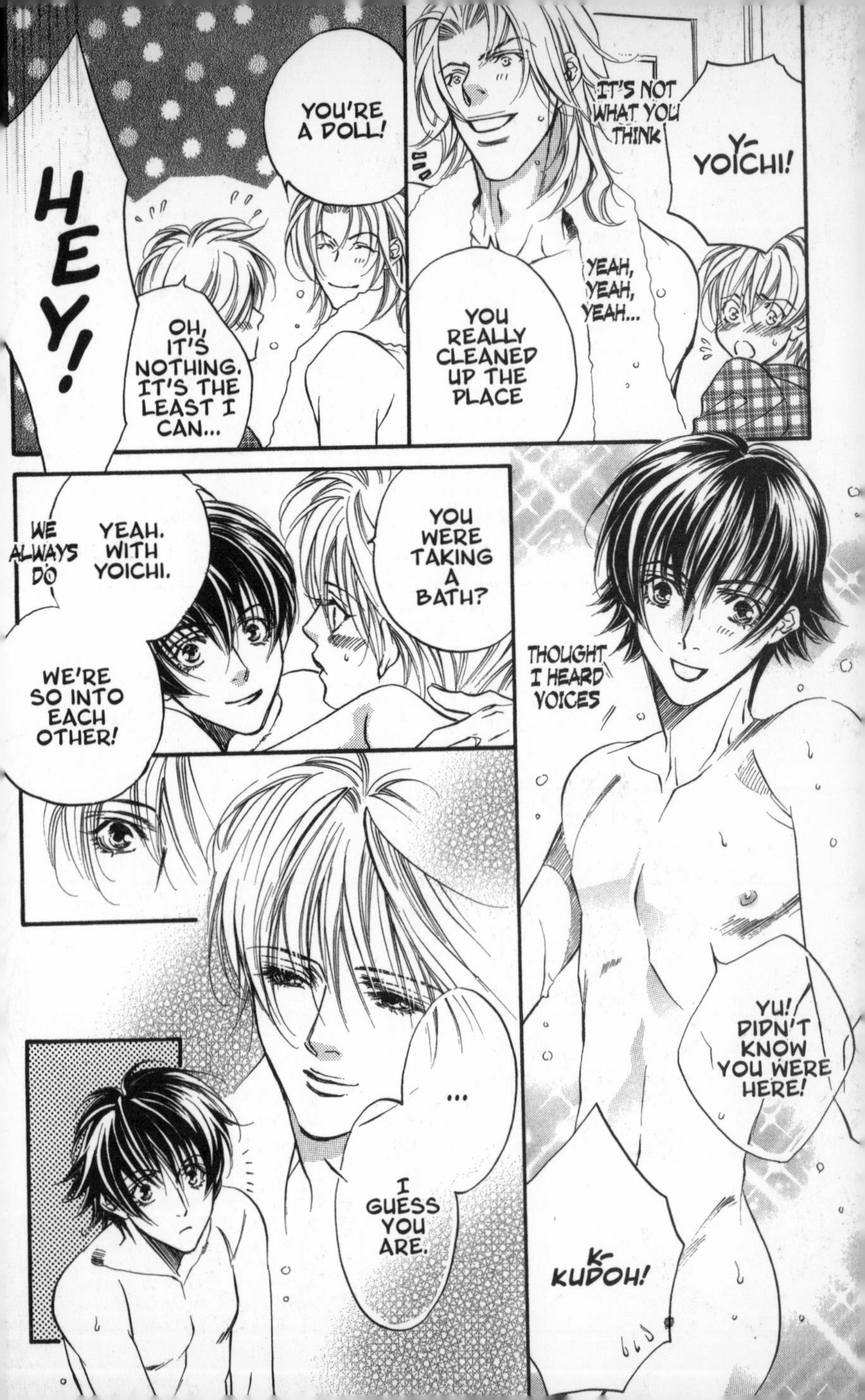
Y-YOICHI!
IT'S NOT WHAT YOU THINK
YEAH, YEAH, YEAH...
YOU REALLY CLEANED UP THE PLACE
YOU'RE A DOLL!
OH, IT'S NOTHING. IT'S THE LEAST I CAN...
HEY!
THOUGHT I HEARD VOICES
YU! DIDN'T KNOW YOU WERE HERE!
K-KUDOH!
YOU WERE TAKING A BATH?
YEAH. WITH YOICHI.
WE ALWAYS DO
WE'RE SO INTO EACH OTHER!
...
I GUESS YOU ARE.

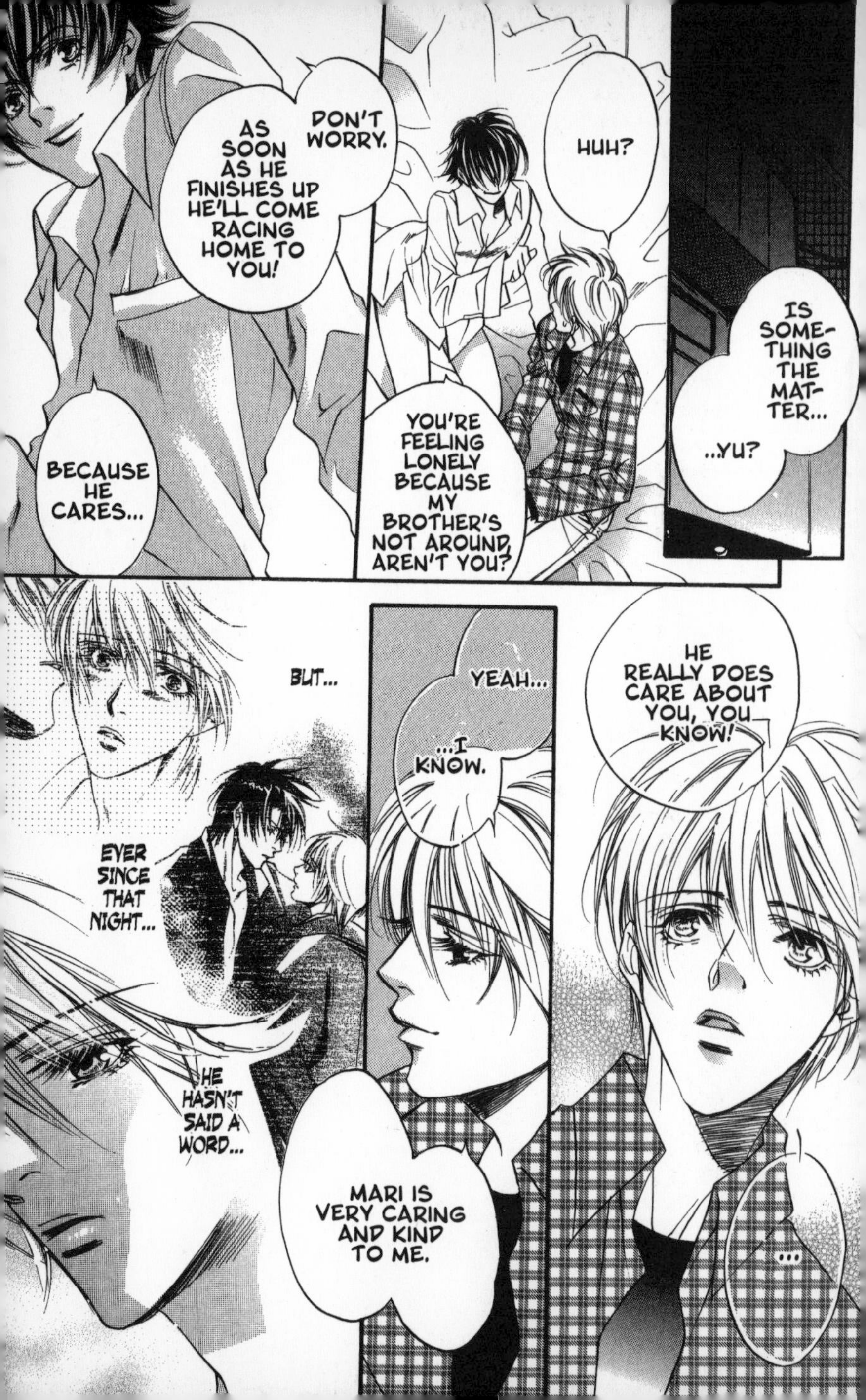
IS SOMETHING THE MATTER...
...YU?
HUH?
YOU'RE FEELING LONELY BECAUSE MY BROTHER'S NOT AROUND, AREN'T YOU?
DON'T WORRY.
AS SOON AS HE FINISHES UP HE'LL COME RACING HOME TO YOU!
BECAUSE HE CARES...
HE REALLY DOES CARE ABOUT YOU, YOU KNOW!
...
YEAH...
...I KNOW.
MARI IS VERY CARING AND KIND TO ME.
BUT...
EVER SINCE THAT NIGHT...
HE HASN'T SAID A WORD...

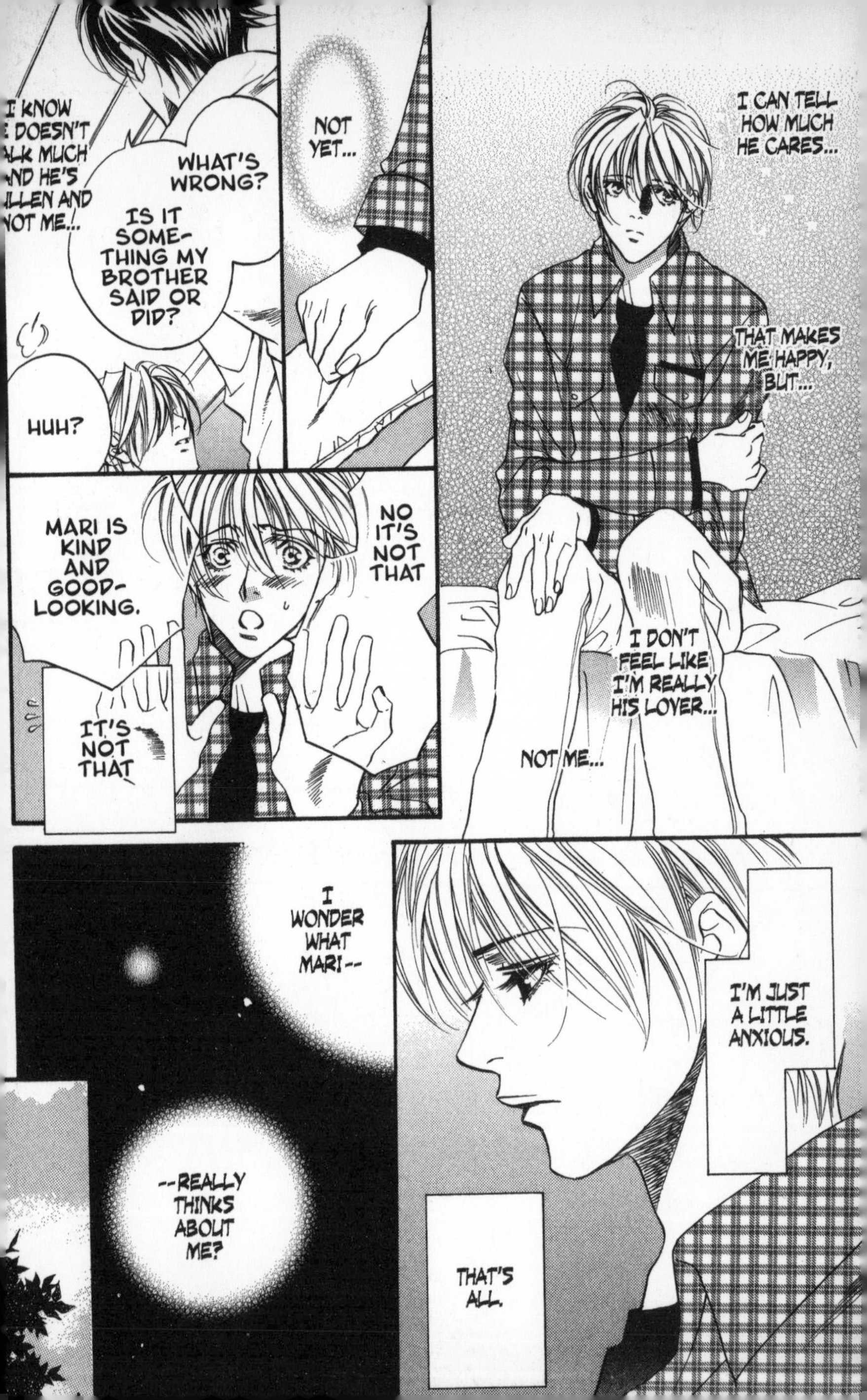
I CAN TELL HOW MUCH HE CARES...
THAT MAKES ME HAPPY, BUT...
I DON'T FEEL LIKE I'M REALLY HIS LOVER...
NOT ME...
NOT YET...
WHAT'S WRONG?
IS IT SOMETHING MY BROTHER SAID OR DID?
I KNOW E DOESN'T ALK MUCH ND HE'S ULLEN AND NOT ME...
HUH?
NO IT'S NOT THAT
MARI IS KIND AND GOOD-LOOKING.
IT'S NOT THAT
I'M JUST A LITTLE ANXIOUS.
THAT'S ALL.
I WONDER WHAT MARI--
--REALLY THINKS ABOUT ME?

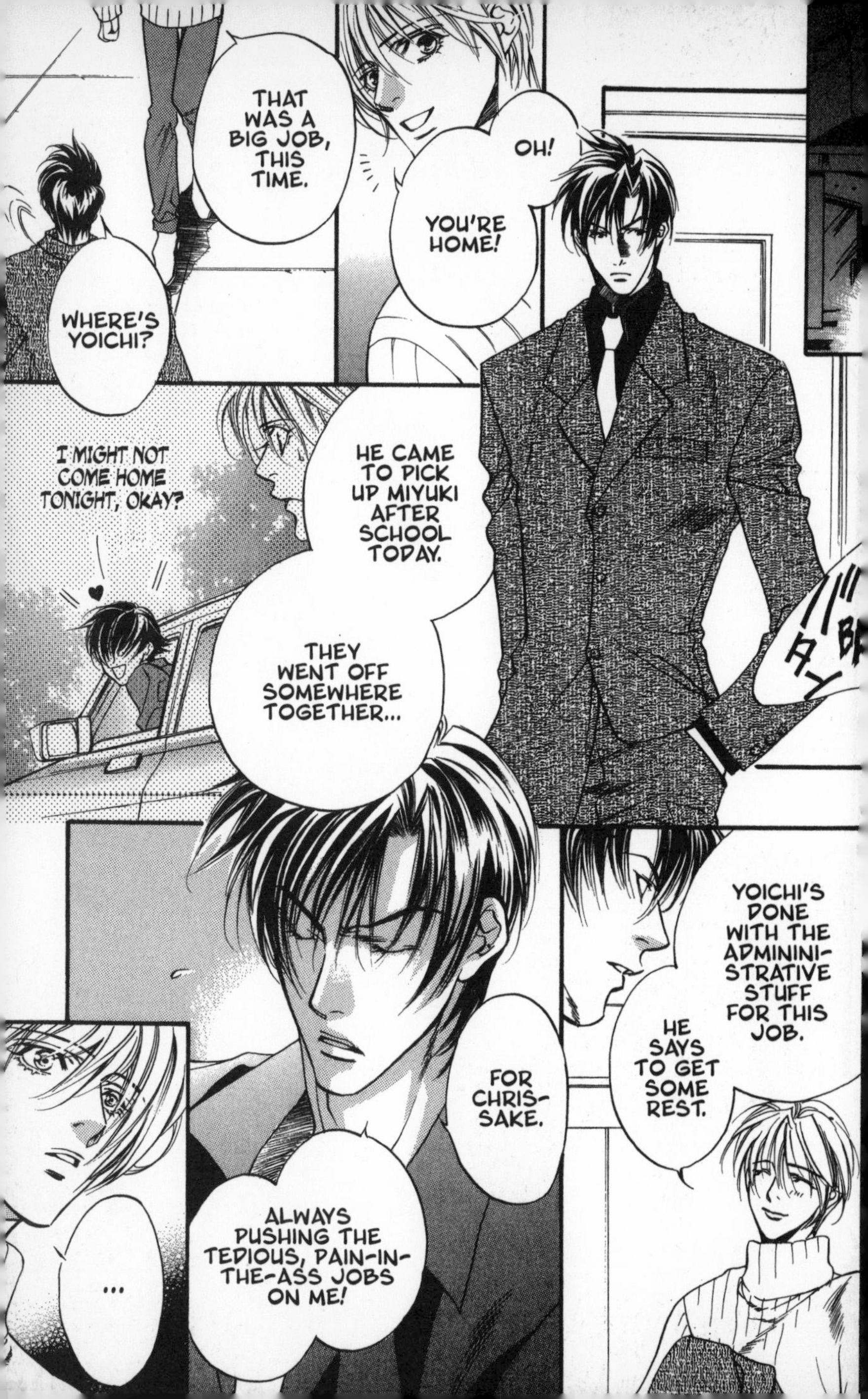
OH!
YOU'RE HOME!
THAT WAS A BIG JOB, THIS TIME.
WHERE'S YOICHI?
バタ BA
HE CAME TO PICK UP MIYUKI AFTER SCHOOL TODAY.
THEY WENT OFF SOMEWHERE TOGETHER...
I MIGHT NOT COME HOME TONIGHT, OKAY?
YOICHI'S DONE WITH THE ADMININISTRATIVE STUFF FOR THIS JOB.
HE SAYS TO GET SOME REST.
FOR CHRIS-SAKE.
ALWAYS PUSHING THE TEDIOUS, PAIN-IN-THE-ASS JOBS ON ME!
...

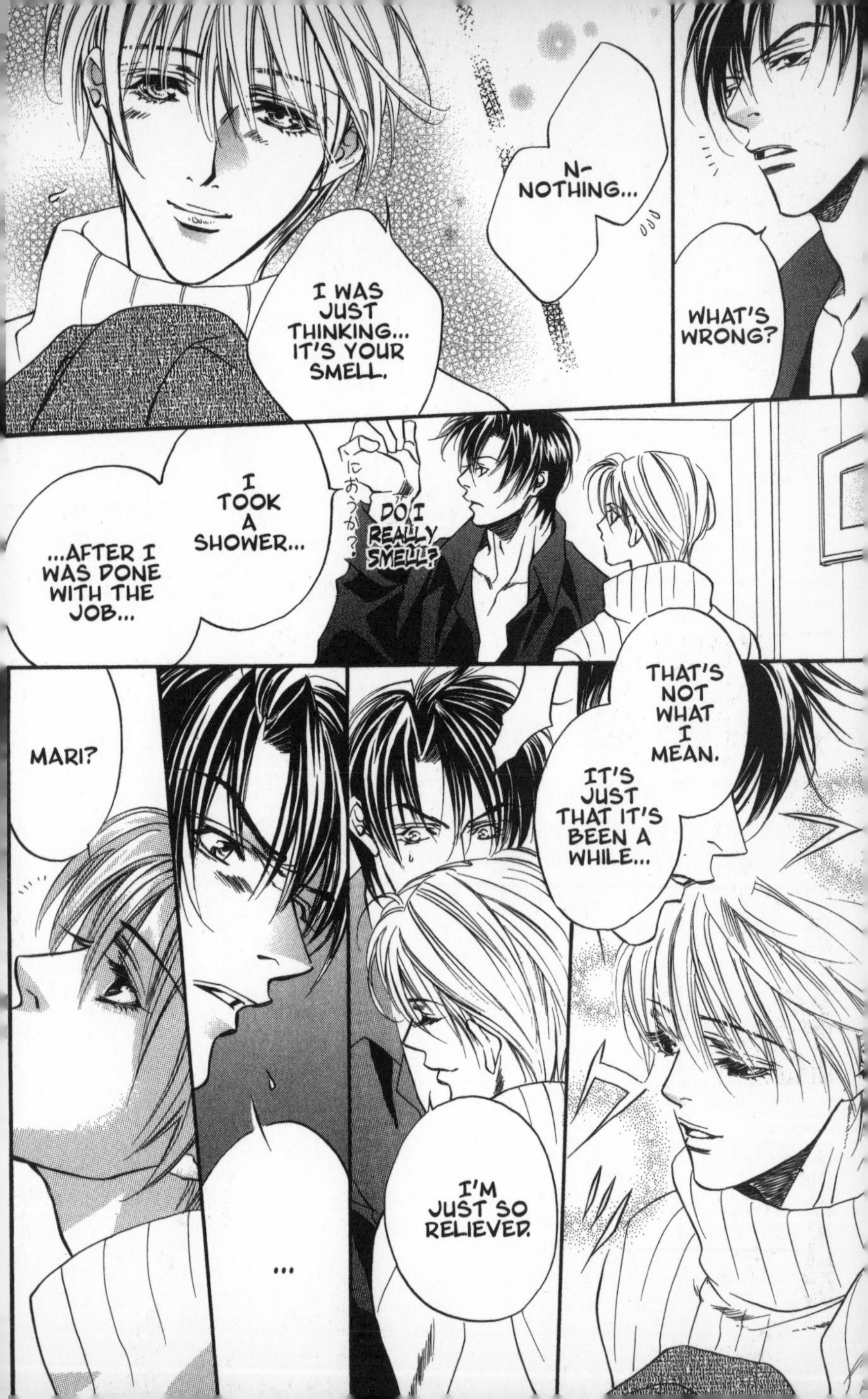
WHAT'S WRONG?
N-NOTHING...
I WAS JUST THINKING... IT'S YOUR SMELL.
におうか？
DO I REALLY SMELL?
I TOOK A SHOWER...
...AFTER I WAS DONE WITH THE JOB...
THAT'S NOT WHAT I MEAN.
IT'S JUST THAT IT'S BEEN A WHILE...
I'M JUST SO RELIEVED.
...
MARI?

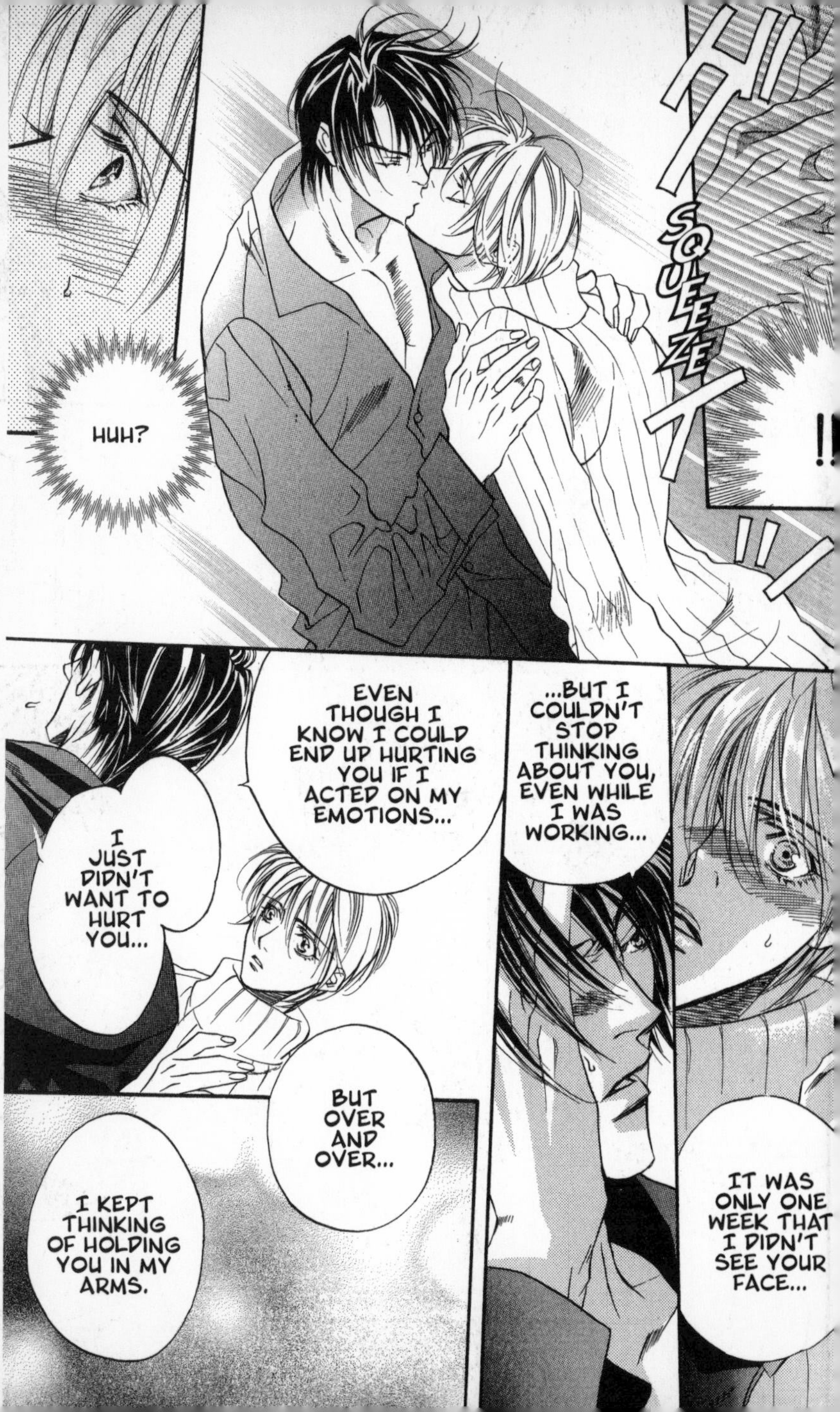

!!
SQUEEZE
HUH?
IT WAS ONLY ONE WEEK THAT I DIDN'T SEE YOUR FACE...
...BUT I COULDN'T STOP THINKING ABOUT YOU, EVEN WHILE I WAS WORKING...
I JUST DIDN'T WANT TO HURT YOU...
EVEN THOUGH I KNOW I COULD END UP HURTING YOU IF I ACTED ON MY EMOTIONS...
BUT OVER AND OVER...
I KEPT THINKING OF HOLDING YOU IN MY ARMS.

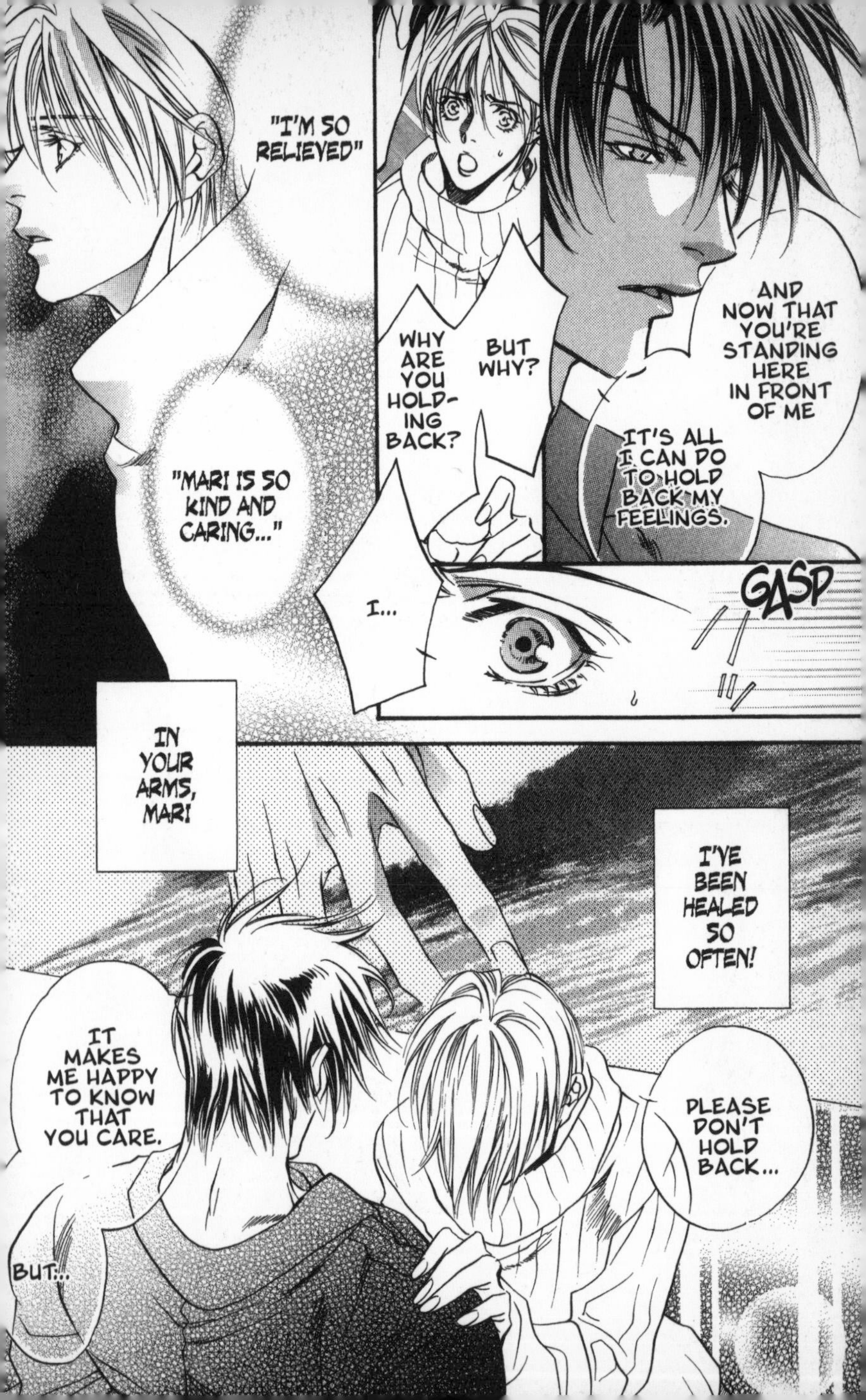
AND NOW THAT YOU'RE STANDING HERE IN FRONT OF ME
IT'S ALL I CAN DO TO HOLD BACK MY FEELINGS.
BUT WHY?
WHY ARE YOU HOLD-ING BACK?
GASP
I...
"I'M SO RELIEVED"
"MARI IS SO KIND AND CARING..."
I'VE BEEN HEALED SO OFTEN!
IN YOUR ARMS, MARI
PLEASE DON'T HOLD BACK...
IT MAKES ME HAPPY TO KNOW THAT YOU CARE.
BUT...

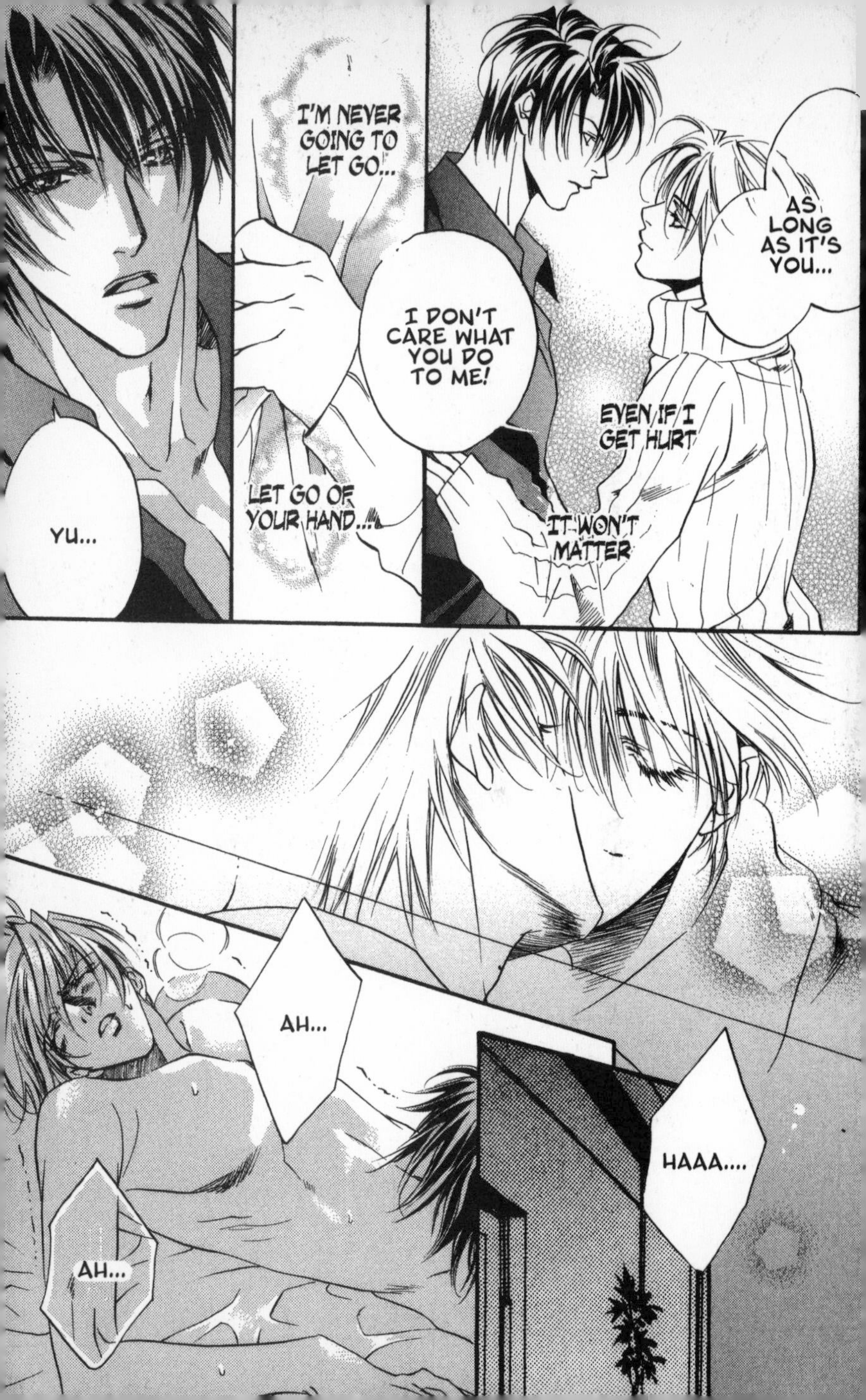
AS LONG AS IT'S YOU...
I DON'T CARE WHAT YOU DO TO ME!
EVEN IF I GET HURT
IT WON'T MATTER
I'M NEVER GOING TO LET GO...
LET GO OF YOUR HAND...!
YU...
HAAA....
AH...
AH...

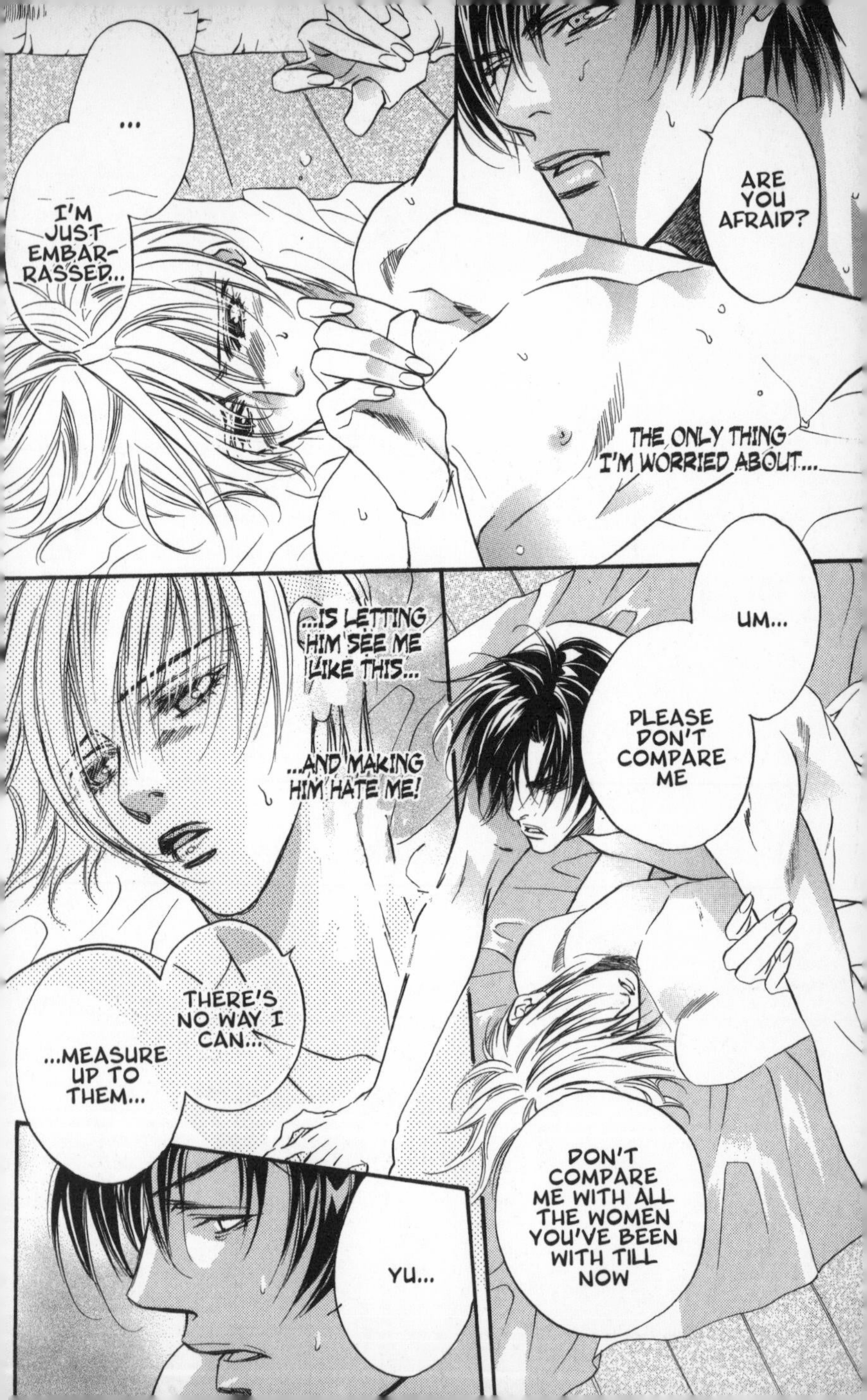
ARE YOU AFRAID?
...
I'M JUST EMBARRASSED...
THE ONLY THING I'M WORRIED ABOUT...
...IS LETTING HIM SEE ME LIKE THIS...
...AND MAKING HIM HATE ME!
UM...
PLEASE DON'T COMPARE ME
DON'T COMPARE ME WITH ALL THE WOMEN YOU'VE BEEN WITH TILL NOW
THERE'S NO WAY I CAN...
...MEASURE UP TO THEM...
YU...

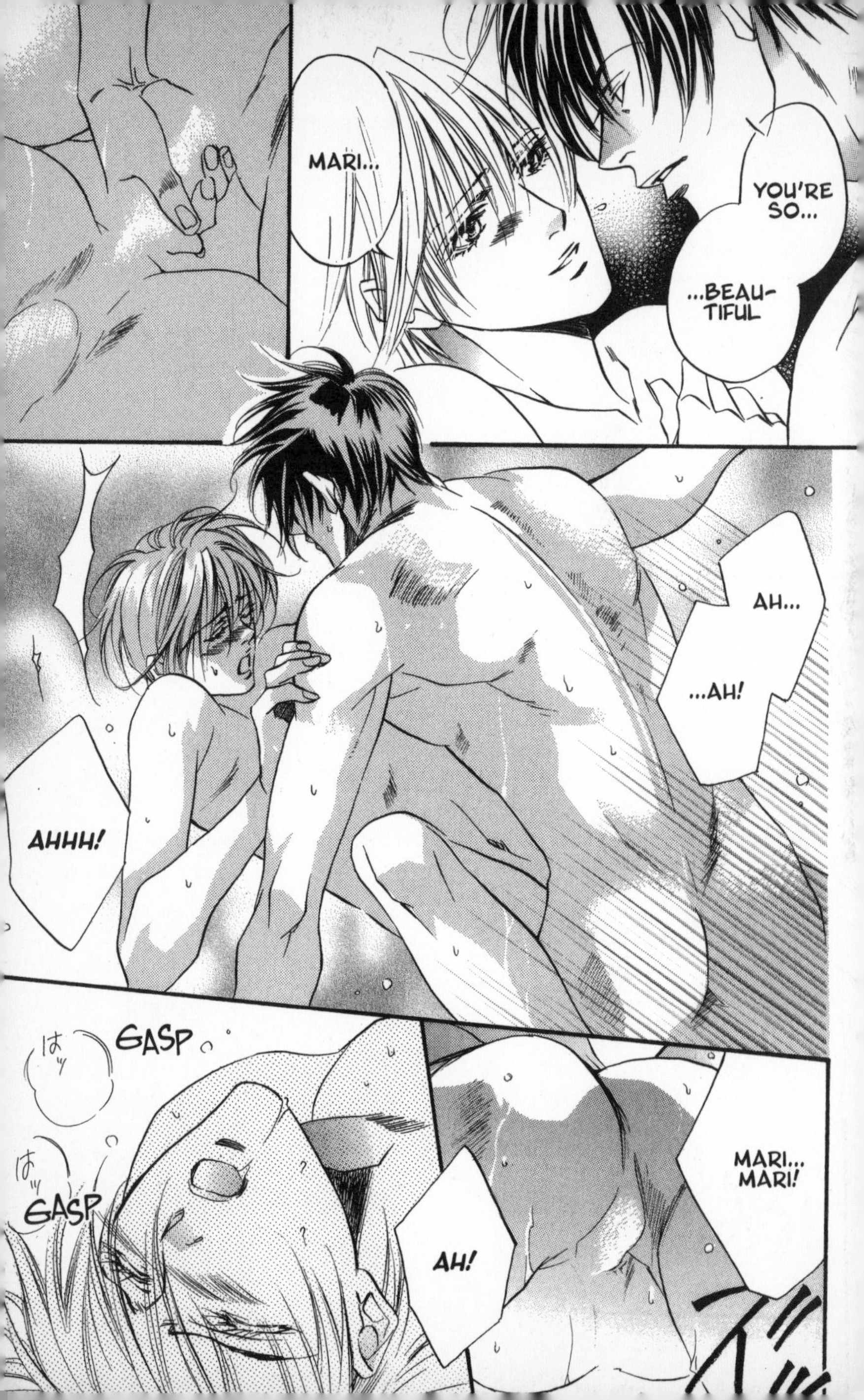
MARI...
YOU'RE SO...
...BEAUTIFUL
AH...
...AH!
AHHH!
MARI... MARI!
AH!
GASP
はッ
はッ
GASP

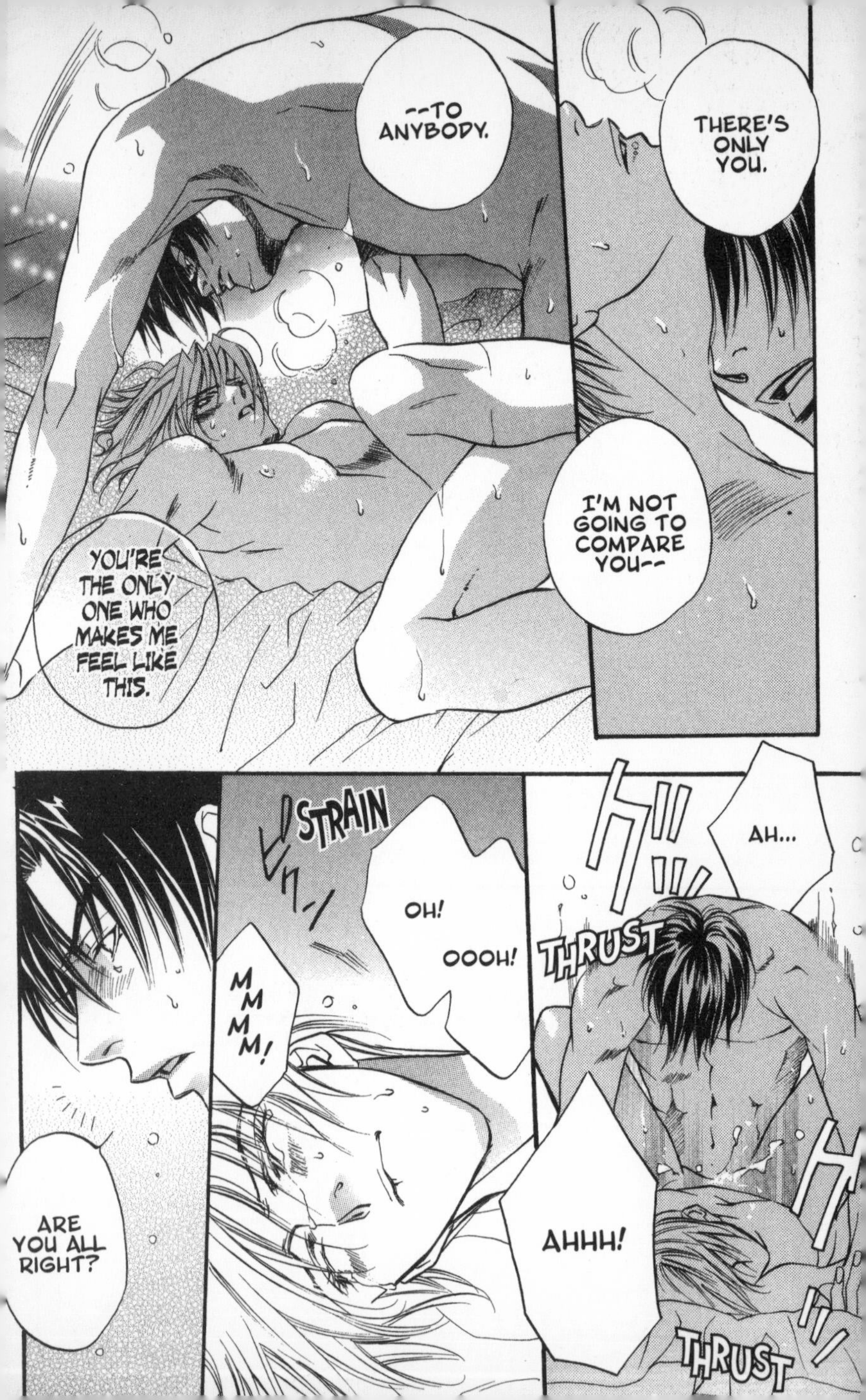
THERE'S ONLY YOU.
I'M NOT GOING TO COMPARE YOU--
--TO ANYBODY.
YOU'RE THE ONLY ONE WHO MAKES ME FEEL LIKE THIS.
AH...
THRUST
AHHH!
THRUST
STRAIN
OH!
OOOH!
MMMM!
ARE YOU ALL RIGHT?

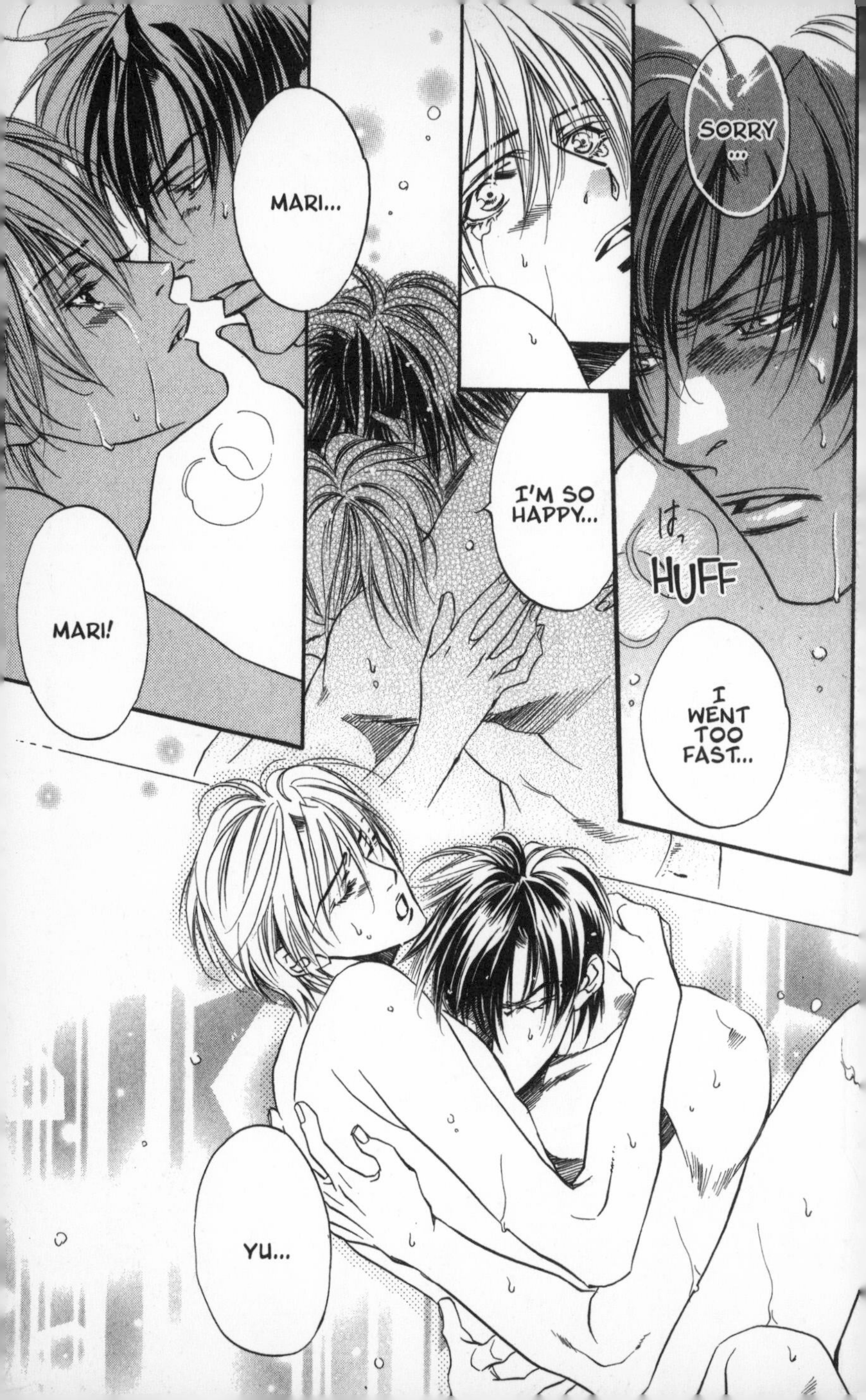
SORRY...
は
HUFF
I WENT TOO FAST...
I'M SO HAPPY...
MARI...
MARI!
YU...

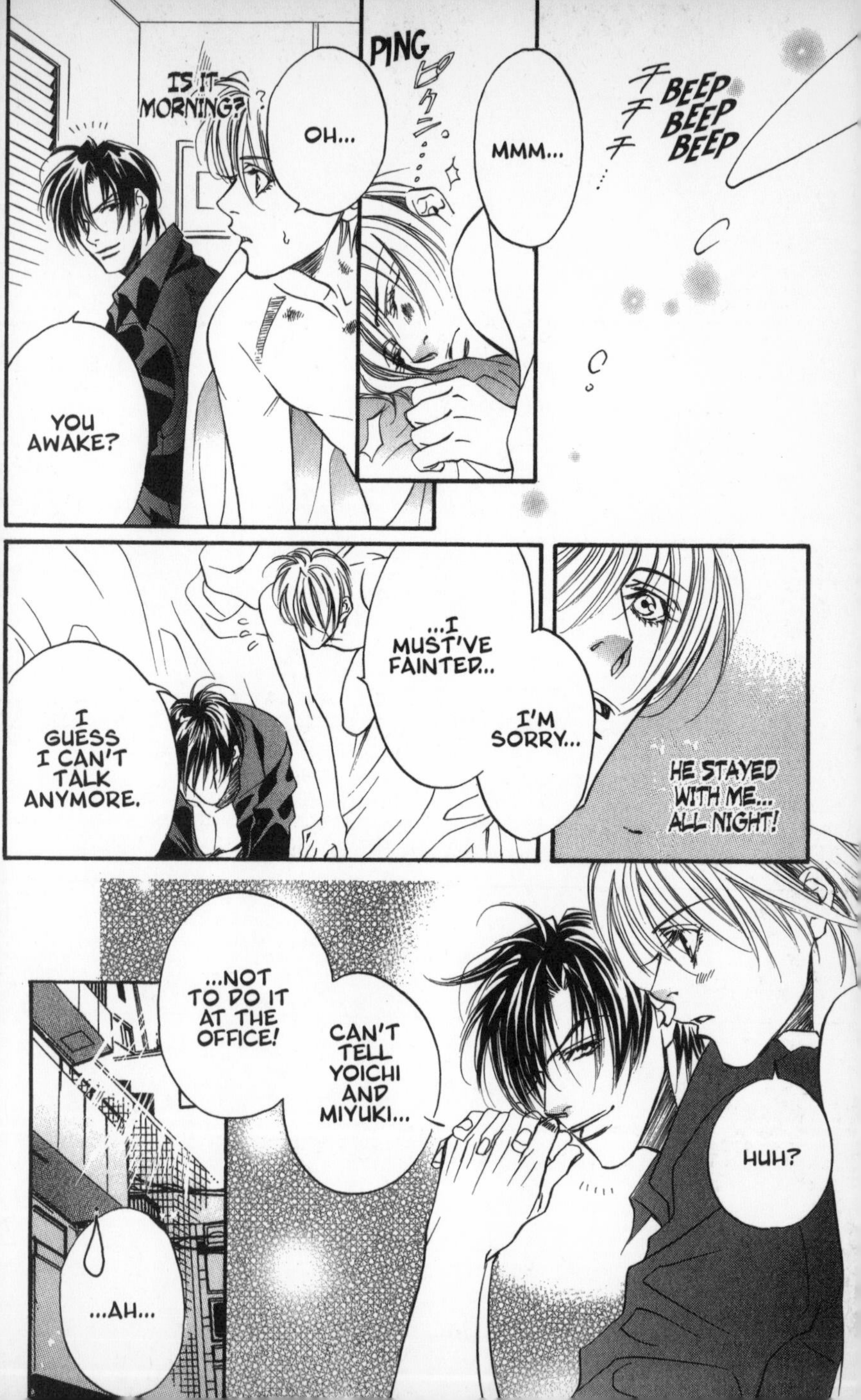
チチチ…
BEEP BEEP BEEP
MMM...
PING
ピクン。
OH...
IS IT MORNING?
YOU AWAKE?
HE STAYED WITH ME... ALL NIGHT!
...I MUST'VE FAINTED...
I'M SORRY...
I GUESS I CAN'T TALK ANYMORE.
HUH?
CAN'T TELL YOICHI AND MIYUKI...
...NOT TO DO IT AT THE OFFICE!
...AH...

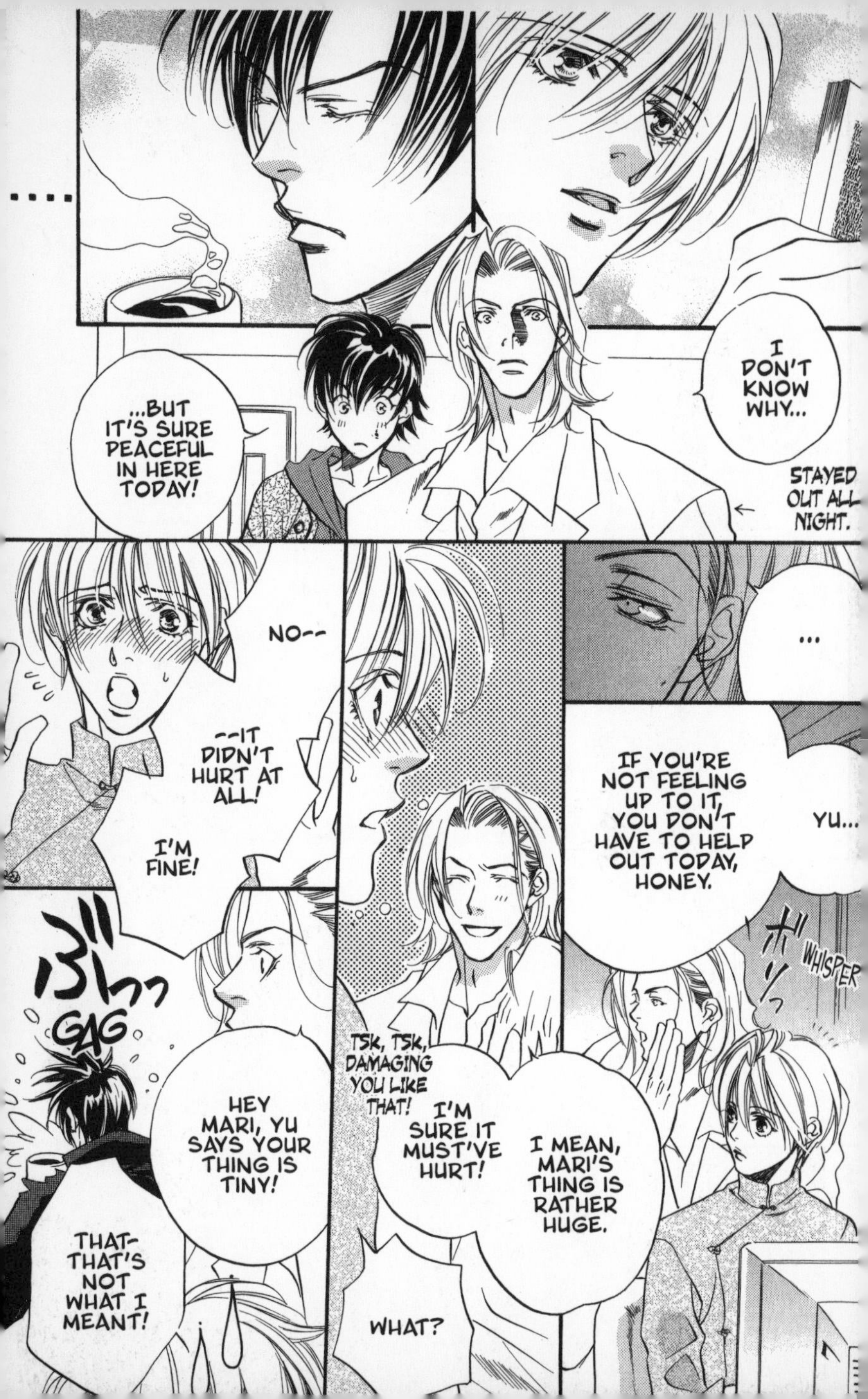
....
I DON'T KNOW WHY...
STAYED OUT ALL NIGHT.
...BUT IT'S SURE PEACEFUL IN HERE TODAY!
...
YU...
IF YOU'RE NOT FEELING UP TO IT, YOU DON'T HAVE TO HELP OUT TODAY, HONEY.
NO--
--IT DIDN'T HURT AT ALL!
I'M FINE!
WHISPER
I MEAN, MARI'S THING IS RATHER HUGE.
I'M SURE IT MUST'VE HURT!
TSK, TSK, DAMAGING YOU LIKE THAT!
WHAT?
HEY MARI, YU SAYS YOUR THING IS TINY!
GAG
THAT-THAT'S NOT WHAT I MEANT!

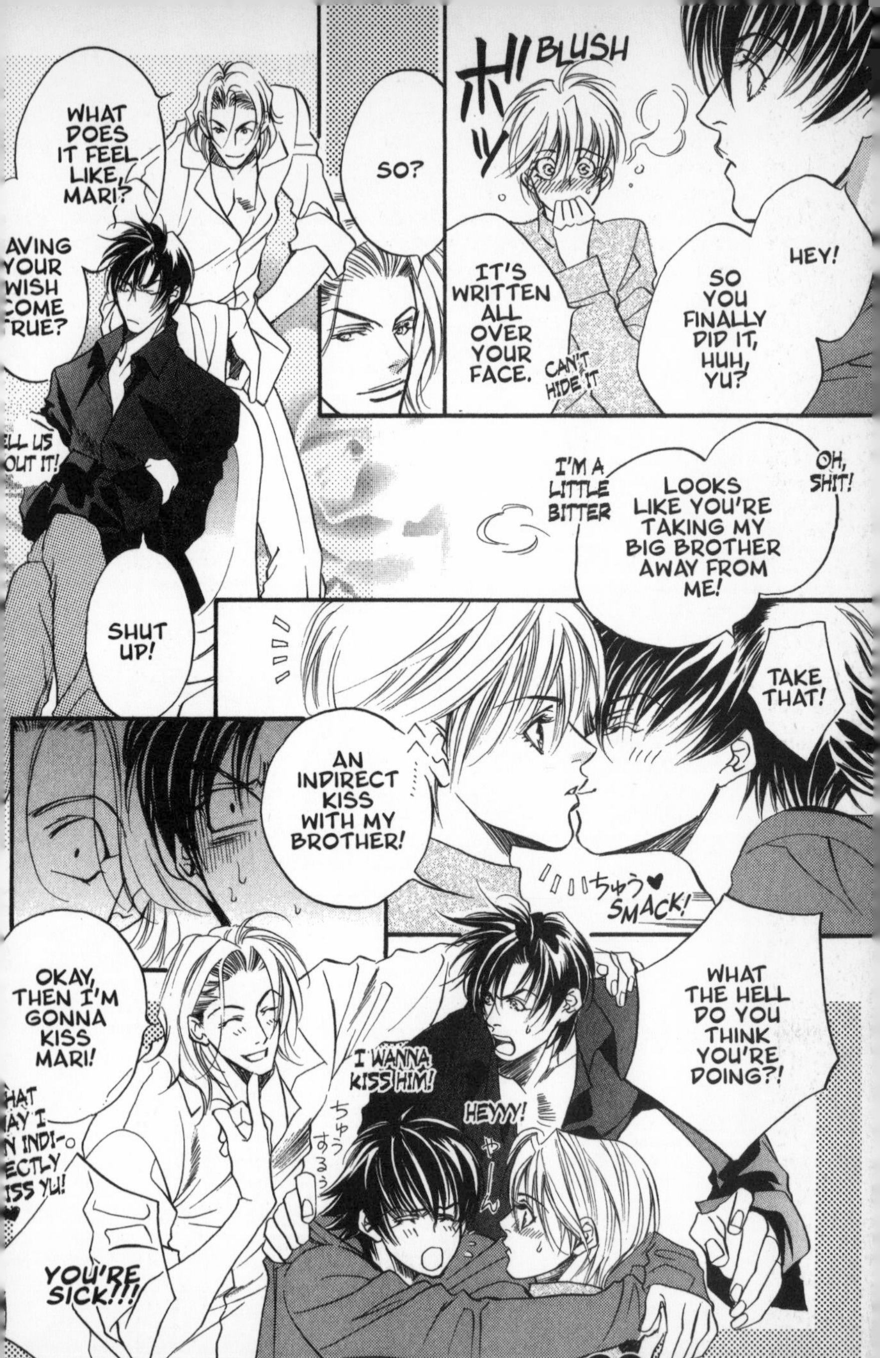
HEY!
SO YOU FINALLY DID IT, HUH, YU?
ホッ BLUSH
IT'S WRITTEN ALL OVER YOUR FACE.
CAN'T HIDE IT
SO?
WHAT DOES IT FEEL LIKE, MARI?
AVING YOUR WISH COME TRUE?
ELL US OUT IT!
SHUT UP!
OH, SHIT!
LOOKS LIKE YOU'RE TAKING MY BIG BROTHER AWAY FROM ME!
I'M A LITTLE BITTER
TAKE THAT!
AN INDIRECT KISS WITH MY BROTHER!
ちゅう♥ SMACK!
WHAT THE HELL DO YOU THINK YOU'RE DOING?!
HEYYY!
やーん
I WANNA KISS HIM!
ちゅうするぅ
OKAY, THEN I'M GONNA KISS MARI!
HAT AY I N INDI- ECTLY ISS YU! ♥
YOU'RE SICK!!!

address.OZ SPECIAL END

GLOSSARY

ABOUT JAPANESE SOUND EFFECTS

In Japanese comics, the sound effects or onomatopoeia vary greatly from their American counterparts. It's difficult to express a sound through the written word. It's just through our cultural knowledge that we know that the word "crash" represents a loud noise of something breaking. If you write the word crash in another language, like Japanese, it comes out as nonsense; much the same way that it would if we translated Japanese sound effects literally. Also, in Japanese comics onomatopoeia represent some things for which there are r sounds like grins, shudders, blushes, feeling of shock, and glompy hugs.

What follows are some representations (the sound effects used in this book with th literal Japanese in Romanji (English letters) give you an idea of just how much things nee to be changed in order to help things read mo smoothly in English.

PAGE 7
The "buzz" of the camera transmitting is represented in Japanese as "Jiiii" while the clicks are "pi pi".

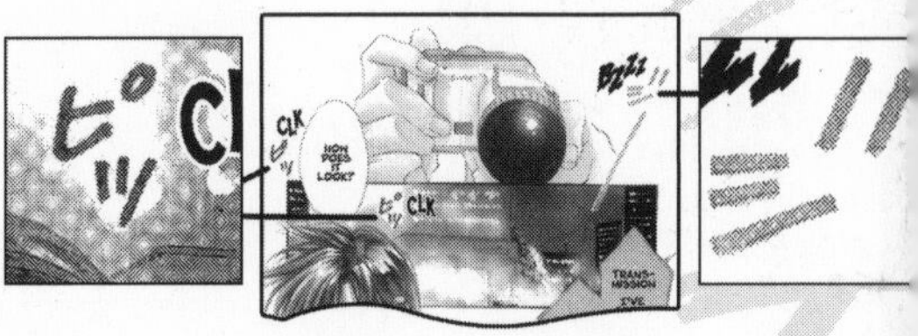
BZZZ
CLK
HOW DOES IT LOOK?
CLK
TRANSMISSION
I'VE

PAGE 13
When Mari falls back into the bed, the "Fwump!" sound is "Dosa"

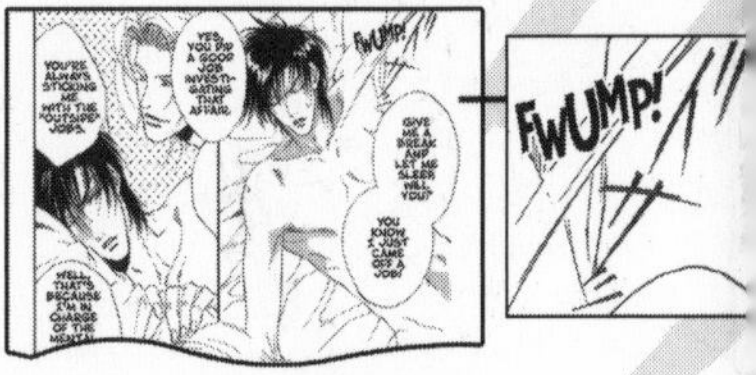
FWUMP!
FWUMP!
YES, YOU DID A GOOD JOB INVESTIGATING THAT AFFAIR.
YOU'RE ALWAYS STICKING ME WITH THE "OUTSIDE" JOBS.
GIVE ME A BREAK AND LET ME SLEEP, WILL YOU?
YOU KNOW, I JUST CAME OFF A JOB!

PAGE 17
Yoichi's hand isn't actually making noise as it waves, but in Japanese it is represented as "hira hira"

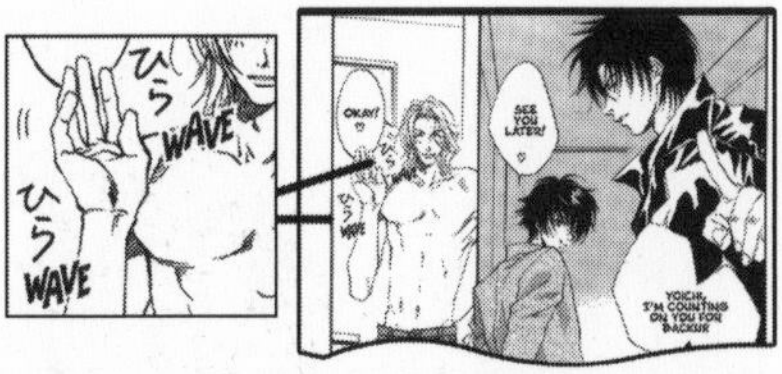
SEE YOU LATER!
OKAY!
WAVE
YOICHI, I'M COUNTING ON YOU FOR BACKUP.
ひら
WAVE
ひら
WAVE

PAGE 24
When a stranger brushes up against Yu it's hard to represent with just an image, the sound effect "GOSO" brings it right home.

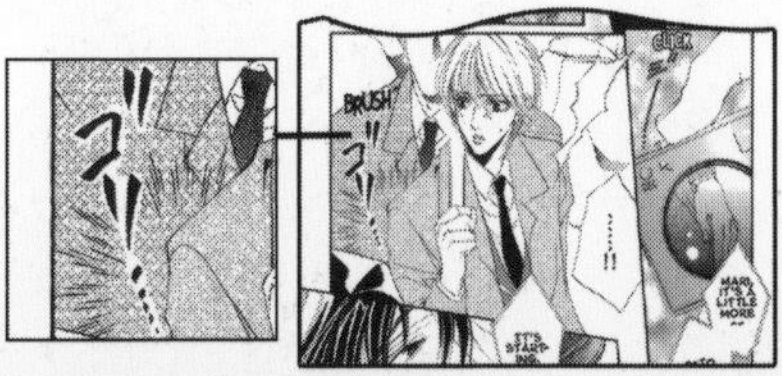
CLICK
MARI, A LITTLE MORE
BRUSH
!!

PAGE 25

To emphasize the shock of being grabbed, the sound effect "GA" is used.

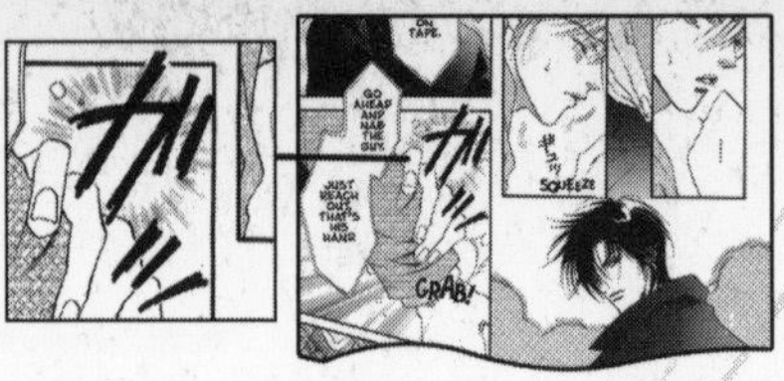
SQUEEZE
GO AHEAD AND NAB THE GUY.
GRAB!

PAGE 25

When someone's arm is twisted it doesn't usually make a noise, but in Japanese it's "GUI".

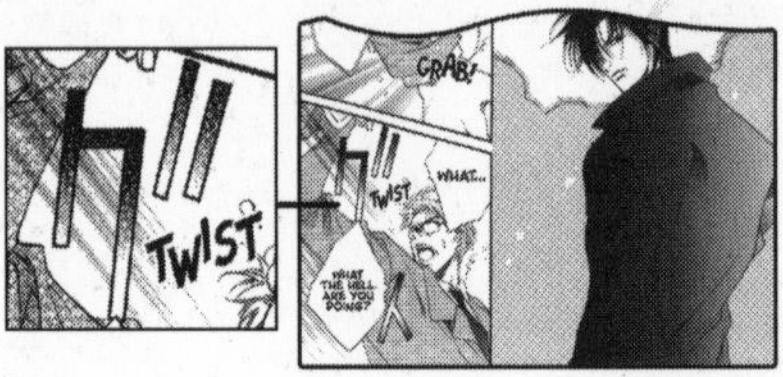
GRAB!
WHAT...
TWIST
WHAT THE HELL ARE YOU DOING?
TWIST

PAGE 30

Pulling out a business card rarely makes a sound but in manga it gets a "PI".

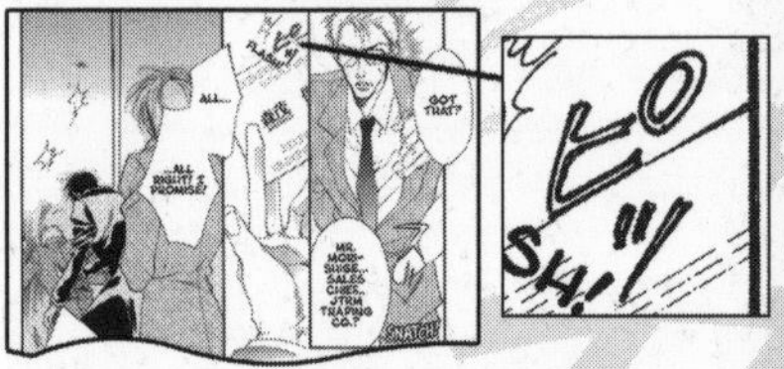
GOT THAT?
SNATCH
ALL...
...ALL RIGHT! I PROMISE!
SHI!

PAGE 46

Perhaps Yu is shivering to the point that his bones are rattling but more likely it's just another manga sound effect "gata gata". Also the way Yu is clinging to Mari is represented by a "GYU"

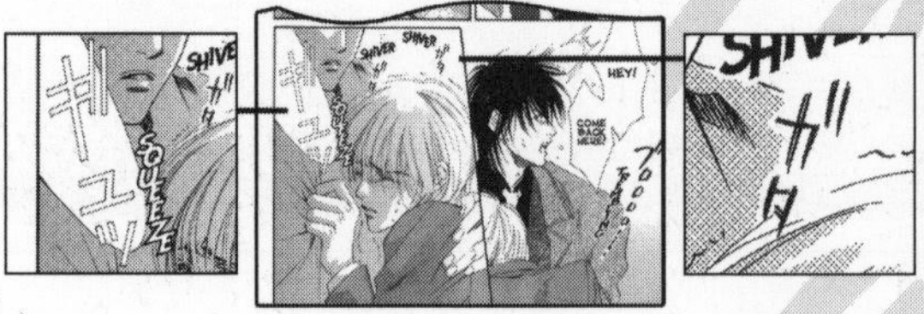
SHIVER
HEY!
COME BACK HERE!
SHIVER SHIVER
SQUEEZE
SHIVER

PAGE 57

Manga has an interesting way of representing blood rushing to the cheeks with "KAAA"

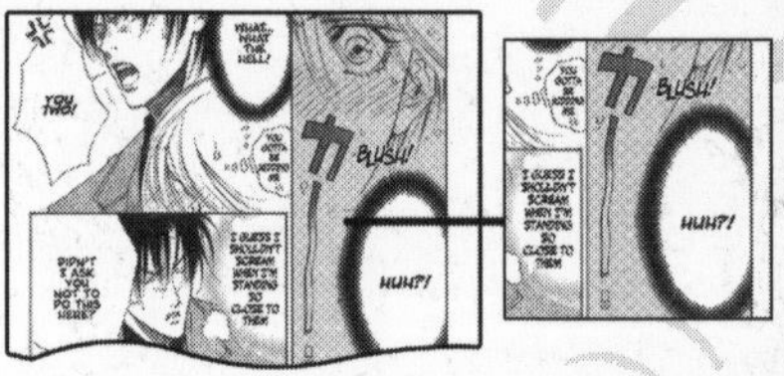
WHAT... WHAT THE HELL?
YOU TWO!
BLUSH!
HUH?!
BLUSH!
HUH?!

PAGE 59

In Japanese comics, even smiles get their own sound effect "nikoh"

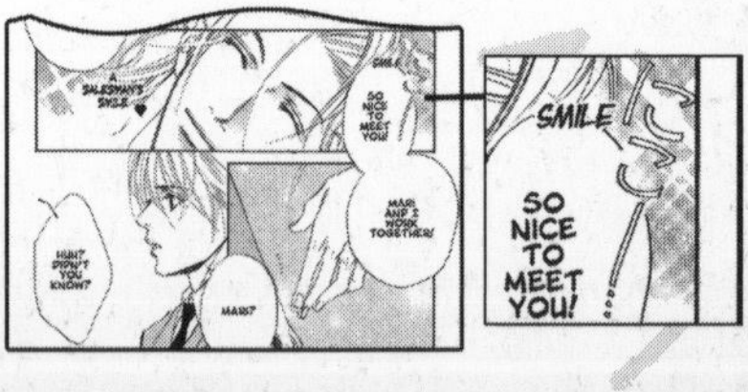
SMILE
SO NICE TO MEET YOU!
MARI AND I WORK TOGETHER!
MARI?
SMILE
SO NICE TO MEET YOU!

LEVEL-C

Mizuki is a popular male fashion model with [a] promising future. CEO Haruno wants to mak[e] him the centerpiece for her latest promotion. [To] lure Mizuki in, she calls on her twin brothe[r] Kazo. He is quick to seduce the youn[g] supermodel, but things soon escalate beyo[nd] business as usual. As Kazo's feelings run wild, [it] looks like true love for him and Mizuki.

DVD • 30 Minutes • 18 & UP
Japanese w. English Subtitles
Cat# KVDVD-0227 • UPC 6-31595-02276-6
SRP $24.95

MY SEXUAL HARASSMENT

Mochizuchi is a young office worker with a knack for falling into bed with his coworkers, clients and bosses. Kept under the thumb of his supervisor, Honma, Mochizuchi does his best to keep the office running smoothly. Will he ever get to be alone with Fujita, the one man who wants him for something other than his body? Or, will he remain as Honma's slave forever?

DVD • 130 Minutes • 18 & UP
Japanese w. English Subtitles
Cat# KVDVD-0309 • UPC 6-31595-03096-9
SRP $29.95

STOP, THIS IS THE END OF THE BOOK!

This book is printed in its original Japanese format, which allows you to experience the story and art in the way they were originally intended. It's important to both the creator and the fan who reads it, so is also important to us.

We hope you enjoy reading this manga. Read from right-to-left starting in the upper right hand corner of the page and if you need help take a look at the diagram below.

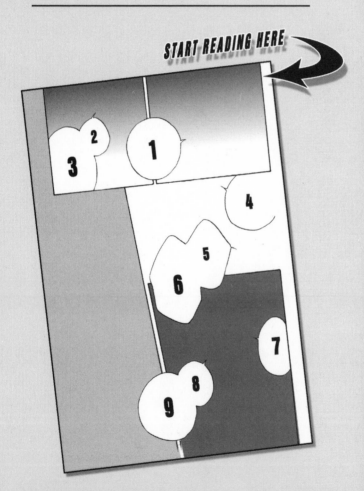

START READING HERE

W A R N I N G ! !

NOW YOU ARE READING LIKE A PRO